COLLIDE

A SWEET ROMANCE

AMANDA SHELLEY

Editor: Sue Soares
SJS Editorial Services
https://www.facebook.com/sue.soares71
Proof Reader: Julie Deaton
Deaton Author Services
http://jdproofs.wixsite.com/jddeaton
Cover Design: Krys Janae
Krysjanae.com

Visit my website at
www.amandashelley.com

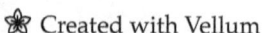 Created with Vellum

CONNECT WITH AMANDA SHELLEY

Want to be the first to know about upcoming sales and new releases? Make sure you sign up for my newsletter as well as connect with me on social media and your favorite retail store.

Website:
www.amandashelley.com
Newsletter:
https://goo.gl/forms/tT8EbQ5YhB7Uuj1Z2
Facebook:
https://www.facebook.com/authoramandashelley/
Instagram:
https://www.instagram.com/authoramandashelley/
Twitter:
https://twitter.com/AmandShelley
Reader's Group:
https://www.facebook.com/groups/AmandasArmyofReaders/

Amazon:

https://www.amazon.com/author/amandashelley

Goodreads:

https://www.goodreads.com/author/show/19713563.Ama

nda_Shelley

Book Bub:

https://www.bookbub.com/profile/amanda-shelley

ABOUT THE BOOK

Falling head over heels was the last thing I expected.

Literally.

Coffee is everywhere - and more than my ego is bruised.

When the handsome stranger I plowed into calls me by name, mortification sinks in.

He rushes off to class. I run home to change, hoping to forget the whole incident.

If only I could be so lucky.

I quickly find it's a small world and Gavin Wallace is completely unavoidable. Everywhere I turn he's there. In my classes. Hanging with my friends.

I've got his full attention and I have to admit, I like it a lot more than I should.

COLLIDE

A SWEET ROMANCE

Life can turn on a dime. The direction you head in when it does makes all the difference!

~ Barbara Delinsky

1

CAMPUS LIFE

CAMPUS IS DESERTED this early in the morning. As I eat up the brick pavers filling the road through the middle of campus, I can't help but fall further in love. At this time of day, brick buildings glisten in the sunlight, and the green grass lining the pathways is inviting. I know I've made the right decision to transfer to Washington State University.

Running down a steep hill as I return to my apartment, I can't help but think about how much my life has changed. Two days ago, I lived at home with my family. With two other kids in college, my parents encouraged me to attend our local community college because my scholarship money would last longer. I'd been able to keep my high school job, live at home, and save money. I made a few friends at school, but I was in high school all over again. It didn't take long to realize I needed a change.

When my sister, Katherine, announced her engagement to Ben last winter, I decided to transfer. My parents encouraged her to move home while she finishes her student teaching. Since their wedding's in December, Ben's moving in afterward. Don't get me wrong, I love Katherine, and Ben will be a great brother-in-law, but this means we're back up to six in our household. Although it's a big house, it's perfect timing for the change I need.

After my run, I stretch again before taking a shower. Anticipating a scorching-hot day, I wear khaki shorts, a green t-shirt, and sandals. I pull my hair back into a loose ponytail before gathering papers to meet with my academic advisor. I quickly eat breakfast before walking to the French Administration Building.

As the evening cools, I eagerly return to campus to see how my schedule flows. On the way home from my self-guided tour, my phone rings. My heart rate picks up with excitement. Caller ID shows it's my sister, Katherine.

"Hey, Kate. How are you?" I've been anticipating her call. Knowing Katherine, I'm sure she's dying to know everything. I can't help the smile that spreads across my face.

As expected, she takes a deep breath and eagerly pumps me with questions. "So, how's your new place?"

"Great, I…" I start to say, but she interrupts before I can answer.

"What's it like? Describe everything and don't leave anything out," she rapidly spits out, causing me to laugh.

I pause for a moment, biting my lower lip, thinking of where to begin. "Well, it's a one-bedroom, furnished apartment right off the edge of campus. It's perfect. There's AC, and the double bed's actually comfortable." I fill her in on the specific details of my apartment. With each detail I add, she seems to have two or three questions in return.

I chose a one-bedroom apartment because I get up early and study late. I don't require much sleep. Five or six hours tops, then I'm wide awake. Thanks to my siblings, I've heard enough horror stories about roommates to easily convince myself as well as my parents, to live alone.

"Did you meet your advisor?" she asks when she's exhausted the topic of my new apartment.

"Yeah, this morning. She's really nice. I'm taking eighteen credits. Oh, guess what? I've been accepted into the education program." I'm beyond excited. Being a transfer student and only a sophomore, I had worried I'd have to wait until next year to start my required classes.

"That's awesome. What are you taking?"

I look at the schedule in my hands and prattle it off to my sister. She's eager to hear about my classes, until I mention geology.

"I thought you'd completed your science requirements," she states, making it sound like a question.

"So did I," I sigh in frustration. "Apparently, I'm one credit short for my lab requirement, so I have to take another class."

Kate moans conspiratorially. "That's sooo frustrating."

"It is," I agree, "but it'll be over this semester." Attempting to sound more enthusiastic, I add, "I'm still on track to get my reading and ELL endorsements. Oh… And you'll never believe this… I can minor in Italian of all things, if I take a class or two."

"That's good, but crazy." There's a brief pause, then she asks, "So, what else did you do today?"

Holding in my excitement, I calmly state, "I got a job."

"You're kidding." Her voice raises in disbelief. "You've only been in town one day. How on earth did that happen?"

"Well... At dinner last night, there was a sign in the window. I filled out the application and brought it back." Still trying to sound casual, I take a deep breath and exhale slowly. "She called me while I was at The Bookie buying textbooks." Knowing Katherine, she'll have plenty to say after this tidbit of information.

"You're kidding?" She surprises me with her lack of commentary.

"I interviewed this morning and was offered the job before I left," I state, sounding kind of smug, rather than as relaxed as I was hoping.

"Wow." She still sounds surprised. "Where at? I mean... What will you do?" she sputters.

I can't control my enthusiasm any longer. I finally let my excitement show as I explain, "It's at an Italian restaurant downtown, called Antonio's. It's right off Main Street. I'm a server, which means I will deliver food, once it's ordered... I start tomorrow!"

"Al, that's amazing!" Katherine sounds like a proud mother. "You have the best luck! I'm so happy for you!"

Switching the focus of our conversation, I ask Katherine about her wedding plans. We haven't talked about them in the past couple of weeks, so there's bound to be an update. I'm one of her four bridesmaids. Like the typical bride, there's always something new to divulge.

Katherine gushes in detail about picking out tuxes, making it sound like a chore. I take this opportunity to let myself into my apartment and make dinner. I respond at the appropriate times, so she won't realize my mouth is full or think I'm not paying attention. She gives me the full update on the flowers, photographer, and DJ. Unfortunately, she seems a bit overwhelmed, even for Katherine. And she's as high strung as they come.

All of a sudden, Katherine gasps, drawing my attention. "You're coming to the bridal shower, aren't you? The bachelorette party's afterward!"

"I'll be there, Kate." Wondering why she needs to ask. I'm her sister, after all. I can't help when, "Why?" comes out of my mouth.

Knowing exactly what I mean, she begins, "Well…" She hesitates as if not sure what to say. "I just thought… Now that you're working, you might not make it," she sighs as if a huge weight has been lifted. I picture her visibly relaxing through the phone and shake my head. Katherine always overreacts, but once things are off her mind, her feathers don't stay ruffled.

"No worries, Kate. I talked with my manager. I'll be there." I shake my head in disbelief. I can't believe she'd think I'd miss her big day. God, I hope this wedding doesn't turn her into one of those crazy brides.

"Oh, that's amazing!" Katherine sounds relieved. I can hear in her voice how important it is for me to be there.

"What are sisters for?" I tease. Changing to a solemn tone, I state, "You're turning, you know."

She hesitates for a moment before asking, "What do you mean?"

"You're on the verge of becoming a crazy bridezilla!" I accuse as I let out a snicker.

Giving her the reality check she needs, Katherine's silent

for a moment, then humbly states, "Thanks, Al. I know I can count on you to keep me honest."

"It's what I'm here for," I say sarcastically and continue to chuckle. She's horrified by the thought of becoming one of those brides who freak out over every little detail. Her best friend did that last summer, and Katherine hated it. Though she still loves her friend, she's vowed never to be like that. I whole-heartedly intend to hold her to it.

We say our goodbyes as I take my dish into the kitchen and clean up after myself. I put my leftovers in the fridge and wash the dishes. Hopefully, she doesn't take my bridezilla comment too seriously. I can't handle the next four months with her obsessing over negative details every time something she doesn't like happens. I love her dearly, but when she's freaking out, she's horrible.

I spend the rest of the evening unpacking. I hang some pictures and organize my bedroom. I go through my bags from The Bookie. After pulling everything out, I curiously look at some of my textbooks as well as other reading required this semester. To pass the time. I pick up *Roll of Thunder, Hear My Cry* by Mildred D. Taylor and begin reading. I'm surprised at how fast I devour it. My thoughts linger on this book as I fall asleep.

After my morning run, I venture to the laundry room of our apartment building and run a load. Just as I put clothes into the dryer, a tall, slender girl walks into the room. She's wearing a navy pair of capris and a turquoise V-neck tank top. Her light-brown hair is tied back in a loose knot. She plunks her large, yellow laundry bag and detergent onto the floor near the washers on the other side of the room. She sways to music heard through her earbuds without any knowledge of my presence. I make a point to close the door to the dryer quietly, hopefully alerting her to my presence, but not startle her. I'm unsuccessful.

"Oh." She gasps loudly, due to the music blaring in her ears. "I didn't see you there." She takes out her earbuds and sorts her bag of laundry into three different machines.

"Sorry for startling you."

She smiles and shrugs. "That's what I get for not paying attention." She lets out a light laugh. "I'm not used to anyone being here so early in the morning. This place is usually vacant at this hour."

"Oh." I shrug, not knowing what else to say.

"I've lived here just over a year. It's the best time to come, especially when classes start. Never come in the afternoon. You're better off going downtown to the laundromat after three." She gives me a warm smile. Her first reaction was just because she was startled, not that she wanted to be alone.

"Thanks for the advice. I'll keep it in mind. I'm usually up pretty early."

"No problem. Are you new to WSU?" she asks, pronouncing it Wazzu.

"I arrived Tuesday."

"That's awesome. You're a transfer student?"

"Yeah, I went to community college last year."

"Welcome." She encouragingly smiles. "I'm Sophie Reynolds. I live in that apartment." She points to the one upstairs about three units away from this room, halfway to mine.

"I'm Alex." I extend my arm in the direction of my apartment. "I live there. It's nice to meet you."

"What's your major?" she asks as she puts detergent in her last load.

"Elementary Ed. What's yours?"

"Poly-Sci." She loads quarters into each machine before starting them. "Are you getting settled?"

"I'm getting there." I shrug. "My parents arrive this weekend to help me finish getting settled, since they couldn't bring me over."

"That's nice of them." Sophie smiles, then she adds, "I'm getting coffee while these wash. Wanna join me?"

"Sure." I smile. I have nothing else to do, and it's a relief to meet some of my neighbors. "Let me get my purse."

"Great. I'll take this to my apartment and meet you in a few minutes. We can walk down the hill, or drive. It's up to you."

"I'm fine either way," I reply, not knowing where the coffee shop is. I know I have four hours until work, so there's plenty of time, no matter what we decide.

"Okay, we'll walk." She gathers the rest of her things and heads toward the door. "See you in a few minutes."

What a relief to finally have someone to talk to. Sophie seems friendly enough and who knows, it might be fun. I quickly gather my things to take to drop off. I change into a pair of sneakers, not knowing how far we're walking. I quickly pull a brush through my hair and tie it back from my face.

Sophie walks into the courtyard as I arrive. "Great timing." She smiles. We cross the parking lot toward one of the dorms. Orton Hall, I think.

"Thanks for inviting me." I match my pace to hers, and

we walk down a small path toward a dorm. "How long have you been here?"

"Oh, I've been here all summer, working and taking a class. It's my junior year, so I've been in Pullman two years so far. I'm originally from Everett."

"I'm from Tumwater. Where do you work?"

"Right here, actually." She grins and points to a small building between two dorms. From the sign, I see it's a daycare. "I work with the before and after-school kids. We held summer camps during the day."

"I love kids. Do you work many hours during the school year?"

"Since it's open from seven to six, I get between twenty to thirty hours each week. It changes depending on my class schedule. Will you work while you're here?"

I clear my throat and grin. "Um... I was offered a job yesterday."

She looks encouragingly at me. "That's awesome. Where at?"

"A restaurant called Antonio's." I make it sound like a question rather than a statement.

"Wow, that's amazing. How'd you get a job so soon?"

I eagerly explain, and we spend the rest of our walk talking about my day yesterday.

As the door to Starbucks opens, a burst of cool air escapes, saturated with coffee beans. A few people are scattered about, but it's not too busy. Sophie approaches the counter and orders a vanilla latte. Then she waits for her latte at the other end of the espresso machine. As I step up to the counter to order a chai Frappuccino, a group of guys walk in.

"Hey, Sophie," one of them calls out in a friendly tone.

"Josh!" she exclaims. "When did you get back?"

"Monday. How was your break?" I hear him reply as I pay for my drink.

Once receiving my change, I turn in their direction and see the one who's apparently Josh, the tall, lanky blond, wearing tan shorts and a blue Polo shirt, reaching out to hug Sophie. The three other guys with him continue their conversation in the line behind me. Sophie picks up her drink and explains the different camps she helped with this summer. I walk to the other end of the espresso machine to wait patiently for my own drink, as they continue to chat with one another.

After a moment, my drink is ready, and I walk toward them. There's a break in their conversation, and Sophie gestures toward me. "Oh!" she gasps. "How rude of me. Alex, this is Josh. Josh, Alex."

Josh smiles as he reaches to shake my hand. "Josh Andrews."

"Alex Manning."

"Alex just transferred. She lives in my apartment complex." She smiles toward me, rolls her eyes, and lets out a little giggle. "We met this morning doing laundry," Sophie interjects before anyone can say anything else.

"Nice to meet you." Josh returns a warm smile.

"You, too."

Josh walks to order his drink since the three others he came in with are finished.

"Do you want to sit for a few minutes?" Sophie casually asks.

"Sure." I shrug, taking a sip of my drink.

She walks over to a table for four that has an identical one next to it. She sits at one end closest to the other table, and I sit across from her. After a few minutes, Josh and his friends walk toward us.

"Can we join you?" he casually asks.

"Sure, Josh," Sophie replies.

As they sit at the table next to us, Josh introduces his friends, "This is Vince, Gavin, and James." He gestures toward them, but not to anyone specifically, so I'm left not knowing which name belongs to whom.

Simultaneously, I hear three different versions of "Hello," from distinctly different voices.

"Guys, this is Alex Manning." Josh gestures to me.

"What are your plans today, Soph?" Josh continues.

"Well... we're in the middle of laundry, so we need to finish it soon, but other than that, not much."

"Want to head to the Dunes with us?"

"Sure, what time do you want to leave?" Sophie asks before taking a drink from her latte.

"Around one?" Josh questions toward his friends. They each nod in agreement.

"Sounds fun. Can you pick me up?"

"Sure," he replies to her, then looks at me apologetically, "You're welcome to come, too, Alex."

"I'd love to, but I have to work," I say with regret.

"Maybe next time," he sincerely states.

"Thanks," I reply, wishing I could've gone to see more of the area.

We visit for a while before the dark-haired one in the green t-shirt stands. He hesitates before saying, "Hey, guys? If we're picking Sophie up by one, we've gotta move." He flashes a gorgeous smile apologetically to Sophie and me.

Until he stands, I hadn't realized his height. He's easily six foot three. When everyone joins him, I foolishly smile when I realize how little I'm paying attention. He isn't the only tall one here. None of them are under six feet.

After saying goodbye, Sophie and I return to our laundry. Sophie explains, "'The Dunes' is a place to swim on the Snake River." She insists I go sometime. "So, how long do you work tonight?" she asks.

"I think until eight." At least that's what the manager said.

"That's not bad. I love the food there."

"I've only tried it my first night in town." I chuckle, continuing to fold a shirt. "It's definitely something I won't mind being around."

Sophie lets out a loud snort. "Well, it would suck if you hated the food you had to serve!"

"Yeah, it would," I agree.

As I finish putting the last of my clothes into the hamper, Sophie giggles. "This was fun. Let's do it again sometime."

"Yeah, it was. Thanks for inviting me." It's nice to know at least one person on campus.

"Hey, I'm going to Spokane tomorrow. You're welcome to come."

"I'd love to, but my parents arrive in the morning. Maybe another time?"

"Sure." She pulls out her phone and asks for my number. I rattle it off, and I receive a text.

"Call me if you want to hang out sometime," Sophie offers.

"Will do."

AFTER SPENDING the weekend with my parents, I'm exhausted. I show them all around campus, where I work, and places in Pullman and Moscow. They fell just as in love with the Palouse as I have. Our favorite sightseeing adventure was at the WSU's Bear Center. I had no idea bears were being researched on campus. It's highly entertaining to watch grizzlies play like kittens, rolling over one another down the hill as they played with the research students.

As expected, Mom goes overboard with groceries. I swear it's as if she's shopping for all six of us back home, rather than just me. Fortunately, most of the things she bought are non-perishable, so I can store them. She knows I love cooking and doesn't want me to go without.

Being nervous about my first day of classes, I spend more time than usual choosing what to wear. After some speculation, I choose a pair of khaki shorts and my favorite blue scoop-neck tank top. I double-check my bag to ensure everything's there and pick out an outfit to wear jogging in the morning.

Lying in bed that evening, I can't help but think about tomorrow. I'll admit, I'm nervous about what my professors and classmates will be like, but it's not too overwhelming. I can't wait to see what happens.

2

ROUTINE

As far as classes are concerned, it's a typical first day. My education classes are small, with only thirty students in each. Each professor takes roll and clearly states attendance is required. As predicted, they introduce themselves, outline their syllabus, and explain major projects for the semester. Somehow, they manage different icebreakers for us to experience. Though everyone's reluctant at first, I meet a few more people. By the end, I can put names to faces in most of my classes.

Work's slower now that students aren't coming in with their parents, but it remains steady. Most customers arrive in larger groups. Time flies because they're full of laughter and conversations as they reunite from being apart over the summer. Andrea, my boss, scheduled less people today, so there's more for each of us to do.

My phone rings as I enter my apartment. I fling my shoes into the hall closet and dig through my purse to answer it in time.

"Hello?" I let out breathlessly.

"Hey, Alex, it's Sophie," replies a cheery voice on the other end. "Is this a bad time?"

"No, I just got in." I walk over to the couch and plop down.

"How's your first day?"

"Good, I had four classes and worked from one to eight. How's yours?" I pull my feet in, curling up into a comfortable position.

"Wow, you're busy!" she exclaims. "I only had three classes and don't work until tomorrow." She hesitates. "Um, are you busy?"

"No, I'm just hanging out," I reply curiously, wondering what she might ask me to do.

"Well, I need groceries, wanna come?"

Even though I don't need anything from the store, and I'm a little tired, I refuse to turn her down three times in a row. "Sure, sounds fun. I just got home and need to change. Can you give me fifteen minutes?"

"No problem. I'll drop by your place when I'm ready to go," she responds.

"Sure, see you then."

While I change, I call my parents to tell them about my day. It's a quick conversation, but it's always good to talk to Mom. As soon as I end the call, I hear a knock on my door.

Sophie greets me with a huge grin. "Ready?" Her light-brown hair hangs in long layers past her shoulders. Her expressive eyes widen, and her brows suddenly raise. "Did I give you enough time?"

"Yeah… Just talking with my mom," I dismissively say. "If I didn't tell her about my first day, she'll hound me later."

Sophie gives an understanding nod. "My mom's the same way." She rolls her eyes sarcastically adding, "Heaven forbid I go a couple of days without checking in."

"I know the feeling," I reply, keeping the same sarcasm as Sophie.

I grab my purse, and we walk out the door.

"I want to head over to Moscow, if that's okay with you?"

"Moscow?" I ask, wondering which store's worth driving to.

"I'm heading to Winco." Sophie shrugs.

"Winco?" I've never heard of it.

Realizing my confusion, she smiles and clarifies, "Winco's a grocery store."

"So you know, my parents stocked my cupboards yesterday, so I'm just going along for the ride."

Sophie grins at me and lets out a little laugh. "Parents are the best. Don't worry, I really appreciate the company."

"So, did you have fun at the Dunes?" I ask.

"It was awesome. The weather was perfect. It wasn't too hot, but warm enough to make the cool water enjoyable." She tells me in great detail about a water fight Josh started. She laughs hysterically from time to time, making me wish I'd gone. Once her laughter settles, she regains her thoughts and continues with the story. It's obvious they had a great time.

"The Dunes are amazing. You need to go sometime." We pull into the parking lot as she tells me another story about roasting hotdogs and marshmallows, once it got dark.

As she shops, we laugh and joke around. She asks about my weekend, and I tell her about my time with my parents.

Sophie's so easy to be around. We only walk down specific aisles since she knows her way around and is the only one shopping.

"So, how do you know Josh?" I ask as we get back into the car to return home.

"Oh." She smiles widely. "He and I met our first semester. We took a lot of the same Gen-Ed classes together."

"I thought you might be dating," I state matter-of-factly, though curious.

"Actually." She lets out a light laugh. "It's funny you should mention that. We've never dated, but always do things together as a group." She smiles thoughtfully, like there's more to the story.

Not sure whether I should pry, "Oh," is all I manage to say, chickening out. I don't know her well enough to ask such personal questions.

She reads my expression and fills me in, without prompting. "You see, there's crazy chemistry between us, but for some reason, we never act on it." She shrugs, making the next statement sound like a question. "I guess we just don't want to mess up a good thing." She shakes her head before continuing, "We've been friends for the last two years. Neither of us have dated anyone seriously, but we do date from time to time."

"Sounds complicated," I reply, still not knowing what to say. I can tell there's more to the story, but I'm not one to be pushy.

"It's not as dramatic as it sounds." Sophie laughs lightly. "We just like to have fun and haven't taken any steps to further our relationship."

"I think I understand." Feeling more comfortable, I ask, "So it's you who wants to stay 'just friends'?"

She sighs and giggles as if my question catches her by surprise. She throws her hair over her shoulders and continues to look at the road. "Well, to be honest, we've never officially talked about anything. We keep it casual. I know I like him, and it could potentially lead somewhere, but for now, I'm happy with the way things are."

"Sounds reasonable." I grin. Then change the subject because we're back at our complex. "Want some help taking these in?" I point to the back seat filled with bags.

"Thanks, that'd be great." Between the two of us, we carry everything in just one load.

As we enter her apartment, music plays softly from the back room. Her apartment's similar to mine, but there's another door off the living room.

"That's Erin, my roommate." Sophie gestures to the bedroom at the end of the hallway.

"Oh. I didn't know you had a roommate."

"Yeah, we met in the dorms, freshman year. We hit it off and the rest, as they say, is history." She smiles as she sets the groceries down on the counter. "You'll have to meet her, she's great." Sophie's quiet for a moment and then says, "She's likely talking on the phone with her boyfriend, James, or she's almost asleep."

"Another time." I smile, not wanting to interrupt. Glancing at my watch, I see it's almost ten. "Wow, I'd better go. I have an early class in the morning."

"Sure. Thanks so much for coming with me." Sophie warmly smiles.

"No problem. Thanks for asking," I sincerely state.

"I know you're new and thought you might want to get out of your apartment," she offers.

After Sophie and I say goodbye, she stands on her doorstep, until she sees me reach my apartment safely. "Thanks again!' she calls out.

"Anytime!" I holler back in her direction as I open the door.

As I enter my apartment, I feel exhausted. I've been on the go since six, and I haven't had a moment to rest. I'm relieved my class doesn't start until nine. If I can sleep in, I'm definitely going to try.

WHILE RUNNING on campus a little after seven Thursday morning, I appreciate how quickly I've settled into a routine. I'm relieved my schedule's manageable. Between going to class, work, and studying, I still have time for myself. As a bonus, I'm able to catch up on any needed sleep on Tuesdays and Thursdays, and still get a decent run in, since my first class isn't until nine.

This morning, I run over to the middle of campus. I run past the clocktower and make my way behind Holland Library, next to the gyms. I check my watch and realize it's later than I thought. Crap. I see steps along the library, which will bring me back to the top of campus. I quickly run up and make my way along the path across the top of the library. Since it's flat ground, I pick up my pace to save some time. I cut around the corner of the building and suddenly, someone's there.

"Whoa," a deep voice calls out as we collide, tumbling

into one another. I see him squeeze the cup of coffee he's holding, and the lid flips up into the air, as we both are knocked to the ground. As if in slow motion, he lands on the ground, the cup he's holding flies up into the air, turns over, and spills its contents everywhere.

"Well, good morning to you, Alex!" the deep voice echoes with sarcasm. The stranger smiles apologetically, quickly making his way to his feet. Once upright, he reaches his hand toward mine to help me up.

"I'm so sorry…" I begin to sputter, but I'm caught off guard by the fact he knows my name. Instead of saying anything coherent, I stare at him, confused.

He reads my dumbfounded expression. "You know, there're better ways to get my attention?" His handsome face splits into a wide smile.

"Um." I bite on my lower lip, not knowing how to respond. Taking a moment to fully assess the situation, his golden-brown eyes scrutinize me. *How in the world does he know my name? Is he in one of my classes?*

I look him over closely. His white t-shirt and khaki cargo shorts have long, jagged, brown streaks and splattered spots all over them. He stares back with wide eyes, filled with concern. He wipes his muscular tan arm on the back of his shirt while waiting for me to respond.

"You okay, Alex?"

Again, I'm confused and at a loss for words. I manage to sputter, "I'm fine… Are you?" My face flushes crimson, and he chuckles loudly.

"Yes, but our clothes may not be." An eyebrow raises in my direction.

His perusal causes me to blush deeper. It's then I realize

the entire front side of my once white tank top is now brownish gray. "Oh," is all I manage to reply, still staring, feeling confused.

He runs his hands through his thick, dark-brown hair. All of a sudden, his eyes tighten while his brows pull together, as if he's deciding something important. Our eyes lock for a moment of silent awkwardness. He finally stretches out his hand to me. "Um, I'm Gavin."

I still can't think clearly. *Did I hit my head?* His eyes hold mine. I shake my head to regain control of my thoughts. He looks vaguely familiar, but I can't place him.

"Hi, Gavin." I watch him apprehensively, noticing his face flush a little.

"Um… We met the other day at Starbucks," he sputters out rapidly, unlocking his eyes from mine to look around nervously. "With Sophie," he tacks on for further clarification.

I consciously blink a few times and inhale slowly while it all comes back to me. "Oh, right!" It comes out louder than I'm expecting, which makes my cheeks light on fire from embarrassment.

"Are you sure you're all right?" he sincerely asks, looking me over, checking for any sign of injuries.

I flex and look myself over, finding nothing hurts. "I'm just a little wet." I smile in embarrassment as I meet his gaze again.

"You're not the only one," he sighs sheepishly. Then he grins widely. "I wish we could have met again under better circumstances."

Not knowing what to say, I fumble with the cords to my earbuds that fell during the fall. "You sure I didn't hurt you?" As I look him over now that he's upright, I realize he towers over my five-foot-seven frame. Geez, he must be at least six foot three.

"I'm fine." He grins widely back at me. "Where are you going in such a hurry?"

"Just finishing my morning run." I shrug guiltily, trying to explain, but still unsure what to say. He simply stares with an unreadable expression on his face. So I prattle out an explanation, the best I can. "There haven't been many people out this early before... And it's later than I thought... I took a shortcut up the back of the library... Picked up my pace..." I take a deep breath and stop rambling my long-winded explanation because he's still wearing a strange look, and I can't help but uncomfortably ask, "What?"

"Nothing," Gavin solemnly states, then takes a quick breath as if he's about to say something else, but nothing comes out. His brows draw together as if he's contemplating something but says nothing. He glances at his watch. "I'd better get to class, or I'll be late."

"Uggh. You don't have time to change? I'm so sorry for not paying better attention." I look up at him and apologetically sigh.

"You weren't the only one." He smiles again, letting a hint of sarcasm leak out. "You'd better get to class, too, Alex. I'll see you around!"

He gives another incredibly gorgeous smile, letting me know he isn't upset and turns to walk toward his class.

"You, too," I reply to his back.

He turns around one last time and grins in my direction, leaving my stomach flipping with butterflies. "This isn't the worst morning I've ever had."

I'm left gaping as he turns and walks toward Todd Hall. It takes a few moments before I can think clearly. Glancing at my watch, once I've regained my composure, I see I'm really late. "Shoot," I mumble to myself in frustration. This *is not* the way to start the morning.

I take the shortest route home. The entire time I replay the awkward scene in my head. Each time, I'm left dwelling on his phrasing of things. Every time, I'm left utterly speechless.

I rush through a shower, get dressed, and pull my hair into a loose knot before gathering my things for class. I return to campus and arrive in my seat as the professor calls my English studies class to order.

Though my mind's on the encounter with Gavin, lingering on his facial expressions, I'm somewhat able to pay attention to my professor and participate when called upon for an answer. My mind keeps wandering to Gavin, though. I can't figure out how to read him... It's as if he found the whole thing comical, or there's an inside joke I'm not privy to. Don't even get me started on how attractive he is.

I walk to geology, eating a granola bar on the way to Webster Hall. I wash it down with my water bottle, then enter the lecture room. I choose a table to sit where the aisle seat is open. I'm still mulling over my eventful morning when the professor begins her lecture. It's about halfway through class when I notice the dark-haired boy sitting to my right, about six or seven people away from me, in the row below.

He's facing the professor. His thick, dark-brown hair's kept trimmed, but barely touches his ears, neck, and eyebrows. From his side profile, I can see the front of his shirt. Yep, he's wearing the same white-splattered t-shirt from earlier this morning.

Immediately, my face flushes crimson, and my heart thuds in my chest, as I realize how cruel the universe is. Gavin's in this class. I quickly take my hair out of its knot, letting it fall to shield my face. I prop my head with my right hand and look discreetly from the holes of my fingers at him again. Mortification doesn't begin to describe my feelings. I have to find a way to leave without him noticing me once class is over. I don't need to embarrass myself any further today.

A few minutes later, I hear him answer a question the professor has apparently asked, though I'm unaware of the nature of that question. *Get a hold of yourself, Alex*. I need to pay attention. I can't afford to be so preoccupied. I have lab this afternoon and surely, it'll help if I listen to the lecture today.

As our professor finishes her lecture, I gather my things. I turn my back to Gavin, trying to stay undetected, placing my feet in the aisle while I put the notes I finally got around to taking into my backpack. The auditorium empties around me. Luckily, there's no one waiting to get out next to me. I take my time to put things away neatly, hoping Gavin's already left the hall. As I stand to walk out, I hear a deep and suddenly all-too-familiar voice call my name.

Shoot! Obviously, I wasn't successful at being unnoticed. I turn around, feeling my face heat as I respond, "Hey," as nonchalantly as I can manage.

"I see you were able to change?" He grins as he looks me over. His perusal makes me flush even hotter.

"I see you weren't," I moan apologetically. I swing my

backpack over my shoulder, and we walk together up the aisle toward the exit.

"It's not so bad. I've been dry for the last couple of hours," he teases.

"I'm glad. I made it home and cleaned up before my first class."

"That's great." He pauses for a moment, then continues in a joking tone. "You managed to get the worst of it, you know." He chuckles, obviously remembering the incident.

Not knowing how else to respond, I whisper, "Oh."

We walk out of Webster Hall together in an uncomfortable silence. Once outside, he catches me off guard by stopping to face me. I take a deep breath, coming to an immediate halt. When I feel brave enough to face him again, I see an indecipherable look on his face. It's a cross between deeply concentrating and a little self-righteous all at the same time. "So, when's your lab?"

Once again, I feel completely inept for the second time today. I manage to eventually sputter out, "Uh, at three today."

"Oh," is all he says as his exquisite, golden-brown eyes lock onto mine, making me feel even more self-conscious. *Why can't I act normal around him?*

Finally, curiosity gets the better of me, and I ask, "Why?"

He beams a brilliant smile at me. "Well, I just want to know if I need to be prepared for class?"

"For?" I draw out, unsure of where he's coming from with his comment.

"I have lab today at three, too. Just wondering if I should bring an extra set of clothes." By now, he's grinning widely.

Is it possible to burst into flames from sheer humiliation?

Finally, I get it under control and let out a little huff of frustration. Sarcasm rolls easily off my tongue. "I don't really think that'll be necessary."

He chuckles at my response. "Well, I guess I'll see you at three."

After a few moments, I manage a delayed response, "Okay."

"Well, I'm going this way." He points back to the top of campus. Though it's a statement, he makes it also sound like a possible invitation at the same time.

Pointing in the direction of my apartment. "I'm over here."

He flashes another brilliant smile in my direction. "See ya!"

"Okay." I shrug and turn to walk home before anything else could be said. I force myself to look straight ahead as I depart, resisting the urge to look back. It's a bit of a challenge, but somehow, I manage.

On my walk home, I become frustrated at how flustered I am around Gavin. I've never had this problem before. All I seem to do around him is sputter and stare. It's uncharacteristic of me. Usually, I have a broad vocabulary, rather than one-word, nondescript answers. I feel completely inept. Maybe I'll be able to avoid him this afternoon during lab.

To pass the time and get my mind off that ridiculous boy, I spend the next two hours cleaning my apartment. I even resort to scrubbing the sink, tub, and toilet, which don't really need it, but it eats up time. Finally, around two, I open a can of soup and heat it on the stove and slowly eat my lunch.

Realizing there's nothing left to do, I grudgingly gather my things for geology lab and make my way back to campus. I have planned my arrival perfectly, allowing little time before class to socialize. I walk into the room and find numerous tables with two stools at each. I force myself not to look around as I enter the room. I choose an empty spot in the back of the room next to a red-headed girl with freckles. As I walk to the table, she greets me with a warm smile.

"May I?" I gesture to the vacant seat next to her.

"Sure, it's yours," she welcomes me eagerly. "I'm Tabatha."

"Hi, I'm Alex." I sit, putting my backpack next to me, feeling relieved. I've successfully evaded Gavin.

When I discreetly glance around, I notice he's already sitting next to a tan, blond-haired guy who looks like he should be surfing, rather than confined in Pullman surrounded by wheat fields. On a positive note, Gavin's ahead of me, so he isn't able to look at me, at least not without extending some effort. On the flip side of that coin, he's in my direct line of sight to the lab instructor, who introduces himself as Ian Marshal, a graduate student. This doesn't help in the slightest. Instantly, I feel myself blush in memory of my earlier awkwardness. *This is going to be a long semester.*

Ian, as he prefers to be called, gives a course overview and reviews the expectations for this semester. I force myself to keep detailed notes, to refrain from being distracted by Gavin. After reviewing the syllabus, Ian discusses the topic of plate tectonics from the lecture earlier this week. He also gives an overview of the geology in Washington State. Thankfully, throughout most of the entire two-hour lab, I'm able to fully concentrate on the lecture and hands-on activity Tabatha and I complete together. Only once do my eyes meet Gavin's. Of course, I'm frozen on the spot as he raises one eyebrow, smiles, and gives a quick nod in my general direction. As soon as I'm able to break eye contact, I force myself to pay strict attention to the lab activity we've been assigned.

As Tabatha and I work on our plate tectonics activity, I learn she's a communications major, who's originally from Spokane. Tabatha and I get along well and are able to finish a little ahead of others. I'm relieved because Ian had mentioned at the beginning of the lab, we could leave once we were finished.

Tabatha and I exchange numbers as we gather our things to leave. While she programs my number into her phone, I come up with a brilliant plan to successfully exit the room without Gavin detecting me. If I casually keep in conversation with Tabatha, I'll be able to safely avoid any interactions with him. I've already experienced more humiliation than I can handle in one day. Remaining as relaxed as I can, I make eye contact with Tabatha and pump her with questions to help her carry most of our conversation. Once outside, I thank her again for all her help and say goodbye.

Relief washes over me on my way home. I'm finally able to relax and take in the warm afternoon. As I reach the dining hall, I see Sophie approaching. I smile and wave. When she gets closer, I see she doesn't have her backpack with her, so she must not be going to a class.

"Hey, Alex! How's your first week going?"

"Great!" *Except for Today.* "How's yours?"

"Good. I think I'm going to like it." She grins.

"Me, too. So… What are you up to?"

"Oh, I'm meeting Josh for dinner at the CUB." She grins a little. "What are your plans?"

"I just finished my geology lab, and I'm heading home." I grin as I remember our conversation from earlier about Josh. "I hope you have fun!"

"Do you work tonight?" she asks.

"No, now that classes have started, I'm only working Monday, Tuesday, and Wednesday, unless they need someone to fill in."

"Want to join me for dinner? There will be a group of us."

Thinking about the last time we ran into Josh and who his company was makes me blush. I try to conceal it the best I can. "Um, I actually have a lot of studying to do tonight. It's my first night off this week." I smile apologetically, then add so I don't sound like I'm avoiding her, "What are you doing this weekend?"

"Nothing, really." She shrugs and speculates my expression.

"Maybe we could do something?" I stammer, trying not to sound so self-conscious to divert her from finding out about Gavin, the real reason behind my blushing.

"Sure, what do you have in mind?" she eagerly asks.

Not having a clue as to what there is to do, I throw my arms up in defeat. I smile and sarcastically reply, "I don't know. I'm new here. What's fun?"

"There's lots of things." She giggles sarcastically back.

"Well, we'll decide this weekend. I'll give you a call later." I snicker. "I should let you go, so you're not late."

"It's okay. Are you sure you can't come?" she pleads.

"Yeah," I sigh, still holding onto my first excuse. "I'll see you this weekend."

"Okay." Disappointment is clear on her face as she looks mine over again. "See you later." She turns and walks toward campus.

"Bye."

3

UNAVOIDABLE

SATURDAY MORNING, I actually manage to sleep in. By the time I leave the house, it's after eight. I run the same path Sophie and I took toward Starbucks, planning to run downtown. When I'm running in place, waiting at a stop light, I see something that stops me in my tracks. Well, not something, someone. Gavin to be more specific.

He's about to enter Starbucks. His back faces me. Even though I shouldn't be able to identify him from this distance, I'm sure it's him. I recognize his towering height, his muscular body, and thick, dark-brown hair. It's the same stance and body that walked away from me twice before and left me gaping. I panic and think of a way to avoid him. I don't, under any circumstances, want to make a fool of myself again.

I make a one-hundred-eighty-degree turn and run toward Moscow. I cross the street about a block away and run up the road I recognize as the one leading me to a grocery store. I know I can then make a big loop and make my way back to my apartment eventually.

Though running usually relaxes me, today I'm guilt stricken and anxious. I feel bad about avoiding Gavin, both Thursday in class, and now this morning. He's done nothing wrong. I'm being ridiculous. I can't believe I'm letting him have this effect on me. I don't even know his last name, let alone anything about him. He's handled things perfectly acceptable, witty even, while I've been a bumbling idiot.

When I arrive back at my apartment later that morning, I honestly don't know how I managed to get here. It's as if my body's on autopilot and my brain's checked out to lunch. I take a long, hot shower and get ready for the rest of my day.

Around ten, my phone rings. Thinking it might be Sophie, I rush to the phone. As I see the caller ID, a smile lights up my face. It's Jacob, my older brother. "Hey, Jake. What's up?" I'm surprised to hear from him. We're pretty close, but we're busy with our own lives and don't get the chance to chat much.

"Not much. How's your first week of classes?"

"Really good. I've met a few people. So far, classes have gone well," I tell him about Sophie, Tabatha, and my professors. We also talk about my apartment, job, and what I think of Pullman itself. I leave out Gavin because I don't want him to tease me like he always does about boys. Besides, there's really nothing to tell. Jacob knows I haven't really dated anyone seriously. I doubt he'll even think to ask me about boys. That's usually Katherine or Mom's job.

"What are your plans for the weekend?" Jacob asks curiously.

"Um, Sophie's coming over for lunch, then we're seeing a movie later."

"Which one?"

"Um, I'm not sure. We'll decide when she gets here." I walk to the kitchen and look through my cupboards, trying to decide what to cook.

"Well, it sounds like fun. I'm glad you're making friends. I've been worried because it's harder to meet people when you live on your own."

"I know, Jake, but I love my apartment. Really, I'm doing fine. You don't have to worry," I assure him.

"Al, that's not what I'm saying," he adds in a light laugh, "I'm just remembering what it was like for me once I moved out of the dorms. I had friends, but it was harder to stay in contact, scattered throughout campus."

"It's actually been amazing, Jake. Things are falling into place the way they should." *Apparently, falling literally at times, too. As I remember the tall, brown-haired boy occupying my thoughts today.*

"Good for you, Alex!" There's a short pause on the other end of the telephone, and then I hear Jacob sigh. "What are your plans later this week?"

"Well, I work Monday through Wednesday and have lab until five on Thursday. Why?"

"Want some company Thursday or Friday evening?" He takes a short breath and sounds like he's thinking of something. Then he adds, "I have a conference on Wednesday and Thursday in Spokane."

"I'd love to see you. I can only offer a couch or my bed, though." Knowing he'd never take my bed from me, I smile to wait for his response.

"I can get a hotel. It's a business trip. I'll extend for the day. I have plans Saturday, so I'll leave Friday afternoon."

"Sounds good! When will you get here?"

"Um… I'm not sure when the conference will end. I'll call when I'm on my way. I'll leave a message if you're still in class."

"I can't wait to see you," I say excitedly. I love visiting with him. We always have fun. We haven't had a lot of time since he moved to Seattle to work as a finance manager.

"See you Thursday. Have a great week."

"Love you, Alex."

"Love you, too, Jake," I say as I hang up the phone and gather ingredients to make chicken salad for lunch.

A little after twelve, there's a knock at my door.

"Hey, Alex," Sophie greets me.

"Hello. Lunch is almost finished. We just need to throw it all together." I smile as we talk toward my kitchen. "You can sit, I'll get everything."

As I toss in the remainder of the ingredients, Sophie sits on one of my barstools. "Is there anything I can do?" she asks helplessly.

"No, not really. What movie do you want to see?"

She smiles a little. "I don't have any idea what's playing. I haven't seen a movie in… I don't know when." She looks as if she is lost in thought.

"We can do something else," I suggest, if she's not into watching a movie.

"No, a movie sounds great. Too bad it's an away game this week. You'll have to go to the football game next weekend." She smiles and then adds, "You do have your sports pass, right?"

"Of course. I'm looking forward to it. It'll be more fun with friends."

"There's a group I always go with. It'll be so much fun," Sophie says enthusiastically.

"Sounds great. So, what do you want to do today?"

"Um…" She takes a bite of salad. "Wow, this is really good. I can't believe you just threw all this together."

"Thanks. It's one of my favorites."

The romantic comedy we want to see doesn't start until four fifteen. To pass the time, Sophie suggests rollerblading along Chipman Trail, that leads to Moscow.

"We don't have to go the whole way there," Sophie teases when she sees my expression as I remember it's an eight-mile drive to Moscow. "It's just a great place to ride that's relatively flat. We'll have fun if we drive to the trailhead. I'm not a big fan of steep hills and rollerblades!"

"Me neither," I whole-heartedly agree, thinking of the painful consequences. "I'll drive." I walk over to my front closet to pull out my rollerblades and wrist pads.

"Let me help you with the rest of these dishes, then we can go to my place and get mine."

When we get to Sophie's apartment, Erin and her boyfriend, James, are just finishing lunch themselves. To my surprise, James is one of the guys I met with Sophie on our trip to Starbucks. I attempt to hide my blush as I come to this realization. *The world's getting smaller and smaller.* I distract myself by watching TV until I can regain my composure.

"What are you guys up to?" James asks once we've all been officially introduced.

Sophie responds before I can, "We're going rollerblading, then to a movie around four."

"Sounds fun. Mind if we rollerblade with you?" He looks at Erin for approval, but she is nodding her head and smiling. "We were thinking of doing that today, too."

"Sure. You don't mind, do you, Alex?"

"Not at all. I can drive, if you'd like?" I offer to the group.

"Do you mind stopping by my place to pick up my blades?" James asks.

"No problem, you'll just have to tell me the way," I respond.

Erin walks into the other room as she calls out, "I'll just be a minute. I want to change and get my things."

Sophie walks into her bedroom at the same time, leaving James and me alone in the living room.

"So where are you from, Alex?" James asks me.

"I'm from the Olympia area," I state, since no one ever knows where I live.

"What do you like to do for fun?"

"Um…" I think for a moment then add, "I like to run, read, hang out with friends. You know, the usual." I shrug.

"Have you found some places to run since arriving in Pullman?"

"Yeah, I have a few different routes I've found so for. Most either are across campus, or downtown."

"Sounds good. Do you play any sports? We have some great intramural teams here on campus, if you're ever interested."

"I've played, but not since high school. Mostly soccer, cross country, and track. I also played a few years of basketball, too." I smile when I realize I don't want to sound too full of myself. But the truth is, I've always been on a team throughout the entire year. That's why I run so much, to burn my excess energy.

"We're always looking for girls to play on our co-ed soccer team. If you're interested, we practice on Thursday and Sunday evenings. It's usually around seven p.m., but it sometimes changes depending on field availability. Games are pretty late though," he adds, sounding hesitant.

"I work until eight Monday, Tuesday, and Wednesday," I sigh, not wanting to get my hopes up if the dates change. It'd be fun to play again.

"No problem. When I say late, I mean, late. We start after around nine," James encourages enthusiastically.

"Wow, that sounds fun." I feel encouraged this might work out. "When's your next practice?"

Sophie and Erin return at the same time to the living room.

"Tomorrow at seven."

"What's at seven?" Sophie interjects.

"Soccer practice." James smiles and raises an eyebrow in her direction.

"Oh, he's always trying to get girls for their team." Erin shakes her head and laughs in my direction. "Did he wrangle you in? I'll warn you, they're pretty intense."

"Oh," is all I manage as I read her reaction. Then I can't help but grin. "That shouldn't be a problem."

James ignores Erin's remarks and seriously asks, "I'll meet you here around six? If that's okay, Alex?"

"Sure, sounds good." I shrug and fumble the keys in my hand, now that everyone's ready to leave.

"Ready?" James turns to Erin and Sophie.

"Let's go," Sophie replies before Erin.

The Chipman Trail's near our apartments, at the bottom of the hill. Like Sophie promised, it's a flat, well-paved path that runs parallel to the Moscow-Pullman Highway. We're surrounded by wheat fields, once outside of Pullman.

Everyone enjoys themselves. We laugh and joke around the entire time. It feels natural to hang out together. I finally feel myself relax and enjoy this experience with new friends. They easily accept me and make me feel as if I'm no longer an outsider intruding on their fun. We end up skating about two miles before we turn around.

By the time we return, Sophie and I have just enough time to drop off Erin and James at Sophie's apartment before heading to the theater in Moscow. We quickly grab snacks at the concession stand and find a place to sit as the movie begins. The theater's only halfway full, so we are easy to find our seats in the dark.

After the movie, we go to a Mexican restaurant. Sophie and I talk about the movie until our food arrives. As I take the first bite of my chicken burrito, Sophie changes the subject abruptly, catching me off guard.

"So, what position do you play?"

Not fully following her, I just stare blankly, waiting for further explanation.

"Soccer. You said you play soccer." She smiles when she realizes how lost I am but continues chewing her food.

"Depends on where the coach wants me." I shrug, trying to stay modest. "I can play everywhere, but usually offense."

"Cool. I play goalie a lot." She chuckles.

"You're on the team, too?" I'm shocked she hasn't mentioned it. "Why didn't you say something earlier?"

"I just didn't think of it, I guess," she sighs and lets out a little laugh. "Now that we have you on the team, we'll be able to have substitutions. The beginning of the season is a few weeks away."

"That's awesome! It'll be nice knowing someone else on the field." I take another bite before I adding, "I'm looking forward to playing again. It's been awhile."

"Good, I'm glad James asked you because I would've if he didn't." She lets out a little chortle, then finishes her burrito.

On Sunday, when I arrive at Sophie's apartment, she and James are dressed and ready for practice.

"Ready?" Sophie asks James as I enter the living room.

"Sure, let's get going." He stands and reaches for his backpack next to the kitchen counter.

Sophie disappears into her bedroom and returns with a bag of her own. "I'll drive, if you want," she eagerly volunteers.

"Where's practice?" I ask curiously.

"There's a field we use across town, next to the high school," James responds before Sophie can.

When we get to the field, five people are stretching. Two girls, the rest guys.

"Hey, guys. This is Alex," Sophie calls to get their attention.

I hear various responses of hello from everyone as they look in my direction. Sophie introduces me to everyone individually while we wait for practice to begin. I'm trying to commit names to faces, but I'm sure it'll take me more than one practice to master them.

"So… Who are we waiting on?" James asks the group as he counts the players.

No one answers immediately, causing James to mumble to himself, "Oh, I know. Never mind..." As he shakes his head, continuing to stretch on his own.

Everyone stretches individually while we wait for the remaining players. James tells the group about some warm-up drills we should do to get us working as a team. We break into two even lines of four and pass the ball to one another, making our way across the field.

I'm working with my partner halfway down the field when I hear James announce, "Well, look who's decided to finally make it."

"It's barely six now," a deep, familiar voice replies. "You must've started early."

When I see Gavin and Josh approach the field together, my heart sputters. It takes my concentration to finish the drill with my partner, Samantha. Thankfully, I have something to distract myself and maintain my composure.

When Samantha and I make it back from the other side of the field, I'm relieved to find Josh and Gavin are halfway down the field, taking their turn. We continue different warm-up drills for thirty minutes. Each time Gavin's near, I make sure I'm busy concentrating on a task, so I don't show how easily he distracts my train of thought. I'm thankful Samantha's skilled because we push each other further and remain busy.

Eventually, Josh calls us all over to pick sides for a scrimmage. I'm on the same team as Sophie, Samantha, Josh, and James. The other team consists of Gavin, Andrew, Paul, and two girls by the names of Carmen and Shannon. I play forward, which keeps me focused entirely on the game. I manage to ignore Gavin, other than when I play directly against him, which proves to be quite interesting.

Gavin and I are intense when it comes to being one-on-one with the ball. I eventually manage to dribble hard to his left and pass the ball to Sophie. She in turn makes a shot at the goal, but it's blocked by their goalie. I'm thankful everyone is even matched on this team. If we play this well against others, we should do really well.

At the end of practice, we all linger to drink water as we gather our things and change out of our cleats. Gavin chooses this time to sit beside me, making me feel incredibly self-conscious.

I greet him with a smile, not knowing what to say.

"Hey," he says as he returns a smile. He takes off his shoes and digs for something in his bag. He finds his water bottle and turns to face me. "So, you play soccer, too?"

"I try." I grin, trying to sound modest, while making a conscious effort to remain coherent around him. Geesh, I can talk to anyone but Gavin. Why does he have this effect on me?

"You're okay." He smiles smugly, locking his eyes onto mine.

I break away and distract myself by looking at my water bottle before I take another drink.

"How long have you been playing?" he asks after taking a drink.

"Since I was six," I admit as I trace the top of my water bottle with my index finger.

"Thought so," is all he replies. *How do I take that? Yeesh, Gavin's so frustrating.* I wish I wasn't a bumbling idiot around him and could respond as quickly as him. *What is it about him that turns me into a complete fool?*

"Are you ready?" Sophie interrupts my pondering.

"Sure, just a sec." I close my water bottle and finish gathering my things.

I turn to Gavin, but he's faster than me. "I'll see you around." He smiles and holds my gaze a moment longer than necessary.

This sends me reeling. I'm positive I'm blushing by now, but I manage to say, "See you," as I quickly get up to follow Sophie and James.

When I catch up with Sophie, she asks, "Did you enjoy yourself?"

"Yes, it's great playing again." I avert my eyes from her to regain coherent thoughts and distract myself from thinking about Gavin any further.

"Boy, you and Gavin are intense when you want something," she states matter-of-factly.

This catches me off guard. "What do you mean?" I sputter out after taking a drink of my water, nearly spitting everywhere.

"Well, you both fight for the ball. It's only our first practice, but we should kick some serious tail with both of you as forwards."

I know she means nothing by this, but I'm suddenly self-conscious. I'd taken her comment to mean my interest in Gavin, causing mortification to set in. "Oh," is all I can reply. He'd killed it on the field. I've never played on a co-ed team before, but I'm sure I was able to hold my own out there. *If only I could do this when I talk to him off the field.*

I'm relatively quiet on the ride home. My mind drifts to

Gavin and the connection we have. It completely unhinges me. How can he do this to me?

When we arrive home, I make up an excuse of needing to study, so I can avoid possible conversations about Gavin. I'm already thinking about him more than I should, and I'd rather Sophie not notice. Maybe I'll fill her in later once I figure him out.

The next day, classes fly by. I'd read the necessary chapters on Sunday, so I easily follow along during the lectures. I arrive early at work and eat before my shift starts. Thankfully, work is busy, allowing me to keep myself occupied.

It's a little before six when my uneventful day changes. I'm bringing out a chicken alfredo and spaghetti with meatballs to one of my tables when I see *him* seated at my destination. He's sitting with Josh, and his back is to me.

"Hello, Alex," his deep voice says smoothly as I approach.

"Gavin," I reply, then focus on the food in my hands. "Chicken Alfredo?" I ask, trying to discern which dish belongs to whom.

"That's me." He smiles warmly.

I place his plate in front of him and put the spaghetti in front of Josh.

Looking slyly at Josh, Gavin asks, "You remember Alex?"

Josh looks a little confused and raises his eyebrows suspiciously at Gavin, but calmly replies, "Yeah, I remember," giving me an encouraging smile. "Hello, Alex."

"Hi," I hesitate for a moment, "Um… Is there anything else I can get you?" trying to stay in control of my voice. I glance between the both of them for an answer.

"No, thank you, Alex," Gavin says as his eyes lock onto mine for a moment longer than necessary again.

"Let me know if you do," I casually reply. Forcing myself to turn away, I focus on serving a few more customers.

A few minutes later, I make my traditional rounds to each table, checking to see how their meals are going as well as if they need anything else. Gavin and Josh are laughing at something when I arrive to ask them, "How's everything?"

It's Josh who speaks first. "Fine, can I have another Coke?"

"Sure. What about you, Gavin?"

"I think…" He hesitates for a thoughtful moment. "I'll have a coffee." He smiles as a chortle escapes. He turns his head directly to look at me for a moment, then winks from the eye Josh can't see.

"Sure," is all I manage, and I catch myself staring at him a moment longer than I probably should. *What on earth was that for?* I try to maintain my composure, though I'm sure my face gives me away with its sudden redness. When the feeling in my legs returns, I walk quickly to the kitchen to fill their drinks.

When I return, they're talking about a project for class. I take a deep breath to calm myself as I set down their drinks. "Anything else?"

"No, thanks," Josh replies while Gavin continues to stir some sugar into his coffee.

"See you tomorrow in class." Gavin smiles again before I turn to leave.

"See you," I reply, feeling unsure of what else I'm supposed to say. My face burns again as I walk away.

As I serve other tables, I can't help but notice Gavin. He

and Josh talk animatedly throughout their meal. I'm serving another customer when Gavin and Josh walk past me to leave. Each smile and nod at me as they go, but Gavin's has a lingering effect.

The remainder of my shift creeps by. For some reason, the restaurant slows down, literally. I'm forced to find busy work to fill the time. It's frustrating because I've been using the rush of customers to avoid thinking about my interactions with Gavin. *Why can't I just be normal around him?*

Around seven thirty, Andrea asks if I'd like to leave early. With nothing left to do, I quickly gather my things and return home.

The rest of the evening is spent writing a paper for my English studies class. I completed most of it on Sunday, but I want to go over it once again before I turn it in. It's only a little after nine when my final copy's printed. Being too early for bed, I pull out my geology textbook to prepare for tomorrow. Geology isn't the most interesting subject, but it keeps my mind off the person I'm not allowing myself to think about. Sort of.

The next morning, I go for a run, as usual. I head over to campus around seven thirty, making great time to arrive at class on time. When I turn to run down Terral Mall, I see him. He's sitting on a bench, reading a book with a cup of coffee in hand. As I approach, he looks up and grins with the most breathtaking smile. He greets me, "Good morning." His deep voice sends shivers up my spine.

I contemplate running right past him, but since he's unavoidable these days, I might as well stop and not be rude. I slow down and come to a halt as I get about a yard from him. "Hey, Gavin," I say out of breath as I take out my earbuds.

"I see you're out early." He raises one eyebrow as he looks me over.

Still out of breath, I admit, "Yeah, I'm on time today."

"Run into anyone today?" Gavin asks, thick with sarcasm.

"Nope, not today." My breath returns to normal as I let my own sarcasm roll out.

"Do you run every day?" he asks as he sets his coffee on the bench next to him.

"Yep," I reply, wondering why he wants to know.

"Oh." This is surprising. He always has a comment for everything. Suddenly, his dark eyebrows pull together as if he's deeply concentrating, yet he says nothing. His gaze lands on me, scrutinizing. *How frustrating. I'm dying to know what's going on in that handsome head of his.*

Though I linger on his dark, golden-brown eyes, I fill the moment of awkward silence by stating, "Well... I should keep running." After another few long moments, I finally break his hold on me. I look toward home and continue, "I don't want to be late for class."

"Sure." Gavin takes a deep breath and stands. "I've gotta get to class, too." He gathers his things and walks in the direction I'm heading. "See you then." He looks down and smiles at me, and my belly flips out of control.

"B... Bye," I mutter and can't help but be in awe of how much he towers over me.

He simply nods. I glance at my watch and readjust my earbuds. I hit play on my phone as I wave goodbye. Keeping my eyes on the brick path ahead of me, I force myself not to look back until I know I'm way out of sight. I go home, take a shower, and get ready for my English studies class.

While walking to Webster Hall for geology, I wonder what's in store for me today. After pondering about Gavin all morning, I've come to the realization that I have to get a grip on things. I need to at least pretend to be normal around him. He's everywhere I go. *He is just being friendly because we have the same friends,* I remind myself sternly.

I'm one of the first to arrive. I choose an aisle seat and pull out a granola bar and my notebook while I wait for class to begin. Within a few minutes, people fill the auditorium. It isn't long before I feel the presence of someone beside me. I look up to see a tall figure staring at me with a smile on his face. Gavin doesn't say anything until I look at him directly. Once again, I'm taken back by his beautiful, golden-brown eyes, dark hair, and perfectly clear skin. My stomach flips, and my face heats.

"Mind if I sit with you?" he asks and gestures at the empty seat.

Holy crap. He wants to sit by me? It's one thing to be aware of him from across the room, another thing entirely to have him in smelling distance. I can't help but notice he has a distinct fragrance to him that makes me almost drool. I look at him, bewildered, and he continues to wait for my response. Finally, after what seems like an eternity, I manage a meager reply, "Sure."

He doesn't say anything but steps behind me and pulls out the chair to sit. He takes out his notebook and gets ready for class. Neither of us say anything and soon, our professor begins the lecture.

With last night's study session, I'm easily able to keep up

with the lecture. Unfortunately, this also means I'm unavoidably too aware of Gavin. Though I try not to, from the corner of my eye, I scrutinize his every expression. Most of the time, he concentrates on the lecture, but occasionally, he appears lost in thought. It's not like we can talk during class, but there's a distinct tension between us. By the end of the lecture, I'm so in tune with him, I can sense every move he makes.

When class is over, he breaks the uncomfortable silence. "So… Do you have class after this?" He gets up and gathers his things.

"No, I'm done for the day," I say as I put the last of my things into my backpack. I step out into the aisle, and we walk out of the auditorium together.

"Do you have another class?" I ask, not knowing what else to say, and it seems like a perfectly acceptable question.

"Yeah, I'm on my way to Carpenter Hall. I have one more class, then I'm done for the day, too."

Once we're outside, we walk together until we reach the street. "Well, have fun." I smile in his direction and turn right, heading home.

"See you later." He smiles and turns left toward his next class.

The rest of the day passes rather uneventful. Work tonight is slower than usual, but steady at the same time, so I'm able to keep myself busy. I study again when I get home, knowing that Jacob's coming Thursday and with soccer practice, I won't have much time.

4

FOOTBALL

ON MY WAY home from work Wednesday, I meet Sophie coming in from the parking lot. She greets me with a warm smile. "Hey, Alex. How's it going?" She waits for me to catch up, and we walk toward our apartments together.

"Good. I just got off work."

"Wanna ride to practice tomorrow?"

"My brother might be in town. Would anyone mind if he comes?"

"Not at all. Erin comes all the time," Sophie shares.

We arrive at the stairs of my apartment as I say, "I'll call about riding together. I can drive. My car's bigger. Though, I'm not sure what we'll be doing beforehand."

"Sounds good." She smiles and waves in my direction. "Have a good night."

"You, too," I reply and ascend the stairs to my apartment.

Once inside, I shower to rid myself from the pasta smell. Then I flip on the TV. There's nothing interesting to watch, but I use it as background noise as I relax and settle in for the evening. Around nine thirty, my phone rings. *Who'd be calling at this hour?*

"Hello?" I answer.

"Hey, Alex. How's it going?" I recognize the caller as Jake, though he seems tired.

"Good. When will you arrive tomorrow?"

"Well, my meeting should end around two, then I'll head straight to Pullman. You have class until five, right?"

"Yeah, that's when my lab ends." I hesitate for a moment then add, "Um, Jake… I've just joined this co-ed soccer team, and there's practice tomorrow at seven. Mind going with me?"

"Not at all. I'd love to watch you play again. Will it last long?" he asks.

"Uh… I've only been once. It wasn't longer than ninety minutes."

"It sounds like fun."

"Hey, I've been thinking…"

"Uh-oh," Jake teases.

"Seriously." I roll my eyes. "I'll leave my keys in my car so you can wait inside my apartment if you get here earlier. Plan on staying with me tomorrow. Then we'll see more of each other. You can take my bed."

"You sure? I don't want to intrude."

"No worries." I let out a little laugh. "It'll be like old times."

"Okay," he says hesitantly. "If you insist. A hotel isn't a bother, either."

"No way. I'm out of class at noon on Friday. We'll eat lunch before you leave."

"Sounds great. See you then."

"Drive safe, Jake."

"Will do, sis."

The next morning, I run into Gavin again during my morning jog, though thankfully, not literally this time. As I round the corner on Terral Mall from the clocktower, I notice him long before I reach him. He's sitting in the same place as Tuesday morning, wearing a pair of brown shorts and a long-sleeved, blue t-shirt, reading a book.

"Morning, Alex." He smiles, giving a slight nod in greeting.

"Hey, Gavin," I pant, out of breath, stopping in front of him.

He takes a drink of his coffee and puts down his book. "Where'd you run today?" His face is filled with genuine curiosity.

"Um… Downtown, then up Greek Row. I'm on my way back home." I'm still panting a little but get it out somewhat smooth.

"Wow, that's pretty far. You do that every day?"

"No, I change it up a little each day." I feel my face heat, and it has nothing do with my run.

"I guess I'll see you in class." He smiles at me and gathers his things.

"See you then," I reply, wondering if he'll sit next to me. As awkward as I feel around him, I secretly hope he does. It's indescribable, the feeling I get when he's around. I can't help but want to figure out why.

Apparently, while I'm lost in my thoughts, he stands to leave. "See you." I watch him for a few moments before shaking my head to clear my thoughts and run home.

My morning goes by in a blur. I'm early for geology, and

I sit in the same place as before. I eat a snack while reading the chapter we'll cover today. It's only a few minutes later when I hear the chair pull out next to me. I look up to see Gavin's handsome face smiling at me.

"Hey, how was your morning?" Gavin asks sincerely.

"Good, and you?" I quickly finish chewing my granola bar.

"Well, I gave a presentation, but I think it went well." He shrugs.

"What was it about?" I ask, trying to remember his major.

"Architectural design," he says nonchalantly.

"You're an architect major." It comes out more like a statement than an actual question.

"Yeah, it's my third year."

"Sounds interesting." It must be exciting to design buildings that come to life in the future.

The professor calls the class to attention. We shift in our seats at the same time to pay better attention.

Today's a little more comfortable than Tuesday with Gavin next to me. It's only awkward when our eyes inadvertently meet, and I have to force myself to quickly look away. Though this only happens a few times, I'm caught off guard each time, causing me to blush a little from embarrassment. *He must think I'm completely nuts, or crazy at the least.* I eventually force myself to not look in his direction at all, to save myself any further scrutinizing from him afterward.

When class ends, he's first to have his things put away. He patiently waits as I gather my things, allowing us to walk out together.

"So… I'll see you in lab." He smiles down at me. Once again, I'm in complete awe of his ability to capture me in just a single glance.

"Yeah, I'll be there." I attempt to sound casual, but not really managing. Inside, I feel like a long-tailed cat sitting in a room full of rocking chairs. My nerves are wound, and I'm clueless for knowing what to say. *Why does he have this effect on me?*

We walk down the steps of Webster and as usual, I walk to the right, he walks to the left. "See you." He waves in my direction.

I wave back in return. "Bye."

Knowing that I won't have much time tonight, I spend my time working on a humanities paper. Thanks to my extra studying, I'm caught up on everything else.

When I arrive at lab, Gavin's already there, which sets my heart racing. He motions for me to join him. Not seeing Tabatha, I slowly walk over and sit, trying to calm my nerves.

"How was your afternoon?" he asks casually as he smiles at my choice to sit with him.

"Good." I let out a sigh of relief. "I finished a paper so I can visit with my brother tonight."

Surprise fills his features. "Will you be at practice?" The full force of his stare is my kryptonite.

"Um…" Not being able to think for a moment, I finally shake my head and manage a "yes," at the same time.

Wow, I'd been doing so good. What's happening to me? How can he look at me that way and be so casual? His brilliant, golden-brown eyes draw me into an abyss. *Get a grip, Alex! You're acting crazy and need to stop before you look like a complete fool.* I scold myself while he says something in return, but I don't catch it.

He's looking at me as if he expects an answer. *Crap, what did he just say?* "Um..." is all I manage.

"Will your brother be at practice?" he asks a little loud, as if he's repeating it.

"Yes," I respond, still staring into his eyes. "That's okay, isn't it?"

"Sure, it'll be fun. Does he play?"

"Yeah." I finally unlock his hold from my stare and force myself to look around the room.

"He can practice, too, if he wants," he offers.

Just then Ian starts class, and we're put to work on another lab assignment. This week, we're observing and measuring earth materials. He assigns our first library module, which is due at the beginning of lab next week. Gavin and I keep fairly busy with this lab until time is almost over. As we pack up our things to leave, Gavin catches me off guard again.

"Want to complete the module together?" He puts the last of his supplies into his backpack as he nonchalantly asks this. Meanwhile, my stomach somersaults.

"Sure..." I manage to say.

"We have that quiz next week, too. Maybe we can get together this weekend?" He runs his hand through his hair and looks around nervously.

"Well, I've got plans with Sophie on Saturday. What about Sunday?"

"Sure, what time's good for you?"

"Um..." I bite my lip, not wanting to suggest an unrealistic time, but knowing me, I'll be working on homework in the morning already. "There's practice that evening, so what about earlier in the day?"

"Sure, it says in our syllabus, the library opens at noon. How does that sound?" he suggests. "I have to spend some time in the architecture studio later that afternoon."

"Good. Will you have enough time for studio?" I ask, not knowing how long the module will take.

We walk out of the lab together as we finish our conversation.

"Well, we could meet earlier, study for our quiz, then go to the science library when it opens. What about meeting at ten?" He smiles before adding, "Then we'll have time to study and complete our assignment." He lets out a small sigh. "Another big project's due next week, and this will give me more time in the studio."

"Where should we meet?" I ask, not knowing where to suggest.

"Holland Library opens at nine. Let's meet there first. I'll wait for you outside, and we'll find a place to study."

"Okay. I'll meet you on Terral Mall," I suggest.

"Great." He turns to open the door for me. "See you at practice." He smiles widely.

I stare at him as we walk outside. I hesitate as I turn toward my apartment. "I'll see you tonight then."

"Looking forward to it." He lets out a loud laugh then turns to leave in the opposite direction. *What in the world is he laughing for?*

As I reach my apartment, I see Jacob's car next to my 4-Runner, and I pick up my pace to see him. He's watching TV on the couch and stands to greet me with a hug when I enter.

"Hey, sis," he says as he lets go.

"Hey, Jake. How was your trip?"

He sighs in relief. "I'm glad it's over. I can only sit for so long listening to someone go on and on about theory when they've never tested it in the real world."

I let out a little snicker. It's uncharacteristic of him to complain about work. "That bad, huh?"

"It was fine until this afternoon." He flops on the couch and powers off the TV. "But it was worth it. I learned a few things."

"When did you arrive?" I ask, walking to the fridge to see about making dinner.

"About an hour ago. I hope you don't mind, I helped myself to a snack while I waited."

"No problem. What sounds good for dinner?" I ask with my head still in the fridge.

"Let's go out… If you don't mind? I know you cook plenty when you're alone," he teases.

"True. I don't get out much," I admit, and he grins wider.

He walks to the counter and sits on a stool. "How about you get ready for practice and we'll grab a bite to eat without having to rush anywhere?" Jacob suggests, knowing I don't like to be late.

"Sure. I'll call Sophie to tell her we'll meet at practice." I grab my phone and walk to my bedroom to change.

When Jacob says he wants burgers, I suggest the Cougar Country Dine-In.

As we reach a booth, Jacob asks, "Have you talked with Kate lately about the wedding?"

"How can I not," I say sarcastically. "I don't think there's been a conversation in the past six months where the topic hasn't come up."

"Me, too." He chuckles. "And I know squat about flowers, cake, or the likes of that."

"That's Kate for you," I sigh. "It's worth knowing she's happy though. She and Ben are great together. I'm looking forward to the bridal shower in two weeks."

"That's great. Maybe I'll come home for the weekend to visit," Jacob suggests as he takes a bite of his burger.

"Sounds like a plan. Maybe you'll help me babysit Maggie's kids," I tease, knowing I'll be entirely on my own when it comes to spending an evening with a couple of toddlers.

I volunteered for kid patrol, since I'm not twenty-one. Kate's friends planned her bachelorette party after the bridal shower, since everyone's already gathered. Her friend, Maggie, has two little girls under the age of three. I used to babysit them when I lived at home when Maggie needed help. They're great kids, so I volunteered. This way, Maggie won't miss out on the party.

"Tempting, but I'll pass." Jacob smirks and takes another bite of his burger. "Besides, I haven't spent much time with Dad or Kai lately. I'd rather hang out with them."

"You're no fun!" I tease. "You're going to miss out!" By now, my sarcasm's extremely thick.

When we arrive at practice, Sophie and James are getting out of her car.

"Need help with anything?" I offer as they walk to the trunk of her little sedan.

"I think I have it, but thanks," James announces.

"Hi, you must be Alex's brother." Sophie reaches out her hand to Jacob. "I'm Sophie. I live in the same complex as Alex."

I interject before anything else can be said and make proper introductions.

James nods in our direction from the back of the car. He grabs the mesh bag filled with soccer balls and says, "Hey," as he closes the trunk.

"Looks like we're the first ones." James walks toward the edge of the soccer field. "I'll set up so we can start once everyone arrives." He places cones in various locations around the field. Meanwhile, Sophie and I put on our shin guards and cleats before stretching.

I look at Jacob and shrug. "There's a blanket in the 4-Runner, if you want something to sit on."

"I'm fine for now. Thanks." Jacob sits next to me as I put on my gear.

Within a few minutes, everyone arrives. Each stretch independently once their gear's on. We're grouped in an informal semi-circle as we do our stretches. Eventually, James comes over and calls us to order. He explains our goal for tonight is to work on dribbling, ball control exercises, and taking the ball from the air. If there's time at the end, we'll scrimmage.

As I get up to join the group, Gavin nods at me with a casual, "Hey." I attempt to sound as natural as possible by matching his, "Hey" in return. Then I walk over to Sophie and Samantha who stand with Paul and Josh, to even out the lines forming.

As we dribble around a line of cones, James wants us practicing our spins and maneuvers around the cones, pretending they're defenders on the field. The goal is to work on our speed and agility. At the end, we're to take a shot at the goal, which seems simple enough.

Afterward, James breaks us into pairs to practice taking the ball from the air. I walk toward Sophie, but she partners with Josh. I look around for someone else, but before I know it, everyone's paired up, except for Gavin and myself. He casually walks in my direction, giving me a sheepish grin. "I guess it's you and me." He kicks the ball as if it's a hacky-sack and juggles it for several bounces before catching it with his hands. "Let's go over here," he suggests a spot in the field that's clear and jogs in that direction.

"Sure," I say, taking a deep breath and jog behind him. *God, let me be coherent and not a hot mess around him.*

When we arrive, he stops and motions to where he wants me to stand. Then he throws the ball high in the air, in my general direction. I take a step and lean back, trapping the ball with my chest, quickly allowing it to drop to the ground. Once I have it on the ground, Gavin's there as the defender. I roll my foot in front of the ball, then swivel to face him directly. Then I explode with a kick to my right, just as he thinks I'm about to go left, and the ball sails down the field.

A quick laugh escapes before he retrieves the ball. "Nice one," is all I hear from behind him. He returns by dribbling the ball with his foot and passes it to me. As I bend down to pick it up, he smirks. "My turn."

I toss the ball into the sky. He quickly traps it and has it on the ground. I step toward him to play defense as he dribbles hard to my right. He then slides the toe of his shoe down the back of the ball and flicks it with his foot, making the ball fly up to his knees. As if it's one solid motion, he swings his foot forward and kicks the ball past me to my left. *It's freaking impressive.*

I jog to get the ball as I compliment his unexpected move. "Great shot."

We continue trapping the ball with our chest for a while. Each time, one of us pulls out a harder skill to get past the other. It's pretty intense by the time James calls us over to practice another skill. As Gavin and I approach the rest of the group, James calls out, "Hey, why don't you two show the rest of us the moves you made as you trapped the ball and got past the defenders? That last one was wicked."

"Thanks," Gavin and I simultaneously respond.

Gavin tosses the ball into the air at me, and I quickly trap the ball with my chest and release it to the ground. I use the tip of my toe to control the ball as I attempt to swivel past him. In an effort not to be outdone, I add his first trick of popping the ball up to my knee and exploding to my right with a follow-through kick. The entire time he defends me meticulously. He sees what I'm doing and attempts to block my final kick. He gets a piece of the ball, but it still escapes him. I'm quite proud of myself as I run to retrieve the ball. When I get back, his arm extends for a high-five. I slap his hand as I run past to sit with the rest of the team. I can't help the shiver of electricity that spreads up my spine with his touch.

James looks at his watch. "Wow, it's later than I thought. There's another team booked after this." He then looks to the rest of us. "We only have the field for another fifteen minutes. Mind if we just head out?" No one says anything, so he adds, "Our next practice is Sunday at seven."

As the group breaks up, I walk over to Jacob where he sits by my bag. He hands me my water bottle as I approach.

"Thanks, Jake." I plop down next to him on the grass. "Thanks for waiting for me."

"Not a problem." He grins. "You had some great moves out there." He motions over to Gavin who now sits about three yards from us, taking off his cleats. "Both of you are intense."

"Were we?" I ask innocently. To get out of the hot seat, I ask, "What do you want to do tonight?"

Jacob lets out a snicker and teases, "Sure." He snickers again. "Whatever you'd like to do is fine." He looks in Gavin's direction for a moment, smiles again, and returns his attention back to me, remaining silent.

"I don't care really." I finish putting on my shoes then suggest, "It's still light out for a while. Want to drive to the top of campus and walk around before going home?"

"Sounds great. It's a clear night. I'm sure the view will be spectacular."

Just then, Gavin approaches. "Great moves out there, Alex."

"Thanks, you, too," I say, trying to look busy by putting the last of my things away to hide my flushing face.

I notice Jacob take in my expression, but I quickly attempt to change it to nonchalance by making introductions. "Gavin, this is my brother, Jacob." I look to Jacob. "This is Gavin."

Gavin smiles and reaches out his hand to shake Jacob's hand. "Nice to meet you."

"Same to you." Jacob returns the smile. "Those were some amazing moves out there."

"Thanks." Gavin smiles humbly, then changes the subject. "How long are you in town for?"

Jacob replies with a shrug, "I head back tomorrow evening."

As we walk to the parking lot, Gavin asks, "Do you have any plans tonight?"

Before I can reply, Jacob fills Gavin in. "We're just going to tour campus. I haven't been here in awhile, and Alex wants to show me around."

"That's a good idea." Gavin looks directly at me with his penetrating, golden-brown eyes, making my heart race and says, "I'll see you around."

It takes me a moment before I can say anything, but after a few seconds, I respond, "Yeah."

Jacob says nothing about Gavin as we leave for our tour of campus. We park near the CUB and make our way across campus on foot. Jacob fills me in on what he's been doing at work, and I tell him about my classes. By the time we return to the car, it's completely dark, though campus is well lit.

When we get back to my place, I excuse myself to take a shower and change into pajamas. I hear him in the living room searching for something to watch. When I return, I find Jacob with a bowl of ice cream, watching television.

"Want some?" he asks as he scoops some into his mouth. "I picked up your favorite."

"Sure." I walk to the kitchen and dish myself some chocolate chip mint. I then walk over to the chair and curl up in it.

"So, have you talked with Kai lately?" I ask as I take a bite.

"Um, I actually talked to him on my way here. I'd called Mom to check in."

"I haven't talked to him since I moved," I sigh with

regret. "Every time I call home, he isn't there. If I try his cell, it usually goes to voicemail."

"He's busy with football and apparently, he's dating a new girl named Jenna." Jacob snickers at the end.

I know there's more to the story by the way Jacob snickers. "Who's Jenna?"

"Oh, she's just a girl in his class. They've only gone out a couple of times. He seems to like her though."

"What makes you say that?"

"Well, he picks her up for school and drives her home. She lives quite a distance from our house. He even wakes up early to get her."

"Wow, he must like her. Kai never gets up early unless a bomb's about to go off."

"Speaking of liking people…" he trails off.

"You're dating someone?" I eagerly ask, thinking there might be someone new in Jacob's life.

He clears his throat. "I'm not dating anyone to speak of." He looks suspiciously at me, which makes me feel self-conscious enough to blush a little.

"Then what are you talking about?" I ask innocently, though it may sound a little defensive.

He says nothing but stares at me, as if he thinks I'm hiding something.

"What?" I finally say, breaking the silence.

"Nothing. I just thought you're dating someone new."

"Jacob, I've only been here a couple of weeks. I barely know anyone." My voice raises at the end, sounding a little defensive. *Okay, a lot defensive.*

"Just curious," he states as he raises his hands in surrender.

"There's nothing to tell," I reassure him in a relaxed voice. "I go to class, work, and when I get the chance, hang out with Sophie."

"You play soccer, too," he states, though it sounds a little like a question, implying something more.

"I've played twice. I hardly know most of the team."

"It didn't seem like that to me," he speculates.

"What do you mean?" My voice now full of sarcasm.

"Well…" He's thoughtful for a moment as if he's carefully planning what to say next. "I didn't see you talking to anyone. You're much too intense for conversation."

"You know how I get when I play sports." I laugh it off and attempt to change the subject. "So where do you want to go for lunch tomorrow?"

He shakes his head briefly as he rolls his eyes, but he doesn't push the subject of my social life any further. He lets out a little huff of defeat, then states, "I don't really care. Let's just drive around until we find a place that looks good."

ON SATURDAY, I spend my morning finishing my paper and catching up on housework. When Sophie calls, we arrange to walk to campus together for the football game. After my call, it's hard deciding what to wear to the game. It's warm now, but it'll be cooler by seven tonight. I also don't want to get sunburnt. I finally decide on black cargo capris with a crimson WSU t-shirt.

As we walk to meet Sophie's friends, I realize I have no idea who we're meeting. When we get to the top of campus and head down the back side of the CUB, I finally muster up the courage to ask.

"So, um... Who are we meeting?" I ask, filled with curiosity and the thought of someone in particular has the butterflies in my stomach doing back-flips.

"There's about ten of us." She smiles and walks along the flat sidewalk next to the stadium. "Oh, here they are." She smiles and picks up her pace to meet them.

At the far end of the sidewalk, are James, Erin, Gavin, Josh, and a few others I don't recognize. "Oh," is all I can manage. *How did I not see this coming?* I think to myself as I say hello to everyone.

We show our sports pass and walk into Martin Stadium. We find seats in the student section near the fifty-yard line, though we end up in two different rows. Gavin, Josh, and the others I don't know sit in front of Sophie, Erin, James, and myself. I'm next to Sophie on the end. Josh sits in front of me with Gavin next to him, allowing me to watch him without being noticed. I can't help but stare through my dark sunglasses. There's something about him I just can't ignore.

As we wait for the game to begin, everyone talks amongst themselves. I take a moment to take in the vastness of the stadium. The student section's filled with crazed fans wearing their Cougar Pride. A sea of red fills the stands. Butch, the mascot, makes his way around the crowd, getting fans pumped for the game. It's hilarious to watch him on the jumbo screen.

"Have you been to a game before?" Josh asks, breaking my concentration from Butch.

"Um, no. It's my first one." I suddenly feel self-conscious

and bite on my lip.

"This should be fun!" he exclaims then turns to clap for the team entering the field. The band plays the fight song, and the crowd around me chants along. Since I don't know the words, I just clap along, hoping to catch on.

The Cougs win the coin toss and choose to receive the ball. After the kick off, they catch it on the fifteen-yard line and bring it back for another ten more yards. On the first down, they manage to gain six yards by running it down the middle. The second down's an incomplete pass. The crowd shows its disappointment with a loud groan. Fortunately, the quarterback regains control of the ball and on the third down, he connects with the receiver, making another eight-yard gain. The crowd's instantly on its feet with cheers.

The announcer starts by boasting "And THAT'S ANOTHER..."

But the fans interrupt with "COUGAR FIRST DOWN!"

The intensity of the fans makes me completely caught up in the rest of the game. The Cougars hold their own and are both ahead and behind throughout the first half. The crowd spends most of its time on its feet. At halftime, we're ahead by four points. Everyone who's not going to the concession stand settles down and sits for the halftime show.

"Having fun?" Sophie enthusiastically hollers in my direction, even though we sit right next to one another.

"Yeah, it's great!" I holler back enthusiastically.

Gavin and Josh stand and look in our direction. "We're going to the concession stand, want anything?" Gavin asks the crowd but ends by locking his eyes on mine.

Sophie hands cash to Josh and says, "I'll have a Coke."

When I realize Gavin's waiting for my response, I pull

cash from my pocket and add, "Me, too, please." As soon as I hand him the money, they both jog up the stairs.

I'm busy watching the band's halftime performance when the guys return. The next thing I know, they're in front of me with snacks and our drinks filling their hands. Josh files in when he returns, leaving Gavin sitting directly in front of me.

Gavin puts his nachos down next to him and hands me my Coke. As he does, he leans in so only I can hear. "Do I need to be worried about this?" He raises one eyebrow at me and lets out a quiet laugh.

"I'm sure you'll be fine," I quietly retort back, so no one can hear. "There's a lid."

"Enjoying the game?" Gavin asks, being serious now.

"It's been pretty intense!" I admit. I love it though. I can't imagine ever missing another home game.

"Yeah, so are we still on for tomorrow?" He dips a chip into the cheese and takes a bite while waiting for my response.

"That's the plan." I smile and take another sip from my soda.

The second half begins. Once again, we're fully engaged by the intensity of the game, leaving little time for conversations of any substance. It's a nail-biter at the end, and my nerves are wrecked. Miraculously, the Cougs pull off a win by a touchdown.

As we gather our things, Josh turns to Sophie. "Why don't we grab some dinner." Though it's a statement, he also makes it sound like a question. He turns to the rest of the group and asks, "What do you think? Dinner?"

Simultaneously, several people talk at once. Erin and

James say they have other plans and so did the other people I never really met, leaving only Josh, Sophie, Gavin, and myself going to dinner.

It takes awhile to file out of the stadium. While we walk, Sophie and Josh make the final details of our plans. Gavin and I contribute when we can, walking behind them. Since our apartments are closer than theirs, I offer my 4-Runner because it's bigger than Sophie's sedan. We drive to Moscow since the restaurants in Pullman are guaranteed to be full after the game.

As it turns out, it's crowded in Moscow, too. We find a Thai restaurant at the other end of town. We have to wait to be seated so we fill the time by talking about soccer and school. It turns out both Josh and Gavin are third-year architect majors. They spend a lot of time in the studio, working on their projects for class. Though they've never been roommates, they met each other in their first semester of classes.

While walking to our seats, Gavin asks, "So, how was your visit with Jacob?"

"Great, it's been so long since just the two of us hung out," I sigh with that realization, but quickly perk up. "I'm going home in two weeks for my sister's bridal shower. He said he'd come to visit then, too." I take my seat next to Sophie.

"Wow! Your sister's getting married? Is she older or younger than you?" Gavin asks with interest, choosing the seat directly across from me.

"Two years older. She's finishing her student teaching this spring, after the wedding."

"You seem happy for her," he observes.

"Yeah, I really like Ben, her future husband, too. They're great for each other, and he's a lot of fun to be around."

"When's the wedding?" Sophie asks with interest.

"In December, during our winter break."

"How exciting!" Sophie picks up her menu but instead of reading it, asks, "So, are you going to be gone the whole weekend when you go for the bridal shower?"

"Um, yeah. I'll return Sunday afternoon. I should be back in time for practice that evening."

"That's good," Josh adds.

"Do you have any plans while you're home?" Gavin casually asks, but his interest makes my bundle of nerves resurface in my stomach.

"Well… My sister's friends are throwing her a bachelorette party after the bridal shower, since they're already in town."

Gavin looks at me with eyes filled with curiosity but only says, "Oh?"

"Well… I'm not going to that." I notice Gavin's eyebrows pull together as if questions are forming. To evade any unnecessary questions, I chuckle and explain, "Everyone but me is over twenty-one. They're going clubbing in Seattle. I've volunteered to babysit for my sister's best friend, so she can enjoy a night out."

"That's nice of you," Gavin sincerely says. His golden-brown eyes draw me in to the point I might be drooling at him, if I'm not careful.

Hoping no one's noticed, I quickly avert my eyes and intently peruse my menu.

Throughout the meal, I avoid looking directly at Gavin as much as possible. I refuse to slip into the role of being incoherent when I'm near him. I find if I don't look directly into his golden-brown eyes, I have a much better chance.

On the way home, Josh asks if I'll drop them at their apartments. I drop Josh off first because it's on the way, then Gavin. Once Gavin's out of the car, Sophie turns to me and stares inquisitively. I ignore her gaping until we're completely out of sight from Gavin.

"SOOOOO?" she asks with exaggeration.

"What?" I reply defensively, keeping my eyes on the road.

"What's up with you and Gavin?" Her voice is thick with speculation.

Dismissively, I reply, "Nothing really. We're in geology together. That's all."

"That's all. I'm sure." Thick sarcasm rolls off her tongue.

"Honestly, there's not much to tell. We've talked a few times before and after class. We're studying tomorrow."

Suspicion is evident, but she concedes with a dramatic sigh. "Sure, if you say so!"

I take this opportunity to change the subject. "So… Wanna ride to practice again tomorrow?"

"Sure," she agrees, but trying to read my face further.

To change the subject, I ask, "Any progress with Josh?"

Now, it's her turn to blush. "Um, not really." She hesitates then adds, "I've been tempted to bring up the subject quite a few times since you and I last talked."

"What's stopping you?" I ask encouragingly, stopping to face her.

"Well, I just get too embarrassed." She takes a deep breath and rambles, "I feel as if there's really something there… I know I feel it… But I'm not sure about him… We're always in a group, so there's never been an opportunity for me to test my theory."

"Well…" I start, but I'm interrupted.

"We've been alone a few times lately, but we get quiet, and it becomes awkward." Sophie lets out a loud groan in frustration. "I just don't know what to do!"

"I'm sure you'll figure it out," I offer in support.

"Yeah, I know." Sophie runs her hands through her long hair and gazes at the floor of the car.

"You know…" I suddenly have an obvious idea. "Why don't you just ask him out and just not mention it being a date?"

Sophie looks up with curious eyes. "What do you mean?"

"Well, just ask him to do something on the spur of the moment when it's just the two of you. Then you can see how you feel toward him when you're alone."

"Humm…" Her eyebrows pull together in serious thought.

"Or, not." I hesitate, watching her reaction. "It's just a suggestion."

Her face suddenly forms an infectious smile. "No, that's a great idea." She contemplates it some more, then adds, "Maybe I'll see what he's doing right before practice tomorrow and if he's free, invite him to dinner?"

"Yeah," I encourage. "Just keep it casual. If you spend some time together, maybe you'll realize what your own feelings are. Then you'll know if your gut instinct's correct."

"Thanks, Alex!" she says exuberantly, as her arms wrap around me in an unexpected hug. "That's great! I can't wait to see what happens!"

5

CATASTROPHE

THE NEXT MORNING, I try my hardest to stay in bed, but like usual, that's an utter fail. To pass the time, I do laundry and go for a run. By eight thirty, my laundry's put away, and I'm sitting in my living room trying to find something to do. There's nothing on TV, so I pick out a book to read for my children's lit class. Unfortunately, I become so engrossed in the book, I don't notice the time until nine forty-five. Crap. I have fifteen minutes to meet Gavin.

With a bit of a panic, I quickly grab the things I need to study for geology, throw on my shoes, and rush out the door. On the way there, I realize I haven't actually seen what I look like today, so I give myself a once-over in the reflection of one of the windows and run my fingers through my hair to make sure it's not sticking up. As I arrive on top of campus, I'm relieved to find I've made it with a minute or so to spare.

Rounding the corner of Todd, I spot Gavin walking up Terral Mall from the opposite direction. He couldn't look better with his dark jeans and crimson hoodie. As our eyes meet, he acknowledges me with a smile, making my heart flutter. *How does he do that?*

I make it to the entrance to the library just a few moments before him.

"Morning, Alex." Gavin smiles as he opens the door for me.

"Thanks. I'm glad you weren't waiting. I got caught up in a book and lost track of time," I admit, suddenly very nervous.

He lets out a little chortle, continuing to make direct eye contact. "Me, too. I went into the studio around seven and got lost in a project."

"So… Where do you want to study?" I ask, looking around the circular-tiled room we entered, not having the faintest idea of where to go.

"Well, there's some group study rooms over here," he suggests as we walk down a hallway.

"Will this do?" he asks confidently as his eyes bore into mine.

"Yes," is all I manage to say from under the full power of his gaze. I can barely breathe, let alone think with those potent, golden-brown eyes locking onto me.

He holds the door open for me and watches me slowly walk through. I finally force myself to break eye contact. I choose a chair on the right side of the table as he shuts the door and goes to the left. We spend the next few moments getting out our geology materials.

My stomach's suddenly tying itself into knots as it dawns on me, I've never been alone with Gavin, anywhere. I feel very self-conscious and am more aware of his presence than ever before. I fight to regain my composure. To have a distraction, I read over my notes from our geology lectures. This allows me to keep my eyes diverted from Gavin, for the time being.

Breaking the awkward silence, Gavin's deep voice slightly startles me when he says, "So... Where should we begin?"

When I glance up, he's looking over his own notes, so I'm able to reply without noticeable hesitation. "Well, so far, we've only covered the first two chapters as well as parts of thirteen and fourteen, where plate tectonics are concerned." Conveniently, I'd taken good notes, so I'm able focus on those.

"Yeah, that's true." Gavin turns a page in his notebook. "But last week, Ian also went into further details about the state of Washington specifically."

"Let's start at chapter one, that way we won't miss anything," I casually suggest, keeping my eyes on my materials instead of the breathtakingly handsome man before me. Now that we're in an enclosed space, I can't help but notice the distinct smell that's uniquely him. It's a mixture of faint cologne mixed with a mouthwatering smell I can't quite describe, making me want to be closer to him.

"Good," he responds as he shuffles some papers on the table.

Thankfully, after my initial awkwardness, I find it's easy to keep from being distracted by his brilliant, golden-brown eyes and gleaming smile because we have so much to cover. By eleven thirty, we're ready for our quiz. I sigh heavily as I look at my phone to check the time.

"Hey... Wanna grab lunch before heading to Owen

Science Library?" Gavin suggests as he stands, stretching his arms out. He looks at his watch. "It doesn't open for another half hour."

"Um... sure." I bite on my lip. "What do you have in mind?"

"Well... Do you want to eat on campus or downtown?" Though he's still gathering his materials, he unexpectedly stops and looks directly at me, leaving our eyes to linger on one another for a long, silent moment. Once again, I'm completely incoherent and unable to say anything in response.

Suddenly, he breaks our stare by shaking his head and diverting his eyes from mine. He hesitates a short moment before continuing. "I... Ummm... Actually... Already completed my project in the studio this morning," he admits sheepishly. "I have some final touches, but other than that, I don't have much to do today."

"Okay," I draw out, taking a moment to comprehend what he's said.

"Let's go downtown," he suggests. "I'm not in the mood for cafeteria or fast food. Are you?"

"Not really," I admit, still unsure what to do or where to suggest.

"Okay. We can either walk or drive."

"It depends on where you want to go," I say skeptically, raising one eyebrow at him when I remember just how far some restaurants are from campus.

"I... Um... Walked to campus this morning, so your car's probably closer," he admits, cracking a smile in my direction.

"No problem. Do you mind if we drop this at my place?" I ask, pointing to my notebook and backpack.

"Not at all." He smiles and holds the door open for me to leave in front of him.

The walk to my apartment's filled with small talk. He asks where I'm from, about my family, and how I like working at Antonio's. I feel as if he's getting to know all about me, but I'm still left in awe and wonder about him. For every question he answers, I have a thousand more in return, but I never quite muster the courage to ask. I learn he's from the Everett area and has an older brother as well as a sister who's married with two kids. I enjoy getting to know Gavin, though I feel I'm forced to reveal far more about myself in comparison.

"Have you been to Sella's?" Gavin asks.

Completely baffled by this question, I respond, "Sella's?"

Catching on that I'm clueless, he gives a little smirk and explains, "Sella's a restaurant that sells pizza and amazing calzones."

"Oh," I start to say but Gavin interrupts my thoughts by pulling his eyebrows together as he steps in my direction.

"Um, you probably don't like Italian, since you work at Antonio's, do you?"

I smile at his concern. "I honestly don't eat at work much, so we're good."

"Sella's it is."

After ordering calzones, Gavin leads me to a table near the window where we wait for them to be served. Taking a drink of my soda, I give myself a moment to look around the restaurant and take it all in. The aroma of pizza sauce and baked bread makes my mouth water. A local rock station plays in the background, and I try to keep my mind occupied, so I don't make a fool of myself in front of Gavin.

"So, when are you going home?" Gavin asks.

"I'll take off a week from Friday, after my last class," I say with excitement. "I get out at noon."

"Wow, you have a nice schedule." He rolls his eyes. "My last class on Fridays ends at two."

"That's not too bad." I shrug.

"Well, I enjoy the class, so it goes fast, but it means I can never leave early. Attendance's required."

Our server comes and greets us with a "Hello" as she places our food in front of us.

I place my napkin on my lap as I take my first bite. It's absolutely delicious. "Wow, this is amazing."

"I'm glad you like it," Gavin agrees, taking a bite of his own steamy calzone.

"What project are you working on in the studio?" I finally get up the courage to ask a direct question now that my nerves have settled.

Gavin tells me he's building a model of a design he's made for an urban setting in a predetermined space in Seattle. He goes into great detail about how they take pictures of the area and fictionally build something within the space they're assigned, while following the requests of their client. Though I don't know much about building and design, he's able to explain it in enough details so I'm easily able to understand.

"Do you spend a lot of time studying fictitious buildings or do you get to see them throughout the entire process?" I ask once he's finished explaining his current assignment to me.

"Well, a little of both actually." He takes a drink of his

soda before continuing, "I'm going abroad in the spring to study in Europe."

"Really?" I say with excitement. "Where?"

He puts down his fork to explain, "I'm not really sure yet. I'm still working on the final details. For the fall, one-third of the class stays here, and the rest goes to Spokane for classes, then we'll travel abroad next spring semester."

"Wow, I've always wanted to travel. I'm thinking of getting an English Language Learning Endorsement, but I just don't know how I could fit a semester abroad into my schedule."

"Well, Dad always says, if you want something bad enough, there'll always be a way." Gavin grins in my direction as if it's a challenge.

"We'll see," I sigh. I change the subject. "What do you think we'll do tonight at practice?"

Gavin and I talk about soccer until we finish eating. Once we're done, we drive back to my apartment, then make our way to the Owen Science Library to complete our lab module. Since we'd spent so much time studying, we complete our assignment with ease.

As we gather our things to leave the library, Gavin asks, "What are your plans for the rest of the day?"

"I'm working on a paper for English studies. I also need to read a book and do a write up for children's lit."

"I guess I'll see you at practice?" He shrugs modestly.

Not understanding why he's asking the question, I give him an *I told you so* look and say, "Yeah, I'll be there."

When we walk out of Owen, he hesitates on the sidewalk. "So… I guess I'll see you then."

Confused and not understanding the expression on his face, I say, "Yep, I'll see you at seven."

"See you." He turns to walk up the hill toward the main campus.

"Bye," I call out as we part ways. I can't help but wonder what his sudden weirdness was all about.

That night at soccer practice, Gavin and I return to being awkward and no longer have conversations. There's a kinetic energy that pushes and pulls freely between us. When we scrimmage at the end of practice, we're on opposite teams. At one point, Gavin and I both go after the ball, and I have to pull out some of my moves to get past him. When practice ends, he comes to sit next to me while we stretch and put on our shoes to go home.

"Great practice, Alex." Gavin lets out a sigh of exhaustion as he takes off his shoes.

"Thanks," I humbly reply, taking off my left shin guard.

"Hey, Gavin, are you ready?" Josh calls out.

Gavin turns to look at Josh. "Sure, be right there."

Gavin turns his attention back to me, which makes my heart race as he shyly smiles. "That's my ride. See you later."

"Bye. See you in class," I reply, not knowing what else to say.

I go back to putting my things in my bag. When I look up, I find Sophie smiling in my direction. I attempt to conceal my embarrassment by glancing at Josh as I ask, "Any progress since our last conversation?"

She giggles with delight and her ponytail shakes rapidly. "A little." Lowering her voice so only I can hear, she whispers, "I'll explain more in the car."

Throughout the entire ride home, she fills me in on the

details of her progress with Josh. She asked him to hang out earlier this afternoon, and they had lunch together. "I think I might be right about something being there," she bursts out once we are in her car.

"Really, why's that?" I encourage.

Sophie's eyes are wide with excitement as she says, "There's this chemistry that's hard to explain. It's like I'm drawn to him, and I have no idea how to stop myself."

"Good for you. Have you told him how you feel?" I probe.

"No," she spits out. "I don't want to risk it if he doesn't feel the same." She shakes her head in denial. "I barely know how I feel. I don't want to ruin it."

"Well, you're never going to know unless you tell him," I remind her.

Our conversation continues for the remainder of our ride. When we arrive back at our apartments, she finally admits that she should tell him soon, so she doesn't have to waste her time pining away for the unknown chance of something happening. When we reach my apartment, we say goodnight, and I head up my stairs.

The next day is a typical Monday. Classes are fairly uneventful, and I feel well prepared for them due to my extra studying. I make it to work a little early, taking the opportunity to have lunch before my shift.

Around six, as I'm serving an older couple, I notice Gavin walking into the restaurant with Josh. They order their food and sit in my section.

"Hey, guys," I address each as I approach them with their orders.

"Hi, Alex." I hear simultaneously from each of them, making all of us laugh.

"Is this becoming your usual hangout?" I tease.

Josh looks at Gavin skeptically, but Gavin just ignores him and simply states, "What can I say? We like pasta," as he shrugs in my direction.

"Well, let me know if there's anything else I can get you," I remind them as I go to pick up another order. As I leave, I hear some hushed whispers coming from them along with deep laughter. *I wonder what that's about?*

Throughout the rest of their dinner, they're in deep conversation about something I'm not made privy to. Each time I stop to check on them, odd stares pass between them as well as a lot of laughter after I leave. If I didn't know better, I'd think they were talking about me.

When they get up to leave, Josh snorts and says, "I guess we'll see you next Monday." He taps Gavin on the shoulder with the palm of his hand, and they laugh some more.

"Night, Alex," Gavin calls out as they leave the restaurant.

Though the rest of the week seems typical, I see more of Gavin than usual. He sits next to me again in geology as well as lab. We continue making small talk, but there's still a lot of awkward silences from time to time.

On Saturday, I get up, make breakfast, and straighten up my apartment before heading out for a morning run. Even though it's October and the weather's cooler, I still run in a pair of black shorts and a green t-shirt.

I'm on my way back home a little before nine when I notice Gavin in the parking lot of Starbucks, across the street from me. As I wait for the light to change, I jog in place at the intersection. He sees me and waves in my direction. I wave back in return and find myself being pulled in his direction. *Maybe I should go over to say hello to him?* I'm about to head in that direction, but I chicken out and simply smile in return. It's amazing to feel the power of his stare from across the street. Electric pulses shoot up my body. The light finally changes, and I jog across the street. I glance at Gavin, who's still watching, which makes me even more self-conscious.

Suddenly, Gavin's face turns to one of horror. I look around to find the source of his drastic change in composure. I see the car rounding the corner, making a right, and barreling into the lane I'm currently standing. Instantly, it collides into me. I don't even have time to scream. It happens so fast. I pull my arms up to protect myself. Then everything goes dark.

6

AWAKENING

FOR SOME TIME, there's only flickers of my memory I manage to hold onto. These flickers include Gavin's horrified face, hitting the hard pavement, and people crowing around as the ambulance approaches. Though I recall this information in bits and pieces, everything's fuzzy with no real sense of a timeline to follow.

The first thing I coherently recall is being in an unfamiliar bed in a darkened room. I hear constant beeping and someone approaching me. Suddenly, I'm more alert, and I take a moment to become aware of my surroundings.

"How are you feeling, sweetheart?" I hear a woman's voice ask as she touches my wrist for a moment.

"Uh…" I manage to moan, "Where am I?"

"You're in the hospital. You were hit by a car this morning." The woman I now recognize is a nurse. "You're very lucky, young lady." She smiles in my direction to put me at ease.

I stare in disbelief when I realize she's said I've been hit by a car.

The woman stops what she's doing and looks at me directly to calm me. "You only have a few minor injuries in comparison to what it could've been. Three cracked ribs, a few large contusions on your right leg, and a mild concussion." She smiles as she takes out her stethoscope, listening to my lungs and heart.

I take a deep breath to digest her words and instantly wish I hadn't. The pain takes what breath I had away, making my entire body cringe. That's when I notice I can't move my right leg. Something's holding it in place.

"Uh," I sigh, feeling confused. "I thought you said I didn't break my leg?"

"You didn't, but the doctors want your leg immobilized to ensure there's no fractures. You'll get another x-ray in a few weeks to determine that for sure," she sighs, then checks my vision with her light. "For now, you'll wear a brace."

"You were very lucky," a deep, all-too-familiar voice says from across the room.

I notice the lengthy body stretched out in a chair on the other side of me. I stare at him in disbelief. "Gavin?"

"What?" He looks at me wide-eyed and full of concern. "Did you expect me to leave you there on the road?"

"No, I…" I start to say but I'm interrupted by the nurse.

"You get some rest. You can discuss this later." She sticks a thermometer in my mouth, and I'm left with nothing to do but stare at Gavin in silence. *What is he doing here?*

When I'm able to speak again, Gavin talks first, his eyes full of concern. "Is there anything I can get you?"

"Ummm," I start to think. "I need to call my parents and let them know I'm all right."

"I can do that for you, if you'd like?" Gavin sincerely offers.

"Do you have a phone I can use?" I ask hesitantly.

"Sure," he sighs in relief and digs for it in his pocket.

Before I dial, I ask hesitantly, "What exactly happened?"

I sense his stress as he recalls the details. "I don't really know. One minute I was saying hello to you while you're waiting for the light. I saw the light change, and you start jogging across the street. Then all of a sudden, a little red car speeds past me. I thought it was going straight, but at the last second, it turned into you and sent you flying in the air about ten feet before you hit the ground." He takes a deep breath and shakes his head in disbelief. "I thought for sure you were seriously injured, but the doctors say it's just some bruising and a few cracked ribs." He smiles at me in relief as he takes another deep breath.

"How long have I been here?" I ask, completely unaware of how long it has been.

"Just a couple of hours." He looks into my eyes and continues, "The doctor said they gave you some medication that'll make you sleep while it relieves your pain."

"Oh," I sigh. "I guess I remember bits and pieces now that you've reminded me." I sit quiet for a moment, taking it all in. "Do my parents know?"

"Yes, one of the nurses looked up their number using your student records."

"Uhhh," I moan. "They're probably panicking. I'd better call them now then."

I reach for his phone and dial.

It barely rings once when I hear Mom's frantic voice on the other end. "Hello?"

"Hey, Mom. It's me. I'm okay," I try to assure her.

From the other end, I hear, "I'm making arrangements now to come over, hon." Worry clearly present in her voice.

"Mom, that's not really necessary," I try to sound convincing. "I only have a few cracked ribs and some bruising. Really. I'm okay."

"You forgot about a concussion," she states sharply.

"Mom, really, I'm okay. There's nothing you can do here," I insist.

The door opens, and a doctor steps in. He's a short man in his mid-forties with gray highlights throughout his once-brown hair.

"Hey, Mom, the doctor's here. I'll call you back. Please don't do anything until I call you." I plead.

"Oh, all right," she resigns. "But you'd better call back soon."

"I will. I promise."

"Hello, Alex. I'm Dr. Newman. I've been treating you since you arrived. You're one lucky lady," he announces.

"Hello," I return his greeting.

"Well, let's get a closer look." He examines my vision, pulse, and reflexes. "You're actually doing well. I'd like to hold onto you for a few more hours of observations, but I really don't see a lot of reason to hold you overnight." He then looks at Gavin. "Mr. Wallace, she'll need a ride home and a lot of rest for the next few days. With the medication she's on, she won't be able to drive until the brace is off and her pain subsides."

"Okay. Thank you for your help," Gavin sincerely states.

The doctor turns to me. "Alexis, do you have a roommate who can watch over you to make sure you can get around okay?"

Before I can answer, Gavin states, "Yes, someone will be there."

I'm left looking at Gavin wide-eyed and confused.

"I'll come by in an hour or so to see how you're doing." The doctor then turns to leave.

"Thanks," I calmly say as he walks out the door. "What were you talking about? I live alone, you know," I remind him.

"I know, but someone will be there. You have friends. Besides, your family will likely come."

"I hope not. I've been on crutches before. They're inconvenient, but not a big deal. They don't need to drive six hours to babysit me. I'll be okay," I argue.

"Someone will be there," he insists, and I can tell it's no use in arguing from his suddenly stern voice.

"I'd better call Mom. Can I use your phone again?" I ask, trying to change the subject.

When Mom answers, and I tell her I'm being released this evening, she's relieved. She really wants to come to Pullman, but with a lot of convincing, I promise I'll be okay and to call her if I need her.

"This is against my better judgment," she concedes after a lot of arguing.

I can't help but grin when I pull out my winning argument. She's hosting a bridal shower next weekend, and she needs to prepare for it now that I won't be able to do all my hosting duties.

"You'll have to miss the shower since you can't drive

home, honey. Are you sure you don't want me to come and get you?"

"Mom, I have classes this week. We'll make arrangements when I get back to my place. It's not like we won't be talking every day. I know you better than that." I laugh but sigh because my ribs revolt against the movement.

"Okay, honey. I'll talk to you later. I love you," she sighs reluctantly.

"I love you, too. Bye." As I hang up the phone, I remember Gavin's still in the room, staring at me.

"I'll take you," he suggests as I hand him the phone.

"What?" I gasp again because I tried to sit up without being careful, and my breath's caught short.

"I'll take you home. I don't have plans next weekend, and you can't miss your sister's bridal shower." His sincerity is impossible to argue with, but I try.

"I don't know... You don't even know where I live," I sarcastically retort.

"You can give me directions," he teases and raises an eyebrow with a smirk.

"We'll see." I try to change the subject, but another nurse walks in to check my monitors and adds something I assume is more medication to my IV.

Gavin steps back and sits in the chair he'd been in. Now that I have a moment to take things in, I finally notice how tired he appears as he leans back in his chair. His face is drawn tight as he folds his arms against his chest and chews on his lower lip. He closes his eyes for a moment and lets out a quiet sigh.

When the nurse exits the room, I watch Gavin for a few more moments before asking, "Are you okay?"

He's caught off guard by my question, but quickly regains his composure. "Yes," he states, looking thoughtful. "Why?"

After careful consideration to my choice of words, I finally say, "You look tired."

Gavin takes a deep breath. As he exhales, he draws out, "Well, it's been a day." He slowly produces a smile that reaches the entirety of his eyes and looks directly at me. Once under the full power of his stare, I'm left speechless. Even in my dilapidated state, I can't deny. The man is gorgeous.

After another long moment, Gavin sincerely states, "I'm glad you're okay." Then his eyes flicker with a bit of amusement in them and sarcasm rolls out. "This seems to be your thing?" He raises an eyebrow and waits for my reaction.

"What?" I spit out, not sure where he's going with this.

"Are you always this accident prone?" He smirks in my direction.

Instantly, I'm defensive and let out a huff. "No!" coming out a little louder than I mean. "You seem to be the common factor." Pointing this out to him, I find myself glaring at him, trying not to breathe deep because it hurts.

Gavin returns my glare with an innocent, but impatient stare, waiting for me to calm down. He then sighs, changing the subject, "You should get some rest. You've been through a lot today." He continues to make eye contact until I concede.

After a few more silent moments, I resign and break the hold of his determined, golden-brown eyes. I sigh and attempt to find a comfortable position. My leg's sore, and the brace is heavy, but I'm able to shift my position and relax.

"Need anything?" Gavin asks, his voice filled with concern.

"I'm fine. I'll just rest awhile." I take in another breath as deep as I can before closing my eyes.

"Okay," Gavin responds quietly, and I hear a backpack unzip, making my eyes pop open in response. "Sorry," he apologizes, "didn't mean to disturb you."

"It's no problem. You know, you can leave if you want. I'm not really much company." Not wanting to put him out in any way, if he wants to leave, I'll understand.

"I know. I'll stay, if that's okay. You'll need a ride home." He smiles in reassurance and pulls out a large textbook.

"Okay." I feel the pain medications taking their toll and suddenly, I feel sleepy. "I'm just going to rest awhile then," I sigh, letting my eyes fall closed.

When I wake awhile later, the room's empty. The only things I hear are the monitors attached to me. Within a few minutes, a nurse enters my room.

"Hello, how are you feeling?" The nurse reminds me of Mom, so I immediately feel at ease. "The doctor will be in within a few minutes. Gavin went to get his car," she says as she collects my vitals and records them on my chart.

"Oh," I say, not knowing how to respond.

The doctor with whom I had spoken earlier comes in and looks at the chart the nurse hands to him. He takes out his light and says, "Please look directly into my eyes," while he directs the light at me from different angles. He then takes both hands and feels the back of my head and neck. I flinch when he reaches a soft spot.

"Well, other than a lot of bruising and your ribs, you seem to be okay, relatively speaking." He steps back, surveying my response.

"Thankfully," I sigh.

"I've spoken with Gavin, and he's agreed you won't be alone for the next twenty-four hours. Other than rest, there's not much we can do for you here. The medication you're on for pain means you shouldn't drive or operate any heavy equipment."

I nod my head to show I'm listening.

Oblivious to my confusion, the doctor continues, "Take your medication every four to six hours to manage pain and inflammation. It'll make you a little groggy but should be manageable."

"What about class?" I ask when I finally get my thoughts together.

"Well, I can write you a note, but if you feel you're up to it, you can go. I'll give you a note to make any accommodations as necessary."

"Thanks." I slowly exhale, relieved that I'm able to go home.

"Now, try not to overdo it. You need a lot of rest, and you have to take it easy to ensure a speedy recovery. I'll want to see you in two weeks for a follow-up appointment to make sure your leg's healing and not fractured.

"Okay," I agree.

"You can take the brace off for showers, but don't bear any weight on it for more than twenty minutes a day. Keep it elevated as much as possible."

I notice Gavin's reappearance. He greets me with a smile, not wanting to interrupt the doctor.

The doctor turns to Gavin. "She's welcome to go whenever you're ready, Mr. Wallace. Please make sure she takes her medication as prescribed and that she's monitored over the next twenty-four hours or so to ensure she's handling them. If there're any problems, call the advice nurse or bring her back to the ER."

"Thank you, sir." Gavin reaches out to shake hands with the doctor.

The doctor then turns to me. "Take care, I'll see you in a few weeks. The nurse will be in to get you settled with crutches and your release papers." He then turns to walk out of the room.

I look at Gavin confused as to why the doctor's telling him everything.

"Hey, how are you doing?" He smiles warmly as he walks toward my bed.

"Okay... I've been better." Sarcasm escapes a little at the end. "Why did my doctor tell you all that?"

"Well..." He takes in a deep breath. "While you were sleeping, I kind of told him I'd be the one watching you." He watches my reaction carefully and then tacks on rapidly, "Because you're my fiancée." He then looks down at the floor sheepishly.

I'm in complete shock, and I'm sure it registers on my face because all of a sudden, Gavin's rapidly explaining, "Well, you see... They wouldn't let me in at first... Unless I was family... And they didn't want to release you with no one at home."

"Okay," I slowly acquiesce, comprehending he's only trying to help.

"Are you okay with this?" he asks in a pleading way,

once again locking his eyes on mine, leaving me unable
to argue.

I can't say anything because I'm not sure what to say. I'm
confused as a million thoughts fly through my head. I want
to go home. I rationalize with myself it's only twenty-four
hours. After thinking about it a moment longer, I ask one of
the many questions sprinting through my head, "Where will
you sleep?"

"You have a couch," he suggests. "Or the floor. It doesn't
matter. I just know from the conversation with your mother
that you want to go home."

I sigh in defeat. He has me there. "Okay."

He grins as he adds, "I've talked with your mom and
assured her that you'll be looked after when you
get home."

"What?" Reeling in shock, I ask, "When did you
do that?"

"She called my phone while you were sleeping." He
looks at me cautiously before adding, "She's worried and
doesn't want you being alone tonight."

"Oh. Thanks. I appreciate that." Knowing that he
probably relieved my mother from unneeded stress.

The nurse comes in with a pair of crutches. "Have you
ever used these?" she asks sympathetically.

"Um, Yeah," I admit, flashing my eyes at Gavin's
reaction. He already thinks I'm accident prone. As expected,
I see him stifle a small chuckle by covering his mouth and
looking away.

"Well, let's make sure you have them adjusted so you use
your hands, not your armpits to support your weight, all
right?" she suggests as she motions for me to stand.

I notice I'm only wearing a hospital gown. Embarrassed, I ask, "Where are my clothes?"

"Well, they're in a bag by the table." The nurse points to a plastic bag. "There's a lot of blood on them and were torn. All your personal belongings are in there, too."

She helps me swing my legs toward the side of the bed, then supports me as I stand. With a few minor adjustments, my crutches are ready. "I'll be right back with a pair of scrubs for you to wear home and your paperwork to check out."

When she returns, Gavin excuses himself, allowing me to change with some privacy. The nurse stays to offer help, and I'm grateful. I can tell my balance is off at the moment. She shows me how to carefully take off my brace and put it back on. I'm shocked to see the scattered bruises and scrapes all throughout my body. There are two bruises larger than my hands on my thigh and calf and ribs. The nurse ensures me they'll heal, and I'll be as good as new before long.

Once I'm dressed, with my brace outside the scrubs, Gavin returns. I sign the paperwork, and the nurse wheels me out to the parking lot while Gavin takes my things and retrieves his car.

A black shiny sedan with tinted windows pulls up to the hospital entrance. To my surprise, Gavin steps out and quickly walks along the front of his car to open the door for me.

He helps me out of the wheelchair and into the black leather seats of his immaculate car. I thank the nurse and so does Gavin as he shuts my door and lopes around to the driver's side to take me home.

7

RECOVERY

WHEN WE ARRIVE at my apartment, I find Gavin carries a bag as well as his backpack over his shoulder. He quickly walks around the car to hoist me to a standing position and hands me my crutches from the back seat. "Do you have your key?"

"Um, they were zipped into my shorts." I search for the bag from the hospital.

"Hold on." Gavin turns and retrieves the bag from the back seat. "Here." He digs through the bag and finds the key in my shorts pocket.

As we walk slowly, or in my case hobble, to my apartment, I quickly become winded, and my entire body aches. Before I go too far, Gavin tells me to "Stop."

Turning my head in his direction. "Why?"

"Please wait here." He smiles pleadingly, then turns and runs toward my apartment. He returns a few short moments later with nothing in his hands.

I gape at him confused when he approaches my left side

and takes my crutches. Before I can protest, Gavin bends and swoops me into his arms with ease. He carries me home as if I'm not five foot seven, weighing one-hundred thirty pounds. He sets me down to unlock the door. He leaves everything on my doorstep and swoops me up again, carrying me to my couch where he gently sets me down.

"That really wasn't necessary," I say acidly as Gavin walks back to the door to gather the things he left.

He ignores my comment, walking toward my bedroom. Before entering, he asks, "Pillows?"

"Yes," I call out as he ducks into the room and quickly returns with two pillows. He helps get me comfortably propped up on the couch.

"Are you hungry?" he asks, walking into the kitchen.

"Help yourself to anything," I suggest, not answering his question.

"Okay, do you want to rest or watch TV?" he asks from the kitchen.

"The remote's over there." I point to the counter in the kitchen.

He hands me the remote, and I flip through the channels, not seeing anything worthy of watching while he bangs around in the kitchen. I must have fallen asleep because the next thing I know, Gavin wakes me by setting a plate on the table beside me.

"Sorry, I didn't mean to wake you. Are you hungry?"

I wasn't, but now that I smell the aroma of chicken and rice in some sauce I'm unfamiliar with, I'm suddenly ravenous. "Um, yeah. Thanks."

I slowly sit up, being careful not to jar my leg or ribs while Gavin hands me a plate.

I take a bite. "Wow, this is amazing. I had all this?"

He suddenly looks self-conscious and turns a little red. "Um... Yeah."

"Where did you learn how to make this?" Curious because he's obviously spent some time in the kitchen.

"My mom." He suddenly looks thoughtful. "She insisted I learn when she found my brother went off to college not even knowing how to boil water for himself." He laughs at a memory. "She forced me to cook with her a couple times a week, so I wouldn't be helpless on my own."

"Wow, she taught you well," I compliment, taking another bite.

"Thanks." He grins and sits with his plate in the chair next to me.

"Want to watch a movie?" I suggest, taking another bite.

"Sure, what do you have in mind?" He looks intently at me, sending my heart sputtering.

"I have some movies on the top shelf of my hall closet, if you're interested." I point to the hall closet as he gets up to check them out. "There's not much, but you can choose whichever you'd like," I call toward the hall.

He comes back and puts one into the DVD player. I wonder which one he's chosen.

"It's a romantic comedy, if that's okay with you." Gavin sits and eats his dinner.

"I won't make it through the entire thing," I sigh.

"You're due for your meds. Can I get them for you?" He stands to walk into the kitchen to get them.

He hands me three horse-like pills and a glass of water. I finish eating as we watch the movie. Though there are characters on the screen, I don't have any clue as to what's happening.

Once I finish eating, nature calls. I attempt to stand, but I realize my crutches are across the room.

Before I can say or do anything, Gavin asks, "What can I get you?"

"Can you get my crutches?"

He quickly stands and retrieves them for me. "Can I help you?"

Embarrassed, I admit, "I need to use the bathroom."

"Oh," he quietly says. "I'll help you get there and then when you're done, if you need me, just ask."

Not liking to feel helpless, I say, "I'll try and if I need you, I'll call. Can you help me through the doors?"

I slowly make my way to the bathroom. It's a bit awkward and off balance, but I manage. As I go to the sink to wash my hands, I notice for the first time my reflection in the mirror.

"Ughh," I moan in frustration. My face has a few minor scrapes and a slight bruise on my right cheek. My long, brown hair's in complete disarray, going in every direction possible but where it should. I look absolutely awful.

There's a knock on the bathroom door. "You okay?" Gavin's voice comes through the door a bit panicky.

"I'm fine. I just realized I need a shower," I sigh as I lean against the counter for support and attempt to pull a brush through my hair.

"Want me to call Sophie to help you?" he offers through the door.

"No. I'll be okay. You can open the door, I'm decent." I give up on my hair and turn slowly in his direction.

"Can you help me get clothes from my bedroom?" I ask, feeling helpless.

We slowly make our way through the bathroom into my bedroom. Gavin stands in the middle of my room, looking awkward and folding his arms across his chest. If I didn't need his help, it'd almost be comical.

"Please open that third drawer?" Once opened, I grab a pair of pajama pants and their matching top. He closes the drawer, and I quickly grab a pair of underwear from my top drawer, trying to be inconspicuous. I don't make eye contact with Gavin until I have them tucked into my folded pajamas. I hand him the pile of clothes, and he sets it all on the bathroom counter while I slowly make my way back to the bathroom.

"You sure you're going to be okay? You've just taken your medication," Gavin points out with grave concern.

"I think I'll be okay," I assure him while I walk over to the tub and lean down to start the water, placing most of my weight on my crutches.

The trickiest part's trying to get in and out of the tub without rendering much weight on my sore leg, *especially being wet*. I try to be as quick as I can, all things considered. When I return to the living room, Gavin stands ready to assist me in any way he can.

"I've got it," comes out in a grunt as I get to the couch. I set myself down and swing my leg up on the couch to lie back.

"Is there anything I can get you?" he offers sincerely.

I try to think of anything I might need, so he won't have to get it later. "No, I think I'm good. Thanks." I then realize that he's paused the movie from when I last left the room.

"Oh, you can start the movie if you want." I watch the movie for awhile but at some point, I fall asleep.

I wake up in my bed, and everything's still dark. The clock on my bedside table says it's 5:24. *Great,* I think to myself. *How am I getting up without waking Gavin?* Relief flows through me when I see my crutches propped against the wall, next to my bed. Gavin seems to think of everything.

I slowly make my way to the bathroom, being as quiet as I can. When I return to my bedroom, I dress into a sports bra, pair of leggings, and a t-shirt. It's a slow process, but somehow, I manage without too much noise. I need my ribs re-taped because my shower and sleep made it fray and no longer stick at the edges. Maybe after Gavin wakes, I'll ask him to take me to get more. Before settling on my bed, I crack my door to let him know I'm awake. He's done enough for me already and deserves what sleep he can get. I pass the time by reading.

Eventually, I hear stirring in the living room. Within a few minutes, I see Gavin as he enters the bathroom from the hall, wearing a different pair of shorts and t-shirt. His hair is rumpled, and he has a sly grin when he greets me. "Morning."

"Good morning." Instead of shutting the pocket door to my bedroom, he walks through it.

"Want your medication?" His voice is deeper than usual but filled with concern.

"Use the bathroom. I'll meet you in the living room." I look to my crutches, but before I can move toward them, he hands them to me. When our fingers accidentally touch, I can't help the shiver that spreads through my spine. After a long, lingering moment where I do nothing but stare into his

golden-brown eyes, I finally remember my manners. "Uh...
Thanks."

Gavin opens his mouth to say something, but hesitates,
causing awkward silence to pass between us. He breaks it by
pointing to the bathroom with his thumb. "I'll be out in a
few." Almost as if he forces himself to walk away, he slowly
turns and walks to the bathroom.

I stare after him for a moment, then slowly make my way
to the kitchen. By the time I arrive, I'm winded. The fact that
I've let my meds lapse longer than I should is evident. I look
for my medication but have no clue where it is.

A deep voice from behind me sends shivers up my spine.
"Did you get your meds?"

"Um... No," I admit, standing near my kitchen counter.

He walks to the fridge and grabs the bag on top. He pulls
out two prescription bottles, hands me three pills then
reaches for a glass in the cupboard and fills it with water.
"The nurse suggested you should take these with food."

"Okay, cereal's in the cupboard," I suggest, not wanting
him to do more than necessary.

"I saw eggs in your fridge, is that okay?" he counters.
"How do you like them?"

"Over easy, but whatever you like is fine." I sit at one of
my barstools while he cooks. I spot an unfamiliar sleeping
bag and pillow on my couch.

Gavin must notice my change in facial expression.
"When I went home, I grabbed anything I thought I might
need. Mind if I shower after breakfast?"

"Of course. Towels are in the bathroom closet." I then
hesitate for a moment before I asking, "Hey, Gavin?"

He turns in response from the stove. "Yeah, Alex?"

"Would you take me to get tape for my ribs?"

"There's some in the bag the nurse gave me. I'd be happy to take you shopping though, if you need anything." He turns back to the eggs and flips them in the pan.

"Thanks. I... Uh... Need help with re-taping my ribs. The tape's starting to fray and itch."

"Can it wait until after breakfast?" He reaches into my cupboard and retrieves two plates. As he plates our food, I notice my kitchen's spotless.

"Wow... You didn't have to do the dishes," I comment as I look around.

He starts the toaster and turns with a smile. "It's not a problem. I made the mess, it's only fair I clean it."

When Gavin finishes our breakfast, I hobble to the couch.

"Oh, I'll move those." He quickly walks over and folds his sleeping bag before I can do anything. "Prop yourself up with my pillow."

I sit, allowing my right leg to be along the inside of the couch. Effortlessly, he props my leg to a comfortable position. As I snuggle into the armrest, Gavin returns to the kitchen.

I can't help but watch Gavin cook. He's skilled in the kitchen, and his arms flex as he handles the pan. Even from behind, I can tell he's athletic. His muscles are well defined and evenly distributed across his moderate frame. He's wearing a white t-shirt with a pair of blue soccer shorts. Though he's barefoot, he towers against the stove. When he turns to bring me my plate, I can't help but smile in embarrassment for being caught staring at him.

"Here you go. Want something to drink?" he offers, returning to the kitchen to get his plate.

"Water's great. Thanks."

As he sits in the chair next to me, he asks, "How are you feeling?"

"Like I was hit by a car," I try to pull off as a joke, but it doesn't go over well.

He tries to grin but solemnly asks, "Seriously?"

I sigh heavily and cringe at the movement. "I'm fine."

He's skeptical but says nothing, and we eat in silence. He breaks the silence by asking, "So... What do you want to do today?"

"My plans have kind of been canceled," I say sarcastically. "But I wouldn't mind picking up a few things."

"Besides that, you'll be resting a lot, too." Gavin makes it sound more like a demand, than a suggestion.

"You really don't have to stick around. I'm fine... Really." Knowing he's had to cancel his plans to be here, I intend to let him off the hook.

"I gave the doctor and your mother my word of twenty-four hours." Then he smirks. "You're stuck with me, so let's make the most of it."

What am I supposed to say to that?

When I don't respond, he adds, "Rest. I'll shower and get ready. Then we'll go anywhere you want." He hesitates, then tacks on, "Within reason. Maybe we'll pick up a movie or something since you're spending most of your day on that couch." He points to it and smiles victorious.

"Okay," I sigh in defeat. "Can you get my book in the bedroom?"

After reading a few pages, my medication kicks in, and my eyes grow heavy. The next thing I know, I awake to find myself covered with Gavin's sleeping bag, and he's studying at the kitchen counter. I take in a deep breath, enjoying the scent unique to him.

He turns his head in my direction. "Hey… How are you feeling?"

I slowly stretch, trying not to hurt myself any further. "Good," I say in a yawn. I feel the irritation of the tape on my ribs and ask, "Hey, Gavin, can you re-tape my ribs?" I ask as I gather my crutches to stand.

When he enters my room with the tape, I'm suddenly very anxious. I'll have to lift my shirt almost entirely or take it off to do this. Though I'm wearing a sports bra for this purpose, it's still uncomfortable for both of us. Neither say anything as we look around awkwardly. Eventually, our eyes lock on one another.

His face flushes as what he has to do must sink in. "Um, how do you want to do this?" he stutters quietly, still holding my gaze with his golden-brown eyes.

A blush spreads over my face, and my tongue ties. Eventually, I regain composure and respond, "Um," I sigh, trying to focus. "I think, if I sit, I'll be able to hold my shirt. If you look at how the doctors have it taped now, you should be able to replicate it."

He hesitantly studies the bandages. I feel Gavin's light touch, making me shudder slightly, not necessarily out of pain but in reaction to his closeness. He gauges my reaction speculatively. "Um… I'll pull this old tape off first." Apprehension fills his features as he bites his lower lip. "It may hurt. You sure you want to do this?"

"Yeah, the tape's rolling and sticks to my clothes."

He's right. It hurts like crazy, but I concentrate on keeping my face clear from emotion, though I slip a few times. Once the tape is removed, he replaces it effortlessly. When he's done, I'm surprised to feel a sense of relief from the sturdiness of the new bandage. Gavin helps me get ready so we can go shopping, by putting a shoe on my braced leg and gathering my purse.

We run a few errands on the way to the store. I stop by Antonio's to give them my doctor's note, and I'm relieved to know they'll hold my job. By the time we get to the store, I'm nodding off. Gavin offers to shop for us and picks out a movie. We spend the afternoon watching a movie; well, he watches while I sleep some more. I had no idea this accident would take so much out of me.

When I realize it's after six, I ask, "Are you going to practice tonight?"

"I hadn't planned on it. You shouldn't be alone just yet," he reminds me.

He can't put his life on hold for me. "The team needs you. We're already one person down."

"Alex, they'll be fine without me." He tries to sound convincing, but I don't buy it. He loves soccer and has been intense at every practice.

"Gavin, you've got to be bored babysitting me. Really, go. I'll be fine for a few hours."

He looks as if he's considering my suggestion seriously but says nothing.

"I'm even going stir crazy, and I live here. Go to practice! I would if I could," I encourage.

He stares deeply into my eyes and stops my argument. "I really don't think you should be alone."

I formulate another argument to convince him. "I'll go with you. I promise to stay on the bench. We'll bring pillows and prop up my leg," I suggest, not wanting to play the role of a complete invalid.

"Alex," he sighs in frustration. I can tell he isn't expecting this. There may be hope yet. His eyebrows burrow together in serious thought. "You really need to rest, and I don't think you'll get much at practice." He shakes his head, and I'm sure he's about to continue his argument, but he surprises me. "Will you promise to stay on the bench the entire time?" He eyes me suspiciously, as if he doesn't believe I'll grant his request.

"Yes!" I reply enthusiastically.

"Well, let's go because we need to swing by my apartment to get my gear," he sighs, clearly realizing my victory.

Eager to be out of my apartment, I'm careful not to overdo things. Of course, everyone's concerned about my accident. Fortunately, Gavin retells the story, so I don't have to explain why I wasn't paying attention to the car as it hit me. I notice he leaves out the part about him waiting on me hand and foot, as well as his overnight stay. Before everyone heads out on the field, Gavin checks on me one last time. His kindness melts my heart.

"Are you sure you're okay?" His eyes are full of concern, searching for any sign of discomfort.

Though this bench is uncomfortable, I assure him I'm fine. It's interesting to watch practice from the sidelines. I pick up a few moves mentally that I hope to use in the future.

From across the field, Gavin checks in on me more than I expect. A few times, he catches me trying to reposition myself and eyes me suspiciously. I can't hide much from him. Once he comes across the field to make sure everything's okay because I'd unconsciously grimaced from a wrong movement. I assure him I'm fine and encourage him to continue practicing. He almost insists on taking me home right then, but James calls him over to help demonstrate a maneuver to the group.

Sophie sits by me while everyone scrimmages, since my absence makes the teams uneven. Her crystal-blue eyes bore into me, and I prepare myself for a loaded question. "So." She takes a deep breath and stares as if seeking an answer to a question she's yet to ask.

"So?" I ask innocently.

"Are you okay?" She's genuinely concerned yet fishing for information. "To be honest, you don't look so hot."

I attempt a joke and laugh it off. "Well, what can I say, I was hit by a car. It's bound to leave a few marks."

"Alex, why haven't you called? I would've been there to help you." Her brows burrow in confusion.

How do I explain this? Looking to the ground shyly. "I haven't... exactly... been alone." My eyes flicker to Gavin before looking at Sophie, whose eyes are wide with suspicion.

She glances to Gavin before continuing to stare at me with a mountain of questions in her eyes. "Why is Gavin overly concerned about you?" Is the one of many, she decides to put into words.

"Well, I guess it's because he wants to make sure I'm comfortable." I downplay the accident as much as possible.

"But why are you here? You should be resting. A soccer field isn't the place for that." Her expression's unreadable, and I'm not sure where she's going with this.

I look down, unsure how to explain. Finally, I say, "Well, it's the only way Gavin would come." I look up guiltily.

"Why does it matter? You've just been hit by a car, literally," she says in surprise.

"Well… You see… He watched it happen. He was at the hospital and has been here ever since," I admit, waiting for her reaction.

"Wait a minute, weren't you hit yesterday morning?" she asks, piecing it all together.

"Um, yeah." I shrug slightly but stop when I realize it hurts.

"So… He's been with you ever since?" Though it's a question, Sophie makes it sound like an accusation, raising her eyebrows at me.

"Yep," is my only response.

She stares at me inquisitively for a while longer. Still looking puzzled, "Is there something you're not telling me, I mean?"

My cheeks instantly heat as I recall the first time I literally bumped into Gavin and the numerous encounters ever since. "Um." I speculate what to divulge. "We have geology together, and we've bumped into each other a few times on campus."

"Oh." Her face is thoughtful before continuing, "So… I'm confused. Why is it important that Gavin's at practice?"

"Well, since he feels he needs to babysit me, I was afraid he wouldn't come otherwise," I finally admit, feeling awkward.

She picks up on the key word. "Babysitting?"

"He seems to have taken it upon himself to feel responsible for me and has been caring for me ever since."

Not knowing what else to say, I shrug, but suddenly wince from the pain.

Unfortunately, neither Sophie or Gavin miss it. Suddenly, they're both asking if I'm okay, though Gavin's still a few yards away.

"I'm fine, just made a sudden wrong movement," I assure them both.

Sophie still looks as if she's filled with loaded questions, but lets them drop, seeing Gavin's presence.

"Alex, let's get you home to rest properly. I'll hurry up and change my shoes, so we can leave. Your medications are in my bag. It's been almost six hours." He quickly goes to his bag and digs for my horse-size pills.

I raise my eyebrows at Sophie, giving her a slight shrug, silently saying, "See?"

Sophie discreetly lifts an eyebrow in my direction and says under her breath, "I see what you mean." Then louder, she states, "If you need anything, please remember I'm here." She gives me a quick hug and walks to her bag to change out of her cleats and shin guards.

"Thanks, Sophie," I reply as she leaves my side.

I turn to see Gavin handing me my medication with his water bottle. "Here you go. Let's get you back home, so you can relax."

On the way home, Gavin finally breaks the now comfortable silence by asking, "Are you staying home from class tomorrow?"

"Well… I haven't thought about it," I sigh, pondering the question. "I think I can make it through my classes. I'm done by noon, then I'll go home to rest if I need to."

"What time's your first one?" Gavin asks nonchalantly.

"Eight."

I can see Gavin's eyes widen from the corner of my eye in response. "Just how many classes do you have on Mondays?"

I see where he's going with this, so I quietly say, "Four."

Without trying to sound like he's making judgments, Gavin continues, "Do you think you can make it that long? Where are they located?"

"My first class is in Todd, then Bryan and the last two are in Cleveland."

"My first class is at eight, too. Would you like a ride, and we'll park under the library?" he asks, keeping his eyes on the road.

"You don't really need to do that. It's not too far to campus."

We pull into the parking lot of my apartment, and he looks me directly in the eyes. "Alex. You get winded walking fifty feet on those crutches. Todd's a lot further than that. It's also up a hill."

Leaving me no room to argue, I sigh. "Okay, but I really don't want to put you out any further."

Gavin smiles, holding onto my eyes. "It's no problem. I'm going that way already. If you'd like, I'll meet you behind Cleveland at noon since I have a break then, too. It'll be a few minutes before I can get there, but it'll probably be easier than hoofing it back here." He raises an eyebrow and waits for my reaction.

"All right." I think he has me there again. "If it's not an imposition."

"I work from one until five tomorrow, so it won't be a problem."

He smiles, relieved I'm taking his offer.

He's never mentioned work before. I curiously ask, "Where do you work?"

"Oh, I work for the College of Business between classes and a few afternoons each week."

"I didn't know that," I quietly respond. He doesn't offer more, so I let it drop. The effects of my medication begin to take effect, and the remainder of the car ride's in comfortable silence.

Once inside my apartment, Gavin helps me settle on the couch. "Do you have homework?" I ask as he walks to the kitchen to get something cold to drink for himself.

"No, I finished everything this weekend."

"Really?" I don't recall him studying much besides in the hospital and a little this morning.

"Well, you've been asleep a lot." He turns to smile at me. "I brought my laptop and my backpack and have made use of my time."

"What about your studio projects?" I ask, making sure he's not getting behind in his classes.

"I finished Friday. I'm good." Gavin smirks as he returns to the living room. "What about you?" He raises an eyebrow in my direction.

"I finished Friday evening, too. Other than showing up for class, I really have nothing due this week," I say with relief.

"Want to watch a movie then?" he asks.

"Sure. You'll end up watching more of it than me." I chuckle, knowing I'll fall asleep against my will again.

I'm surprised the next morning to find I'm in my own bed when I wake a little after six. I slowly hobble to the bathroom, take a shower, and slowly get ready for my day, dressing in another pair of leggings and a t-shirt. As I'm putting on my shirt, there's a knock on my bedroom door.

"Just a sec," I call out to the door. When I'm decent, I call out, "Come in."

I sit on my bed as Gavin shyly enters my room. "Hey, I've made some breakfast if you're interested. Mind if I take another shower?"

"Thanks. You didn't have to do that."

"I've been awake for awhile. When I heard you get up, I started cooking," he admits quietly.

Gavin drives me to the top of campus. Though I don't want to admit it, I'm grateful. It's honestly hard getting to my classes. My professors are understanding when I'm a few minutes late, especially since I hand them a doctor's note when I arrive. To be alert for classes, I purposely skip my medication. Though my mind's clear, I'm paying the price when I reach my final class. Thank God, I've made it through. I'm completely exhausted when I wait for Gavin at noon.

"Hey," he greets me as he assists me into the car. "How was your day?"

"Exhausting," I admit as he shuts my door. He is a sight for sore eyes, and I can't help but watch him as he gets into the car.

"I'll have you home in no time," he says as he starts the car and drives to my apartment.

On the way home, I realize I haven't spoken to my mother since the hospital. Wondering aloud, "I'd better call Mom before falling asleep. She's probably a bundle of nerves by now."

Gavin suddenly looks down sheepishly. "Oh, she's called."

"What do you mean?" I ask, suddenly confused.

"Well…" Gavin looks sheepish. "She's called at least twice a day since you've been home, but you were sleeping, so we didn't bother you."

Still confused, I ask, "Why haven't I seen any missed calls on my phone?"

Now that we're at my apartment, Gavin looks directly at me, his eyes flicker to a darker shade of golden brown. "She's calling my phone."

Now shocked. "Why on earth is *my* mom calling *you*?"

Covering his smile, Gavin averts his eyes and says, "She wants you to rest. She's very concerned. Since you've slept most of the weekend, she asked me to call when it wouldn't disturb you. She knows you'll call when you feel better." He tries to reassure me.

"Why haven't you mentioned this?" I ask in disbelief as Gavin helps me out of the car.

His eyes fill with concern. "Are you mad?"

I think about it for a moment. "No, I'm actually grateful."

"You should call her, she misses you," he suggests as we make it to my apartment.

"Have you told her you're staying with me?" I ask hesitantly.

"Um, yeah. Your mom asked me to. Apparently, Jacob had good things to say and wanted me to look after you," he humbly admits.

Shock flies through me. I stand here, leaning against my crutches, my mouth gaping at him, unable to say anything.

Seeing this, Gavin approaches me hesitantly and changes the subject. "Why don't you sit, and I'll get your medicine."

I do what he asks because I'm exhausted and wiped out from the day, not necessarily from what he's just revealed. While he's in the kitchen, he makes roast beef sandwiches and brings them over with two glasses of milk.

"Here you go." He hands me my sandwich and medication. He holds onto my drink until I pop the pills into my mouth. Then he sits next to me to eat his lunch.

"Thanks," I say quietly and eat my sandwich. "I think I'll take a nap when I finish with this. I'm beat."

"You sure you'll be okay? I'll call someone to stay with you, if you'd like?"

Beginning to glare, I'm stopped short when he backtracks. "Never mind. You'll be fine for a few hours, I'm sure."

He looks at his watch. "I need to go. Anything you need before I leave?" His features fill with apprehension.

"No, I'm good. Thanks."

Gavin stands and takes his plate to the sink. "I'll be back around five. I've left my number on the counter. If you need anything, just call."

"I'll be fine. Thanks."

"Okay, take care," he says as he walks toward the door.

The sound of a knock wakes me a few hours later. I slowly shuffle to the door, expecting Gavin. I'm pleasantly surprised to find it's Sophie.

"Hey, Alex." She smiles in greeting. "Did I wake you?"

"I need to get up anyway. Come in." I open the door further and make my way back to the living room. "Would you like anything to drink?"

"Sure, what do you have?" she asks as she stops at the kitchen.

Realizing Gavin shopped last, I respond, "I'm not sure, just help yourself."

She pulls out a soda and asks if I'd like one, then sits in the chair adjacent to me as I pull my leg carefully onto the couch and face her.

"So how was your day?" I ask, trying to avoid being the focus of attention.

She pulls her feet into the chair with her as she takes a sip of her soda. "It's a typical Monday. I went to class and worked this afternoon. What about you?"

"It could've been worse. Even though I'm really sore, I made it to all of my classes by holding off with my meds until this afternoon, so I wouldn't fall asleep. It's really frustrating."

"You'll be better soon," Sophie encourages.

"Yeah," I sigh, but wince. "It's just hard being dependent on people."

"It'll be okay," she sympathizes. "Can I help you with anything while I'm here?"

"Um... I can't really think of anything." I'm caught off guard by her sudden change in subject.

"Are you still going home this weekend?" Sophie asks with genuine interest.

"I hope so."

"Want help packing? I can't imagine it's easy on those crutches."

She has me there. "Yeah, it's a little difficult," I slowly admit to both her and myself. "Before packing, I need to do laundry." I groan in frustration. "I'm running out of sweats to wear under this brace." I point to my leg in disgust.

"Alex… What do I look like, chopped liver?" She smiles at me accusingly, then cocks an eyebrow in my direction. "Unless, you'd rather Gavin help?"

Nope. No way. He's already done enough. Sophie's a lifesaver. Gavin has no business doing my laundry. With a sigh of defeat, I sigh. "That'd be awesome."

Sophie stands suddenly. "Show me what needs to be done."

"No!" She abruptly stops me by putting her hand in the air. "I'm perfectly capable of finding your clothes. Just tell me from where you are." She points to the couch sternly.

"My laundry's in my room, and I need to make sure my towels are washed. We ran out."

Sophie's eyebrows raise in an accusation, but I interrupt her thoughts. "With Gavin staying here, my supply's limited."

Sophie nods and walks into my bathroom. Within minutes, she returns with a basket full of clothes, including my bedsheets.

"I really appreciate this, Soph." I attempt to get up again, but Sophie gives me the stink-eye. I concede, "Laundry detergent and a roll of quarters are in my hall closet."

Within minutes, she's out the door, and I'm left to my own devices. I look for something to watch on TV, but nothing stands out. In all too short of time, Sophie returns to visit with me in the living room.

"So," she announces as she sits next to me again. "What's really going on with you and Gavin?"

My face burns, and I don't know what to say. "I told you,

he's just a friend. He's been a huge help since my accident. He promised my mom to keep an eye on me."

"Um, Alex," Sophie hesitates. "That's not what I meant," she states as if I'm being obtuse.

I look at her dumfounded. "What do you mean?"

"Well, are you sure you're *just friends*?" Sophie asks as she bites her lower lip.

"Yeah, what else would we be?" I ask rhetorically.

Sophie says nothing but stares intently at me.

"Really, nothing else is going on. He's taking care of me, that's it." I sound a little defensive, even to myself, at the end.

"Okay," Sophie sighs. "If you say so." She doesn't sound convinced but lets the subject drop.

She changes the subject to soccer. Soon, there's a knock on my door. Sophie rushes to answer it, and Gavin's voice fills the hall. He doesn't seem surprised to see her. As they walk down the hall together, he asks, "So... Have you eaten?"

"Not yet," I admit from the couch.

"Well, I think there's plenty of leftover chicken and rice if you want some. Sophie?"

"Sure, sounds great," she admits as she sits in the chair next to me.

"What have you been up to?" Gavin asks to no one in particular.

Sophie and I glance at each other, trying to determine to whom he's speaking. It's me who finally answers, "You know the usual, running a few miles, homework, maybe even some squats afterward." Sarcasm drips as a grin spreads across my face.

Gavin grimaces in my direction, then turns to Sophie for a response.

"Well... I'm helping Alex with laundry as we speak. Why?"

"Well, if you're hanging out, I'm going to head to the studio, so I can get ahead this week."

"Gavin, you should go regardless," I say, not wanting to be a burden.

"It's no problem, Gavin. I'll be here," Sophie replies, not acknowledging my comment.

Gavin adds a few vegetables to make dinner stretch between the three of us. Then as discreetly as he can, he assures I'm okay before leaving for the studio to work for a few hours.

After he leaves, Sophie eyes me suspiciously, but says nothing. She makes sure I take my medication and retrieves my laundry as I watch TV. When she returns, I find she's already folded everything, making me feel completely helpless. Though she protests, I get up to show her where things belong. It's overwhelming to realize I have such a good friend in her.

Sophie insists on staying to watch a TV program we've started while I take a shower. When I hobble out to the living room, we watch another of my favorite programs. By this time, I'm extremely tired and can barely keep my eyes open. The next thing I know, I'm waking up in my own bed the next morning, having no recollection of how I got here.

The next few days, other than for my short distances between class, I'm hardly left alone. Either Gavin or Sophie drive me to or from campus and hang out with me in the evenings. Though each have told me they haven't planned anything, I hardly believe it's coincidental. When Gavin needs be at the studio to work, Sophie miraculously appears before or shortly after he leaves. Gavin sleeps on my couch the entire week as well.

Each day, my family checks in and makes arrangements for the bridal shower this weekend. On Tuesday evening, we're discussing the need for my sister's friend to find other arrangements for a babysitter when Gavin interrupts and renders me nearly speechless.

He volunteers to babysit two kids he's never met. He claims since it's short notice, and I'll be there to help him, it should be a walk in the park. Mom and my sister both think it's an excellent idea and can't wait to meet him in person. *Could he be anymore perfect if he tried?*

On Thursday afternoon, I stay on campus between class and geology lab because it's silly to have someone drive me home only to return a few hours later. I make use of my time studying in Cleveland Library. When Gavin meets me before lab, he looks me over with care.

"Hey, Alex. How's your day?" Gavin asks with genuine concern. "You seem a bit tired."

"Um," I say after staring into his golden-brown eyes. I can't lie to him because he's good at calling my bluffs, so I admit, "Just a little."

"Are you sure you're up for a two-hour lab? I'm sure you haven't had any meds today... Have you?" he accuses as I take a sharper than usual breath, ascending the stairs to Webster Hall.

I must take longer than I should because Gavin's voice fills with frustration. "Alex, you'll never fully recover if you don't rest."

"I know. I'm fine." I try to sound convincing. "I'll take it on the way home. I need to concentrate. All it does is knock me out, as I'm sure you've noticed. I don't have homework tonight. I'll sleep later." I sound as if I'm whining by the end of my rant.

Before we take our seats, he goes to grab a stool that's been vacant this entire semester. He places it next to the table in front of us. "Here, this will help keep your leg elevated."

I'm about to protest, but Ian calls the class to order. As it turns out, the stool is necessary because it's more difficult than I imagined to sit with a brace on. Unfortunately, there's a steady pulse running through my leg and chest, so I have to concentrate harder than usual on our instructions. Thanks to Gavin's efforts on our lab, we finish early.

After class, Gavin insists I wait while he retrieves his car, parked by Carpenter Hall. It's only a short wait. I'm able to hobble discreetly out to the parking lot by one of the dorms without alerting him as to how much pain I'm actually in. Thankfully, he meets me there in no time. While I wait, I take my medication and sit on the wall of a flowerbed near one of the dorms.

As usual, he gets out of his car to assist me into the passenger side. Trying to hide my pain, I maneuver my way into the car, but it's a completely wasted effort. After stowing my crutches in the back seat, Gavin returns to the driver's side. From the corner of my eye, I watch him scrutinize my every move, sigh, then shake his head in annoyance. I say nothing. It seems as if neither of us want to mention my current condition. When we enter my apartment, he brakes the silence by asking me what I would like for dinner. By then, I'm so exhausted, I honestly don't care if I eat.

Relaxing into the couch, I lie my head back, closing my eyes, eagerly waiting for my meds to kick in. The next thing I know, Gavin taps my shoulder and hands me a plate with a grilled tuna fish sandwich and a scoop of cottage cheese.

"Here, you need to eat." He sets the plate on my lap and looks sternly into my eyes. "You're supposed to take your meds with food. You don't want an upset stomach on top of everything else that's bothering you, do you?" he asks rhetorically.

"Thanks," I groggily say, taking a bite of the cottage cheese. It takes all my concentration to keep my eyes open. As soon as I've chewed my last bite, I rest my head and my eyes lose the battle they've been waging.

BRIDAL SHOWER

As WE PULL out of the parking lot after Gavin's last class Friday afternoon, he casually asks, "So what's the plan for this weekend?"

"Um…" *Where do I begin?* "Tonight, we'll hang out with my family. Tomorrow is the shower. I need to finish some things for the games, but other than that, I'm set. Then tomorrow evening, we'll be babysitting while everyone goes out. On Sunday, we'll have a family brunch and take off in the afternoon… If that's okay with you?" He agreed to babysit but didn't commit to the entire weekend. *Crap. I hope it's okay.*

"Wow… Let me know what you need help with, and I'm there, okay?" he promises. Relief washes through me, and I sink further into the comfortable passenger seat.

"So… Since we're spending the weekend together, tell me about your family." Gavin smiles but keeps his eyes on the road.

"What do you want to know?" Where do I even begin?

"For starters, you can tell me where you live. Then I'll know how to get there in case you fall asleep." He smirks quickly at me before returning his eyes to the road. Geesh. Have I been sleeping that much? "I assume this is the way because unless you live in Idaho, it's the only way to any major road," he teases lightly with a thin smile spreading across his lips.

"Ha Ha. Very funny. I live south of Olympia. We'll go over Snoqualmie Pass to Highway Eighteen. Head south on I-5, until Olympia. *If I'm asleep at that point*," I say a little louder than necessary, "Wake me because I live in the boonies, and you'll miss some turns." I sarcastically tack on at the end to prove the point.

"Okay, I'll do that." He smirks at my reaction but leaves it at that.

"Tell me about your parents," he suggests after a few minutes of listening to the stereo.

"Well… As I'm sure you know… Their names are Charlotte and Kurt. They met in college and have been married for almost thirty years, this summer. Dad works for the Department of Transportation, and Mom works at the Thurston County Courthouse.

"You've already met my brother Jacob. He works in a finance office in Seattle. Katherine's absolutely my best friend. If she's a little pre-occupied with the wedding and turns slightly into a bridezilla, please don't hold it against her. She's not usually that way." I look at Gavin to see his reaction.

"She met Ben while attending St. Martins and have been together for about two years."

"Okay, I'll keep that in mind." He smiles, then looks back to the road. "Don't you have a younger brother, too?"

"Yep. Kai. He's a junior in high school. He's the typical teenage boy who's into girls, hanging out with friends, and playing sports."

"Which sports does he play?" Gavin asks as he turns right onto a road between two wheat fields.

"Football, basketball, and soccer year-round," I hesitate for a moment when I remember that Gavin's meeting my *entire* family this weekend. "Um, Gavin…"

"Yes," he draws out, waiting for a response.

"I should warn you… My ENTIRE family is here this weekend," I say with reservation.

"You said everyone will be home," he adds with a quizzical face as if he's wondering what's the big deal.

"No. I mean, my *entire* family." He has no idea what he's getting into. I've never even brought anyone home before, other than friends from high school. He being here is a big deal. "Grandparents, aunts, uncles, cousins, long-time friends of the family. It's a couple's shower. Everyone's invited." I sigh when I realize the extent. "Might as well be a family reunion," I finally admit, shaking my head.

"Well, at least I'll only have to do it once." He laughs once aloud, though I don't really understand why.

"Yeah, you can say that again," I sarcastically retort.

He's quiet for a moment as I contemplate the thousands of questions about my accident, let alone the fact that I've brought Gavin.

"Everything okay?" Gavin's voice fills with concern.

"I'm fine," I assure him. "Just thinking about all the questions everyone will bombard me with tomorrow."

"I'm sure you'll be fine. They're probably just concerned." His words calm me. "Fortunately for you, the only part of your accident that remains obvious to everyone else is your leg. Your face has virtually healed, almost impossible to notice. There's no scars, just a faint bruise if you're really searching, but it's nowhere near obvious."

"Thanks, Gavin. I appreciate your support." Honestly, injuries are the least of my worries. There's no way I'm telling him he's the root of my fears. How the heck will I explain him to my family? There's no need to make him worry, so I let the subject drop.

Throughout the drive, we laugh and joke as we listen to music in the background. All is fine until he makes the statement, "I'm sure you've dated a lot." My face instantly turns red, and I can't find words to tell him the truth, if someone paid me a million dollars. God, this is embarrassing.

Unfortunately, Gavin's learned to read my tells this week, prompting him to ask more questions. I'm not sure what's worse, the fact that he's asked or what I have to tell him. "No... I haven't... really... ever been serious... with anyone." Trying not to sound too pathetic, I inform him I've gone to dances, though usually with a group. Throughout our entire conversation, Gavin's wearing a faint smile, as if he enjoys watching me squirm.

Eventually, I turn our focus to him before he reveals every secret I have. "So... Have you dated a lot?"

He shrugs a little and replies, "Well, like you, I dated a little in high school and went to dances, but there's no one in particular. For the past few years, I've gone out a few times, but it's usually just as a group of friends."

"Why?" comes out of my mouth before I can stop myself.

Gavin turns his head slightly to the side and sheepishly smiles before saying, "No one's ever caught my interest."

Seriously? After spending any amount of time with Gavin, I find it hard for anyone not to like him. I'm positive he's had girlfriends. He's likely downplaying it, for my benefit. I stare in disbelief. When my mouth catches up to my brain, I ask, "Really? You've never had a serious girlfriend?" I pay close attention to his facial expressions to see if there's any change.

He glances in my direction and shrugs. "Nope, the opportunity never presented itself." Then he focuses his attention on the road. *What the heck? Has he been living under a rock?* This baffles me.

When we pull into my driveway, I'm surprised to find my entire family rushing out to greet us.

Before I'm out of the car, Mom calls my name, practically running toward us. As soon as Gavin helps me to my feet, Mom wraps me in a hug.

"Oh, Alex, you've scared me so much. Are you sure you're okay?" Her voice fills with grave concern as she looks over every inch of me.

"Really," I pant, "I'm fine, but you don't need to hug me so tight. I'll still be here tomorrow." She suddenly lets go and laughs. Her attention turns to Gavin, who stands awkwardly beside me. Within a heartbeat, she's hugging the life out of him, too.

"You must be Gavin. It's so nice to finally meet you in person. I can't tell you how grateful we are for your help. Thank you so much for watching Alexis."

"It's no problem, ma'am," he assures her. "It's the least I could do."

Dad breaks in, "Well, Alex isn't the easiest to take care of. I'm sure you've had your work cut out for you!" Snickers erupt from the rest of my family. *Geesh! It's not like I've been that difficult.*

"Dad!" I call out in embarrassment, but my protest is lost on everyone.

Dad holds out his hand to Gavin. "I'm Kurt. It's nice to meet you."

"Sir. Gavin Wallace." They shake hands with wide smiles.

"Well, let's get everyone inside," Mom calls out.

"I'll get the things from the car," Gavin suggests, and Dad offers to help.

Once inside the living room, Mom's in full coddle mode. She insists I lie down to put my leg up.

"Mom," I sigh. "I just spent six hours in a car. Give me a moment. Besides, I need to get up to use the bathroom."

From across the room, Gavin catches my eye. I give him an *I told you so* glance, and he winks in return, and my stomach flutters.

"Alex, what's it like being hit by a car?" Kai asks excitedly. *Only a teenage boy would find this a thrilling topic.*

I deadpan, "It's something I wouldn't recommend." This brings laughter from everyone but Mom, of course.

Kai pleads, "Tell us what happened."

Before I can begin, Gavin clears his throat and fills in the details about the car speeding down the street, turning at the last moment and sending me flying across the pavement. He doesn't exaggerate or give too many details, but thankfully, it pacifies Kai's curiosity. I appreciate Gavin doesn't mention the extent of my original condition. There's no need to worry my family further.

"Oh my goodness," Mom whispers. "I don't know how we'll ever thank you enough for being there for Alex." Mom rushes to him and hugs him once more, leaving him to stand awkwardly after she releases him.

"It's no problem. Really," Gavin assures her.

Dad notices Gavin's still at the entrance to the living room. "Well, get in here and make yourself comfortable."

"Okay." Gavin grins, looking around for a place to sit. With Jacob, Kai, and Ben on the other couch and Kate sitting in one recliner, the only spot that's left is Dad's recliner or next to me on the couch.

To put him out of his misery, I offer, "Sit here." I pat the spot on the couch next to me, but he hesitates.

Kai laughs at Gavin's hesitation. "You're already tired of her?"

I throw Kai an angry glare, but he doesn't notice. What a brat. I start to protest, but Gavin interrupts.

Gavin clears his throat and simply states, "Not at all."

"Seriously?" Kai's eyes widen. "I'd be sick of her if she didn't get to run for that long." Causing the room to once again erupt with laughter.

"I haven't been that bad." I defend myself.

Gavin shrugs. Then his voice couldn't sound more sincere if he tried. "She's not that bad, Kai. But then again, she's been sleeping most of the time." He pats my good leg to assure me he's only joking. I'm not sure who notices, but with his piercing eyes, I could care less.

"What are you going to school for, Gavin?" Ben breaks in,

changing the focus from me. I could almost kiss him, I'm so thankful.

"I'm a third-year architect major."

"That's interesting. Do you know where you want to work when you're done?" Dad interjects.

"Well, I've done a few internships already, but I'm leaving my options open. This summer, I'm working for a firm outside of Seattle. I'll live at home to save for my semester abroad, next spring."

"So… You live in Seattle," my sister, Katherine, concludes.

"Lake Stevens, but it's close enough to commute." Gavin sits back, relaxing a little. His leg slides closer to mine, and I can suddenly feel his body heat radiating through my leggings.

"Where are you studying abroad?" Mom's eyes widen with delight. She loves to travel, and I can only guess the number of questions she'll ask.

"I'm still waiting for all the specifics of the plan. I've chosen four destinations in Europe. The university will make the final arrangements. Once I get there, I'll either live with a host family or get a place of my own. I don't have any preference."

"Will you be done with school when you return?" Jacob probes.

"No, it's a five-year program. Next fall, I'll either be in Spokane or Pullman, then go abroad in the spring. I'll return the following fall to Pullman, for my final year."

"Sounds interesting." Jacob asks questions about Gavin's program at school. Gavin answers every question thrown at him with ease.

I watch Gavin comfortably interact with my family. They've been easy on him, so far. Relieved, I relax, but eventually nature calls. I grab my crutches to stand.

Gavin stops his conversation and asks, "Need any help?"

"I'm fine," I assure him. "I'm going to shower and unpack my things."

He stands, walking over to my bags. "Where do you want these?"

"Um…" Feeling everyone's eyes on me, I continue, "Just follow me, and I'll show you."

Before leaving the room, Gavin turns to my family and asks, "Um… Where's the nearest hotel?"

Dad instantly answers, "We won't hear anything of the sort. There's a bed in the den. It's located at the second door to your left down that hall. Charlotte's prepared everything for you."

"Oh," Gavin whispers in surprise. "Thank you."

Once upstairs and out of earshot, Gavin quietly asks, "Alex, how are you doing? Really… Don't sugarcoat it," he warns, piercing my eyes and me to my spot.

Knowing it's pointless to lie, I stare until my mouth catches up with my brain. "I'm a little sore. I'm really stiff from the car ride, but I'm okay. Honest."

He holds my gaze for countless heartbeats. Once he must realize I've told him the truth, he smiles. "It's about time you stop hiding things from me."

"I… Uh… Haven't meant to," I concede, still trapped by his golden-brown eyes, unable to pull away.

He grins widely. "I know. You're definitely stubborn when you choose to be."

Not knowing what to say, I grimace in frustration.

"Do you want help putting things in your bathroom before I go?" Gavin asks, setting my bags on the bed.

"Um…" Where to begin. "If you wouldn't mind putting my skirt and top in the closet, that'd be great."

He sees my pajamas on the top of my bag and sets them aside for me. Then searches my closet for hangers.

"Thanks," I say as he finishes. "Can you set those pajamas and my grooming bag on the counter as you walk down the hall? I'll get there in a few minutes." I stand in the middle of my room awkwardly as he grabs the things I asked for. "I think I'll take off my brace in here."

"I can help, if you'd like." He sets the things down on my bed and bends down to unfasten the Velcro on my brace. He removes it, placing it on my bed. "There." He then looks at me questioningly, "Need anything else before I leave?"

"Nope, I'll be downstairs to take my medication before going to bed."

Without another word, he picks up my things, turns, and walks out of the room.

I take my time in the shower, letting the knots dissolve from my body. By the time I return, forty-five minutes have passed. Upon entering the kitchen, I hear Gavin and Mom's voices. Pans clanking so she must be cooking. As I round the corner, I'm surprised to find it's Gavin who's cooking while Mom sits on a barstool, leaning against the counter.

"Hey," Gavin calls out as I enter the room. "I thought you might be hungry. Your mom said you've always loved breakfast for dinner, so I'm making eggs and toast."

I eye her suspiciously and she quickly insists, "I was more than happy to cook, but Gavin insisted I relax." She glances hesitantly at me once again. "You know me, the moment anyone else around here wants to cook, I'm more than willing to let them."

Feeling awkward, I wonder what else they've shared about me in my absence. I feel myself blush, so I force myself to look away from them.

Gavin picks up a plate and slides an egg onto it alongside a slice of buttered toast. "Here, have a seat and eat. I'll get your medication if you want."

I have no idea what to say. "Um, it's upstairs in my purse." He walks out of the room, returning with my entire purse a few minutes later. I spot Mom from the corner of my eye, smiling with approval.

"Here you go." Gavin hands my purse to me and walks to a cupboard near the sink. "Where are your glasses?"

"Right there." Mom points to the one on his left. He opens it and fills a glass with water before handing it to me.

"Gavin, you don't have to do this." I protest.

"I'm already up." He slightly smiles, knowing I'm getting frustrated. "No worries."

"Well… Are you going to eat?" I say defensively.

"I had something while you were in the shower." He leans back against the counter, folding his arms across his chest.

Not wanting to make a scene, I let it drop. Mom changes the subject, to who's arriving tomorrow. When I finish eating, we return to the living room. By now, Katherine and Ben have left the room and Jacob, Kai, and Dad are watching something on the Discovery Channel. Gavin settles into the spot on the end of the couch while Mom sits in her recliner, leaving me the rest of the couch Gavin isn't occupying.

"Want to lie down?" Gavin asks before suggesting, "I can sit on the floor."

"No, I'm fine for now." Knowing I won't last long either way, I contemplate going straight to bed, but I'm unsure about giving them the opportunity to talk about me again. I settle into the armrest of the couch. Gavin takes a throw pillow from between us and offers to place it under my leg. As I watch the program, my eyes droop. I try to fight it, but it's no use. Within minutes, I'm fast asleep.

The next morning, I wake up confused. I'm in my childhood bedroom and have no idea how I got here. The clock tells me it's barely past six. Knowing I have a lot to do, I make my way to the bathroom to get ready. Once downstairs, I notice a light in the living room. Unsure of who's up at this hour, I slowly make my way to investigate. To my surprise, it's Gavin. He's fully dressed in a pair of khakis and a navy-blue polo shirt, reading a textbook.

"Oh," he says, startled as I turn the corner. "I hope I didn't wake you."

Confused because I hadn't heard anything, I stare at him. "Well, I was actually afraid I might've woken you."

"Nope, your parents showed me the downstairs bathroom last night, so I got ready before the rush comes. Growing up with my brother and sister, it was always a fight for the bathroom once everyone was awake." He grins, motioning me to sit beside him.

"Well, I'm usually the early bird around here. I'm surprised to see anyone alive at this hour." I sit on the opposite end of the couch to face him directly. "I usually let them sleep until after eight." I snicker.

"Well, since it isn't even seven, can I get you something to eat?" he asks quietly.

"We could cook breakfast for everyone?" I suggest in the form of a question. "Then once everyone's up, we'll decorate the house for the shower."

Gavin returns his book to his backpack and stands. "Well... Show me the way. You can help... From the barstools," he teases.

We begin by brewing Mom's favorite coffee. "This is sure to get her up."

"So how many are here today?" Gavin asks.

"Eight," I say as I run through a mental list, making sure no one's forgotten. "I usually make a quiche or something like that. It's easier to prepare for a group this size. If you get out the ingredients, I'll help with the chopping." I point to a cupboard below him. "The cutting boards are in there and the knives are on the counter."

He empties the contents we'll need from the fridge onto the counter near me. Then he sets the oven before asking, "Where's the pan you like to use?"

Within a short time, the room fills with the aroma of coffee and bacon frying on the stove. The quiche is made in record time. Gavin covers the large pan with foil before placing it in the oven. He sets the timer for forty-five minutes and washes the dishes by hand while we wait for it to cook. Is there anything this guy can't do?

"Anything else we can add to breakfast?" he suggests after drying the last dish.

"Well..." I ponder, looking at the enormous bowl of fruit on the table. "What about fruit salad?"

"Where's a bowl?" Gavin asks, turning to retrieve the

cutting boards and knives from the cupboard he had just replaced them in.

"You're incredible, you know." I can't help but stare at him in amazement. I don't think my brothers would even consider doing any of these things.

Gavin smiles widely, blushing a little. "I've been told that before."

This catches me off guard, and it's my turn to blush, realizing he might have taken my comment in an alternative way. I stammer for a moment, trying to regain my thought. "I... Uh... Just meant that I appreciate your willingness to help my family."

He says nothing, but simply holds my gaze and smiles.

I'm not sure how long I'm captured by him, but suddenly, Jacob's voice echoes from the hall. "Wow, that smells great." He enters the kitchen wearing flannel pajama bottoms and a t-shirt. Gavin's busy slicing fruit and putting it into a bowl.

"Wow, you're athletic, and you can cook," Jacob comments toward Gavin. "You're even an early riser." He eyes me suspiciously as he adds, "Hummm..." but says nothing more.

Gavin looks up, appearing unsure of what to say. "Um..." He finally adds, "Thanks. I hope we didn't wake you."

"Oh, nothing but my stomach woke me this morning." Jacob laughs. "Not even this twerp's getting up at the crack-of-dawn routine will wake me if I'm tired enough." He gives me a little nudge and grabs a piece of fruit I'm slicing.

"Hey." I threaten with my knife, but he pops the nectarine into his mouth before I can do anything.

It's only moments later my parents, Katherine, and Ben saunter into the kitchen. Each is surprised to see Gavin and me cooking. Everyone but Mom assumed it was me. The only person yet to make an appearance is Kai.

"Should someone get Kai?" I suggest as Gavin takes the quiche out of the oven.

"You snooze, you lose," Jacob sneers as he sneaks another bite of fruit.

"He'll sleep till noon, if you let him," Dad volunteers.

Mom walks around the counter and gets plates to set the table. Katherine retrieves the silverware. Mom suggests dishing the quiche from the table, as everyone takes their usual chair. Gavin sits next to me, and my heart picks up its pace. I glance around, hoping no one notices. Soon, our meal is filled with light conversation and laughter. The quiche is a hit, and everyone gives their compliments.

Eventually, Kai stumbles into the kitchen wearing a t-shirt and shorts. "Anything left?" he pleads as he rubs his eyes and slumps down in the chair on the end.

"Barely," Ben teases, taking another scoop for himself, though leaving plenty for Kai in the pan, causing everyone to laugh.

After breakfast, Gavin volunteers to help clean up, but Mom and Katherine suggest we start on the decorations. Mom brings everything we need into the living room. I'm pleased to find she bought some plants to give away as door prizes, too. I sit on the couch and decorate the plants with tissue paper while Gavin hangs the remaining decorations. I can't believe how patient he is with me throughout the day. Dad and my brothers are grateful for him, too; it means they don't have much to do throughout the morning.

"So how are you really doing?" Gavin asks as he scrutinizes my body movements as I get into the car to run our errands.

I don't say anything, knowing it'll give me away. Instead, I ask, "Do you think we should stop by the mall before getting the cake?"

Before putting his car in gear, he pins me with his golden-brown eyes. His eyebrows narrow, and his lips form a grimace. "Sure... That's no problem." Then he takes a deep breath and tries again, "Alex..." He waits until he has my full attention.

"Yes." I widen my eyes, trying to appear as if I don't comprehend what he's getting at. Of course, in doing this, I get lost in his deep, golden-brown eyes, abolishing all train of thought.

"You're overdoing it," he quietly states.

"What do you mean?" I say, still locking my eyes onto his.

A smile flashes across his face for a brief instant. "For starters... You're an awful actress." By the time he finishes, a smirk spreads widely across his face. My attempt at maintaining my composure is faulty at best, but I say nothing. "Secondly, you need to rest. You're in pain, aren't you?" His deep voice sends chills through my spine.

"I can't spend my day sleeping..." comes out nearly in a whine. "I need to have coherent conversations and..." I protest, but Gavin interrupts.

"You should still take your medication." He raises an eyebrow, waiting for further objection.

I attempt a compromise instead, "I promise if there's time

before the party, I'll take a nap. I'm okay… Honest. If the pain gets worse, I'll take it."

Gavin runs his hand through his thick, dark hair and takes a deep breath but says nothing. He stares at me, speculating my promise.

"I promise, I won't overdo it," I plead, hoping to sound convincing.

After another long moment, he puts the car in reverse and backs out of the driveway. "Okay, but will you also try to rest after shopping, too?" he quietly asks.

"If you think you can find your way, I will." I smile, realizing I'm about to get my way.

We make a quick trip into the mall, and I find something from my sister's registry within a few minutes. After we pick up the cake, Gavin stops at a gas station to fill up his car.

"I can make it from here," Gavin states as we exit the freeway. "You can rest now."

I want to protest, but I realize I probably could get a short nap in and then maybe he won't push the issue when we get back home. To my surprise, even without medication, I fall asleep quickly, not waking up until we enter our driveway.

"Do you want help getting upstairs so you can sleep more?" Gavin asks before getting out of the car.

I notice a car in the driveway. "Um… Guests are arriving." I yawn as I point to the car in the driveway. "That's my grandparents."

As I walk through the door, Grandma calls my name. "Oh, Alexis." She gasps and walks to hug me. "Oh my goodness! Are you okay?"

"Yeah, Grandma. I'm fine. It's great to see you." I lean on my crutches to return her hug.

When she pulls back, Grandma looks me over with care. "Let's sit, honey. You look tired. Tell me how this happened." She walks me into the living room and insists I put my leg up.

This is the first of many times I repeat my story today. I may as well get it over with. By the time I finish, Gavin appears in the living room.

"Hey," I greet him. "This is Grandma Manning." Gavin smiles as he walks to greet her. "Grandma, this is my friend from school, Gavin Wallace."

"It's a pleasure to meet you, Gavin." She reaches out her hand to shake Gavin's.

"You, too, ma'am." Gavin smiles in return.

She glances between Gavin and me before asking, "So how did the two of you meet?"

We're both quiet as we glance at one another briefly. Before he can say I literally ran into him, I spit out, "We're on the same soccer team and have a class together."

"Thank you for taking care of Alexis this week. Charlotte's told me she would have gone crazy without your reassurance and help." She stands to pull him into an unexpected hug. "Thank you so, so much."

Gavin humbly replies, "You're welcome." When he glances in my direction and my face flushes, I look away before anyone notices.

Since I've never brought anyone to family functions before, everyone's eager to know everything about Gavin as well as my accident, though the jury's out on which order is their priority. This scene repeats itself countless times throughout the day every time Gavin's introduced to someone new.

Before too many people arrive, Katherine suggests I go upstairs to help her change as well as get myself ready.

The instant Katherine and I are finally alone together, she prompts, "Soooo?"

"What?" I ask innocently, not wanting to be bombarded with details.

"Why haven't you told me about Gavin?"

"There's not much to tell," I try to appease her.

"Alexis Marie Manning, even Jacob who's completely inept when it comes to reading relationships, could tell when he visited that *something* was going on between the two of you." Her eyes are narrow slits and full of accusation.

"What?" My defenses rise, and I protest. "He has no clue!"

"This is me, Alex. Spill it!" Her eyes widen into a plea. Knowing Kate, she won't back down anytime soon. So, unless I want this drawn out publicly, I might as well give her some details, then she'll leave me alone.

"When did you first meet?"

"At a coffee shop with a group of friends." *Technically. Though I didn't really remember,* I remind myself.

Unfortunately, Katherine can always tell when I'm holding back. "ALEX?"

I should've known better. UGGHH! "Well, I guess you can say I ran into him." I turn red as I remember the incident.

"Ran into him?" she asks for clarification.

I might as well come clean. I take a deep breath and tell her the entire, embarrassing story. I go on to explain how he coincidentally appears everywhere. She suddenly laughs when I tell her he's entirely unavoidable.

Not knowing what she's laughing about, I defensively ask, "What?" for clarification.

"You like him," she states simply as her smile widens.

"Kate," I protest, but then reality hits like a ton of bricks. All I can say is "Oh" as my mind whirls with awareness. I hadn't even told her about practice or him taking care of me. *And she can already tell I like him?*

"He likes you, too, Alex," she says quietly.

"What are you talking about? He feels obligated to take care of me because he literally saw me being hit by a car! With Mom talking to him all the time, he probably feels guilty. AND because he's an honorable person, he's living up to the promises he's made." My voice fills with frustration by the end.

Katherine says nothing at first, but a sarcastic smirk spreads across her features. Eventually, when she realizes I'm not confirming her suspicions, she rolls her eyes as she slyly states, "Whatever reality you want to live in, is fine with me."

"Will you just help me get dressed?" My tone is clearly petulant, but I can't help it. After an audible sigh from her, she helps me put on my leggings, skirt, and blouse. She even offers to braid my hair since it's difficult to do leaning on crutches.

Once downstairs, I play my role as host the best I can, by greeting people and making small talk. As predicted, I replay the same conversation with my grandmother over and over, which is never any less embarrassing. Fortunately, the part about how Gavin and I met isn't repeated often because many haven't made our connection. He spends the majority of the time talking with Jacob.

Though Gavin isn't near me as I hobble around the room, I'm completely aware of his presence. From time to time, I find his eyes from across the room. I can sense his concern as his eyes deliver the unspoken question of 'how are you doing?' It's incomprehensible how acutely aware he is of my pain level. I've managed to keep a brave face, but know he sees completely through my façade.

When it's time to open gifts, he comes to sit next to me. "Hey, Alex," he greets me with a warm smile that makes my heart race. "Can I get you anything?"

"Um..." No point in hiding the truth. "I could use some ibuprofen and maybe a glass of water?" He gives me a disapproving look, but before saying anything, I continue, "It's in the medicine cabinet upstairs." His features darken as if he wants to argue. I quickly plea, hoping he'll understand. "I can't go to sleep now."

He lets out a sigh. "I'll be right back."

While Gavin's gone, Mom hands me a pad of paper and a pen to write the gifts down for my sister. Her concern's evident, but I assure her I'm fine. Katherine and Ben open gifts just as Gavin returns, bringing a glass of punch with him.

"Thanks." I take the pills quickly, washing it down with the punch. As the party continues, I quickly find ibuprofen has about the same effect as a PEZ dispenser. I hold my head high and smile through the now-throbbing pain. By this point, Gavin senses I'm bluffing and doesn't leave my side. He predicts my needs, and I hardly have to lift a finger for the remainder of the party.

When all that's left are my immediate family and the friends my sister plans on going with to the bachelorette party tonight, I lie on the couch, propping my leg up. I take this time to personally introduce Maggie to Gavin now that we're alone, so that she'll feel comfortable with us while we're watching her girls this evening. "Where are Monica and Grace?" I suddenly realize I haven't seen much of them today.

"Oh, they're outside with Kai playing in the yard. They've been following him all day."

"He's great that way. Are you sure you don't mind us watching the kids here?"

"No, it shouldn't be a problem. I brought Monica's playpen, and Grace will sleep anywhere when she's ready. She loves using her sleeping bag."

"Is there anything specific we should be aware of?" Gavin asks Maggie. "My niece and nephew are about the same age, and they like having stories read to them before bed, as well as their favorite blankets."

"Well..." Maggie thinks over his question. "Typically they bathe, and we read a story. Sometimes, I let them watch one cartoon. They're pretty easy. I'll set up the playpen before I leave because it can be tricky."

"Thanks," Gavin and I both say at the same time, making Maggie giggle.

"Really, you shouldn't worry. I've watched my sister's kids countless times. Besides, Alex's entire family will be here, too."

"I'm not sure how late I'll be." She raises her eyebrows as if she thinks the late hour might be a problem.

"I thought you guys were staying in a hotel?" I say with confusion.

"Well, we were, but I don't want to make you watch the kids all night," she admits.

"It's not a problem. Alex and I are fine watching your girls. Like I said, Mr. and Mrs. Manning will be here, too," Gavin reassures her.

"Okay. If you insist. The girls get up early," she warns.

"Do you know Alex at all?" Gavin teases. "She wakes up at the crack of dawn. I'm sure we'll be fine." Maggie glances from me to Gavin with wide eyes. Crap. She must suspect something. But if she does, she stays quiet.

9

BABYSITTING

AFTER MY SISTER and her friends leave for Seattle, Monica, Grace, and Gavin play in the living room with a box of toys Mom pulls out. I prop myself up on the couch, trying to ignore my aches. Finally, Grace announces, "Alex, I'm hungry."

"What are you hungry for?" I ask.

"Macaroni and cheese!" She beams, putting her arms up in the air, making her enthusiasm melt my heart.

"I think we can manage that," I confirm.

"I'd be happy to make that for you, Miss Grace." Gavin winks as he walks into the kitchen.

"Thank you! Thank you! Thank you, Gavin!" Grace exclaims as she follows him to the kitchen. "Can I help?" she asks eagerly.

I hear from the hall, "Well… we'll see. What can you do?" Gavin inquires enthusiastically.

When dinner's ready, Gavin comes to get Monica, and I follow them to the kitchen.

"Um… We may want to take off their clothes," I suggest as I sit at the kitchen table. Gavin looks as if I've lost my mind, so I explain, "They'll both want to feed themselves. Trust me, it's better they eat naked since we don't have any bibs."

He takes my suggestion without another word and sets both of the girls up to the table at their own chair. He grabs two plates from the counter with macaroni and cheese and finely cut up pieces of fruit for each of the girls. Once he serves them, he brings over plates for us.

As predicted, the girls love feeding themselves, especially Monica. She's not as skilled at using her spoon and quickly becomes frustrated. Eventually, she's eating with her hands. Before we know it, macaroni's everywhere. In her hair, on her chest, some even manages to make it into her mouth. Gavin tries to clean her with a warm rag when she's finished, but it's a futile attempt.

Through an escaped giggle, "Um, Gavin," I sigh. "I think you'd better give up and just plop her in the tub."

The minute I say tub, both girls scream with delight, especially when they hear bubbles are involved. Mom walks in, surveys the kitchen, and offers, "If you two put them in the bath, I'll clean up here."

"Thanks," Gavin says as he holds Monica out at an arm's length, trying not to get food all over himself in the process. I do my best to stifle my laughter as Grace and I follow them to the bathroom.

I convince Grace to use the potty while Gavin adjusts the water temperature and puts the soap Maggie has in the diaper bag for bubbles. He quickly takes off his shoes and socks so they won't get wet if the girls splash. He must be used to kids, if he knows that trick.

When Gavin sees my attempt at washing macaroni off Monica is futile, he suggests I sit on the toilet and let him help. I find leaning against the counter's more comfortable with my crutches, so I visit with the girls from here. Once all the food is off them, Gavin sets in to washing each of their hair. While he focuses on Grace's hair, I notice Monica hold her breath and grunt. *Oh my!*

"Um, Gavin," I gasp loudly. "I think Monica's about to…" He flies into action when he, too, sees what I've warned him. In one fluid swoop, he lifts her from the tub, water dripping everywhere. He pivots on one foot and turns to place her on the toilet.

All I can do is gasp out another warning when I see her efforts drop to the floor, just in time for Gavin's bare foot to squash into it.

"EWW…" Gavin hollers, looking down at his foot, wondering what to do with it.

Though I shouldn't laugh, I burst out in hysterics. My ribs ache terribly, but I still can't stop. I'm left staring at Gavin in disbelief. He's now balancing on one foot, trying not to put his soiled foot anywhere. Monica's startled, sitting naked on the toilet as Grace yells from the bathtub, "Gavin stepped in poop!" repeatedly between bursts of laughter. I'm stuck leaning on my crutches, and there's nothing I can do to help him. So of course, I laugh some more.

All this commotion brings my parents and brothers running to see what's the matter. Suddenly, this medium-size room now has eight people in it. Once my parents and brothers realize what's wrong, they burst into hysterical laughter themselves. By now, I'm on the verge of tears, not because of the pain necessarily, but because it's just too funny.

Mom regains her composure the fastest. "Here, Gavin. I'll take care of Monica." She then turns to my brother, Jacob, who's the closest to the bathtub. "Jake, take Grace out of the tub, so Gavin can wash his foot." To make room for everyone, Dad and Kai giggle to themselves as they exit the bathroom.

"Thanks, Mrs. Manning," Gavin says quietly, letting go of Monica. Somehow, he's kept a hand on her the entire time, so she wouldn't fall off the toilet. He stands upright, holding an arm out against a wall as he balances on his clean foot.

"Jake, let the water out of the tub before taking Grace out to get dressed," Mom says, wiping Monica clean before wrapping a towel around her and walking out of the bathroom to make room for Gavin to move.

"I... Am... So sorry," I attempt through bursts of laughter. Gavin stares at me in disbelief before shaking his head and laughter erupts from him as well.

"It's... O... Kay..." He still rocks with laughter as he hops to the bathtub on one foot. He places the dirty foot in the tub and lets the water run over his foot. "I think I may just take a shower if that's okay with you." He looks at me for my response. "It might just be easier."

"I'll get you a towel." I giggle and start for the linen closet in the hall. I bring it back between one arm and my crutch. Gavin's still vigorously cleaning his foot. "Want me to get you a change of clothes?" I suggest.

"Alex." He raises an eyebrow in my direction. "How

would you do that? You're barely holding a towel," he accuses through escapes of giggles.

"I'll ask someone to bring your bag," I chortle in return and turn to leave.

Dad meets me in the hall with Gavin's bag as I exit the bathroom. "I figured he'd probably just want to wash completely." He grins, walking past me. "I know I would."

While Gavin showers, I change out of my dress into a comfortable pair of pajama bottoms and a t-shirt. Then I go downstairs to help Mom get the girls dressed. By the time he returns, the girls are playing again on the living room floor.

"Hey, honey," Mom says to me, "Would you mind if Dad and I went to a movie with your brothers?"

I look to Gavin, knowing I'm of little help to him. He nods at me before answering, "I think we can manage. Go... Enjoy your evening," he reassures Mom with a devastatingly handsome grin. "Hopefully, the worst is behind me."

Mom bites her lip to contain her laughter. "Are you sure, Gavin?"

"Mom, we're putting the girls down in a few minutes. It'll be easier if you're gone anyway," I reassure her.

"What about you, Alex? You look exhausted."

I notice the line that forms between her eyebrows when she worries. "Mom, I'm okay. Once the girls are down, I'll rest, too."

"Really, ma'am. We'll be fine," Gavin reassures her.

After my family leaves, it's a piece of cake to put the girls down. Gavin places Monica's playpen in the study so she's not disturbed when everyone comes home. He also puts Grace's sleeping bag on the floor next to the playpen as Maggie suggested. We read the girls a book their mom brought for them. Then we sit in my parents' recliners and rock the girls to sleep while watching cartoons. Fortunately, they're asleep within minutes. Gavin carefully carries each girl to the study, returning with a glass of water and my medication. I look at the clock, and it's only eight thirty.

"You're exhausted and likely in a lot of pain." He raises an eyebrow, challenging me. "You have no excuse now," he accuses.

I know better than to protest. Besides, my body's internally screaming at me for some relief. "Thanks, Gavin." I take the medication willingly. "For everything. You've been amazing today. I appreciate your help with everything." I get up from the recliner, deciding the couch is more comfortable.

Gavin hands me a pillow from the chair for my head and places another one under my leg. "No problem. It's the least I could do. You've done pretty well yourself, you know. I'm amazed you're coherent. You must be exhausted beyond belief."

"I'm okay," I sigh in heavy relief, sinking further into the couch. "I'll rest on the way home tomorrow."

"Can I get you a blanket?" Gavin asks before sitting on the other couch.

"Thanks," I say as he brings me the one Mom drapes over the couch.

"Mind if I watch TV?" Gavin asks before returning to Dad's recliner.

"No, not at all," I mumble.

I think Gavin says something else, but I'm not sure. I wake up the next morning in my bedroom upstairs, once again, unaware of how I arrived. As I roll over, I see the clock says 5:23. I hope it was Gavin who carried me, and not Dad or my brothers. That'd just be far too embarrassing.

To stop worrying, I head downstairs to wait for the girls to wake. I shoulder my backpack with me to study as I pass the time. Eventually, I hear one of the girls talk. Before I can get up to check on them, Gavin exits the study with Monica in his arms.

He doesn't see me because his back is toward me as he walks to the kitchen. She babbles something to him and he responds, "Are you hungry?" She squeals with delight in response. "Let's change you first. Then we'll see what there is to eat." By now, he's out of my line of sight, but I can hear them talking softly as he changes her. My heart swells as I take in his kindness.

I put my books back into my bag before making my way to the kitchen. By the time I arrive, Monica's sitting at the kitchen table, and Gavin's pouring a few Cheerios onto the table for her to eat.

"Morning," I whisper as I enter the kitchen.

"How'd you sleep?" he asks with concern.

"Good, I feel much better. I've been up for awhile. I hope I wasn't the one who woke you."

"Monica's been awake for awhile. She was getting restless, so I thought I'd take her out of the room before Grace woke up."

"Good idea." I smile, sitting at the table.

"Can I get you anything?" Gavin asks as he gets himself a glass of milk from the fridge.

"Um... I think Mom wants to make us brunch before we leave. Maybe just some toast?" I suggest.

"Sure. I'll have some, too." He grins and sets to making

the toast for the two of us while Monica feeds herself happily.

"Butter's in the cupboard, and there's jam in the fridge. Could you put peanut butter on mine?" I request as I point to the cupboard. "I could use some protein."

Before sitting himself next to me at the table, he refills his glass of milk and offers to bring me a glass. We eat silently for a while, watching Monica chase her Cheerios around the table before eating them.

Mom comes down a little before seven and doesn't seem surprised to see Gavin, Monica, and me at the table. She greets us and works on breakfast. We offer to help, but she insists we play with Monica. Mom brings some plastic bowls and spoons over for Monica to play with, and she pretends to make breakfast for us. Gavin checks on Grace but returns saying that she's sound asleep.

By the time Jacob and Dad arrive, the aroma of coffee, bacon, and pancakes fill the room. Mom places the pancakes in the oven to stay warm while she starts on the eggs. Katherine and Maggie show up around nine, joining us all in light conversation at the kitchen table.

"Grace is still sleeping?" Maggie questions when she realizes her oldest daughter is nowhere to be found.

"I keep checking on her, but she's zonked," Gavin offers.

"Kai must have worn her out!" Maggie exclaims.

"Or Gavin," Mom suggests from the stove behind us.

"So… Were there any problems?" Maggie asks sincerely.

"Not really," I say as a smile spreads across my face as I look at Gavin.

There's a loud chuckle from Jacob. "For you," he finally bursts out.

Maggie looks from me to Gavin, puzzled. I glance at Gavin, and I lose it. I can't control the laughter that erupts. It hurts, but I couldn't stop if I tried.

"What?" Maggie shouts over me, her face filled with concern.

I tell her about the bathtub incident. By the time I get to the end, she's in hysterics, along with everyone else in the room. Our laughter brings the sound of little feet running down the hall.

"Mommy!" Grace exclaims, seeing Maggie at the table. She runs and climbs onto her lap to give her a big hug.

"Hey, sweetheart. Did you have a good night?" Maggie asks after kissing Grace on the forehead.

"Yes! I slept in my princess sleeping bag, next to Monica."

"Okay, guys. Let's dish up," Mom suggests. Mom puts serving forks on the blueberry pancakes and places a variety of topping choices on the counter.

"Can I get you a plate?" Gavin whispers to me before getting up from the table.

"Sure. I'll have two pancakes with butter and cool whip on them. I'll have some bacon and eggs, too."

As soon as he fills my plate, Mom takes it from him, replacing it with an empty one for himself. She walks mine to me, gives me a kiss on the forehead, and says, "Here you go, honey. How are you feeling today?"

"Not too bad. I know I'll rest more in the car."

"Gavin, are you staying with her until she's off her medication?" Mom asks, catching me off guard by her choice of topic.

"Ummm…" Gavin looks at me and then to her before replying, "We haven't really discussed it."

"Mom, I…" I start to say, but she interrupts.

"I'd appreciate it if someone stayed with her until she's at least off her medication. They knock her out." She glances to Dad before continuing, "We'd feel more comfortable knowing someone was there. I've thought about coming over myself but know she wouldn't hear of it." She glances accusingly at me, to show me how serious she is. *No, I don't.*

"I don't need a babysitter," I complain, though it's lost on them.

"If she needs me, I'm happy to help," Gavin offers.

"Then it's settled," Dad states as if there's to be no more discussion. He quickly changes the subject. "When are you heading back, Jacob?" Dad takes a bite and waits for a response.

"Before three. I have to prepare for a meeting tomorrow."

Dad turns to me. "What time are you heading out, kiddo?"

I look to Gavin, and he only shrugs in response. "We'll head out before noon. Gavin has practice at seven tonight," I remind him.

"We'll see you off, then Jake and I can head to town," Dad suggests, glancing at Mom for any objections.

10

DISCLOSURES

"So now that you've met my family, tell me about yours," I probe as we drive along the country road to the freeway.

"What do you want to know?" He smiles in my direction.

"Well, for starters..." I hesitate, wondering where to begin, then blurt out, "Everything." I let out a quiet laugh when I realize how intense that sounds, so I backtrack. "I don't know anything, so whatever you want to share's fine." I hope I didn't sound too insane.

"Well, my brother Will's eight years older than I. He works for a law firm in Seattle. We used to be a lot closer, but with our schedules and me living across the state these past few years, we mainly see each other on holidays.

"Elizabeth's happily married to Phil. She's about six years older than me. They got married about seven years ago while she was in college. She became an RN, but currently works part-time, so she can stay home with their kids. Phil's an investment banker. Their kids are amazing.

Mason turned four last month, and Gretchen will be three in November. I visit them whenever I can. They seem to grow a foot between each break. I miss them like crazy." Gavin's voice trails off, and he appears as if he is reminiscing about something enjoyable as he changes lanes.

Since Gavin's quiet for a moment, I ask, "So... Where'd you grow up?" He smiles but is silent as we merge into traffic on the freeway.

"Well, I was born in Chicago. My parents moved to Washington when I was two, for Dad's job, and we've been here ever since. He's worked for corporate offices of different airlines throughout the years. Currently, he works for Delta. Because of this, we've traveled to some amazing places."

"Wow, how exciting." I want to ask more, but Gavin continues without any prompting.

"My parents always took us on family vacations either by car or plane. When I was little, we used to camp all the time. My parents liked to keep us in touch with the basics of life, from time to time. Mom always took us on road trips if Dad was away on business. Of course, on trips to Chicago, we flew to save time and the sanity of being in a car with three kids for hours on end," Gavin sighs and then smiles widely as he starts to tell another memory.

"But one summer, Mom decided we should see more of the country, other than just from the air. She insisted we drive across the entire country to experience it in person." Gavin pauses for a moment, shaking his head slightly. "Huh... I must have been about six or seven at the time. I remember Will being frustrated because he had to leave his girlfriend behind for three weeks. He had to have been at least fifteen because he had his learner's permit. The only thing that made him happy during the entire trip was when he could drive. Liz couldn't understand why we were driving across the country when we could easily fly. She made the best of it by taking pictures with her new camera my parents bought her before we left. I was excited because I wanted to see all the national parks." Gavin chuckles quietly before continuing.

"Mom was the best. She always cranked up the radio and made everyone sing along. She'd have us play games and found ways to make three weeks of being in a car very entertaining, at least for me. She could make up songs that would have the entire family rolling in their seats from laughter. She also planned out each day so that we would have at least one major point of interest along the way. It's probably one of my favorite family trips." Gavin continues to smile at the memory as he looks out the window of the car.

"Sounds fun. Tell me more about your mom. She sounds amazing."

A wide smile spreads across his face. "Mom was awesome. As you know, she could cook like no other. She loved to experiment with new recipes and have plenty of people to use as her guinea pigs. If you think I can cook, you have no idea what she could do." He glances in my direction and shakes his head.

"Growing up, she always volunteered for field trips, helped in the classroom, and did everything she could to help us kids see the value in education. She helped us with our projects... Boy, did we have some projects..." Gavin laughs aloud. "She never minded if we invited our friends over after school. Our place was the hangout for everyone in the neighborhood. There were always plenty of snacks to go around. She was like a modern-day June Cleaver."

I suddenly realize everything Gavin's telling me about his mom is in the past tense. Not wanting to pry, I finally get up the courage to ask, "Um, Gavin?"

"Yeah?" He smiles, still thoughtfully looking out the window.

Still unsure of how to word my question. "Umm... You keep saying, *was*..."

He takes in a breath and shrugs. "Oh, I forget you don't know." His tone is more solemn than before.

"Know what?" I ask hesitantly.

"Um... My mom died the summer after I graduated high school."

"Oh," I mumble, not knowing what to say. Without thinking, "What happened?" quietly escapes my lips.

Gavin inhales slowly. "Well... During my junior year, she was diagnosed with stage four ovarian cancer."

I take in a deep breath. Not knowing what to say, I just stare at Gavin, searching for the right words to come to me, but they don't.

Though he doesn't look at me directly, Gavin appears to be deep in thought for a moment before continuing, "She was unbelievable. She stayed as positive as she could throughout the entire process. Knowing that both Will and Liz had already started their own lives, she did her best to make sure I was well taken care of." He pauses again and grins widely. "You know, even though I knew she was dying, some of my best memories of her were at the end."

He takes another deep, steady breath and continues, "When she found out the odds weren't in her favor, she did her best to make sure we all went through the grieving process while she was still alive. She constantly talked about our futures and made us all promise that no matter what happens, we'll continue to work toward the lives she had helped each of us start for ourselves. Of course, her death was hard on everyone. But for some reason, her persistence to force us to continue our daily lives helped in the end. Each of us, in our own way, have made peace with the situation and are trying to follow our dreams the best we can." Gavin's eyes flash in my direction, checking my reaction before telling me more.

"She had a complete hysterectomy before starting chemo. If Dad was out of town on business, I was the one who'd take her, since I was out of school for the summer. To help get our minds off things, we usually sat through her treatments together and talked about my future. She made me promise to follow my dreams of going to school and becoming an architect. Live life to the fullest, and never take anything for granted." Wow. She sounds amazing. No wonder Gavin's turned out like he has.

Gavin takes a deep breath, then continues before I can wrap my head around anything to say. "We also talked about family, friends, and potential relationships. She insisted I wait for the right girl. She told me once I find that girl, don't hold back. She'd seen too many young people repeatedly have failed relationships because they treated them too casually. She wanted better for me." Gavin shakes his head and chuckles lightly to himself.

"Don't get me wrong, she insisted I experience dating

and getting to know different people by going to dances and hanging out with my friends, along with other important rites of passage. But she insisted I refrain from seriously dating anyone, unless I was indisputably ready to be committed to them."

Gavin's voice becomes softer. "Toward the end, she knew her treatment wasn't working. The cancer had spread to her liver and lungs. She eventually refused treatment, wanting to live out her remaining days at home. Her goal was to watch me graduate and spend as much time with our family as possible. She managed to make it about three weeks after my graduation."

Gavin's face livens up as he recalls, "She was so proud when I received my diploma. Until her last breath, she never said anything negative and always talked about our future."

When Gavin finishes, the car remains silent. Gavin looks thoughtfully out the window. I can't imagine going through anything like that, and I'm not sure what would be appropriate to say. Finally, Gavin breaks the silence with a chuckle.

"What?" I whisper with grave concern. A wide smile spreads across his face, which confuses me even more.

"I guess I've never told anyone that before." He laughs lightly once again before shaking his head.

I stare at him in disbelief and whisper, "Then why now?"

He shakes his head as he whispers, "I don't know."

We are both quiet for some time. I stare out the window, not focusing on anything as I take his story in.

"Hey, Alex," Gavin whispers.

Matching his tone, "Yeah?"

"Thanks for listening." Gavin looks briefly in my direction, then smiles. "I appreciate it."

"Anytime," I whisper in response, returning a smile.

Gavin turns on the stereo, and we listen to music in comfortable silence as we drive over Snoqualmie Pass. There's snow on the highest hills, and it's obvious that winter's fast approaching.

As we descend the pass and approach Ellensburg, Gavin asks, "Are you hungry?"

"I'm getting there. Want to stop in Ellensburg?" I suggest.

"Yeah. Mind if we get something other than fast food?" he asks, looking at his watch.

"Anything's fine with me." I shrug.

He pulls off the exit, and we find a family style restaurant near the freeway. He helps me out of the car, and we walk side by side into the lobby. The hostess seats us quickly. Gavin holds out my chair for me as I sit and places my crutches on the floor beside me.

After we order, Gavin asks, "Have you taken your medication today?"

When I don't say anything, he eyes me suspiciously. "Alex, how do you expect to recover if you don't take care of yourself?"

Taking it as a rhetorical question, I choose not to answer that one either. I'm not in the mood to be babysat. The waitress brings us our meals, and Gavin pins me with pleading eyes. "Alex, will you please take your meds? You were in pain when you walked in here."

This brings my defenses out in full force. "You know, you don't have to do all this!"

Gavin's eyes widen with surprise. "What?"

"The driving me around, taking me shopping, making me dinner." I don't want him to feel obligated to spend time with me, and I think it's time I finally let him off the hook. Besides, I don't need to be told what to do. It's so frustrating.

He opens his mouth to say something, but quickly closes it. All of a sudden, he begins to blush a little. What is he blushing for? With a sheepish look, he quietly states, "You know, Alex, it's not a coincidence that I've been at the coffee shop each morning or eating dinner where you work."

Now I'm the one who's confused. I stare at him wide-eyed, and my breath quickens. "What... Do... You mean?" I sputter out, making each word sound as if it is its own sentence.

Still blushing, his golden-brown eyes pierce me on the spot. "I don't *have* to do anything."

Where's he going with this? My mouth gapes as I continue to stare.

He takes a deep breath. "I knew you work at Antonio's and that you run every morning."

"How?" is all I manage to think, let alone say.

"Well." He suddenly looks slightly uncomfortable again, then simply states, "I asked." He shrugs, and his eyebrows raise, attempting to look innocent.

Still unable to respond, I bite my lower lip, letting what he's said sink in. His eyes grow wide with concern when I finally respond with a soft, "oh."

Nervously, he looks around the restaurant and remains silent. Then he turns to face me directly. With the full force of his brilliant stare, he states, "I like you, Alex." He then takes in a slow breath, watching my reaction. "I'm not doing this out of any obligation."

Trying to make sense of his words, I hear them replay in my mind. I feel the intensity of his golden-brown eyes, but I'm still left speechless. My eyes widen, and my heart races. Is he really saying this?

"The truth is, I'd probably be doing these things eventually, even without you being injured or needing my help," he states matter-of-factly.

The part about needing help brings my defenses back. "I... Um... Don't need help," I partly sputter out.

"Yes..." He hesitates. "Yes, you do." His eyes are tight and serious for a fraction of a second, then they relax. "You're quite stubborn when you want to be. I see that." By now, a slight smirk spreads across his face.

I begin to protest but am unsuccessful. He interrupts me, "But that's not my point." He clears his throat, and his face becomes serious as he continues to penetrate me with the full force of his eyes. "My point is, Alex, is that I really like you." He takes another long, steady breath and continues, "After this weekend and meeting your family, maybe even more so."

I let out my breath because I realize I had been holding it. "Humph," sharply escapes as I exhale. I can't help the smile that spreads across my face as I tilt my head slightly to the side, now becoming aware of his meaning.

He looks a little apprehensive as he finally asks, "Well?"

How do I respond? I'm completely bewildered and feeling so many emotions simultaneously that I can't even think, let alone respond appropriately. I let go of the hold his eyes have on mine and blink a few times while my mouth gapes open. "Me, too," is all I can manage.

This brings a look between shock and bewilderment to

Gavin's chiseled features. As if he's at a loss for words, he mimics my response earlier and says nothing but, "Oh." He runs his hand through his hair, and we stare wordlessly at one another, no longer feeling awkward.

Who knows how much time passes, but the next thing I know, our waitress is standing at our table, asking something I haven't heard. She must have repeated herself because Gavin breaks our gaze to focus his attention on her.

She appears annoyed. "Would you like anything else?" she says louder than necessary.

"Um, no," Gavin politely replies. I shake my head no in response to answer her.

"Should we get back on the road?" Gavin suggests.

"Sure." Gathering my purse, I reach for my crutches, but Gavin beats me to them. Instead of handing them to me, he holds out his arm for initial support, then returns them to me. Just the touch of his skin against mine sends shivers across my body. I'm not sure if he says anything on the way out to the car; all I can hear is my pulse roaring through my ears. I've never felt this way about anyone, and I have no idea what to do about it.

When we're on the freeway, I realize my leg's sore and my ribs ache, so I pull out my medication. From the corner of my eye, I see Gavin smile and shake his head slightly. I wash my horse-like pills down with water before sitting back to relax in the seat. Gavin turns on the radio again and soft music fills the car.

I turn my head slightly toward the window, getting more comfortable. I place my left arm on my lap while my right arm rests comfortably across my chest. I take as deep of a breath as my ribs will allow and sink into my seat. Suddenly,

I feel the warm touch of Gavin's large hand being placed over my mine. Our fingers find one another with ease as they interlock comfortably. I glance at him briefly, returning his smile before rolling my head back to its previous position and drift off to sleep.

11

WAKE UP CALL

AFTER BEING COOPED up in the car all day and spending the majority of my time in bed this past week, it feels exhilarating to get out and move about. After returning from practice, Gavin suggests we go for a walk on campus. I've gotten good at keeping a fairly normal pace on my crutches. Often, I sense he's gauging if I'm overdoing it, but he says nothing. I desperately need to exercise and if this is my only outlet, I'll gladly take it.

Though our conversation is casual, most of our outing is kept in comfortable silence. I need to concentrate on where I place my crutches since mud puddles are scattered all around us. After about twenty minutes, I feel tired. I suggest we make our way back, and Gavin gladly approves.

After helping me get settled into the car, he shakes his head in disbelief. "Wow, you can be reasonable."

How do I take this? My mouth gapes, causing him to chuckle so loud, the car vibrates. I feel my jaw tense as I realize he's laughing at me. "What do you mean?"

"Alexis, you're quite stubborn when you choose to be. I'm surprised you actually listened to your body and didn't try to overdo it. That's all." Gavin stares innocently and waits for my defenses to retreat.

Once again, I'm completely speechless and in awe of the captivity his hold has on me. Neither of us say anything for some time. I contemplate what this means on the way back to my apartment.

Not feeling sore, I go to bed without my medication. Unfortunately, I'm wide awake by four thirty the next morning. After staying in bed as long as I can, I get up, use the bathroom, and get my book. Crap. I left it in the kitchen. Not wanting to disturb Gavin, I make my way to the counter without turning on any lights.

Hearing Gavin stir on the couch, I nearly gasp when I see him. From the dim light of my bedroom, I find him lying on his side. One arm is over the back of the couch while one foot nearly touches the floor. This cannot be comfortable. Since I'm wide awake and won't be sleeping for some time, someone may as well get use of my bed. I hobble over as quietly as I can on my crutches. I nudge his shoulder. He's quickly alert, sits straight up, and stares at me in a panic.

"Hey," I whisper, not wanting to startle him any further. "Go and sleep in my bed. I'm wide awake, and you look extremely uncomfortable."

Gavin stares at me unfoundedly. So, I repeat myself, "Gavin, really. Go sleep in my room. I'll be reading for awhile, and the couch is far more comfortable for me."

Hesitantly, he asks, "You sure?"

I motion to the couch. "It has to be more comfortable than this."

Seeing he's not going to budge, I raise my voice louder than I intend, "Gavin. Go sleep in my room."

He yawns and mumbles something like, "If you insist," before stumbling into my bedroom. "Wake me around seven?"

"Sure, my alarm's already set for then, but I hardly ever use it."

Gavin mumbles something else as I hear him flop onto my bed. I shake my head as I sit on the couch. It's much cooler than usual. I turn on the lamp before nestling my way into his sleeping bag and adjusting his pillow behind me. As I snuggle in, I can't help but notice Gavin's pillow smells faintly of him. I take in a deep breath and let myself enjoy the moment. I open my book and begin reading. After a couple of chapters, my eyes feel heavy. Knowing my alarm will wake Gavin if necessary, I allow myself to drift off to sleep, savoring his musky scent and the comfort of his sleeping bag.

The next thing I hear is music from the alarm in the bedroom. This forces me instantly upright. Crap. I never expected to sleep the entire time. Not wanting Gavin to see I've fallen asleep, I get up as quickly as I can with my crutches and make my way to the bathroom. I hear Gavin fumble with my alarm clock and can't help the smile that forms.

Knowing there's not much time to be ready for my eight o'clock class, I skip my morning shower. I forcefully pull a brush through my tangled, brown hair and let it lie on my shoulders when I finish.

As I get ready, I can't help but think of how I found

Gavin this morning. We need to have a serious talk today. He's already doing so much for me, I can't let him lose sleep over me, too. Hanging off the end of my couch the way he was can't be comfortable. Though I appreciate his company, I need to convince him it isn't necessary to put himself out so much.

When I finish with the bathroom, I quietly knock on the door of my bedroom, so I can grab a change of clothes. There's no sound, but I hear him stir slightly. "Hey, Gavin," I try again in a whisper.

A muffled "Yeah" comes from the other side of the door.

"Mind if I come in?"

"Um..." I hear the movement of blankets. "Yeah, no problem."

As I enter the room, Gavin sits on the edge of my bed with the blankets pushed behind him. His back is to me, but I see him rub his hands through his hair and yawn as he greets me. "Morning."

"Did you get much sleep?" I make my way to my dresser and search for another pair of sweats and a t-shirt to change into.

"Need any help?" he offers. "Um..." He hesitates as he looks toward the clock beside my bed, and panic fills his features. "Your first class is at eight, right?"

"Yeah, I won't take long. Sorry. I should've woken you sooner. I lost track of time." When was the last time I let myself sleep in?

It'll be such a relief when I can wear more than leggings. Not that I'm much into fashion, but having the same couple of outfits means doing laundry more often.

"Everything okay?" I hear Gavin approach my left side on his way to the bathroom.

"Just getting tired of this brace. I can't wait until Friday."

Gavin melts my heart with a reassuring smile. "It'll be here before you know it. I'm going to take a quick spin. I'll be ready in a few minutes to drive you to class." He doesn't wait for my response as he walks into the bathroom, shutting the door behind him.

On our way to class, I see Gavin stifle a yawn. I guess now is as good a time as ever to broach the subject. So... how'd you sleep last night?"

"Fine."

"Gavin, you looked pretty uncomfortable this morning. You need to sleep in a proper bed. You're more than welcome to go home at night. Honestly, you don't need to babysit me."

"Alex, I'm fine." He stares out the window, avoiding eye contact.

"But," I plead.

To finalize his argument, he stares directly into my eyes and adds, "I made a promise to your parents that I'd stay with you as long as you're on meds."

Remembering his long legs sprawling across the couch, I'm determined not to put him out any further, so I quickly suggest, "What about your place? I can sleep on your couch. I'm shorter and I've fallen asleep on mine for most of the last week anyway."

"Alex, I don't really think that'd be a good idea."

"Why?"

"Well, for starters, you need all the rest you can get, and

secondly… I live in a studio apartment." He holds my gaze with determined eyes.

"So?" I whisper, not knowing how to take his argument entirely. "Gavin. After I take that medication, a wrecking ball could come through the place, and I wouldn't be any wiser."

I see his eyes lighten slightly as he bites his lower lip, deliberating. At first, I think he's going to argue more.

"My couch is actually a futon," he adds slowly. "It probably isn't that comfortable."

"Neither is falling off mine," I contest.

Gavin's quiet but the look on his face shows he's nowhere near giving up on this argument. So, I'm surprised when he adds, "Well, I could take my futon, and you'll sleep in the bed."

"Do you fit entirely on your futon?" I accuse. "Gavin, when was the last time you actually slept in your bed?"

We both know it's the night before my accident. I know he can't argue with my logic.

"You need your rest if you want off those things." He points to the crutches between us. Boy, he's good. He knows exactly how to push my buttons by pointing out what I want most.

"Gavin, *you* need good sleep, too! You're already doing so much for me, I feel bad. I fit on couches, you don't. It's simple." I take a deep breath before giving him the only options I'm willing to accept. "Either you sleep in my bed, and I stay on the couch, or we go to your place. The choice is yours, but you're not sleeping on my couch this evening." I'm amazed I never take my eyes off him throughout my entire argument, and a smile forms on my lips.

Gavin looks away briefly before returning his eyes to me with a sigh. "I guess we'll go to my place," he slowly concedes, shaking his head in disbelief. "We'll need to pick up a few things at the store since I haven't gone in over a week." He sounds like the last part was more for himself, rather than directed at me.

"Fine." I smile smugly.

He lets out another surrendering breath. "Want me to pick you up after work? I'll make dinner before we study."

"Sounds great," I say with a victorious smile. "I'll pack some things while you're at work. Anything in particular I should bring?"

"Just clothes, your toiletries, and anything that will make you more comfortable. I should have everything else."

That afternoon, there's a knock at my door. Knowing Gavin would just come in, I go to answer it. I'm greeted by Sophie's enormous grin.

"Hey, Alex," she greets me with a hug, and we walk back to my living room together. "How was your weekend?"

"Great." I fill her in on the details of my sister's bridal shower as we make our way back to the living room.

Sophie notices the bags packed next to my bedroom "You haven't unpacked yet?"

"Oh, those are for tonight," I say dismissively.

"Going somewhere?" Her eyes widen with speculation.

"Well, I came out last night and found Gavin practically falling off the couch, so I convinced him to sleep in his own bed tonight."

"Alex, aren't those your things?" I look to the pile and see my sweatshirt and pillow on top. There's no denying the purple bag's mine.

"Um, yeah," I say, suddenly self-conscious because she's eying me suspiciously.

I tell her about my argument with Gavin earlier this morning when she interrupts, "Is something going on between the two of you?"

This catches me off guard, and I'm left struggling for a response and my mouth gaping open.

"Tell me everything," she demands with an enormous 'I thought so' smile spreading across her face.

"There's not much to tell," I admit honestly.

"Well, then, what *is* there to tell? Anything happen between the two of you this weekend at your parents'?"

"Not really. We just babysat kids of my sister's best friend and hung out with my family." I laugh at the memory of Gavin and Monica in the bathtub.

"What?" she practically shouts.

I tell her about the bathtub incident. We're practically rolling out of our seats when I explain the expression on his face after he put his foot down. "He took it so gracefully, you should have seen it, Sophie," I say through repressed laughter. "He was amazing the entire weekend. He was even a great sport when everyone took turns harassing him."

"So, you like him." Sophie surmises.

I chuckle softly. "Who wouldn't." I feel my face blush as I remember our conversation at the restaurant.

"Alex?" Sophie accuses once again. "What happened?"

Realizing I've already let the cat out of the bag so to speak, with my reaction, I fill her in on the rest. Sophie's practically laughing out of her chair again when I tell her how he forcefully told me he liked me.

Not understanding her reaction, I defensively ask, "What?" for clarification.

"I knew it!" Sophie exclaims. "I tried telling you this before you left. You feel the same, don't you?" She throws another accusing glare in my direction.

"Um, yeah," I admit quietly.

"So, did anything else happen?"

"No, nothing. We haven't talked about it since."

"Won't that make it awkward at his place?"

"No, it shouldn't. I just want him to sleep on a bed that fits him." I suddenly feel a little defensive. I don't want her to get the wrong impression. "I'm going to sleep on his futon," I add to further clarify.

"Why aren't you just staying here?"

"It's a long story." I roll my eyes and shake my head. "But the short version is, he made my parents a promise, and he isn't the type to make promises lightly. He's pretty honorable that way, I've noticed."

"Yeah, that's Gavin for you." She gives me an understanding smile and doesn't press the issue much further. "You'll tell me if anything happens, right?"

"Sure, but I doubt it will. I still need my pain meds to sleep well at night and as you know, they knock me out." I smile, recalling the last time she was over and I passed out before the beginning credits of a show. "Gavin's just a decent guy who made a promise to take care for me." There's not much else to say on this subject, so I switch the subject to her. "What did you do this weekend?"

"Not much. I hung out with Erin and James on Saturday. Yesterday, I spent my day at the library researching a paper and went to practice last night." She pulls her feet into her chair and sighs.

"No Josh?"

She lets out a disappointed breath. "No, he went home for the weekend and didn't get back until right before practice."

"How was practice? I feel like I'm missing out on so much."

"There's a game Wednesday. You should come!" she eagerly suggests.

"I can't wait to be out of this brace," I groan in frustration. "My body's in dire need of exercise. This brace is so confining."

"Your appointment is on Friday, right?" Sophie sounds hopeful. "Maybe you'll get it off?"

"Let's hope so. I can't stand just lying around all the time." I've tried not to take my medication as much, but every time I hold off, I pay for it later.

"Alex, you need to take it easy. Your body will heal faster, if you do." Sophie eyes me skeptically.

"I know," I reluctantly admit. "It's just frustrating."

"Will you be at the game this weekend?"

"I'm planning on it but have to see how I feel. I heard some guys talking about it in class today. It should be a great game against Oregon."

"Uggh, don't get me started. You can't miss this game!" She then looks at her watch and abruptly stands. "Yikes. I need to go. I'm supposed to meet Erin to go grocery shopping. Need anything before I leave?"

"No, I'm fine. Thanks. I'll see you later." She walks down

the hall, and I call out, "Just leave it unlocked. Gavin will be here soon."

I hear a chuckle as she hollers, "Enjoy your babysitter!" She opens the door and is gone before I can think of a response.

After Sophie leaves, I hobble into the kitchen to see if there's something I can make for dinner that won't involve much coordination. Leaning on my crutches, I poke around the fridge and come up with some ingredients to make a casserole. I set into assembling it while balancing against the counter with my crutches. It's frustrating to maneuver my way around the kitchen, but with persistence, I'm successful. Just as I'm finishing, Gavin knocks on the door. Before I can turn to greet him, he enters the kitchen.

"Hey, smells good. What are you making?" He looks down at me and smiles.

"Casserole."

"Need help?" He sets his bags down and walks over to where I'm standing.

"Well... we can either eat here or take it to your place. Then we can study while it cooks. What do you think?" I spread grated cheese on top while I wait for his decision.

"Mind if we stop by the store on the way? I'm out of milk and anything worthy of eating for that matter." He reaches out and grabs a small pile of cheese with his fingers.

"Hey," I tease and push his hand away before starting to shred more. I look up to see Gavin grinning widely at me with a mouthful of cheese. "Do you want a slice?"

"Sure," he says as he grabs another handful of grated cheese and laughs.

"Well," I chortle, "get me a knife." I grate more cheese to

fill the vacant spot on the casserole. "While you're at it, grab the tinfoil out of that drawer." I point to the one behind him.

Gavin tears off a piece big enough to put over the dish and waits for me to hobble out of the way before placing it securely on top of the casserole. He raises an eyebrow and grins slyly. "If you can do all this on crutches." He points to the casserole. "I'm curious to see what you'll do without them."

"If you're lucky, you might find out one day." I poke at him with my finger while balancing forward on my crutches entirely.

"Hmmmm." He smirks, holding my gaze. For a moment, I'm caught in them and unable to think clearly. He slowly inhales, though it seems all too soon to break the connection between us by asking, "So…are you ready?"

"Huh?" I muster, still lost.

He shakes his head, laughter escaping again. "Are you ready to go to my place?"

"Sure." I suddenly comprehend. "My things are in the hall."

"I'll grab your things then come back for the casserole." He looks at me for a moment longer than probably necessary before hauling my things out in one trip. He's back before I can look around to see if I've forgotten anything.

He walks into the kitchen as I'm in my bedroom. "Do you need anything else?"

"No, I'm good," I call out. I make my way to the couch to put on a sweatshirt before heading out.

As he settles into the driver's seat, he glances in my direction with a smirk.

"What?" I'm suddenly defensive.

"I'm just humoring you," he states matter-of-factly and shakes his head slightly.

Not really understanding the meaning behind his comment, I wait for further explanation. He takes in a deep breath, sighs, and remains silent. It's very frustrating, but I'm not willing to press the issue either, so I let it drop.

12

A CHANGE FOR COMFORT

WHEN WE PULL into the driveway of his apartment, Gavin parks under the carport next to a green Honda Civic. I start to get out of the car, but he's next to me before I make any progress. Gavin hands me my crutches from the back seat as I finally make my way to an upright position after pulling myself up from his low car.

"Let me grab the casserole, and we'll set the oven. I'll come back to get the rest," he suggests as he leads me down a path on the side of his building. When we reach the other end, I find we're actually entering the house from the back, in what used to be a daylight basement. He unlocks the door and steps aside for me to enter first.

I feel a little awkward as I step into the large, open room. I'm not quite sure what to do with myself. I take a few moments to look around before continuing. Gavin walks toward a moderate kitchen area and sets the casserole on a wooden table. His smile's genuine when he suggests, "Make yourself at home. I'll get everything."

In his absence, I realize his apartment's almost the same size as mine. Though there aren't any walls, he has distinct spaces around the room. The kitchen's made up of cupboards lining half of one wall, with the stove on an adjacent wall near the corner. There's a round wooden table barely big enough for four chairs around it. To the right of the kitchen are double doors that I presume is a closet on the other side.

I can't miss the king-size bed on the opposite wall of the entry. A large hunter-green comforter spreads across it. Even from here, it's inviting. It has to be much better than my dwarf-size couch in comparison. On each side, there are mismatched end tables with a lamp on the right side along with an alarm clock.

The rest of the area makes up a living room, complete with a television, stereo, and futon, set up like a couch. A small coffee table sits in front of the futon.

Having seen my brother's apartments in college, Gavin keeps his remarkably clean. Though it's getting dark, I can tell there's ample light from the two large windows in the room during the day. The ceiling's also higher than I anticipated, making the room seem even larger. There're a few things out of place, like shoes next to his bed and some mail on the counter, but overall, I'm impressed.

"This should be everything," his voice calls out, and I jump in surprise. I'd been so preoccupied with everything in his apartment, I never heard him come in.

"Oh, sorry. Didn't mean to startle you." Gavin sets my things down against the small wall between the couch and his bed. He points to the room behind the wall. "The bathroom's in there if you need it. There's a full tub and towels are under the sink. If you need anything, just ask. Give me a sec, and I'll get my geology things out so we can study. Will you be more comfortable at the table or on the couch?" He walks to the stove. Before I can answer his previous question, he asks, "What should I cook this at?"

"Um." Which question do I answer first? "Three-fifty, for forty-five minutes." I figure that one is more pressing. "If you don't mind, I think I'd rather put my leg up on the couch since I've been standing a lot today."

"Want a pillow?" I nod, and he walks to his bed, grabbing the only pillow left, and retrieves two more pillows from our bags. He helps me get settled, then places the extra pillow at the end of the couch. His musky scent saturates the room and is stronger in such proximity. I take a deep breath to take it all in. God, he smells so good. I finally gather my wits and state, "You have a nice place," as I exhale.

"Thanks, my sister helped decorate it. Dad bought the furniture," he points to the bed and couch, "and I've picked up the rest over time. It seems like an overkill, but as you know," he smiles sheepishly in my direction, "I don't exactly fit on standard-issue furniture." He puts the casserole in the oven before returning to the couch. "Originally, I only had the extra-long futon, but my sister thought I needed a proper bed and a couch for people to sit on if they came to visit. Who was I to argue? You know how sisters can be." He shrugs as if that explains everything.

"Yeah, I know." Remembering Katherine when she's determined makes me smile. "Trust me."

Gavin brings over both of our backpacks and sinks into the far end of the couch. "So where do you want to begin?"

"Let's start with igneous rocks and volcanoes, then move on to sedimentary rocks, as well as weathering and soil."

"I see you've already gotten started," he accuses lightly.

"Well, I did the required reading for tomorrow this weekend, but I haven't gone over my notes much."

We spend the next forty-five minutes discussing our notes from the lecture and comparing it to the text. When the timer goes off, we're pretty much finished. Gavin gets up to remove the casserole.

When we finish dinner, Gavin clears our plates and washes the dishes by hand. I realize he doesn't have a dishwasher. I get up, making my way to stand beside him. "You wash, I'll dry," I suggest as I pick up a towel and lean forward to balance on my crutches.

"Well, what do you want to do now?" he asks once we're done. He returns to where we're studying and puts his things back into his backpack.

I glance at my watch and realize it's only eight o'clock. "I'm not sure." I look to him for suggestions.

He's still sorting through his backpack when he responds, "Want to see what's on TV?" He zips his bag, placing it near the door, and returns to the couch. "How's the leg?"

"It's fine," I automatically respond. The truth is I'm sore from not taking any medicine. My ribs are stiff, too. It's so frustrating to have to take this medication.

"When was the last time you took your meds?" He raises his eyebrows at me, accusingly.

"Yesterday," I admit quietly. I then quickly add so that there's no further discussion on the subject, "I'll take it in a bit."

Gavin walks to the kitchen and brings back a tall glass of water. "Which bag is it in?"

"I'm fine. I really don't need anything right now," I try to sound as convincing as I can.

He stares me down disapprovingly. "Which bag, Alex?" he repeats with a tone not to be argued with.

I shake my head, giving up. I point to its location. "My duffel bag." He brings me the bag so I can retrieve it myself, then replaces it against the wall.

He sits on what's left of the couch when I pull my leg back around to rest on the pillows. He picks up the remote, but before he actually turns on the TV, he asks, "Want to go to the game this weekend?"

"Um." It takes me a moment before remembering the football game's this weekend. "Sure, sounds fun. Hopefully, I'll be rid of this." I point to my brace and grimace.

He chuckles once at my response. "Either way, I hope you have warm clothes. It's supposed to snow this week."

"What?" I ask in disbelief.

"Oh, I forgot." He laughs lightly. "It's your first winter here." He turns on the TV and looks for something to watch as he continues, "Well, it's a little early but the end of October's not that unusual, I guess."

"Oh." I knew there were distinct seasons, but I never thought there'd be snow before Halloween. "I've brought warm clothes," I say aloud as I wonder if they'll be enough.

Gavin finds a show on the Discovery Channel and doesn't respond. After a few moments, he jumps up and starts for the kitchen. "Hey, want anything while I'm up? I'm grabbing a soda and chips."

"Sure, sounds great." I decide I might as well use the

restroom and change into my pajamas if we're settling in for the night. My medication will kick in shortly, so I might as well be prepared. I look around and feel a bit awkward because I won't have my bedroom to change in. Judging from the exterior walls of the bathroom, there isn't much room to maneuver with my brace and crutches. When Gavin hears the Velcro from my leg brace, he turns and his voice fills with concern, "Alex?"

Embarrassed, I quickly ramble an explanation, "I'm changing into my pajamas and wasn't sure how much room you have in your bathroom. I didn't want to fumble with my brace in there and…" I trail off, not really sure what else I should say. My eyes finally meet his.

"Need any help?" Gavin's perplexed features show he's not comprehending my dilemma. Apparently, he hasn't thought about the logistics of how I get dressed every morning. I've been fortunate to sit on my bed to do most everything but in the small, confined spaces of a bathroom, I'm sure it won't be the same.

"Um…" I hesitate, not knowing what he'd be able to help with. "I think I'll be fine. Thanks." He stands in the middle of the room, hesitating as if he's unsure what to do next. "Get your snacks," I suggest as I set my brace beside the couch.

It's a little harder than I imagined getting dressed in the bathroom. When I finally exit, I find Gavin has put a small pile of blankets along with a set of sheets on the floor near the futon. I make my way back toward the couch.

"Want me to make the bed?" Gavin comes from behind me and sets a bag of chips beside the two sodas on the coffee table.

Realizing there's no place for him to sit if he does, I suggest, "Later. Let's watch TV for now." I put my brace over my pajamas. "What are we watching?" I say as I finally finish tightening the last strap on my thigh.

"I haven't found anything." He sits at the far end of the couch and flips through the channels, pausing on each one to give me a chance to take it in. "This okay?" he finally asks when we get to an episode of *Survivor*.

I nod in approval, though I've never watched an entire episode. Ben loves the show, so I've caught bits and pieces back home with Katherine. Instantly, we're sucked into a food challenge that intrigues, yet disgusts both of us. Each of us squirm and gag a few times at some of the ridiculous things the challengers have to endure to win the immunity challenge. The topper's when they eat a plateful of fish with their heads still attached.

"EEWWW!" I finally say aloud, turning my head away from the screen.

This brings Gavin's attention back to me suddenly. "Want me to change the channel?"

"No, I just can't believe they're eating that. It's so disgusting!" I laugh in astonishment.

"I know, it's pretty bad!" he agrees, chuckling.

I adjust my body to get more comfortable, but it's no use. Gavin sees this and asks, "Want to lie down? I'll move to the floor. Or you can put your legs on my lap?"

He's already doing so much for me, and I don't want him to be put out any further. "Stay where you are. I'll scoot down further." The moment I put my legs on Gavin's lap, I'm suddenly ultra-sensitive to his presence. He crosses his hands over his chest as I nuzzle my way against the back of the couch and the armrest. I adjust my pillows and finally find comfort.

"Need a blanket?" Gavin suggests as he picks up one from the pile near the end of the couch.

Before I can say, "Sure," it's already over me. It must be one of his because I'm suddenly engulfed with his delicious scent. Though it's light, I draw in a deep breath, wanting more. How can one person smell so good? After a few moments, he rests his arms over the blanket on my legs. This sends a slight shiver up my spine. Thankfully, Gavin takes this as me being cold. I hide my embarrassment by nestling the blanket closer to me around my neck and avoiding eye contact by focusing on the television. This, however, does little to keep me from thinking about him.

I hear him take in a deep breath and relax further into the couch. Neither one of us has spoken about our conversation in Ellensburg. My mind's suddenly filled with flashes of our conversations from this weekend. I linger on the moments when Gavin had locked his eyes upon mine, leaving me utterly speechless. I feel myself blush as I recall my embarrassment. Once again, I'm thankful my face is blocked by the blankets to keep from being noticed.

"Hey," Gavin calls my attention to him. "Tomorrow afternoon, I need to spend some time in the studio. I'll go after geology, and I shouldn't be too much longer after work. Want me to drop you off at your place at noon?"

"I have a paper I need to finish. I'll just bring my laptop and finish my research in the library. If I get done before you, I can walk back to my place."

I shift the blankets so I can see him giving me a

disapproving look. "Alex, that's a long walk." He rolls his eyes and shakes his head at me.

"I need to finish my paper. You get off work around five, right?" I already know this, but trying to make my argument convincing, I continue, "Why don't you go straight to the studio to work on your project, and I'll catch a ride from someone when I'm finished?" I'm not sure who will be available, but I add, "I'll call Sophie for a ride if I need one," to make it so Gavin has nothing to argue about.

Gavin eyes me suspiciously but concedes for the time being. "I'll drop by Cleveland between work and the studio to see if you need a ride. If you're not there, I'll meet you back at your place."

"I'll be fine. I promise," I try to assure him.

"Do you need anything from your apartment to finish your paper?"

"I don't think so. I brought it to work on, not knowing if you'd need to study this evening." I shrug in an attempt to sound casual.

"I'm okay for tonight. I'm ready for our exam tomorrow in geology and everything else isn't due until the end of the week," he sighs and pats my good leg once. "I may read a little later before going to bed."

"I can move. I don't want to keep you from anything." I start to get up.

"Alex." He lightly presses on my legs, and I stop moving. "I told you, I'm fine." Gavin smiles, and it reaches his golden-brown eyes. I'm left staring helplessly at him for a few moments. He gives me a reassuring wink. "I've studied enough for now. Let's just watch TV." He continues his gaze until I resign, sinking comfortably back into the couch.

Feeling the effects of my medication, I relax my body further. He flips the channel to another show, but by now, I'm hardly paying any attention. I hear a small chortle escape from his lips as I drift off to sleep, being too tired to find out his reason for laughing.

The next morning, I find I'm extremely comfortable and well rested. It takes me a few moments to recall where I am. What throws me off is the room looks different from this perspective. Upon further inspection, I realize I'm not on the couch, but in Gavin's bed. I look in the direction of the couch and find that he's made the futon into a bed and is sleeping under the covers I used last night. He's sound asleep and appears comfortable, which is drastically different from the scene yesterday morning. I do my best not to wake him as I make my way to the bathroom. As quietly as I can, I brush my teeth and shower. Thankfully, I'd left my bag in here when I changed last night, so I don't have to go into the other room to get anything. I zip through my shower, though it takes more time than necessary to get dressed afterward in such a small space. I keep my brace off because that's asking too much from this confined space.

The clock on his bedside table says 6:40 when I exit the bathroom. Thankful for the light streaming through the window, I notice Gavin's changed position in the bed, but appears to be undisturbed. Being careful not to put too much weight on my leg, I hobble without my crutches to get my book from yesterday. My leg's definitely not ready to be walked upon. I manage to keep my winces silent as I put as little pressure as possible on it. I make it back to his bed and turn on the lamp near me to its lowest setting, without disturbing Gavin's sleep.

A while later, I hear a faint, "Hey" as Gavin stretches and turns in my direction. In a yawn, he continues, "Have you been up long?"

"No, not really."

As he swings his legs over to the edge of the bed to sit up, I realize he's only wearing a pair of shorts. Though I attempt to give him some privacy, I find his bare chest reveals his athleticism more than I could've imagined. His muscles are well defined over his long frame, and I can't force myself to look away. He gives me an impish smile as he stands and continues to stretch.

"Morning, Alex," he offers after he yawns. For a short moment, he looks a little puzzled as he stares at me for a moment, stopping at my sweats and brace-less leg. "You've showered?"

"Um..." I hesitate for a moment. "I tried not to wake you."

"I didn't hear a thing, apparently." He smiles and lopes over to the kitchen to get a glass of water. "Where's your brace?"

"In the bathroom. It was too loud to put back on," I admit quietly.

Gavin gives me a slightly disapproving look but says nothing as he walks to the bathroom and shuts the door. After a few moments, I hear the water for the shower turn on and the toilet flush. I pick up the book I'm reading to pass the time.

Within a few minutes, Gavin appears with only a towel wrapped around his waist. My jaw has a mind of its own as it drops to the floor. Gavin in a towel is something to be seen. Thankfully, he misses my ogling as he walks to his closet, retrieves his clothes, and returns to the bathroom to change. I try not to watch but find myself entirely aware of each distinct movement.

To distract myself, I try once again to read my book, but find it's impossible to concentrate. Fortunately, I don't have to keep up that pre-tense long because he comes back out, fully dressed, holding both my crutches and brace in each of his hands, bringing me back to reality. "And just how did you get out here without these?" His tone is slightly sarcastic, but definitely one of concern.

"Um…" I'm not sure how to explain. "I didn't want to wake you."

"But injuring yourself again would be so much better." Again, the sarcasm's thick, but I'm beginning to think there might be more.

"Well, no," I start to sputter, but I'm interrupted again.

"Alexis Manning, you're utterly impossible." Gavin's voice now sounds stern.

Not knowing how to respond, I just stare, wide-eyed, defenseless.

Gavin breaks his serious demeanor, shaking his head. A smile twists upon his face. "They warned about this." He raises one eyebrow and hesitates before coming to sit beside me on the edge of the bed, placing my brace on the other side of him at the end of the bed.

"What do you mean?" I pick out his last comment.

He shakes his head from side to side and smiles before bringing on the full force of his eyes. "Never mind. Forget that," he whispers. Making sure he has my full attention, he brings his left hand to my chin, tilting it slightly so I have nowhere to look, but at him. It wasn't necessary, but the point's well taken. Wordlessly, he stares as if he's contemplating how to word his next statement. Finally, he takes in a slow breath and exhales slowly, saturating me with his cool musky scent. "You need to focus on healing, not whether you wake me." He brushes a few fallen strands of my hair behind my ear with his right hand and waits to ensure his point is made. Though, there isn't any need. When he looks at me like this, I'm putty in his hands. I can barely make a coherent sentence, let alone argue with him. All I can do is agree.

Our eyes stay connected for awhile before he breaks the trance by reaching for my brace. "Well, we'd better get going if I intend to get to class on time. Want me to help you with this?"

Realizing the time, I sputter, "I... uh... sure."

He grins widely at my acceptance. I hear from under his breath, "Maybe there *is* hope for you."

Instinctively, my lips purse in protest, but he stops me by placing one finger upon them. "Just kidding, Alex. Relax." He eyes me playfully before helping me finish putting on my brace.

TO CELEBRATE DOING WELL on our geology exam, Gavin suggests going to lunch at a cafe on campus. Afterward, he offers to show me this infamous studio he works so much in.

"Welcome to my second home," he states when we arrive at the correct floor in Carpenter Hall. I can't help but be in awe of the office-like setting. There're cubical walls, drawings of various projects as well as three-dimensional models scattered around.

"Wow."

"Trust me. It's not that impressive when you spend as many hours here as we do." He points to the other table next to his. "That's Josh's desk."

"Oh." Not realizing how close he and Josh must be. No wonder they come to Antonio's as often as they do; they're just leaving campus.

He grabs a few things from one of his drawers and guides me to the exit.

As we walk past a girl with dark, pixie-like hair and dark-rimmed glasses, she stands and greets us. "Hey, Gavin. How's it going?" Seeing me, her smile widens. "You must be Alex." She holds out her hand in greeting. I lean forward on my crutches to extend an arm in return. "I'm Alyse. It's a pleasure to meet you." How does she know me? I glance at Gavin.

"You, too," I manage to say, but I'm still at a loss for many words.

Sensing my confusion, she clears her throat, gaining my attention. "I've heard a lot about you."

"Oh, thanks." I wonder what she's heard.

Then she gushes, "The guys talk about you non-stop. Especially, your killer soccer moves. They've been bummed you can't play." She motions to Gavin, and I can't help but notice he's blushing. What's up with that? "And Wallace here… well, he's told us how amazing you are in general." She chuckles loudly. "You must be a good influence on him because I've never seen him more prepared for class since your accident. I'm glad you're on the mend."

"Thanks, Alyse," Gavin interrupts. "I hope someday I can repay the favor," Gavin jokes under his breath.

Alyse gives him a "What did I do?" look and lets the subject drop.

Not knowing what else to do, I say, "It's really nice to meet you, Alyse."

"We should get going," Gavin suggests, avoiding all eye contact. "I don't want to be late for work."

As soon as we're out of earshot from Alyse, Gavin apologizes, "Sorry about that."

"What?" I ask innocently.

"She really means well, but sometimes gets a little carried away. We've all been in the same classes since freshman year. Like I said, we spend a lot of time together so we're aware of what goes on in each other's life. Hope she didn't make you feel uncomfortable."

"So… You've talked about me?" I tease.

Gavin flashes an awkward glance in my direction, grins sheepishly, and almost whispers, "Maybe a little."

"Hummm." I suppress a laugh. "I hope it wasn't bad."

"No, not really. Everyone was in the studio the day of your accident. They ask about you." His face shows there's more he's not telling me.

"Uggh! Have you told them I'm a horrible patient?" I joke as we exit the elevator.

"No, I just report your progress and say that I've been helping you out a little."

"Your version of a little and most everyone else's seems to be vastly different. I don't even know where I'd be without you here." I shudder at the thought. I could just picture one or both of my parents hovering over my every move or having to drop out and go home for the semester. "I really do appreciate all that you've done for me," I say with sincerity.

"No worries, Alex. It's not a problem." He matches my sincerity, then adds in a mischievous tone, "You're not that bad to be around." He pokes me lightly in the shoulder with his index finger. "Even if you do get up at ungodly hours."

"Hey, I…" I attempt to argue but am cut off.

Gavin laughs loudly as we exit Carpenter Hall, walking toward Cleveland. "Sorry, couldn't help that one…" He gasps in air, before adding, "I knew it would get a reaction." After a few minutes, he changes the subject. "Did I tell you I'll know in the next few weeks where I'll be studying next year?"

"No. Do you mean here in the States or abroad?"

"Both. I'll find out my placement for both semesters."

"Wow, that's exciting. What's your preference?" I ask eagerly as I concentrate on the abrupt curb before me.

"I'm hoping to stay here fall semester, then I'm good with what I get." Seeing my situation, he steps down first, ready to support me if necessary.

"Why is that?" Why doesn't he care where he's assigned in Europe?

Gavin stops walking and looks at me. "Well, I have an apartment and a job here. Also, Josh and James are planning to do the same."

"That's great if you can stay with your friends." I haven't given it much thought to how close they are with one another.

Gavin glances in my direction. "Doing okay?"

"Yeah, I'm fine."

"So, what's elementary education like?" Gavin asks, interested.

Isn't it self-explanatory? Okay... where do I begin? "I'm basically taking classes to prepare me to become a teacher. I might get an ELL endorsement and possibly a reading endorsement."

"ELL?" he questions.

"Sorry, teacher jargon. English Language Learners. It's strategies to help those learning English. It'll go hand in hand with teaching students how to read."

"Wow, that sounds interesting. Do you have to speak another language to get that degree?"

"Not really, but it helps. I've taken Spanish and Italian all through high school. It's mainly to teach strategies to new language learners, to help them acclimate to our culture," I explain.

"Would it help if you experienced something like that yourself?"

"Probably, but I've never thought about it like that. You make a good point." Suddenly, what my academic advisor said comes to mind. I'd love to travel, but I'm not sure how to manage it.

Gavin interrupts my plotting, "Mom used to always say everyone should travel abroad while they're young. She spent a semester abroad and encouraged each of us to do the same. My sister and brother both studied in Europe."

"She's right. We're only young once." I've always wanted to travel abroad, but I've been too determined to finish school that I haven't given it much thought.

LATER THAT EVENING, Gavin suggests going for a walk so I won't be so stir crazy. We carry a casual conversation as I hobble around his neighborhood on my crutches. He fills me in on a project he's working on in the studio. I'm still amazed all the work that goes into a fictitious community, for the sake of design. I could probably draw it, but heaven help me build a three-dimensional model. That's where my skills end.

When my arms get shaky, I suggest we turn around.

"Wow, you can be reasonable," Gavin teases.

As we turn around, going down the slight incline, I find I need to grip my crutches tighter, so they don't slip out from underneath me on the bit of gravel on the pavement. This takes all my concentration, and I become silent.

"Everything okay?"

"Yep," I quickly reply. "Just don't want to fall."

Gavin stops in front of me and asks, "Want a ride?"

"I guess I could wait for you to come get me with the car," I concede when I realize my arms are becoming the consistency of Jell-O.

"Alex, I'm not going to leave you on the side of the road in the dark." He laughs lightly at my absurdity. "I'll carry you, of course."

What... the... what? Why on earth would he carry me? We're quite far from his apartment. "Seriously?" I ask, dumbfounded.

He rolls his eyes and shakes his head in annoyance. "I thought you'd be this way," he sighs heavily, "You're rather light, you know... And I wouldn't be slinging you over my shoulder. Give me *some* credit." He lets out a heavy sigh.

I say nothing but stare at him, waiting for further

explanation. I feel my lips purse, and my eyebrows pull together. He's so frustrating.

"I'll either carry you in my arms or if you're up for it, on my back." He smirks, keeping his arms on my shoulders.

"That's not necessary." I set out to make my way around him. In my haste, I don't see the patch of gravel under my left crutch, and it starts to slide out from underneath me. I steady myself with my good foot as Gavin simultaneously catches me from the side.

Gavin says nothing but holds out his hand for my crutches. I reluctantly hand them over and wait for him to make his next move. He puts them together and hands them to me. Before my next breath, he bends down and swoops me into his arms before walking briskly back to his apartment.

After a few yards, Gavin whispers into my ear, "This isn't so bad, is it?" I scowl at him but am stopped by his sudden laughter. "I've got to hand it to you. You're stubborn." He lets out a loud belly laugh, shaking me entirely.

"Humpff." Arguing will only prove his point.

When we reach his apartment, he sets me down to retrieve his keys. Tears threaten, so I hastily head to the bathroom for privacy. It's infuriating needing help. Since there's no room, I sit on the lid of the toilet and stew. Eventually, I clumsily change into pajamas. As I finish, I hear a light knock on the door.

"Alex?" Gavin's raspy voice fills with concern. "You okay in there?" It takes all I can not to lash out. *Apparently, I'm not as calm as I thought.* I stand and force myself to look at my reflection and remind myself it's not him I'm mad at, but the situation. If only I'd been paying attention to that stupid car,

I wouldn't be in this predicament. I finally manage, "I'm fine," and after another long moment, I hear his receding footsteps.

Realizing this bathroom isn't the place to put my brace on, I slip it between my arm and my crutches. Leaning forward on my crutches and opening the door with my free hand, I hobble ungracefully to the bed. I throw the brace a little harder than I anticipate to the bed and turn to sit on the edge of the bed, as a grunt escapes. I stare at the wall for a few moments before repositioning the brace hastily onto my leg. Once I feel I have better control of my feelings, I turn to face Gavin who's been sitting on the couch, watching the entire show.

He's leaning back with his legs stretched out past the coffee table. His arms fold loosely across his wide chest, with his eyebrows raised. Now, I'm not only embarrassed, but furious at myself for my fit. We stare in silence for a few moments before he quietly asks, "You done?"

Sheer humiliation flows through my body and my haunches rise. "With what?" escapes through my teeth more acidic than I anticipate.

"Apparently not." He smiles slyly, and a low chortle escapes.

His facial expression doesn't change as he holds my gaze. Somehow his golden-brown eyes are effective at disarming my temper. My heart slows down, and my roaring temper fizzles. Before long, I'm simply lost in his eyes from across the room. As if there's a magnetic pull between us, Gavin stands and slowly walks to me. When he's within an arm's length, he stops. He reaches out and pulls me to a standing position. Holding my hand for

support, he bends his head slightly and whispers,
"I'm sorry."

His closeness causes me to wobble. Since all my weight is
on my left leg, instinctively, I put out my injured leg for
support, but Gavin takes a step closer at the same instant,
catching me with his other arm. He pulls me in closer, and I
find myself in his embrace. I bury my head in his chest and
say nothing for some time while his strong arms wrap
around me. I feel him press his face to the top of my head
and hear him take in a deep breath before he whispers, "I'm
so sorry, Alex."

Keeping my arms around him, I look up at his face.
"What do you have to be sorry for? I'm the one who should
be apologizing."

Sympathy crosses his features. "You have every right to
feel frustrated. This has to be so hard on you. If I were you, I
would've been throwing a fit from day one. I know you're
not used to being taken care of, and it bothers you. I
apologize if I've done anything to offend you."

How can he know me so well? "Gavin, you haven't done
anything wrong. In fact, you've been a perfect gentleman
this entire time. You're right, I'm not used to being taken
care of, and it's frustrating to wait for my body to heal. Sorry,
I threw a fit. I shouldn't be so ungrateful. I can't thank you
enough for all you've done for me."

His mouth pulls around the edges into a grin. One hand
brushes hair out of my face while he holds my eyes with his.
Suddenly, there's a sense of smugness about him that doesn't
fit his mood. "You know…" He takes in a slow breath.
"You're kind of cute when you're mad." He smiles as if he's
waiting for my reaction.

I pull away to protest, by putting my arms on his chest, but his arms clamp together in the middle of my back, and I'm firmly held in place. It's then I realize he must be supporting my entire weight because my feet have no friction against the floor they're lightly resting upon.

My heart pounds out of my chest as I look anywhere but at him. When he finally has my full attention, "You're welcome," lightly escapes his lips as he bends forward, pressing his warm lips to mine. *Holy Crap. Gavin's kissing me.*

What starts out as a slow but steady kiss, ignites a flame inside me. I lock my arms behind his neck and pull myself closer to him as our lips and tongues dance together. Sparks fly, and everything around me is forgotten. I feel weightless as I enjoy everything there is about Gavin. All too soon, he sets me down on my feet and reluctantly pulls away with a wide grin spread across his face. "So... I guess my apology's accepted."

I open my mouth to speak, but he presses his index finger to my lips long enough to calm me before replacing it with his lips once again. By the time he releases me, my mind's spinning, and I'm literally off balance. I sway against the bed behind me, but Gavin steadies me by wrapping his enormous arms around me in a tight hug once again. He kisses the top of my head and guides me to sit on the bed. He takes a step back and asks, "Are you okay?" He looks me over to fully gauge my response.

I can't think coherently. My thoughts race around so fast, it's hard to pick any one thing to focus on. I shake my head, saying a silent yes.

Gavin hands me my crutches and asks, "Sit on the couch with me?"

"Sure." Gavin holds out his hand to steady me as I stand. He helps me prop my leg up on the coffee table with a pillow before sitting directly beside me. He reaches for my hand that's resting on my lap while he puts his other behind me. I find myself comfortably sinking into the couch and resting my head upon his chest. I inhale his musky scent and swoon. Is it possible to get drunk from simply smelling a man?

We sit together for some time before Gavin asks, "Want your medication? You look exhausted."

I glance at the clock and realize it's after ten. Suddenly, I feel the effects of the day. "Sure. Thanks."

He returns to almost exactly this spot. I can't help but nestle my head on his chest and relax. He presses his lips onto the top of my head and whispers, "Go to sleep, Alex. We'll talk more later."

The next day, classes fly by, and I spend the afternoon at my apartment waiting for Gavin to get off work. Since he's playing soccer this evening, I've made spaghetti for dinner. We haven't talked about last night, but I can't say it hasn't been far from my mind. Who could forget a kiss like that? The thought alone sends shivers down my spine.

I hear Gavin walk through the door just as the phone rings, and he answers.

"Hello?" There's a long pause. "Great... No... she's right here... Sure, I'll think about it... It's no problem." He laughs and is quiet for awhile. "I'll definitely consider it... Really, it hasn't been a problem." Another chuckle. "Yeah, you were right about that. She definitely can be." By now he's coming down the hallway to the kitchen. I mouth, "Who is it?"

Gavin grins widely. "Well, she's right here. Want to talk

to her?" He covers the phone with his hand and whispers, "It's your mom," before handing me his phone.

"Hey, Mom! How's everything?" I say a little too enthusiastically. Gavin grins, shaking his head and walks into the living room to sit on the couch.

I haven't talked with Mom in a day or so, so she bombards me with questions. Without giving me an opportunity to answer, she asks, "How are you? Are you in pain? Have you been taking your medication, Alex? Are you…" She takes a breath, and I can't help but laugh.

I interrupt her before she can set herself into a panic attack. "I'm fine, Mom. I go back to the doctor Friday, remember? I'll know more then. Stop worrying about me." I shake my head in frustration.

Mom continues, "I'm just so thankful Gavin's been there to help you."

"He's been great, that's for sure. You really need to stop worrying. I'm fine. I'll be home in a couple of weeks for Thanksgiving."

"Speaking of Thanksgiving. You should invite Gavin." *Wow. Didn't see that coming.*

"Um, he has his own family, you know," I state a little defensively. He's probably sick of me after all our time together. Besides, as much as I want to be around him, I don't know if I want to subject him to another family gathering.

"Seriously, Alex. At least extend the invitation."

"I'll think about it," is all she's getting from me. Before she can hound me further, I ask, "Any updates on the wedding?"

Mom takes the bait and gushes over the details she and

Katherine have completed this week. I respond at the appropriate moments and am thankful she's taken her focus off me. I'm still lost about how I feel toward Gavin, and I'd rather not be in the hot seat at the moment.

When she takes a break from going over the details, I can't imagine the stress she must be under. I grumble under my breath, "Geesh, I think I'll just elope, thank you."

"Alexis Marie Manning. If you even think of such a thing, you'll be sorry!" she yells sternly through the phone.

"Just joking, Mom." I chuckle at her expense. As I look to Gavin, I realize I've talked long enough. "Hey, Mom. I need to get going. I need to do a few things before I watch the soccer game."

"Alex," she says in an accusing tone, "You're not overdoing it, are you?"

"I'm fine, Mom. Promise."

We hang up the phone, and I head to the couch and flop down next to Gavin, who's turned on the television, watching something on the Discovery Channel.

"What are your plans this weekend?" Gavin asks during a commercial.

I'm perplexed because I can't fathom why he'd be asking such a ridiculous question. He knows my schedule better than I do, especially when I'm on crutches. "Um, just the game on Saturday. Why?"

"Would you be interested in going to Spokane on Sunday?" He glances over casually

Still not seeing where he's going with this, I continue, "It'd be great to get out of town. What do you have in mind?"

He smiles slightly. "Oh, just a few errands. I thought you'd love to get out of here, and I'd like your company."

"You're not sick of me yet?" I tease, causing him to grimace.

Instead of arguing, he nearly whispers, "Not even close," making my heart race.

Before he can say more, I interject, "I'm game with anything that doesn't involve me having to lie around and rest all day."

"Sounds like a plan. Let's eat, then head over to Josh's. I told him I'd pick him up. Grab a blanket for the bleachers. It's pretty cold if you're not playing."

After picking up Josh, we arrive on the field to find the majority of our team warming up on one half of the field. Gavin helps me get settled before heading off to warm up. As much as I enjoy watching them play, I have to admit, I'm jealous I can't be out there. I try not to show it, but I can't be positive that Gavin hasn't seen through my act. He frequently glances in my direction, but I can't read his expression. After a few minutes, I realize there's barely enough players on our team, and guilt seeps in. If only I'd seen that car… they wouldn't be short players. I take a deep breath to calm myself. I can't change the past.

After the game has been going on for a few minutes, Erin comes to sit by me. "Hey, Alex, how are you?"

"Better," I admit. "Hopefully, I'll be rid of these on Friday." I point to my brace and crutches.

"I'll keep my fingers crossed for you." She sincerely smiles. "Mind if I join you?"

"Not at all." I scoot over, so she can join me on the blanket Gavin laid out.

"Thanks. I've got one in the car if it gets too cold." She sits on the bench beside me, and we get lost in the game.

"So, Sophie tells me Gavin's been staying with you," Erin casually states as she watches the other team make a shot, but it's deflected by our goalie, Andrew.

"Yeah, he's been amazing," I say quietly.

Erin smiles. "Gavin's always the perfect gentleman, isn't he?" Suddenly, Erin's on her feet screaming, "WAY TO GO, JOSH!"

Not realizing Erin knows Gavin, well. I'm caught off guard. When the game settles down, I continue, "Yeah, he's a gentleman, all right. Do he and James hang out often?"

Erin lets out a loud laugh. "Oh, he hasn't told you? We're in the architecture program." She smiles and rolls her eyes. "By this point, most of our classes are together."

Feeling silly for not making the connection, "Oh," is all I manage.

"We met our freshman year in class, and since Sophie and I were roommates in the dorms, we've been close friends ever since," Erin sighs and light laughter escapes before shaking her head. "I guess we'd have to be, to spend as much time as we do together and not kill each other." She seems incredibly amused about something, then her mood shifts to thoughtful. "It's great to see Gavin happy. He deserves it."

"What do you mean?" I ask apprehensively.

"Well." She stops for a moment to watch Samantha take a shot at the goal but misses. Erin lets out a sigh before continuing, "I don't really know how to explain it, but we've never really seen him take such an interest in anyone before."

Under my breath, I mutter, "It's probably because he literally saw me being hit by a car."

She shrugs her shoulders. "That may be a part of it, but it's definitely not the only reason." Suddenly, she's on her feet cheering for James, who's just taken a header, assisting the ball in the direction of the goal.

The rest of the game is intense. Though neither side scores, there are several near-miss attempts. Both Erin and I completely get caught up in the game.

When there's only a few minutes to go, James passes the ball to Josh, who fakes out his opponent. The ball sails through the air to Gavin, who's at the corner of the goal post. Gavin drops the ball to the ground, rolls it behind with his toe, and flicks the ball to his knee, where he swiftly strikes it over the goalie's head and hits the back of the net in the top corner. The crowd roars with excitement. Gavin flashes an enormous smile in my direction before he quickly resumes his position in the game. The remainder of the game is intense, but neither team manages to score. The referee calls the game, and our entire team celebrates the victory.

As soon as everything's settled, Gavin jogs over to me with a grin plastered on his face. As he approaches, I make my way to my feet, leaning on only one crutch and call out, "Great move out there!"

To my surprise, Gavin doesn't stop in front of me. Instead, he stretches his arms out and embraces me in a hug which lifts me entirely off the ground, forcing my crutches to fall on the ground beside me. "Thanks for showing it to me; that move was awesome," he whispers in my ear and pulls back to quickly kiss me on the mouth before setting me back down.

Once on the ground, I realize neither of my crutches are within reaching distance. Gavin reaches out and hands them to me. Once he makes sure I'm balanced, he excitedly hugs me again, exclaiming, "Wow! What an amazing game!"

By now, Sophie, James, and Josh have gathered around us. Everyone's high-fiving or hugging.

"Who wants to celebrate?" James ecstatically asks the group. The team erupts in cheers.

"Our usual place?" Josh suggests, and the rest of the group gathers their things and heads to their cars.

Knowing that I can't keep up to their pace, Gavin hands the keys to my 4-Runner to Josh. "We'll meet you at the car." He turns to Sophie. "Want to ride with us?"

"Sure, I caught a ride with James and Erin. Let me tell them, and I'll meet you there." Sophie grins widely and jogs in their direction.

"Well, what did you think?" Gavin asks when we're finally alone.

I smirk. "I probably could've done better."

"You wish!" Gavin places his arm over my shoulder and hugs me from the side. I can't help but giggle as I hobble toward my SUV.

As we enter Gavin's apartment after an evening of celebration with the team, Gavin chuckles to himself. "That was some game, wasn't it?"

"Yeah, it was pretty intense to watch from the sidelines." I turn around to face him.

Suddenly, he's right behind me, his face chagrin. "I'm…

Um… Sorry." He takes a deep breath then rambles the rest, "About kissing you like that out there. I just got so excited. I hope I didn't do anything I shouldn't have." He looks down shyly at the floor and waits for my response.

Crap. What do I say? He was entirely caught up in the moment. I should probably let him off the hook. "It's okay," comes out in a whisper. I slowly meet his eyes, fearing what I'll see. "I would've done the same thing," I exhale loudly, releasing my pent-up energy.

"Oh." He exhales slowly and looks anywhere but at me. Geesh… Could this get anymore awkward? Finally, he breaks the connection and looks toward the bathroom. "Well, I should probably shower. Want to go first?"

"Um, yeah, I'll just be a few minutes. While you're in the shower, it's easier to get dressed out here, so I'll change then."

When I return, Gavin has his back to me at his closet, wearing nothing but his soccer shorts and holding another pair in his hands. His muscles are well defined, and I can't help but stare at him in awe. Thankfully, I pull my jaw off the floor before he notices.

Completely oblivious, he walks past me before turning to say, "Um, I'll knock before I come out, so you're decent."

Amazingly, I change without much trouble. By the time Gavin knocks on the door, I'm reading on one end of the couch. "I'm decent."

Though it's a futile attempt, I force myself to focus on my book as Gavin walks across the room, wearing only a pair of long athletic shorts. After putting his clothes in the hamper, he turns and asks with interest, "What are you reading?"

"Oh, just something for fun. I haven't really gotten far into it." I close the book, not wanting to be rude.

"Well…" He stretches in a yawn. and I can't help but watch his abdominal muscles flex. "Keep reading, I need to do a little of my own." He shakes his head. "Though I wouldn't say for fun." He picks up a large textbook, then goes into the kitchen to get a large glass of water.

"Oh." I start to get up from the couch, realizing he might want his bed.

"Need something?" Gavin asks as he looks around to see what I might possibly need.

"I… Uh… thought you'd want to study on the couch, so I'm moving for you."

"Um, Alex…" Gavin's sarcasm spills out, "I'm not that big. There's room for both of us. No need to get up." He sets the glass on the small coffee table. "Want some?"

"Thanks. Can you get my medication? I forgot to take it."

"Sure." Within a minute or so, he's sitting comfortably on the other end of the couch, with his long legs sprawled out and crossed over one another.

Though I try to consume myself with my book, it's hard not to steal glances at Gavin. His muscular chest rises slowly as he breathes. His musky scent is stronger, fresh from the shower and his hair's in disarray, as if he's toweled off and forgotten about it. His arm grazes my bare foot as he reaches to turn his page. His warm touch sends shivers up my spine.

Apparently, I'm not subtle about my reaction because he feels me tremble. "Need a blanket?" His quick glance my way catches me staring. Crap. My cheeks heat as a blush creeps over me. There must be a God because he merely throws his comforter over me and returns to reading.

When I manage to find my voice, I thank him and forcefully go back to reading my book. I eventually manage to comprehend the text on the page, though it's a bit of a struggle. Soon, the effects of my medication kick in. I mark my place and stretch before reaching for my crutches.

"Going somewhere?" Gavin glances from his book, holding a finger on his place.

"Yeah. I'm calling it a night."

I hobble to the bed and crawl under the covers. It takes a few minutes to get comfortable, but eventually, just as I settle, I hear "Goodnight, Alex," from across the room. I hear another page turn in his book. I reposition myself so he can't see my face, smile, and drift off to sleep quickly, thinking about Gavin.

13

THE FIRSTS OF MANY FIRSTS

"WHAT A RELIEF," I sigh as I hit save on the eight-page paper I've worked on all afternoon. I'm in serious need of a mental break. Since Gavin's still at practice, I curl up with a blanket and flip on the television to see what mind-numbing show I can enjoy, but not pay close attention. I settle on *A Walk to Remember*. I'm just at the part where Jamie reveals to Landon that she's dying, so naturally, I'm on the verge of tears when Gavin walks in.

"Hey," he calls out as he shuts the door and stops in mid-motion when he sees my tears spill over. Slowly, he asks, "Everything okay?" He waits for my answer before moving a muscle, it seems.

Embarrassed, I laugh. "Yeah, just watching a movie." I wipe my eyes to attempt to cover any evidence of my sappiness.

"Oh." His muscles visibly loosen as he sets his bag down and comes to sit beside me. He still wears his sweatshirt, hat, and gloves. His cheeks are rosy, so it must be colder than I realize outside. When he sits on the other end of the couch, he asks, "Which movie?" since it's at commercial.

"*A Walk to Remember*," I sigh. "How was practice?"

"Cold." He takes his gloves off and lays them on the coffee table.

"Besides that?" I wait for more information.

"The usual. We only have one more game next week, then we're switching to indoor league after Thanksgiving break. Most of our team switches over, but some choose to stick to the outdoors."

"Sorry I wasn't much help this season."

Gavin laughs lightly and shakes his head. "It's not like you could help it." He pats my leg and rests his arm across them. "Will you stay on the team?"

I shrug. "If they'll still have me."

He raises an eyebrow. "Oh, they'll have you." He then looks back at the TV. "Should I get some tissues?" he asks sarcastically.

"Why?" I ask, suddenly defensive.

He winks slyly. "If I recall correctly, it's a tear jerker. Or at least it was for my sister."

"I think I'll manage." I smirk.

"Well, I'm freezing. I need a hot shower. I'll be out in a few."

"Okay," I say as the movie comes on.

I'm so into the movie when Gavin returns, I hardly notice the tears have formed once again. He doesn't say anything but brings me a box of tissues from the kitchen counter. Mortification spreads like wildfire. Why do movies like this always get to me?

A light chortle escapes from his mouth. "It's okay. Liz

and Mom are the same way. For some reason, they love movies that make them cry. Mind if I sit with you?"

"Not at all. Want some covers?" I offer since they're taking up most of the couch.

"I'm good for now." He sits on the other end of the couch, just beyond my feet, pushing the blanket back in my direction. We watch the remainder of the show in silence.

"How's your leg?" Gavin raises an eyebrow in my direction. "I mean, what do you think the doctors will tell you tomorrow?"

Well, since there's no glossing over this question, I shake my head and with a heavy heart, admit, "I honestly don't know. I've been really good about not walking on it, except for that one time earlier this week." I wince at the memory. "Based on how I feel, there's no way I'm getting out of this brace." I groan in frustration. "The bruising's still everywhere. I'm not sure if you've seen it lately, but now it's a gnarly shade of bluish-green. It also appears to have spread out. The worst part is still on my thigh, though my calf isn't much better. I hope it's not actually broken." I take a deep breath and finally look to Gavin.

He's silent as his features pull together, and his lips slightly pucker. Whatever he's concentrating on, it's taking a lot of thought. After a few moments of silence, I can't take it anymore. "Gavin?" I ask, wondering if he's heard a word I've said.

"Sorry… Just thinking about how you'll take what the doctor says." He takes a deep breath and exhales slowly. "You know, Alex, there's a good chance you'll still be wearing that tomorrow."

"I know," I sigh and shake my head in disgust. "I just

want to heal quickly, but my body may have other plans." I look up and finally admit what else is bothering me, too. "I don't want to be a burden to you either. I'm doing better without medication, but still can't go without it. I'm too sore by the end of the day, if I do."

Gavin shakes his head slightly and repositions his body so he's facing me on the couch. His golden-brown eyes bore into mine. Leaving no questions. "Alex, you're not an imposition. You should know by now that I'm not doing this out of obligation. I wouldn't feel comfortable knowing you're alone and knocked out. Who knows what could happen then?"

It's a rhetorical question, I know, but I can't help the sarcasm that slips out as I try to lighten the mood. "Uh… I sleep."

"True, but your entire apartment building could be on fire, and you wouldn't be any the wiser." He tilts his head with a slight smile, waiting for my rebuttal, but after a second, he continues in a solemn tone. "It's either me or someone from your family. I won't be offended either way. I don't want to force myself upon you either. Don't say anything now but think about it."

He's quiet for a moment and then continues, "Alex, I enjoy spending time with you. I'm looking forward to when you're able to choose to spend time with me, rather than feel forced. As you know, before the accident, I'd planned to ask you out." Gavin pauses and shakes his head. As if he is speaking to himself, he mumbles, "I just hope you're not sick of me by then."

When his words register, my mouth drops in shock. Millions of thoughts run through my head. Eventually, I respond a little more than I should, "For the record, I never feel forced to stay with you. I enjoy your company, too." I think to myself before continuing, "Yeah, in the beginning, I didn't like feeling babysat, but ever since our conversation in Ellensburg, my perspective changed dramatically."

Gavin looks sheepishly to his feet and with a voice a little louder than a whisper, asks, "So, you weren't upset when I kissed you after our walk?"

"What?" Why would he ask that?

Gavin rambles out an explanation. "I don't want you thinking I'm taking advantage of you. I mean... I ... I never intended to upset you. I just... didn't want you getting hurt..."

"Gavin," I interrupt. "You've been a perfect gentleman. I'm the one who threw a hissy-fit. I should apologize to you, not the other way around."

"Oh," Gavin whispers.

"Uggh!" I groan. This is so frustrating. Where do I begin? How do I tell him what I'm thinking when I'm not even sure how to describe it myself?

"What?" Gavin's features fill with concern.

I shrug and let out a deep sigh. "I give up." I take a deep breath and calm myself before continuing, "I get so tongue-tied around you. From the moment I ran into you that morning on campus, you've been so articulate, debonair, and have shown nothing but respect. All I do is fumble about and appear needy. I truly appreciate all your help, but I often wonder if you're just doing it because you *are* a gentleman. I don't want to force myself upon you either."

"So, it's settled." Gavin's calm, his face smooth and unreadable.

Completely confused, "What's settled?"

He looks directly into my eyes and holds them for a moment before an enormous smile spreads across his face. "We want to be together."

Several thoughts scream through my head, but I simply whisper, "Yes."

"Well, then, I have a confession to make." Gavin bites his lower lip and waits for my reaction.

Puzzled, I ask, "You do?"

"I'm dying to take you on an actual date." He reaches out his hand to mine. "When we go to Spokane on Sunday, can we consider it as one?"

I feel as if I'm about to explode with the amount of emotions flowing through me. Eventually, I gather my wits and say, "Sounds perfect."

"Great." Gavin smiles widely, then raises an eyebrow as if there's more to reveal. "Mind if we keep our plans a surprise?"

I snicker, wondering what he'll come up with. "Sure."

Gavin chuckles happily and holds my hand as we watch the next show.

The next day, just as I open my music notebook to look over my new assignment, I notice a pair of long legs stop in front of me. I look up to see Gavin's beautiful face grinning at me. I can't help but smile in return. "Hey," I say barely above a whisper as I rein in the butterflies swarming in my stomach. *Will I ever get used to how good looking Gavin is?*

"I see you've got a new brace." He smiles warmly, then raises an eyebrow in my direction.

"You're pretty observant. The good news is that nothing is broken. The bad news is I have to wear this for the next week or so. I have another appointment next Friday to see how things are going. The best part is I get to take this one off at night," I sigh with relief.

"I'm happy for you, Alex. But you know I would have skipped class to take you to your appointment at Student Health." Gavin smiles widely as I gather my notebook into my backpack.

"Gavin, it's closer than some of my classes from Cleveland Hall." I stare at him in disbelief, but instead of letting him say anything, I change the subject. "On the way home, can we drop by Antonio's so I can let my boss know what's going on with my leg? The doctor wants me to take my medication until the pain and swelling subside, so he's given me another note to give to my boss."

Gavin reaches out his hand to assist me in standing. "Sounds great."

As I expected, Andrea's more than understanding about my injury. She wishes me a speedy recovery and tells me she'll hold my job until I'm able to return. With it being close to the end of the semester, business has been slow, so there's been no need to replace me. I thank her graciously and return to the car where Gavin's waiting.

He hangs up the phone as I enter the car. "Josh asked if we'd like to hang out with him and Sophie this evening. What do you think?"

"Sounds fun. What are we doing?"

"Um, I'm not sure. Maybe hanging at Sophie's."

"Does Sophie know he invited you?" I ask, not wanting to intrude on anything she's planned.

"Well... She was there when he asked, so I'd hope so." Gavin chuckles. "Why would that matter?"

Not wanting to betray her confidence, I dismiss it as an errant thought. "Oh, just curious." Gavin waits for me to continue, but I change the subject. "Let's invite them to your place. How does dinner and games or a movie sound?"

WHILE DINNER COOKS, I assemble some order to my exploding duffel bag. Then I fold the blankets Gavin's been sleeping with and pick up my toiletry bag from the bathroom. By the time I'm done there, Gavin's standing behind me.

"You don't have to do this. The great thing about a small apartment is it can be cleaned within minutes."

"I know." I look around to see what else I can do to help Gavin.

"Um, Alex, why don't you sit," Gavin suggests. "Dinner's in the oven and…" He then glowers teasingly at me. "You'll only get in the way."

Instinctually, I want to argue, but when I look at his goofy grin, I stop in my tracks. "What!" I exclaim.

"Nothing. You're just predictable, that's all." He grins earnestly and places his index finger under my chin to raise my eyes to meet his. He then bends his head slowly toward mine and stares into my eyes and whispers, "I kind of like that."

I stare into his golden-brown eyes for a long moment, trying to remember how to respond. "Um…" is all I mumble.

He holds my gaze a fraction of a second longer, then shakes his head as if to clear it. "I should get back to dinner."

He takes a deep breath. "Please sit. I'll have everything picked up within a few minutes." He raises a brow until I resign to the couch.

Soon, the aroma of chicken enchiladas fills the apartment, making my mouth water. Gavin has the place picked up and has placed my things in the closet next to his dresser. Just as he sits next to me, there's a knock at the door. He chuckles, shaking his head as he answers the door.

"Hey, guys," Josh calls out as he steps through the door with a bag in his hand. "Wow! What's for dinner?"

"Chicken enchiladas. Hey, Sophie. You can just put that on the counter," Gavin suggests. Sophie holds a pie of some kind in her hands.

"It's apple. Hope that's okay. We also brought ice cream and salad." She places the pie on the counter and grabs the ice cream out of the bag Josh holds to put it into the freezer.

"I knew he wouldn't disappoint us," Josh teases as he pushes Gavin on the shoulder. "This man can cook."

We all laugh, and Gavin shakes his head. "At least I'm good for something." He grabs a kitchen chair and brings it near the couch where I'm sitting, for me to prop my leg. "It's going to be about another half hour before it's ready. Want to sit?" He motions to Sophie. He then returns to the kitchen and hands a bowl to Josh who is now making the salad.

"I see you got a new brace," Sophie observes as she sits on the couch next to me. "What did the doctor say today?"

I replay the story I told Gavin, though I skip the part about my medication.

"I'm sorry, Alex. I know you wanted it off. But it'll go by fast." Sophie gives an encouraging smile.

"Well, it is what it is. I'll have to make the best of it." I smile and attempt to change the subject. "So what games did you guys bring?"

"Cranium, Pictionary, and a couple of card games. Josh rented a movie, but I don't remember what it's about."

"*Covert Ops*," Josh interrupts. "It's about an elite agent who's deep undercover and inadvertently falls for the daughter of the man he's pursuing. It's supposed to be good."

"Yeah, I've heard about that." Gavin sets the table, checks the oven, and continues talking with Josh in the kitchen.

Slightly quieter, Sophie asks, "So, how are things?" She raises her eyebrows and looks in the direction of the guys.

I take her hint and grin widely as I reply with a slight snicker, "Good and you?" Now eying Josh.

Sophie shakes her head and laughs lightly. "Making progress, I think."

Still slightly under my breath, I ask, "We didn't interrupt your plans this evening, did we?"

Louder than I expected, she says, "Oh, no. It was my idea to get together tonight. I thought you could use some fun." She leans forward and pats my good leg. "Gavin said you'd probably want some entertainment because you've been trapped with him for the past few weeks."

"Really?" I laugh loudly. "Maybe it's him who needs the fun!"

Sophie swats her hand at me. "Don't be too hard on him. He's just looking out for you. Besides, I've missed you since you've been here."

"Dinner's ready," Josh calls out as Gavin dishes each of us an enchilada. Thankfully, this brace bends a little so it's finally comfortable to sit in a regular chair, and I don't have to prop my leg up.

As soon as we're seated, Josh challenges, "So, ladies, what'll it be tonight? Guys versus girls?" He reaches over to high-five Gavin.

"We'll have to watch out for them." Sophie giggles. "They're two peas in a pod and share the same brainwaves."

"If you think we're too much for you, I'd be glad to be your partner, Sophie," Josh offers teasingly and puts his arm around her shoulder, drawing her in for a half hug.

"What?" I pretend my feelings are hurt. "No one wants to be my partner?" All three pair of eyes flash to mine, which smile deviously in return. Laughter explodes around the table.

Once everyone settles, Gavin takes a deep breath. "So it's you two against Alex and me." He looks for my approval, then adds, "If you haven't figured it out, she's quite competitive. Hope you brought your A-game." He chuckles as he pats my knee under the table and sends shivers up my spine.

"Always do." Sophie grins widely.

After we clean up dinner, we choose to play Cranium because it has a little of everything in it. As we set up at the kitchen table, I whisper my only concern to Gavin, "I hope you're good at charades because there's no way I'm going to be in this condition."

He winks in return and melts my heart. "Gotcha covered!"

It turns out, it's probably best the guys are on separate teams. Sophie and I both are dominant forces and probably would've won very quickly, or at least that's what we keep telling the guys when either of us guess an answer correctly. We rub it in any chance we get.

Throughout the entire game, I almost roll out of my seat in laughter. Josh, Gavin, and Sophie are hilarious to watch as they do their best to conquer the board. It's almost as if they know each other so well, they practically finish each other's sentences. In the rare moments I'm not actively engaging in the game, I see their closeness and am thrilled they consider me to be an equal among them. Even though we've only known each other for mere weeks, I'm certain this friendship will last.

Josh and Sophie end up winning, but only by one question. Sophie suggests we watch the movie before it gets too late, and she falls asleep. Josh warms up the apple pie and dishes the ice cream while Gavin and I go to the couch. Before I can get there, Gavin pulls the couch out from the wall so that everyone has a direct view of the television. I sit on the right end of the couch, and Sophie sits on the other.

"Do you want a chair, so you can prop your leg?" Gavin asks. Before I can respond, he also asks, "Mind if I sit on the floor in front of you?"

"Sure," I say, pulling my left leg in and extending my right out onto the chair. "Can you hand me my pillow?"

By the time Gavin starts the movie, Sophie scoots to the middle of the couch, and Josh takes the other end, after handing each of us our dessert.

Gavin grabs another pillow from his bed and uses it to prop himself up against the couch. As the movie starts, he nudges my leg and mouths, "You okay?"

I smile in assurance, and he settles in to watch the movie.

About halfway through the movie, I realize I need to

move, or my leg will be numb. I tap Gavin on the shoulder and whisper, "Excuse me, I need up."

He stands and offers his hand to help me up.

"Want us to stop the movie?" Sophie offers.

"No, thanks. I'm just needing to move. Gavin, you can sit on the couch if want," I suggest.

"I'm fine on the floor," he states.

"Then can I join you? My leg's going numb."

"Sure." He smiles and sits back on the floor, offering his hand for support as I make my way to the floor.

Sophie pulls her legs onto the couch. "Here, you guys can lean here."

"Thanks," Gavin and I say simultaneously. Gavin moves over a little, making room for me to lean back against the couch, and we continue the movie once again. I glance up at Sophie to make sure she has enough room. She winks in return and smiles.

When Gavin moves closer, I'm suddenly extremely aware of his every movement. He shifts again, and our arms touch one another. My heart races, not knowing what to do. I calm myself by taking a slow, deep breath. I hear a slight chuckle escape from Gavin. He reaches out and takes my hand. My eyes dart to his. He grins widely, intertwining our fingers, giving a quick squeeze before returning his attention to the movie.

Eventually, I relax and get into the movie again. By now, I'm a little tired, and my leg begins to ache. I sink further against the couch, getting more comfortable. Gavin lets go of my hand, and I look to see if something's wrong. He glances down and places his other hand in mine while the one closest to me surrounds my shoulders, pulling me closer to his chest. My body stiffens in response.

In a low whisper only I can hear, Gavin states, "You're tired. Relax."

He presses his head slightly onto mine as if he's kissing my head and squeezes me slightly. I let out a quiet sigh. After a few minutes of listening to his deep breathing and steady heartbeat, I do as he says. Turning slightly on my side, I sink further into his chest.

The next thing I know, Josh's standing to stretch. "Well, that was a great movie. Did you guys like it?"

"Yeah! My favorite part was when the girl found out he's an agent and protected him instead." Sophie laughs. "What about you, Alex?"

Sitting up abruptly so she wouldn't notice I'd fallen asleep, I just agree with her. "That part was amazing." I yawn and stretch as Gavin makes his way to his feet before helping me to a standing position. He points to my crutches, and I nod. "Thanks."

"Wow!" Josh suddenly roars. "It's already after midnight. Are you done with that final draft for our structures class? I'll have to spend most of tomorrow at the studio." Josh shakes his head and sighs.

"Um, I still have a few finishing touches. It shouldn't take me long."

"You guys will be at the game tomorrow, right?" Josh asks enthusiastically.

Gavin chuckles. "Of course. Why?"

"Let's meet at Sophie's, and I'll drive the two of you to the game," Josh eagerly suggests. "You can save our seats while I drop off my car and walk with Sophie."

"Sounds good." Gavin smiles.

"I'm not an invalid," I mutter. "I can walk, you know." I elbow Gavin in the side.

"Yeah," Gavin huffs out sarcastically. "And that worked out so well for you last time in the ice." He gives me a devious smile as if he's challenging me to argue.

I feel my jaw clench when I realize he's right. To spare myself from further embarrassment, I sigh in defeat. "Thank you for the ride, Josh."

"No problem," he replies as he gathers his things.

"We'd better get going. Thanks for having us, Gavin." Sophie walks over and hugs him. "See you tomorrow," she says as she hugs me.

"Anytime. I know you guys only come around for the food!" Gavin mocks.

"Well, someone has to eat it," Josh teases. "Got everything, Soph?"

"Just getting my purse." She walks to retrieve it as Josh waits to open the door for her.

"See you tomorrow," I call out as they exit Gavin's apartment.

"See you at the studio, Josh," Gavin calls out as he slips his arm around my waist from behind me just as the door shuts.

"Well, that went well," he whispers in my ear, pulling me closer to him.

"I had a lot of fun." I take in a deep breath and savor his musky scent and find myself in an uncontrollable yawn. "Did anyone notice I fell asleep?" I ask as embarrassment washes through me.

"Probably not. Your change in breathing was my only

clue." He gives me a tight squeeze from behind. "How are you feeling?"

"I'm tired and a little sore, but all right."

"Well." He points to the bed. "Get some sleep. I'll do the dishes before bed." He leans down and kisses my cheek before releasing his hold.

He suddenly looks a bit sheepish. "I... Uh... Hope you don't mind but after talking with Josh, I need to spend more time in the studio. Mind if I go in the morning?"

"Not at all. Will you drop me at my place? I need to do laundry and finish a project for children's lit. What time do you want to leave?"

"Let's just play it by ear and see what time we wake up." He snickers. "God knows you'll be up before the roosters."

Before I can protest, he bends to kiss me briefly on the lips, catching me off guard. "I had a great night, Alex. Thanks."

Thankful my crutches completely support my weight for the moment, I smile up at him. "Me, too!"

As soon as Gavin leaves my apartment to go to the studio, my phone rings. "Hello?"

"Hey, it's me," Sophie greets. "I just ran into Gavin outside. I'm not interrupting you, am I?"

"No. If you're not busy, why don't you come over. I could use your help."

Sophie coughs, and her tone fills with disbelief. "You're actually asking for help?"

"Yes." I laugh lightly. "I'm known to do that from time to time."

"What do you need?"

"I... Uh... was hoping you'd help me with laundry and help me pick out an outfit for tomorrow?"

Obviously confused, she asks, "What's tomorrow?"

"Gavin's taking me to Spokane," I state as nonchalantly as I can.

"What for?"

"He wants to take me on an official date!" I crack at the end, my excitement no longer contained.

She squeals to share in my excitement. "I knew it! I'll be right over." She hangs up before I can say anything else.

What does she know? The thought runs through my brain until I can ask her in person.

"What did you know?" I demand as soon as she enters my apartment.

"Ever since that first soccer practice, I knew you guys liked each other."

"What do you mean?" I say defensively, wondering what she's talking about.

"Well... You guys were so intense." She chuckles at the memory. "He'd asked where you worked, and Josh said they've been to the restaurant a few times. Also, I've NEVER seen Gavin ask around about a girl, so I figured he must be into you."

"You knew this... And didn't tell me?" I nearly screech in shock.

Sophie shrugs dismissively. "I tried, but you wouldn't listen."

Crap. She's right.

"You guys hang out all the time, so what's the big deal about tomorrow?"

I sigh, wondering where to begin. "Apparently, he'd planned on asking me out before my accident and wants this to be our official first date... One I choose to partake in, rather than feel obligated." Shaking my head at the thought, I laugh. "You're right, he's a gentleman."

"He has been since the day we met." She laughs, then clears her throat and continues, "It's really nice to see him happy. He deserves it." She pins her eyes on me. "And so do you!"

"Thanks." I smile sheepishly.

"Where's he taking you?" Sophie eagerly asks.

"Um, he wants it to be a surprise." I shake my head, realizing my mistake. "I should have at least asked him what I should wear."

"Well, that would've helped, but it might've ruined the surprise," Sophie teases.

Once inside my bedroom, Sophie insists I sit and let her pilfer through my closet. She quickly goes through the rest of my clothes, since there isn't much to begin with. "What about this?" She pulls out a long, black, A-line skirt that hangs just at my knees and a blue fitted sweater. "You could wear those cute, black leggings with the lace at the end that you wore for your sister's shower."

I nod in agreement. "Those should work."

"Here, try these on."

When I'm finished changing, I hobble over to the full-length mirror on the back of the bathroom door, without my crutches. It hurts but is manageable.

"You look great!" Sophie compliments.

I have to admit, it isn't bad. "Thanks for your help. I really appreciate it. What about those black flats near the back of my closet?"

"Those will be great, and you won't freeze to death if you're outside," Sophie teases. "Do you have any tights? They might be warmer than leggings."

"No," I sigh, liking the idea of my feet being warm.

"I'll take you to the mall if you'd like?"

The trip to the mall's relatively quick, since I find what I'm looking for at the first store. When we return to my apartment, Sophie helps me do my laundry as well as a few other chores. Around two, she goes home to finish some homework before the game.

At the game, it's absolutely freezing. Thankfully, I'm layered so only my face feels the fierce temperature. As we wait for Sophie and Josh to return, Gavin sets one blanket on the bench and leaves the other in the bag. He breaks open the hand warmers he bought for this occasion and suggests I place them in my boots before my toes have a chance to get cold.

"I won't need these tomorrow, will I?" I joke as I finish tying my shoe.

Gavin laughs loudly. "Nice try." He raises an eyebrow. "I'm not giving you any details." Placing his arm around me, he pulls me closer. "No, these won't be necessary."

"Good to know." I lean my head toward his chest and watch the players warm up on the field. It feels amazing to be in his arms.

Suddenly, we hear "Smile!" from Sophie who stands in the aisle and takes our picture. "Wow. This is great!" She looks at her screen, then plops down in front of me. I start to pull my leg back. "Oh, don't bother, Alex. There's plenty of room. I'll sit here so you can stretch out."

"Thanks again for dropping us off," Gavin says to Josh.

"It's the least we could do," Josh announces as the fight song begins, and we stand to sing along.

The entire first half of the game's a nail-biter. Both teams score two touchdowns, but the Cougs pull off a field goal in the final seconds. Oregon's a tough team, but we're holding our own. Just as the teams head for the locker room, Gavin whispers in my ear, "Don't talk about our lead to Josh, or he'll be worried they'll *Coug It.*" Confused about the term, I start to ask but Gavin places a gloved finger in the air and shakes his head before whispering, "Josh is *very* superstitious. I guess we all are." He hesitates for a moment then laughs quietly in my ear. "It means holding the lead until almost the end, only to end up losing."

"I see," I whisper back with a smile.

The remainder of the game's insane. I'm on my feet, cheering loudly as I've officially become a fan. Neither team scores until the last two minutes of the game. Oregon's on the forty-yard line, and their quarterback's about to be sacked. When all of a sudden, he throws a Hail Mary down the field, only to have us intercept it and run back for a touchdown. The crowd goes wild, especially when we get the field goal and lead by ten. Everyone jumps up and down, high-fives one another, and gives out hugs. Oregon miraculously scores a touchdown, with the extra point, but we're still ahead by three. When the Cougs receive the ball, everyone's on pins and needles until the clock slowly runs out, giving the Cougs a well-deserved victory.

I'm caught up in the moment when Gavin turns to

celebrate with a hug. My hands cup his face, and I plant a kiss squarely on his lips. He tastes delicious, like hot cocoa and Gavin all wrapped up into one. The next thing I know, I'm off the ground as Gavin's arms wrap around my waist to close the distance between us. When I finally pull back to take a breath of air, Gavin smiles devilishly and asks, "Are you a fan yet?"

14

FIRST DATE

THE NEXT MORNING, I actually sleep in. When I look at the clock, I have to do a double-take because I'm sure it has to be wrong. I roll over and stretch quietly, not wanting to wake Gavin.

"Good morning, sleepyhead," Gavin's deep voice calls from across the room, sending chills up my spine, though I'm not cold. I'm surprised to find him at the kitchen table, fully dressed in a pair of khakis and a black V-neck sweater, reading a textbook. "Ready for breakfast?"

"Sure," I say as I take in how handsome he is.

"Want to take off after breakfast?"

"I guess I'd better get ready then," I tease.

"I'll just finish this chapter, then make breakfast. French toast and bacon okay?"

"Wow! Cold cereal is fine, too."

"I'm in the mood for French toast." He smiles once before going back to his book.

Unfortunately, I take a lot longer than normal to get

ready. My hair takes forever to lie flat around my shoulders. I place a small French braid along the side in the front to keep it out of my face. Though I've never worn makeup in front of Gavin, I put on eye shadow, mascara, and lip gloss. I figure if I'm in for a penny, I might as well go in for a pound. We will only have one first date.

When I maneuver out of the bathroom without my crutches, I'll admit I'm extremely embarrassed for taking so long. But my efforts are worth it when my eyes land on Gavin.

"Wow," Gavin whispers as he crosses the room. "You're definitely worth the wait." He bends down and kisses me lightly on the cheek, making my knees go weak and my heart race. "You're beautiful." He holds out a bouquet of flowers. "These are for you."

Shocked at his apparent effort, I simply tilt my head up toward his and smile. "Thanks. They're beautiful." They are a mixture of roses, carnations, and some other flower in various colors. I take a deep breath and sniff, letting their fragrance saturate me. *How did I not notice those?* "Wait, when did you get these?"

Gavin's smile shines. "Yesterday, while I was out."

I smile gratefully and whisper, "Wow! You're amazing."

"I have moments." He cracks a devious smile, reaching his arm around my waist to assist me in walking easily toward the table. "Let's eat."

The drive to Spokane passes with ease. Gavin and I listen to music and fill it with casual conversation. Well, it was casual until Gavin's tone changes dramatically.

"You know what's funny?" Gavin chuckles to himself.

"No." Intrigued with the sudden change of tone, I eagerly ask, "What?"

Gavin reaches for my hand and intertwines our fingers. "Remember the day of your accident?" He winces at the memory, but smooths into a serene smile. "My plan was to call you after I got coffee. Then I saw you... I was working up the courage to talk to you."

"Why?" I whisper, tracing the contours of his hand with my free hand.

"Well..." A nervous laugh escapes. "I've already told you this, but I wanted to ask you out so I could get to know you better. I had it all planned out."

Putting it all together, I ask, "So today?"

"It's basically what I had planned," he admits, "but with a few modifications."

"Modifications?" I raise my eyebrows in interest.

"Well, I wasn't exactly planning on you being here for breakfast. It's a little hard to surprise you when I'm with you all the time." He glances toward me and winks. "Thankfully, Sophie made it so I could get a few things done without you knowing."

"You planned that, too?" I spit out.

"No. Sophie was coming to visit you already, but I used the time to finish a few things."

Speaking of Sophie, my conversations with her and Erin and their apparent knowledge of Gavin's social life replay in my mind. I almost let it drop, but curiosity gets the best of me. "So... You were going to ask me out?" Nerves battle in my stomach, and I almost let the subject drop.

"Uh." He glances at me from the side. "I just said that." He then turns to read my face for a second. "Why?"

"But you don't do that often," I state quietly.

"This is the first time I've asked you on an actual date." Confusion fills his features, but he adds, "I hope it won't be the last." He glances over to read my expression further.

"Um, that's not what I meant," I sigh. *How do I say this?*

"Alex?" he questions. When I don't respond right away, he adds, "I'm not following you." His eyes burrow together as he appears to concentrate.

Where do I begin? "Well…" I take a deep breath. "I was under the impression dating isn't something you do often."

"It isn't," he states matter-of-factly and glances once again in my direction before returning his eyes to the road.

"Then…" I begin hesitantly, "why me?" I look down at our hands as I wait for his answer.

Gavin shakes the car with laughter. "I haven't been able to get you off my mind." He takes a deep breath and calms himself. "You made a good impression."

I gasp as the memory. My voice drips with sarcasm. "Who wouldn't remember being plowed over and wearing coffee all day. I wouldn't forget that either."

A deep chortle escapes before Gavin exclaims, "That is something to remember! Especially how mortified you looked when you realized I was next to you in geology. But that's not what I'm referring to."

What does he mean? I quietly mull over the events of that first day. "I don't know what you mean," escapes in a low whisper.

"Well, it's a combination of things." Gavin smiles widely, glancing in my direction before returning his eyes to the road. "Though you're strong willed and quite stubborn when you want to be, you're also smart, strong, independent, and have a good direction of where you're going in life. Aside from myself, you're probably one of the most competitive people I know, not to mention you're an amazing athlete. You're also kind, compassionate, and self-less. On top of all that, you're one of the most beautiful people I've ever met."

Gavin inhales quickly as he watches the road. After a few moments, he continues, "When I'm around you, I feel different. Like... something I've never felt before. It's almost as if I'm completely unhinged and yet stronger at the same time. It's hard to explain." He shakes his head as if he's searching for the right words. "When I'm not around you, I find myself thinking about you. Sure, I've had crushes on people before, who hasn't? It's never felt anything like this..."

His eyes flash toward mine for a fraction of a second, then back to the road. "At first, I thought I was being ridiculous. There's no way you'd feel the same. When I couldn't take it anymore, I was determined to find out one way or another by asking you out." He takes a deep breath and sighs.

"But then that car came out of nowhere, and you were sent flying across the pavement..." Gavin shakes his head from side to side slowly. "This may sound weird, but after I knew you were okay, it was almost impossible not to tell you how I felt. I was worried you wouldn't feel the same..."

"But that didn't happen," I interrupt quietly.

"I know!" Gavin is suddenly ecstatic. "For some strange reason, you actually like me, too!"

"But I was such a freak when we first met. I barely kept

my thoughts coherent," I admit fervently. "I'm surprised you didn't think I was a klutz or a bad omen at the least."

"Don't take this the wrong way. I'd never want anything to happen to you, but I have to admit I've enjoyed spending time with you. Yes, at first, it was out of obligation, but after the first day or so, that's hardly the case. How could you not see I was falling for you?" Gavin takes in a deep breath and almost nervously laughs. "So, in a way, I'm actually kind of glad this accident of yours brought us together."

"You are?" I blurt out. "I've been worried you'll be sick of me."

"Hardly," Gavin scoffs as he exits the highway and merges onto a freeway toward Spokane. "Sure, I wish it would have been under better circumstances. I don't know how most relationships work, but this fast track we've been on is definitely one worth riding. I wouldn't have changed a thing. Would you?"

I take a moment to think about his revelation. A part of me is in awe of his feelings. Sure, I'd prefer to be injury free, but I don't think we would've connected this way if I hadn't. I sigh and admit with a smile, "No. No, I wouldn't." He squeezes my hand again and my nerve endings are on hyperdrive. To calm myself, I take a moment to look out the window.

Spokane's much bigger than I realized. Tall, brick buildings line the freeway and the side streets are congested the way I would expect in a busy city. We drive a few blocks and turn toward the convention center. I'm a little shocked when we pull into the Double Tree parking lot. "We're going to a hotel?"

"Technically. Though we're only going to a restaurant

inside the lobby." He parks his car in one of the closest spots and is out to help me within moments. "You'll want your coat, it's chilly out here." Like the gentleman he is, Gavin assists me with my jacket before handing my crutches to me. As we enter the lobby, he directs me to a restaurant in the corner called Spencer's. Gavin gives his name to the hostess. She shows us to a cozy booth at the far end of the room, handing us our menus once we're settled.

Looking over the pricey menu, I'm unsure what to order. I can't believe Gavin's taking me here for a first date. I'd be fine with a home-cooked meal, as long as I spent time with him.

"Anything look good?" Gavin looks up from his menu and smiles.

"Um, how did you hear of this place?" I ask, still trying to decide.

"It was my parents' favorite restaurant. Dad still makes us stop when he's in town."

"Oh." *What do I say?* Butterflies churn in my stomach as it sinks in. *This is his parents' favorite restaurant.*

"They have killer steaks and the potatoes can double as footballs. I'd love to split one with you. There's no way I can eat one myself, but the potato bar's fantastic."

The waiter comes to explain about the specials and takes our order.

When the waiter leaves, I whisper, "You know you didn't have to do all this?"

Gavin raises an eyebrow in my direction. "Um, yeah, I did. I only get one chance to make a good impression, and I want to make every moment count."

"I already have a good impression." I return his smile.

"So you're good there." I can't help but giggle as I find myself being drawn deep into his eyes.

"Maybe." He quietly laughs. "But I'm not taking any chances."

When our food comes, the portions are huge. I'm thankful we're splitting the potato because it takes up half my large plate, and the toppings from the portable potato bar are heaping. Gavin offers to share his asparagus which I eagerly accept. The moment I bite into my steak, my mouth waters as the flavor explodes. This could easily become my favorite restaurant, too. Gavin's parents have amazing taste.

As we leave the restaurant, Gavin asks if I'd like to walk through the park.

I pull out my gloves and headband ear warmers from my jacket pocket and put them on before going any further as Gavin pulls out a black hat and gloves from his.

We cross over a wooden bridge, and I suddenly hear water gushing. Spokane Falls is beautiful as it rushes under us. We walk to the middle of the bridge and stop to take it all in. His arms slowly envelop me from behind, settling around my waist. I close my eyes, savoring the moment. This has to be the best first date, ever.

After what feels like only a few moments, Gavin sighs. "Let's keep going. You don't want hypothermia." Keeping one hand on the small of my back, he gently leads me in the direction we came. Instead of going back to the hotel though, he guides me down a path further into the park. I look up to him for clarification, and he simply smiles. We walk until I see a large building. Upon further inspection, it's an IMAX theater.

"Up for a movie?" Gavin sheepishly grins as we walk

toward the ticket counter. I nod in approval, and he gets us tickets. I have no idea what's playing, but if this is what he's planned, I'm more than eager to go along for the ride.

"Want popcorn or something to drink?" he asks as we enter the theater. I can't stand the thought of eating anything, for fear I'd burst, so I politely decline. He gets a large Coke and some napkins before ushering me down a hallway. We enter the theater from the top of the auditorium, hobble down a few rows, then make our way to our seats. He takes off his jacket, laying it in the seat next to him before assisting me with mine.

Gavin takes my hand as we settle in to watch the movie. As the movie starts, Gavin pulls my hand up to his mouth and kisses it lightly, sending shivers down my spine. *How can something so innocent have such an effect on me?* Before lowering it, he lifts the armrest between us, placing it behind us and pulls me closer to him. I instinctively lean my head toward his chest, and we watch the movie.

I suspiciously glance to Gavin when the opening credits roll. It's based on a Nicholas Sparks movie.

He whispers with an innocent smile, "You seemed to like the last one." He motions to the cupholder he's filled with napkins. "Don't worry, I've got you covered."

True to form, the movie draws me in. As Gavin predicted, I tear up. Unless you're emotionally stunted, who wouldn't? Thankfully, he doesn't say anything but squeezes me lightly. I don't think I could like him anymore than I do at this moment.

As we walk back to his car, Gavin states, "This isn't really part of the date, but would you mind stopping by the mall? I need to get a present for my niece. Her birthday's coming, and there isn't much of a selection near Pullman."

How sweet. "How old is she?"

He opens my door to his car. "She'll be three."

"What do you want to get her?" I think, running through ideas of my own.

"Liz says she's really into dress-up and princesses." He rolls his eyes and shakes his head.

Laughing, "What little girl isn't? That should be pretty easy to find, especially with the holidays coming up."

"Speaking of holidays, what are your plans for Thanksgiving break?"

"Um… probably going home and hanging out." Suddenly, I remembered my mother's invitation. "You're welcome to come for Thanksgiving. Mom wanted to make sure you knew you're invited. Don't feel obligated. I told her you likely had plans with your family."

"Hummm." Gavin's expression is unreadable.

"What?" I call out.

"Well… I was just about to invite you to my family's cabin for Thanksgiving. We'd spend the remainder of the weekend there before returning to school." His eyes widen as he waits for my response.

Without thinking it through, "Okay," comes out slowly, and a smile spreads across my face.

"Are you planning to go to Apple Cup?"

"Uh, yeah. It's only the biggest game of the year."

"What would you say to me driving you home Sunday and picking you back up on Wednesday. Then we'd only have one car."

"Um…" Suddenly, the extent of his invitation sinks in. "Gavin, when you say family, who exactly do you mean?"

"Just my dad, brother, and my sister's family. Maybe my grandparents, but I'm not sure yet. They don't like to drive in bad weather."

"Where exactly is your cabin? Will we be camping?" I say hesitantly.

"Oh, just outside of Leavenworth. No, we won't be camping. It's got running water, electricity, and all the amenities of home." He snickers and bends down to kiss me lightly on the lips. "We've had it since I was a kid. I've spent a lot of summers and vacations there."

"Just checking."

Our trip to the mall is short. We quickly find a fancy dress for Gretchen, and Gavin insists on buying her a tiara to go with it. When we return to the car, I realize I'm starting to get hungry again. "Hey, Gavin, can I treat you to dinner?" I tease as he helps me into the car.

"You must be reading my mind." He shuts the door and walks to the driver's side. "But, the day's still mine to plan," he teases with delight. "You can have your turn next time."

He puts the car in drive without giving me any further clues as to what he has in store for me. We drive silently back downtown toward the convention center. We turn on a side street and stop outside of the restaurant called The Onion. As we walk in, I notice the restaurant's busy, but we don't have to wait to be seated. We order burgers and fries and continue a casual conversation throughout the meal, oblivious to anything around us.

When we leave, I'm surprised to find it's started snowing. A thick blanket has covered the sidewalk and is accumulating on the trees next to Gavin's car. "It's so beautiful," I whisper in awe, taking in my surreal surroundings.

"Yeah," Gavin states apprehensively as he places his hand on the small of my back as if ready to catch me at any minute. "Are you doing okay with those crutches?"

"I'm fine," I begin but stop when my right crutch slides about an inch. "Maybe I should hand you these and just walk without them?"

Gavin reaches out his arm as I hand him my crutches while placing his other arm firmly around my waist before we take another step. He lets out a low chuckle. "Well, there's some advantages to not using these." He squeezes me lightly, and we continue to the car.

As we reach his car, Gavin unexpectedly turns to face me. Using the full force of his delicious, golden-brown eyes, he stops me in my tracks. He cracks a slight smile and leans the crutches against the car. Without saying a word, he brushes a strand of hair from my face and rests his warm hand behind my neck. He bends down slowly and kisses me gently on the lips.

I completely lose myself in the moment. I don't care that it's snowing, the street's crowded, or that it hurts to stand. I throw my arms around his neck, running my fingers through the back of his hair, and I pull myself closer to him. To make up for the height difference, Gavin pulls me up by the waist so that my feet dangle in the air as he kisses me passionately. A loud horn blasts from behind us, and Gavin pulls his face away breathlessly. An enormous smile fills his features, and he leans forward to kiss me once again lightly before setting me down on the ground.

He pulls me in for a hug as he whispers, "Alex, we should probably get going."

I groan slightly, still holding onto him. "If you insist," I murmur.

He bends down to kiss me lightly on the cheek and hugs me one last time before releasing me with a throaty chuckle. "Trust me," he shakes his head and rolls his eyes, "I'd rather not stop, but I think we'd better get on the road before the weather gets much worse." He points his finger to the sky to remind me about the snow.

The snow is heavier as we head south. By the time we reach Pullman, everything is as if it's asleep on a cloud. The thick layer of snow illuminates in the darkness on the surrounding hills. The city streets themselves have recently been plowed, and Gavin maneuvers the way to his apartment with ease.

Gavin quickly climbs out of his car and assists me to his door. Instead of going for my crutches in the back seat, he patiently waits for me to feel comfortable standing. "Do you want to try it now?" he asks, looking unsure of my decision.

"The more practice the better." I shrug as I pull my jacket around myself tighter. Gavin slips an arm around my waist, and we walk toward the door. Though it's warmer than I expect, I cringe in shock when the snow melts quickly into my tights. I'm definitely wearing boots on both feet tomorrow.

Gavin unlocks the door, still holding onto my waist, and we step into a warm burst of air. He shuts the door behind us and offers to take my jacket as we reach his kitchen table. Laying both of our jackets over separate chairs, he then quickly returns to where I'm standing. "Can I get you anything?"

"Um..." I hesitate, not wanting to end our official date early. "Would you be offended if I excuse myself and take off these wet tights?"

He suddenly looks down and sees fluffy snow still clinging to my tights. "You should have said something."

I resist making a smart comeback and simply turn to limp toward the bathroom. When I pass his bed, I take off my brace. Within a few minutes, I return from the bathroom to find Gavin still standing in the kitchen, looking over his mail. He puts it down as I reenter the room, greeting me with his gorgeous smile.

"Feel better?" he asks as he closes the gap between us.

Though I feel unsteady without my brace or crutches, I do find it easier to walk toward him than the last time I walked on my own. Once I meet the full force of his eyes, I can hardly think of anything but being near him. With only a few long strides, he stands before me, penetrating me with his dazzling, golden-brown eyes. I can hardly remember my name, let alone his question. I take in a deep breath, but nothing comes out.

"Alex, are you okay?" Concern is evident on his face.

"What?" I take another short breath, regaining conscious thought. "Oh... uh... I'm fine," I manage in a whisper.

He places one hand on my shoulder as if to steady me. "Are you sure?" he prods, still looking somewhat skeptical.

"Gavin, I'm fine," I manage in my strongest voice.

He stares at me for a moment longer as if he's assessing my response before his eyes relax, and he's back to simply being smoldering. He takes a deep breath and softly whispers, "It's been an unbelievable day. Thank you."

"You've definitely made an impression." The words barely escape my lips as I bring my hand up to push his dampened hair out of his face. I trace my hand along his jawline and rest it on his chest, shifting my weight onto my good leg, bringing me closer to him.

"That was the goal," he teases as he lightly places his arms around me. He slowly bends and kisses me softly on the lips before pulling only his head back to continue to look me in the eyes.

I take in a deep breath and savor his musky scent as I run my hand along his broad, muscular chest, confined in his sweater. He's irresistible. I find myself pulling him closer with my free hand. As I tilt my head up to reach my lips to his, I find it's not much of an effort because he's closed the gap between us. His lips move slow and sensual as they press against mine. They linger in just the right places, intoxicating my every breath. My heart pumps through my chest as I reach firmly for his neck and pull myself even closer to him. I can't get enough of him.

As if reading my mind, Gavin lifts me effortlessly off the floor. I pull my good leg up and lock it around his waist as my other rests on his hip to keep my lips at the same level as his. One arm clings to his shoulder while my other hand caresses the back of his hair.

When we're both gasping for air, Gavin holds me tightly as his lips trace across my cheekbone and bury into the crevice of my neck. Slowly, I release my hold on his waist, and he sets me down. I rest my head upon his chest. As I fight to regain control of my breath, I feel my heartbeat between my ears, instead of his. When my breathing is under control, I look up to find a beaming smile reaching Gavin's eyes, welcoming me. "Wow," he whispers softly as he pecks me once again on the lips.

I suddenly feel nervous and bite my lower lip as my eyes widen. "Yeah," I whisper in return while we continue to stare wordlessly at one another for another long moment.

Gavin finally breaks the silence with a smirk. "So, I take it you're okay?"

It takes me a moment to remember the question he asked earlier. "Yeah." I smile widely and feel my cheeks continue to burn. "I'm definitely okay."

With a hint of sarcasm, he says, "You definitely leave an impression." Gavin grins smugly as he awaits my reaction.

"I… Umm… Don't… Ummm," I sputter. But Gavin places his index finger over my mouth, stepping closer to me.

Gavin whispers tenderly, "Don't worry so much, Alexis. It was…" He releases his finger and moves his hand to my chin as he pulls me closer to him and kisses me lightly on the lips. "Absolutely amazing."

"I couldn't agree more." I take in a ragged breath and slowly exhale.

15

BACK TO THE DAILY GRIND

JUST AS I slam the door to my apartment, my phone rings. I groan in frustration as I locate it. From the caller ID, I see it's Katherine. Sighing into the phone, I say, "Hey, Kate."

"And hello to you, too!" she mocks. She knows me too well. "Having a bad day?"

"Uggh! You could say that." I hobble across the room to the couch and plop myself onto it before saying anything else. I take off my brace and throw it on the floor beside me.

"What happened?" she demands.

"What didn't happen?" I snip at her. I take in a jagged, deep breath before unloading. "It snowed last night so Gavin and I took the bus this morning, which was fine. I've found my crutches are useless in the snow, so I just wore my brace instead. Once again, not a problem. All was going well at my first class. But after that, I didn't manage to make it to the other three on time. Most of my professors were understanding, but it's embarrassing walking in late and having to hobble to my seat."

"I'm sure they understand." Katherine tries to sound encouraging.

I ignore her comment to continue my rant. "I managed to soak myself on the way to my last class because I slipped on the ice and slid down a small hill, landing in a pile of snow." I hear a giggle escape from Katherine but again, ignore it. "This poor guy stopped to help me, and we both slipped and fell twice before we could stand." I feel myself fume at the memory of this. "UGGGAHH! He laughed it off and thankfully no one was hurt, but I had to walk even slower to my last class, making me even later! Not to mention the fact I had to sit in wet clothes for an hour."

I hear Katherine stifle another snicker on the other end, which only infuriates me further. "Then it took me almost an hour to get back to my apartment!" I'm practically yelling by this point.

Katherine's quiet for a long moment, giving me time to calm down before quietly stating, "I thought Gavin drove you to and from campus."

"He has been but since we took the bus, I told him I'd just meet him here, not realizing it would be that difficult." I groan again in frustration. "Apparently, I was wrong!"

Katherine laughs again, putting me in my place, the way only a sister can. "Oh, Alex, you're so stubborn!"

"What do you mean?" My hackles rising.

"I mean, you're too strong for your own good. It wouldn't hurt you to ask for help once in a while. Or did you even think about that?"

"What did I need help for?"

"You do have other friends at school, right? You could've asked one of them to drive you back to your apartment."

"They all have classes, too!" I sharply retort, trying not to see her side of the argument.

Katherine lets out a heavy sigh. "Alex, you could have waited on campus for them."

"I just wanted to be home," I begrudgingly huff out.

"Well, you're home. Are you happy now?" Katherine teases, and another chortle escapes from her mouth.

As I stew about my response, I decide it's best to change the subject. Kate's not the one I'm infuriated at. I shouldn't take it out on her. "So..." I take a deep breath to relax. "Was there a reason for your call?"

"Yes, brat. When are you coming home next week?" Her tone is much less antagonizing.

"Well..." I sink further into the couch. "Apple Cup is Saturday, so we'll be home Sunday."

Katherine doesn't miss a beat. "We?" she asks skeptically.

"Um, Gavin's coming home with me for the first few days of break."

"Oh." I can hear the surprise in her voice. "I thought you'd be able to drive by then. Mom will be thrilled to have him here for Thanksgiving."

Nervously, I shake my head and come straight out with it. I might as well have a practice run before I break the news to Mom. "Actually, he's asked me to spend Thanksgiving with him and his family at their cabin in Leavenworth." I wait for my information to sink in and prepare myself for the barrage of questions I'm sure is to follow.

"I thought you were *just friends* with Gavin," Katherine states, mockingly. I'm sure there's an enormous grin forming around her mouth. "Apparently, things have changed since you were home last." A faint snicker escapes.

"Yeah, well, you could say that." I laugh nervously, hoping I'll be able to get away with divulging as few details as possible. Knowing Katherine's persistence, I'm sure I'll eventually tell her almost everything she wants to know.

"Hummm…" she sighs into the phone, and I can tell she's winding up. "Enough to meet his family, eh? Things must be pretty serious." My silence only prompts more questions from her. "Just how serious are they, Alex?" Katherine demands.

Where do I begin? "I don't know. I mean… We've only been hanging out and officially have gone on one date, but it's heading in that direction."

"What do you mean officially?"

"It's a funny story really." I can't help but laugh at the memory, "Um… Gavin was about to ask me out and had this whole date planned on the day of my accident. Of course, you know that didn't happen."

"Okay," she slowly states. "I still don't get what you mean by official then." Though it's a statement, it sounds more like a question.

I shake my head, remembering she hasn't exactly been privy to the past few weeks, so I have to backtrack.

"Well, he didn't ask me out or anything at first because he felt I was already being forced to be with him. He wanted to make sure I had an option of being with him. But that all kind of changed on our way back from your shower."

"Why? What happened on the way home?"

"Long story short. We admitted to liking each other." I shake my head at the memory.

Katherine takes a deep breath but doesn't say anything. I brace myself for what she may come up with. After another few seconds, she finally asks, "So why did you need to go on an *'official date'* then?"

Grinning as I remember Gavin's explanation, I explain, "This probably won't make a lot of sense to you, but it just has to do with how he was raised. I have to admit, it was the best date I've ever been on!" I almost squeal in excitement by the end. I find myself wanting to reveal my favorite moments from yesterday.

"So what did you guys do?" she eagerly prompts.

I spend the next few minutes going over every detail of my date. Though if given the choice, I probably would've revealed far less, but she pumps me with questions and being too caught up in the moment, I divulge almost everything. I do, however, keep my reactions to everything to a minimum, wanting to keep some of my favorite memories from yesterday only for me.

"So all you did was kiss and go to bed?" Kate finally asks, though she insinuates as if there may be more.

"Yep." I smile, still remembering every moment.

"Your own bed? By yourself?"

"Yes," I slowly state, but it sounds more like a question. Why does she assume there is more?

"Just checking, though I wouldn't blame you if you did. Gavin's gorgeous, romantic, and quite the gentleman."

"Yes, quite the gentleman," I forcibly remind her of that point. "It isn't like that, Kate. You know I've never..." I blush with embarrassment. Why would she even think such a thing?

"You can't blame me for asking," Kate teases cheerfully. "Being together almost twenty-four-seven for three weeks, a lot could happen!"

"Gavin's been nothing but a perfect gentleman."

"So… Is there chemistry?" Kate probes.

I can't help but giggle. "Oh, that's not a problem. Trust me," I sigh and flashbacks of last night play through my mind. I sigh at the memory as a smile spreads across my face. "There's definitely a strong connection."

"What?" Kate asks as if she thinks there's something I'm holding back.

"I don't know." I take a moment to figure out how to put what I feel into words. "It's not just a physical connection… it's much more. I… I've never felt this way about anyone. It's almost as if I'm completely unhinged, yet stronger at the same time. It's hard to explain…" I trail off, still trying to find the right word, I use Gavin's from last night.

"Do you know how he feels?" Kate sincerely asks.

"I think so… though it's hard to believe he could possibly feel the same." I shake my head at this realization.

"Alex, you didn't see the way he looks at you." She laughs before continuing. "AND that was a few weeks ago!"

"If you say so." My sarcasm's thick.

"Oh!" Kate suddenly exclaims. "I just realized I'm supposed to pick up Maggie to get the bridesmaid shoes."

The thought of those three-inch, spiked heels makes me cringe. "You're going to kill us all, you know."

She dismisses my worry with a loud laugh. "You'll be fine. Don't worry. See you this weekend!"

"Okay, tell Mom I'll call her later about my plans." I take in a deep breath as exhaustion takes over me. "I'm ready for a nap."

I wake to the sound of my front door being unlocked. Knowing it's Gavin, I stay settled on the couch. When he enters the living room only a few short seconds later, a wide grin spreads across his face.

Unfortunately, I greet him with a yawn.

A loud chuckle fills the room. "How was your day?" Gavin asks sincerely.

"Okay," I state, not wanting to relive the memories any further. "How was yours?"

He comes over to the couch, and I sit up to make room for him. "Mind if I join you?" Gavin asks as he stands where my head once was.

"You can lie back down, if you want. I have some amazing news!" He motions for me to lie my head back against his chest once he's settled. He grins while I shift myself to get into a comfortable position.

"What?" My curiosity is aroused.

"Well, I just found out I've been placed at the University in Florence next spring!"

"Florence, Italy! I've always wanted to go there! *Ho seniti to Firenze è sorprendente!*"

Gavin's eyes are wide in astonishment. "Excuse me?"

"I've heard Florence is amazing!" I translate for him.

"You speak fluent Italian?" he asks, still obviously shocked.

"Um, I'd hardly say fluent, but I could probably get around." I shrug. *"Dove è lastanza da bagno?"*

"And that would be?" Gavin mocks.

"Where's the bathroom?" I shrug again.

"Wow, who needs a dictionary when I've got you. I wonder if I could get a suitcase big enough for you to fit in?" he teases as he bends down to kiss me lightly on the lips.

"You never cease to amaze me." He plays with a few strands of my hair.

I roll my eyes, shaking my head slightly. "I have moments."

"Anything interesting happen today?" He smiles conspiratorially.

"Not really. I talked with Kate before taking a nap."

"Oh, James must've been mistaken then." He raises an eyebrow at me with a suddenly accusing look, which confuses me. "I was under the impression you may have gone for an interesting ride?"

My face burns in mortification, but I try to keep my composure. "He told you that, did he?" I neither confirm nor deny the accusation.

"He said you were all right, but that you'd found a faster way to get down the hill." Though Gavin holds a straight face, I can tell he's near the point of convulsing with laughter.

"Oh," is all I can say if I want to keep my same composure.

"He was going to offer you help, but someone else beat him to it. By the time he would have been able to help, you two were actually standing, and you were stalking off in the other direction."

I bury my face in my hands, too embarrassed to look at him. "It was so awful. One minute, I was moving along at my already gimpish pace, and the next, I was on my backside about fifteen feet down the hill into a big pile of snow."

Gavin squeezes me tight, bending down to whisper, "I'm

just glad you're all right." He kisses my forehead lightly and waits for me to face him.

After a few more seconds, I pull my hands from my face and find his eyes suddenly locked onto mine. "Thanks," I whisper. We sit here in silence for some time while Gavin runs his fingers through the back of my hair. I could stay like this for an eternity and still be just as content. Eventually, my stomach rumbles, breaking the silence, and I bite my lower lip from embarrassment.

Gavin grins widely. "Want to head back to my place for dinner?"

"I'm sure we can scrounge something here," I tease, not remembering what's available. I start to get up, but Gavin pulls me to him in a gentle hug.

"I didn't mean this instant," he whispers and laughs lightly into my ear. He kisses me lightly on the forehead, and I feel myself relax. "So how was the rest of your day?"

I tell him about the papers I have due as well as a project. He reminds me we have another quiz in geology to study for as well as a lab module.

"When do you want to go to the library for that?" I ask, realizing there isn't a lot of time before we leave for break.

"We could go tonight?" Gavin shrugs then adds, "If you're up to it. Then we'll go back to my place and start our other homework."

"Only if we drive to campus. I'm not walking back to campus today," I insist.

Gavin chuckles and agrees. "So, Alex, what do you have in there to eat?"

THE NEXT MORNING, Gavin meets me outside my first class to walk to geology together. As I approach, confusion fills my face. "How did you get here so fast?"

He adjusts my hat and brushes a strand of hair under the side before bending forward to brush a quick kiss across my lips, making my heart race. He takes my arm in his. "I had an exam this morning, so we got out early. Thought you might want some company." He raises an eyebrow in my direction, waiting for an argument.

How does he know me so well? If I wasn't afraid of falling on my backside, I'd protest. Snow covers the campus and where it began to melt yesterday, slabs of ice have replaced it. The sky's crystal blue and the sun shines brightly, making me squint as we exit the building. I shiver as the cold hits me like a wrecking ball. "I thought the sun would make it warmer," I protest as I grip a hold of Gavin tighter, not wanting to fall.

"Um." Gavin snickers. "No clouds means it's too cold for snow," he informs me regretfully. "Should make for an interesting game this weekend."

"I'll bet." We walk over another icy patch in the road, and I take a moment to fully concentrate before continuing. "Want to eat again at my place tonight?"

"Sounds good. I need to go into the studio for a couple of hours. Would seven be too late for dinner?"

"Not at all. I'll make a casserole and finish my paper. Hopefully, I'll also get the chance to do a few things around my apartment that I've been neglecting, too."

As soon as class is over and we have bundled ourselves up, Gavin reaches for my hand. We walk slowly out of the lecture hall. When we're out of the building, Gavin asks, "Can I bring your car back to campus after I drop you off?"

"Why wouldn't you? It's not like I can drive it," I quickly retort, pointing to my brace.

"Thanks. It'll save me a ton of time. Need anything from the store? I need to pick up a few things."

"Other than groceries, I think I'm good. Thanks for asking." We arrive at my 4-Runner, and Gavin realizes he needs to scrape the windshield before we can go.

"Why don't you get in and start it. I'll start scraping," Gavin suggests, handing me the keys. It only takes a few minutes since Gavin can reach nearly across the entire windshield.

Not wanting to work on my paper just yet, I spend some time cleaning my apartment. I make dinner, so that all I have to do is put the casserole in the oven. Then I clean my bathroom and sweep the apartment. I eventually pull out my paper and get to work. Just as I'm finishing, there's a knock at my door.

Sophie greets me with a smile and a hug. "I ran into Gavin on campus. He said you'd be home this afternoon. I'm not interrupting anything, am I?"

"No, not at all. Come in."

"So… How was your date?"

Stopping in my tracks, I turn to face Sophie. "It was absolutely amazing!"

"Really, what did you do?" she probes eagerly.

I tell her everything. Like Kate, Sophie asks multiple questions, pulling out just as much if not more information.

When I finish, she squeals, "Oh, Alex, I'm so excited for you! You guys deserve each other! I've always known Gavin to be a gentleman, but I never imagined how far he'd go. Wow… That's an amazing first date!"

"I know!" I can't help but reel in the excitement of my memories. Especially the ones I've kept to myself. "He's unbelievable!" I linger on my thoughts a while longer before realizing Sophie's still smiling at me. "What?" I say a little defensive.

"It's nothing." She smiles. "I can tell you really like him, that's all."

"That obvious, huh?" I suddenly feel a little self-conscious.

"Oh, Alex." She laughs loudly. "I've known probably before you even knew yourself!"

"What do you mean?" I demand.

"Even before your accident, I could tell something was going on… Don't worry. I know he didn't have any idea. I kept my opinions to myself." She smiles and shrugs dismissively.

Knowing there's no point in denying it, I sigh. "I've never felt this way about anyone. I never in my wildest dreams imagined I would find someone like him."

"He's quite the catch," Sophie agrees cheerfully.

"Speaking of catches, how are things going with Josh?" I probe eagerly.

Now, it's Sophie's turn to blush. I'm unsure how to take her reaction, so I wait for her response. She suddenly grins widely. "They, too, have taken an unexpected turn!" She shakes her head in disbelief, leaving me unsure of what's going on.

"So???" I probe.

Still shaking her head. "Well, after a lengthy discussion…

We finally admitted we've felt something for one another for quite some time but were afraid of it changing our friendship."

"And?" I prompt her, still unsure of the outcome.

"We've decided to risk it!" She beams, suddenly no longer containing her excitement.

"That's wonderful. You would've internally combusted if you didn't tell him how you felt soon," I tease as I walk over and hug her. "I'm so happy for you!"

"He'll be over later to hang out after he finishes at the studio."

"Have you eaten?" I ask when I realize it's almost time to set the casserole into the oven.

"No, I'm waiting for Josh."

"I've made plenty of casserole if you want to join us for dinner. Gavin's supposed to be here around seven. Then we're just going back to his place to study for a geology exam."

Sophie looks at me hesitantly. "Are you sure? I wouldn't want to interrupt."

Shaking my head in disbelief. "Sophie, I wouldn't have asked if you were. Besides, it's not like Gavin and I haven't seen each other every day for almost three weeks. The more the merrier!"

"I told Josh to pick me up here, knowing I'd be coming to visit you. He'll be here soon. Can I wait and ask him first before giving you an answer?"

Rolling my eyes, I say, "It's not like I'm going anywhere. Besides, it's just a casserole. Not a seven-course meal or anything."

"You're the best, Alex!" Sophie beams from the couch.

I make my way to the couch just as there's a knock at the door. I look to Sophie and raise an eyebrow. "I believe that's for you. Gavin has a key." I crack into a giggle at the end, seeing the excitement on her face.

Sophie is already off the couch and on her way to answer the door. From the hallway, I hear, "Hey, Josh!" and the sound of the door closing before they come together down the hall. "Alex invited us to dinner, if you'd like?"

"What are we having?" Josh eagerly asks as he greets me with a smile. "Hey, Alex!"

"Chicken casserole and a salad, if you're interested," I volunteer.

"Gavin's?" He raises an eyebrow, questioning.

I shake my head and grin. "You'll have to settle with mine."

"I guess I can risk it," Josh teases. "I have a stomach of steel!" He pats his hand on his stomach and grins widely.

I roll my eyes and smirk. "Wow! Thanks for the vote of confidence!"

"Naw… Just kidding. Gavin said you're an amazing cook."

"He did? What else have you been discussing behind my back?"

"Nothing I'm sure you don't already know." He cracks a smile. "I've never seen him so… I don't even know how to describe it…"

"I was just telling Alex that," Sophie chimes in. "Gavin's really… I wouldn't say changed… but different since Alex came around."

Feeling embarrassed that they're talking about me as if

I'm not even in the room, I can't help but ask, "What do you mean... changed? Is this a good or bad thing?"

"Oh, definitely good," Josh assures me. "It was so much fun to watch him when you first met. He kept asking me to go to Antonio's but wouldn't tell me why. Then when I found you worked there, it made sense. Especially, after seeing the two of you on the soccer field." A low chortle escapes his mouth before continuing, "That was entertaining!"

Sophie laughs. "You can say that again!" She looks at me and winks.

"I'm glad I'm here for your entertainment," I scoff, pretending to be hurt.

"I've never seen anyone as competitive as Gavin... or able to ground him, if that's the right word, you know?" Josh looks at Sophie for reassurance. "The change definitely isn't a bad thing. It's just a change." Josh places his hand on my shoulder, reassuring me of his sincerity.

"If you say so," I tease and hobble into the kitchen to make the salad.

"Want help?" Josh offers. Both Sophie and I look to one another, surprised.

"Sure, if you want to make the salad, you're more than welcome to."

I place the casserole into the oven. "This will be ready in forty-five minutes." Sophie and Josh make the salad within minutes and place it into the refrigerator. "Gavin said he'd be here around seven."

"I think he was close to heading out when I left." Josh smiles in return. "Can I grab a glass of water?"

"Sure, there's soda in the fridge, too."

"Thanks. Water's good."

Before he can ask, Sophie reaches for a glass and asks, "What were you working on tonight?"

"Oh, just a model for that project I was telling you about last week." As Josh fills her in on the details, I hear Gavin walk in the door.

"Hey, man!" Josh calls out. "Long time no see! We're crashing dinner. Hope that's okay."

"No worries." Gavin smiles as he sets his backpack and coat in the hall. He walks to where I'm standing in the living room, hypnotizing me with his golden-brown eyes and gorgeous smile. "How was your afternoon? Finish your paper?" he asks as he places an arm around my waist.

It takes me a second to respond, "Yeah, I finished it."

"Great." Gavin beams. "How long until dinner's ready? I'm starving!"

"Twenty minutes," Sophie responds before I can.

We visit around the kitchen counter until dinner's ready. I find this to be comical because Sophie and Josh are leaning against the counter in the kitchen, leaving the barstools for Gavin and myself. I guess when you're among friends, it doesn't matter who the hosts are.

When dinner's ready, they actually serve us before we go into the living room to eat our meal. The next two hours are filled with laughter and friendly conversation. At times, I laugh so hard it hurts. Especially when my downhill shortcut comes up.

By the time Gavin and I get back to his place, it's after nine thirty. "Are you sure you're up to working on geology tonight?" Gavin asks as we sit on his couch.

"Yeah, I think we'd better," I sigh. I don't like the thought of it hanging over my head. Even though I'm tired, I'd rather finish it sooner than later.

The module itself doesn't take long to complete. Within the hour, we move on to studying for the exam. By eleven, we're finally at a point where we feel we're done. As I'm about to get up and put my book back into my backpack, Gavin takes it from me, placing it on the coffee table.

"Will you sit with me for a few minutes before going to bed?" He pulls me back onto his chest. Instantly, I sink further into him comfortably. He wraps his arms around me and intertwines his fingers with mine. It's then I feel the toll of the day set in.

"So how was your day?" I finally ask now that we're alone, without distractions.

"Good. I got pretty far on my project at the studio. I also had time to work on the paper due Tuesday after Thanksgiving. If all goes well, I'll be able to relax and just enjoy Thanksgiving break."

"Me too!" I chirp. "I have to finish a project for my children's lit class, and I'm free! I'm going to stay on campus tomorrow until it's finished. I'm meeting with my group for another project at three, so I'll make use of my time."

"Sounds good." I feel Gavin take a deep breath and exhale slowly.

I slowly trace the contours of his hand with my fingers as I lie against his chest, listening to his slow and steady heartbeat. After I contemplate whether or not to disturb him, I finally whisper, "Gavin?"

"Yeah?" he whispers slowly in return. I can tell he's only moments from falling asleep.

"Um…" I hesitate, not wanting this moment to end. "Want me to let you sleep?"

I start to pull away so I can see his face, but Gavin embraces me tighter. I look up, feeling slightly shocked to see him fully grinning. "Not so fast," he teases.

"I thought you were falling asleep!" I laugh quietly.

"I may have been, but I'm awake now!" Gavin exclaims as he runs his hand along my cheek, resting it on the base of my neck. He stares into my eyes, leaving me almost breathless and entirely at a loss for words.

Without any conscious thought, I turn my entire body to face him. While his hand still rests upon my neck, I pull my good leg up onto the couch and lean forward onto my knee, closing the gap between us. I trace my finger along the shadows of Gavin's cheek, still maintaining constant eye contact. With my other hand, I run my fingers through the side of his short, thick hair, and an inviting smile spreads across his face.

Taking my time, I swallow a breath filled with his intoxicating, musky scent and exhale before bending forward to reach his lips. Closing my eyes, I'm lost in all that is him. Gavin's attuned to my onset of emotions and returns my lingering kiss in a way that's so intense, I'm left feeling mindless. He wraps his enormously strong arms around my body, caressing my hair and neck. Every touch sends an electric current running to nerve endings I've never known exist.

Eventually, I pull my lips away, completely breathless. Not wanting to let go, I place my head on his chest, and he cradles me in his arms. For another long moment, we listen to both our ragged breaths in silence, as they slowly calm.

Eventually, I'm mesmerized by the constant strum of his heartbeat. Once it's slow and even, I relax further as Gavin runs his fingers along the side of my face.

With a low murmur, Gavin breaks the silence. "I could definitely get used to this." I feel him inhale deeply and kiss the top of my head.

"So could I," I sigh, not wanting this to end. I run my fingers lightly across his chest, and he quietly laughs. "What?" I inquire softly, wanting to be in on what he's thinking.

"Nothing really." I feel him shrug. I lift my head slightly to see his face. He's smiling as he strokes my face. "I was just thinking about this weekend."

"What about it?" Still not seeing what's humorous.

"Well, even though it's only been a few weeks since I met your family, it's almost as if it were a lifetime ago." He bends down to kiss me lightly on the forehead. "They're going to wonder why you aren't sick of me yet."

I can't help but laugh. "More likely, it's the other way around. They've lived with me my entire life. They know how annoying I am," I tease.

Gavin takes another deep breath and exhales slowly. "I'm going to miss this," he solemnly states.

Not sure what he means, I study his face, but I'm left with no insight. Instead, I keep our humorous tone. "What? Are you sick of me already?"

His deep laughter shakes my entire body. "No, Alex. I just realized I'm going to miss you not staying here when you're better."

Not being entirely sure as to how to respond, I simply reply, "Oh." I haven't thought about this. I've been so focused on being better, that I hadn't considered I'd see less of Gavin. I don't know how I feel about this. "I'm sure you'll be happy to sleep in your own bed for a change," I tease as I still consider this new revelation.

Gavin studies my face. I can tell I've given my thoughts away when I see his eyebrows pull together. "It's not like we won't be seeing one another." He lifts my chin up to his and kisses me softly. When we pull away, a grin spreads across his face, and he chuckles. "Besides, I'll gladly take the couch if it means spending more time with you."

16

THANKSGIVING BREAK

WE'RE ready to drive out of Pullman early Sunday morning. Snow covers the ground, though the roads are clear. I'm sipping on my latte while Gavin fills the tank of my SUV. Gavin's coffee steams from the cupholder beside me.

"Everyone must be recuperating from their parties last night." Gavin laughs as he climbs into the driver's seat.

"Yeah, that was some game. I still can't believe the Cougs pulled it off! I'd thought for sure the Huskies would win when they made that last field goal!"

"Me, too! That Hail Mary at the end was absolutely amazing! Apple Cup's never a game to miss. No matter how the season's going. You never know who'll pull off the win," Gavin chuckles, recalling the memory. "Thankfully, we won, so we won't be teased about it over Thanksgiving."

"Why?" I ask, completely confused.

Gavin shakes his head and laughs again loudly. "My brother, Will, did his undergrad at U-Dub, and it's been a rivalry between us for some time. Though it's all in good fun." He smiles, turning down the temperature of the car.

"I can imagine!" I exclaim, knowing how siblings can be. "Mine are bad enough without the college rivalry," I tease. I notice there's a song I like on the radio, and I turn up the volume to listen to it.

Gavin laughs lightly. "How did your mom take it when you told her about coming with me for Thanksgiving?"

"Um, Kate had already told her, so she wasn't surprised. My parents are okay with it, or at least they seem to be. This isn't the first Thanksgiving one of us has missed," I assure him. "It was as if she expected it. Apparently, everyone knew we liked each other, but us." I blush, recalling the conversation with Mom.

"Really?" Gavin seems just as surprised as I was.

"Yeah."

"Well, at least they're okay with things." Gavin grins widely, reaching for my hand to squeeze it.

"Oh, I'd say they're more than okay with things," I tease. Ecstatic's more like it. I laugh at the memory of Mom's response. "You left quite an impression."

"Did I?" Gavin asks innocently.

"Like you didn't know," I tease.

"Um… speaking of impressions…" Gavin suddenly sounds unsure of himself, and I see him grimace slightly. "I talked with my sister yesterday, and they won't be able to make it to the cabin until Thursday around noon."

"That's too bad," I state, still not understanding Gavin's sudden change of mood. "Is something wrong?"

"No, but that means she won't be cooking dinner as planned," he states quietly.

"Okay?" I draw out, trying to get him to explain what the problem is.

Gavin lets out a deep breath in a sigh. "I told her that I'd take care of things since neither Will or Dad are decent cooks." He suddenly grins widely at me as if I should know what's coming next. "I was hoping you'd help me out."

I shake my head in laughter. "Why on earth do you seem so concerned about asking me?"

"Well… it means… we'll have to spend most of Wednesday cooking instead of traveling. So, we'll need to leave earlier than we'd originally planned. My sister wants us to stop by her house in Seattle to pick up the turkey she bought, along with a few other things." Gavin rolls his eyes as if there's something else he's not sharing but continues before I can ask. "We'll also have to go shopping again on the way to the cabin to pick up everything else. Will your parents be upset if we leave earlier?"

"I don't think so. They knew I would be gone by Wednesday."

Gavin takes in a deep breath and yawns. "Good. I was worried they might be upset since you're already not home for Thanksgiving." He's quiet for a moment as he yawns again. "Hey, mind if we stop to get some coffee in the next town? For some reason, I'm not waking up well."

"I'm sure it has nothing to do with the fact we stayed up until almost two watching a movie last night," I tease. "I told you we could have waited a little longer and let you sleep in. You didn't need to get up when I did."

"I know, but I wanted to get on the road," he sighs heavily.

"I can drive, if you want? I went to the doctor on Friday.

Now that I'm no longer wearing any brace, and I haven't taken any medication since Friday afternoon, I should be up to the task."

"Are you sure?" Gavin asks hesitantly. "I'd be fine with some coffee."

"I do know how to drive in the snow, Gavin," I say with a hint of sarcasm. "Besides, I'm wide awake, my leg feels decent, and I haven't taken any meds in days."

"Okay," Gavin sighs heavily again. "I'm beat. I'll just pull over at the next road we come to."

I drive the remainder of the ride home. Thankfully, the pass is clear, even though it starts to snow. By the time we reach North Bend, the snow's turned to rain. "Welcome to the West Side," I sarcastically comment to Gavin, turning on my wipers for the first time.

"Yeah! On the bright side, it'll be warmer here and we won't have to dress in so many layers," Gavin teases in return.

It's only a little after one when I pull into my driveway. To my surprise, Jacob's car is among the cars in the driveway. We're greeted by Kate and Ben at the door.

"Do you need help with anything?" Ben offers Gavin and me as we enter the door. Gavin has both of our duffel bags over his shoulder while I carry my school backpack and purse.

"Nope," Gavin replies, "I think we've got it."

"I thought there might be piles of laundry in the car," Ben mocks as he shuts the door behind us.

"There are such things as laundromats," I jibe in return, knowing that Kate was notorious for saving up her laundry to bring home a couple of times a month. And she only lived across town.

"But home is free!" Kate swats her hand at Ben, knowing the comment was for her benefit. "Hey, Al." Kate steps forward, giving me a hug. "It's great to see you walking on your own again."

"No kidding," I sigh heavily. "Crutches and snow don't mix."

"Ha!" Dad shouts out, hearing our conversation as he enters the room. "I'll bet there's a good story in that!" He reaches out to hug me then turns to extend his hand to Gavin. "Gavin." They finish shaking hands. "It's good to see you again."

"You, too, Mr. Manning."

"Please! Call me Kurt." Dad insists. "Do you want help with that?" he asks, pointing to the bags on Gavin's shoulder.

"No, thanks. I know where they go." Gavin smiles in my direction as he grabs the backpack from my shoulder.

"I can get th…" I start to say, but Gavin's already walking out of the kitchen.

"So, how was the drive?" Dad asks as he settles into a kitchen chair.

"Good, it snowed on the pass, but the roads were clear."

"How are you holding up, kiddo?" he sincerely asks as he pats me on the arm, motioning for me to sit.

"Much better," I insist. "The doctor says I can drive as long as I'm not taking my medication."

"Have you been overdoing it?" Kate accuses.

"What do you think?" Gavin scoffs as he re-enters the kitchen with Mom. The room explodes with laughter.

"Hey, I've been good!" I protest loudly. I look at each of my parents. "Honest, I have!"

"It's okay, Gavin." Mom pats him on the shoulder. "I'm surprised she's healed this soon. She's a horrible patient and doesn't really know the meaning of the word rest. I'm sure you did the best you could."

"I tried," Gavin states sincerely before grinning in my direction.

"We're sure you did!" Dad exclaims. "Stopping Alexis once she has her mind set on something is like trying to change the direction of the wind. There's no use! She can be quite the force of nature when she wants to be." Once again, laughter fills the room.

"Thanks for the warning," Gavin jeers, walking to lean against the counter beside me. "She's seemed pretty set on healing though. Thankfully, that's been her primary focus."

"See! I told you I've been good!" I snicker at everyone.

"Hey! Look who's walking on her own!" Jacob calls out as he enters the kitchen from the hallway. He walks over and gives me a huge hug, nearly lifting me off the floor.

I pretend to cough. "At least my ribs have healed," I tease.

"Oh, sorry, Alex." Jacob's voice suddenly fills with concern.

"My ribs are fine, Jake. Don't worry!" I poke him in the stomach. "Had to get it in while I could!"

Jacob looks to Gavin. "Gavin. Nice to see you again." He reaches out to shake his hand.

"Jacob." Gavin grins, returning the welcome.

Kai stumbles into the kitchen wearing only a pair of basketball shorts. His hair looks as if he had slept under his pillow, rather than on it. "Hey, Alex. Gavin. Mom, are we planning on anything for lunch, or should I help myself?"

Mom sighs heavily. "Can you wait twenty minutes?"

"No problem. I'll grab a snack." Kai walks over to the fridge and grabs a large pile of sliced lunch meat from the fridge before returning upstairs. "I'll be in the shower."

"Okay, you do that." Dad snickers sarcastically. "I hope you don't waste away in the meantime!"

"Hey, Alex, want to head into town to try on those shoes I was talking to you about?" my sister eagerly calls out from across the kitchen.

"Um…" I hesitate, scanning the room to see Gavin's reaction. "I'm not really sure we should subject Gavin to a shopping trip with you," I tease half-heartedly, knowing that Katherine will literally shop until she drops or the stores close. Though I've never seen her too tired to shop.

"Who says Gavin's going with you?" Jacob jeers. "No one deserves that torture." Jacob grabs a sandwich from the pile in front of Katherine, and she swats at his hand. "Besides, we need his help around here. Mom wants us to decorate the house for Christmas this afternoon."

"With the five of us guys, it should be quick," Dad points out. "Who knows, maybe we'll be able to catch the end of the game."

"Have you even asked Gavin if he wants to do that?" I protest, thinking it's rude of them to expect a guest to put up the plethora of Christmas decorations. I know my parents want to go all out this year because of the wedding. Who knows how long that will take.

"Actually, I volunteered." Gavin grins, loping over to pull the chair next to me before sitting.

"Are you sure?" I whisper. "You don't have to." Eying him accusingly, making sure this is something he really wants to do.

"Go. Have fun with your sister," he whispers and gives me a quick wink. "I'm sure you're dying to shop for shoes." Ha. He knows me well.

"Gee, thanks!" Sarcasm rolls thickly from my mouth. "I hope to return the favor someday."

Kate and I leave after lunch and drive to Tacoma. As predicted, we shop for much more than just shoes. She finds the perfect going-away outfit, clothes for her honeymoon, as well as gifts for the other bridesmaids. After being dragged through the entire Tacoma Mall and some of the out-skirting shops, we manage to find the "perfect" pair of black shoes for me.

I do my best to remain perky and upbeat the way any good sister and bridesmaid should. I don't even complain when she suggests I try on a pair of three-inch stiletto heels. Contrary to my first impression, they're almost comfortable. What surprises me most is I can walk in them without appearing ungraceful. Her other bridesmaids are wearing heels, so Kate pitches her best campaign to convince me into purchasing them. She claims these would be the "perfect" shoes for the wedding. The way I figure it, I only have to wear them for pictures, the ceremony, and a little at the reception, then I can chuck them under a table somewhere. If this is what she wants, who am I to resist?

After we close the mall, we grab a quick bite on our way home. We pull into the driveway a little after nine. To our surprise, we're greeted with twinkling lights lining the driveway and outlining the house. The guys had even managed to get the high peaks of the roof covered in lights. Our favorite family decorations are scattered throughout the yard and house. It's a spectacular sight to see.

Before Katherine can put the car in park, the kitchen door opens, and Ben steps out to greet us. "What do you think?" he calls from the porch as we get out and grab the numerous bags from our trip.

"It's amazing!" I shout back.

"This will be perfect for the wedding!" Katherine squeals as she runs toward him in excitement. She reaches him at the base of the steps, and they embrace in a long hug.

With my hands full of bags, I squeeze around them to make my way inside. When I open the door, Gavin greets me with a welcoming smile before standing to help me. "Here, can I help you with these?" He grabs most of the bags, leaving me with only one for each hand.

"Sure. We'll set them on the table. I'm sure Kate wants to show Mom her treasures from the day." Once my hands are free, I turn to face Gavin with one eyebrow raised. "So… How was your day?"

"Productive." He grins. "Like the lights?"

"Yeah. They're beautiful. I haven't seen the house like this in years. Dad usually gets burnt out after awhile." Realizing Gavin probably spent the entire day on lights, I ask hesitantly, "Did that take all afternoon?"

"Only a few hours. It was fun. Your brothers are hilarious!" He laughs at some unknown joke. "We finished in time to watch the second half of the Seahawks game."

Gavin sets the bags down on the table and laughs, pointing at the countless small bags. "Did you find shoes?"

Before I can answer, Katherine and Ben come in holding

hands and giggling. "And then she looks as if I've suddenly grown three heads…" She bursts into full-out laughter.

Great! She's telling Ben about my shoe experience. I can always count on her to relive my least favorite moments. "Hey, in my defense, those first shoes were hideous, not to mention a death trap!"

Katherine takes in a deep breath. "Yeah, but you should've seen the look on your face…" She convulses again, leaning forward onto a chair for support.

"I'm sure I was hysterical," I mumble as I walk to the fridge to look for something to drink. I pull out some juice and turn to walk toward the cupboard for a glass while Ben and Katherine gather the bags left on the table and go in search of my mother.

When I turn around, Gavin's leaning against the opposite counter from me with his arms folded across his chest, grinning. "So, was it that bad?" he whispers.

"Uggh." I release the breath I'd been holding. "It wasn't that bad… but we would've been there for hours if the stores didn't close early because it's Sunday."

"So… Shopping isn't your thing?" Gavin teases lightly, taking a step closer to me.

I sigh softly. "I don't mind shopping, if there's a purpose. But to search every store for *ideas*, isn't really my cup of tea. Maybe I'm just tired from the trip. It's hard to be a supporting bridesmaid when Kate can't make up her mind on anything." I grimace, remembering the many shops we went through several times to compare ideas. "When I get married, I want to keep things simple. Make a decision and stick to it, you know?"

"Hummm." Gavin chuckles and places his hand on my shoulder. "Long day, huh?"

"You can say that again," I whisper.

"Come here." He pulls close and embraces me in a well-needed hug. Once my head rests on his broad chest, I feel myself slowly relax. I take a deep breath, intoxicating myself in his musky scent. I turn my head, listening to only his steady breathing and heartbeat.

"Thanks," I whisper into his chest. "I needed this."

"Anytime." A soft, deep rumble comes from his sternum.

Our moment's interrupted by footsteps in the hall. Gavin releases his arms from me but remains standing at my side.

"Hey, honey." Mom's enthusiastic voice comes through the door a second later. "How are you feeling? You look tired. Kate should've known better than to keep you out shopping so long."

I sigh heavily. "You know Kate. She shops 'til she drops."

Mom gives me a quick hug. "It's good to have you home. I've missed you!"

"You, too, Mom," I whisper.

"Well, I just came to get something to drink, and then I'm heading to read in bed. Your dad's already asleep." She opens the cupboard behind me then turns on the water at the sink. "What are your plans for tomorrow?"

I look at Gavin with wide eyes, and he shrugs in return. "I'm not sure we have anything planned other than hanging out here."

"Well, you'll have the house to yourselves since Dad, Ben, and I are working and Kai's in school." She takes a drink before continuing, "Oh, and I think your sister has an appointment early tomorrow morning. Hopefully, we won't wake you."

I laugh at the thought of that. More than likely, it'll be me waking them up. "I'm sure that won't be a problem."

"I wasn't referring to you, dear." Mom rolls her eyes at me. "Gavin, I hope you're not a light sleeper." She chuckles, turning to look in his direction.

"I'm sure I'll be fine. Thanks again for having me."

"You're more than welcome, Gavin." She walks toward the hall then turns to say, "Goodnight. If you're the last ones up, make sure everything's locked up, okay?"

"Will do, Mom," I call out as she walks down the hallway.

I return my eyes to Gavin's. "Feel like watching some TV?" I don't really care what we do, but I'd like to relax and I'm not quite ready for bed.

"Sure." He shrugs, taking my hand as we walk down the hallway together.

"Where is everyone?" I ask when we find the TV on, but no one in the living room.

"Um…" Gavin hesitates, thinking my question over. "Jacob took off earlier since he has to work tomorrow, and Kai's finishing homework in his room, I think." He looks around the room and appears to be listening for a moment. "I'm not sure where Kate and Ben are."

"I hadn't realized Jake was leaving today. I would have at least said goodbye."

"Oh, he said to say he'd see you at the wedding." Gavin offers an apologetic smile.

Sitting on the couch, I find myself naturally curling up toward Gavin. I twist my fingers into his before grabbing the remote with my other hand from the end table. "What do you feel like watching?" I ask as I flip through the channels.

"It doesn't matter." Gavin yawns. "I likely won't be able to watch much of it anyway."

"You can go to bed if you'd like," I offer, feeling guilty for keeping him up. It's then I look into his eyes and see how tired he looks. His eyes are a dark shade of brown, slightly puffy around the edges. His hair appears wind blown and tussled aimlessly. Even though he looks exhausted, he couldn't be more attractive.

"I'm good for now. Besides, you just got home," he teases lightly as he pats my leg with his other hand.

I find a show we agree looks interesting and lean back further onto his arm to watch it. After a few minutes, he lifts his arm, placing it entirely around me, allowing me to lean onto his broad chest. "Comfortable?" Gavin murmurs as he squeezes me lightly in a side hug.

"Yeah," I quietly sigh in return.

Apparently, he isn't the only one exhausted from the day. It's only a matter of minutes before I hear his breathing deepen while his firm muscles relax. As if we're connected, mine do the same, and I find myself losing the battle with my heavy eyelids.

I'm not sure how long it is, but eventually, I hear a deep voice whisper, "Alex," and I'm jostled slightly. "Hey, Alex. We should go to bed."

I slowly wake in a groggy state to see Gavin's gorgeous smile beaming down at me. "Hey, sleepyhead. Go to bed. You need some sleep."

Reality sucks, and this isn't a dream because a dream wouldn't make me leave this state of utter bliss. I reply in a froggy voice, "Okay." I glance at the clock, and it says one fifteen. "Wow, I must have fallen asleep. Sorry."

There's a light rumble under my head. "No worries. I did, too." He then looks at the television. "Um, someone else turned off the television and placed two blankets on us."

I'm suddenly aware of my surroundings. "Really?" I hadn't even realized I was covered.

"We should probably get to our own beds. I don't want anyone to get the wrong idea about us." Gavin suddenly sounds slightly nervous.

"I'm sure whoever it was, doesn't," I sigh, wondering who it might have been. "We should get to bed though. It's pretty late."

"Need anything before going to bed?"

"No." I look around the room. "I think everything's upstairs." I lean up toward him and caress his face lightly. "Night, Gavin. See you in the morning."

He bends slowly to kiss me lightly then whispers, "Night, Alex."

We walk hand in hand to the den where I kiss him once more. "See you in the morning," I whisper with a smile. Without another word, I turn, walk upstairs, change, and quickly fall asleep.

It isn't even five when I first wake the next morning. I hold off as long as I can but by 5:25, I can't take it anymore. I have to get out of this bed. I quietly change into a pair of running pants and make my way to the bathroom before heading downstairs. On the back porch is my old pair of running shoes and head lamp. I slip them on then walk back to the kitchen to leave a note saying I've gone running.

I take a moment to stretch well, once I'm outside. I know

I'll have to take it easy this morning. It's been nearly a month since I last ran. I cringe at the memory of my accident, but quickly brush past it, remembering how drastically life has changed since then. The doctor's cleared me for all physical activity, but who knows how long it'll take to get back to my pre-accident state of athleticism.

As I slowly jog down my driveway, I notice my right leg's tender, but nothing problematic. My ribs feel slightly tight but more like I'm out of shape than from any injury. Sighing heavily in frustration. It'll take some work to get up to full speed again. I start down the all-too-familiar path along the road by my house. I'm not ready to run on the road just yet. It's dark, and I hate the thought of being in another accident. I shudder at even the thought. My family would never forgive me.

Once on the path, I stretch my legs into almost a full run. I feel the endorphins kick in as I settle into a somewhat normal pace. Unfortunately, about a half mile down the road, I feel winded, which is incredibly frustrating. I'm used to running miles, not yards. UGGAH!

Wanting to scream, but knowing it's pointless, I shake my head in annoyance and slow my pace. *Baby steps,* I remind myself. *Baby steps.* Knowing I shouldn't overdo it, I begrudgingly turn around and jog much slower than usual back home. *I'll get through this,* I repeat over and over until I'm calm once again. When I get home, I stretch and realize this run went better than I'd expected. It shouldn't take too long to get back into shape. It isn't until I reach the steps that I notice the lights on in the kitchen. I grin and jog up the steps to open the door.

Expecting Dad to greet me, I'm surprised to find a

different, yet all-too-familiar voice welcoming me home. "Morning, Alex. How was your run?" Surprised, I look up to see Gavin fully dressed in a pair of jeans and white t-shirt. His hair is slightly damp, so I know he's already showered.

Still slightly out of breath. "Uggh, I've been better, but it feels great to be back at it again."

"I can imagine." He meets my tone. "I haven't run in quite awhile either. You know, I would've gone with you," Gavin offers sincerely.

"I know, I just didn't want to wake you." I walk past him leaning against the counter and reach in the cupboard for a glass. He already has the sink running by the time my glass is available. I fill the cup, then take a quick drink. "Thanks. Is anyone else up?" I ask, looking toward the hall.

"I think someone is up, but I'm not sure who. They have yet to make an appearance." Gavin grins, walking to the fridge to look inside. "I was about to make some breakfast, want any?"

"Sure, but I'm going to take a quick shower first."

"Will anyone else eat if I make it?" Gavin pulls out the carton of eggs and milk and places them on the counter. Then reaches back into the fridge for bacon and cheese.

"Do you really need to ask?" I tease. "You were a hit last time."

Gavin chuckles as he closes the fridge. "I'm just making scrambled eggs with everything in them. It shouldn't take too long."

"Sounds amazing!" As he speaks the words, my stomach reminds me how ravenous I am. I laugh and shake my head. "I'll be right back." Before he says another word, I walk quickly out of the kitchen to shower and get ready for the day.

Thankful to be dressed in anything but sweats, I prance down the stairs in a pair of jeans and red V-neck sweater. In my rush, I pull a quick brush through my hair. Before entering the kitchen, the thick aroma of bacon draws my attention and quickens my pace. Gavin's back is to me, stirring the pan when I enter the room. I saunter quietly to stand behind him. Apparently, I'm quieter than I anticipate because he doesn't acknowledge me. I slip my arms around his waist, causing him to jump.

Spatula still in hand, he pivots in my arms to face me. His eyes wide with shock, a grin quickly emerges. Together, we take a step away from the stove without conscious thought. Reaching up onto my toes, I return his delicious smile. "Need any help?" I offer, not letting loose of his exquisite, golden-brown eyes.

"You could make some toast, if you'd like. All I have to do is finish frying this bacon, then add the eggs." He bends down slightly to kiss me lightly on the lips. "Breakfast will be ready in about ten minutes," he whispers as he pulls only his face away.

"Okay. I'll get out some plates while I'm at it." I squeeze him lightly then release my hold on him.

"What's the agenda for today?" Gavin asks as I pull out the bread and place it into the toaster.

"Is there anything you'd like to do?" I turn my head to read his response. I haven't made plans. My primary focus has been getting that ridiculous brace off and spending time with Gavin.

Before he can respond, the sound of footsteps

approaching and Mom's voice fill the hallway leading to the kitchen. "Kai, you'd better get a move on!" She takes the remaining steps into the kitchen without waiting for a response and directs her attention to me. "Good morning, Alex!" My mother turns the corner then stops suddenly, and I hear a slight gasp. "Oh, Gavin, you didn't have to do all this."

"It's not a problem," Gavin states humbly.

Mom laughs quietly to herself as she walks over to hug me. "I actually thought it was you cooking." She notices my note on the counter and eyes me suspiciously. "Running, are we?"

"Yep." She should know me by now. "The doctor cleared me for all physical activity. I thought I'd try on a surface that isn't covered in snow," I tease.

Mom shakes her head. "I know. Just don't overdo it."

She gives me her famous stink-eye, and I promise. "Okay, Mom," I sigh. "I won't." She doesn't let up until I add, "promise."

Within a few moments, the kitchen fills with busy bodies and loud voices greeting one another. My parents, Kai, and Ben graciously accept the breakfast Gavin's prepared. As soon as they clear their plates to the sink, they rush out the door. Kate takes her time with breakfast and offers to clean up the kitchen afterward, saying it's the least she could do. Then she takes off to town to run errands of her own.

After the whirlwind chaos, Gavin and I suddenly find ourselves alone at the table in the quiet kitchen. Gavin grins and reaches for my hand. "So, what's the plan for today?"

"At some point, I'd like to pick up a few things in town." I sigh heavily at my memory of yesterday and quickly clarify, "I don't want to spend the entire day shopping, but I need to get a wedding gift for my sister and Ben."

"That can be arranged." Gavin smiles widely. "Is there a good bookstore around? I'd like to pick up a few things on Italy since that's where I'm going next spring."

We spend the majority of the day driving around Olympia and its surrounding areas. I show Gavin where I went to school along with my favorite places. We eat lunch at my favorite restaurant on the waterfront, watching boats go in and out of the marina. The weather's actually decent enough for us to take a walk around the boardwalk along Puget Sound. By the time we return, there's barely enough time to pull together dinner for everyone. It's absolutely a perfect day.

On Tuesday morning, it's barely five when my internal clock wakes me from my all-too-comfortable bed. Knowing it's extremely early to be making noise around the house, I force myself back to sleep, though my efforts are entirely useless. I dress for jogging in the first warm outfit I find, heading downstairs to use the restroom at the other end of the house.

On my way back to the kitchen, I notice the light is on, and the door to the den is open. Slowly, I peer into the room. To my surprise, Gavin's sitting on the edge of the fold-out couch wearing a pair of gray sweats and a long-sleeved blue t-shirt. "Morning, Gavin," I whisper, making him aware of my arrival.

Gavin glances in my direction with wide eyes. But within a fraction of a second, they soften as a wide grin spreads across his face. "Hey, Alex." He holds my eyes with his from across the room. "Sleep well?"

Nervously, I shrug. "Yeah, but as I'm sure you're figuring out, I don't sleep long. I'm heading out for a run. Care to join me?"

Gavin's eyebrows pull together slightly. "Are you sure? I don't want to intrude."

"On what?" Sarcasm rolls thickly off my lips. "Gavin, for the record, if I didn't want you to come, I wouldn't ask." I chuckle lightly before adding, "Besides, it's more like a jog these days. I'll probably slow you down."

Gavin rolls his eyes and shakes his head, closing the gap between us in two short strides. With a light laugh, he places a hand under my chin, raising it so my eyes meet his. "Alex, sometimes you're impossible!"

Picking up on his playful tone. "I have moments!" I grin in return, cocking my head to the side, placing one hand against his chest. His muscles are firm through the soft cotton of his shirt.

"I'm sure it'll be fine," he sighs lightly before bending to brush a kiss on my lips. "I just need to grab my shoes."

Once outside, we each stretch silently, knowing my parents will be disturbed if they hear noises outside the house. After a few minutes, we jog out of the driveway, onto my familiar path, lit only by my headlamp. The path is wide enough for us to run side by side. Within a few moments, Gavin matches his strides to mine, and all that's heard is the crunching of gravel under our feet.

I feel much better today, though I'm hardly back to normal. Soon, I find a manageable pace I'm able to maintain.

"So, how far do you usually run in the mornings?" Gavin asks through his controlled breath.

"It all depends on how much time I have. Though it's

usually at least five or so…" I trail off for a few paces then realize I'm still not up to speed.

"What?" Gavin laughs loudly. "You don't think I could keep up with you?"

Suddenly remembering our intense competitiveness from the soccer field, I join in the laughter.

"That's not what I meant. I haven't been able to run for the past month. I'm far too out of shape for that today."

"Well, it's good to hear you're not overdoing it," Gavin sincerely replies and is quiet for a few strides before admitting, "To be honest, I think it's been at least that long since I've run myself."

"Ha…" I chortle nervously, trying to joke. "I really have been a nuisance, haven't I?"

Gavin raises an eyebrow and laughs. "Well, I've definitely experienced some changes!"

That comment stops me short in my tracks. "What do you mean?" I pant out heavily as I look up to his eyes for a response.

Gavin stops about a half stride ahead of me. He's breathing hard as he turns abruptly in my direction and rolls his eyes. "Change is a good thing, Alex. Trust me. I just didn't see you coming."

"Of course you didn't. I plowed you over!" I return before giving it any conscious thought.

This makes Gavin suddenly laugh hysterically. "That's not what I mean," he spouts out between gasps of air. "I'd been completely content before I met you." I'm about to protest, but he reaches his finger over my lips and stops me with a smile and shrugs. "I just didn't expect to find someone like you. Someone I can't imagine NOT being around all the time, that's all." He holds my gaze for a moment before adding, "By the way, you haven't stopped me from anything... I just don't like to run when there's ice on the roads. You're not the only one who has slid down hills unintentionally." He playfully winks at me.

Leave it to me to overthink things. I shake my head, reaching out to swat at his shoulder, but end up only brushing it slightly. "So, have you had enough of a break, or are you ready for more?" I turn quickly and dart down the path almost at my top speed.

"So that's how you're going to play it." Gavin laughs, and I hear him quickly approaching. His long strides make it easy to catch up with me, especially since at full speed. By now, the sun's making an appearance, but the path isn't well lit. He shoots past me in a matter of seconds and remains that way for a few minutes.

Eventually, he slows down, letting me catch up. By the time I do, I see a wide grin spread across his face. "If this is you injured, I'm toast when you fully recover!" Gavin teases and matches his stride to mine.

"You know it." I laugh at even the thought. I'd pushed it to catch up; thankfully, he'd slowed down at the end. I take a quick glance around and realize we've already run about a mile and a half. "We'd probably better turn around. I'd hate to overdo it this morning," I state, rolling my eyes. "Besides, my parents will be up soon. I'd like to see them before they go to work." We slow our pace to a walk then turn around and run again in the other direction.

By the time we return home, I can feel how out of shape I've become. Thankfully, I went further today than yesterday. I'm sure it has to do with Gavin. Once inside, I rush upstairs for a quick shower and change into a pair of jeans and my favorite blue sweater while Gavin uses the bathroom downstairs.

By the time my family comes downstairs, I already have breakfast mostly made. Today, it's French toast. Kai's relieved to eat something other than cold cereal.

"Thanks, Al," he cheers as he finishes his third helping and rushes off to school. "You, too, Gavin! See you tonight!"

As soon as Kai leaves for school, Mom asks, "What are your plans today?"

"Kate wants us to help her with party favors and other than that, just hang around here. I'll fix dinner again tonight, so don't worry about anything," I encourage her with a smile.

"You kids taking off tonight?" Dad inquires as he gets up to rinse his plate at the sink.

I look to Gavin for affirmation before responding, "Nope, not until the morning."

Dad lets out a low chuckle. "If you don't mind, I'll say my goodbyes tonight since you'll likely be out of here before the neighbor's rooster can crow." The room fills with laughter as he gives me a quick hug. "You two have some fun today! See you tonight." Dad grabs his coat from the rack next to the door and heads off to work.

I turn to Kate once everyone leaves. "What do you need help with?"

Kate enthusiastically prattles off a list of things a mile long. I sigh, wondering how much we'll get accomplished. Hopefully, we'll check multiple things off her to-do list, so she can enjoy these next few weeks before the wedding.

Within a few minutes, Kate puts us to work making

decorations for the wedding. We tie red ribbons on every bottle of bubbles she could find. Then we move on to the parting gifts for guests.

Around noon, Gavin offers to make lunch for us. As soon as he leaves the room, Kate gives me an all-too-familiar look, and I know there's no way I'll avoid the onset of questions to come. "Wow, he's amazing, Alex," she whispers as soon as she knows Gavin's out of earshot.

I can't help but laugh. "Yeah, I know! We wouldn't be nearly as far on your 'projects,' if it weren't for him."

Kate shakes her head and continues through her laughter. "That's not what I meant. He's smart, kind, great with the family, and an awesome cook." She takes a deep breath then blurts out, "Not to mention breathtakingly gorgeous. And you should see the way he looks at you!" She accuses with a warm smile.

"I'm sure you're exaggerating." I feel myself blush deeply, doing my best to downplay the situation as much as I can, but it's useless. "He's an upstanding guy. I'll give him that much." I laugh nervously before continuing with my argument, "He's such a gentleman, too." I remind her with a warning glance.

She reads my warning and continues, "Are you excited to meet his family?"

"Nervous, more likely. You know I've never gone away with anyone to meet their family. I just hope they like me," I admit meekly.

"What's not to like?" My sister reaches out her hand and places it on mine, squeezing it lightly. "You're quite the catch, too, you know." She holds her smile until I reciprocate it. "Besides, if Gavin's been subjected to our family the way he has and still wants to come around, I'm sure it won't matter to him what they think of you." She releases my hand and pats my leg next to her.

"That's not really helping, Katherine." I shake my head, trying to gather my thoughts. "I'm just so… I don't know… nervous… I'm usually pretty confident, but it feels different meeting his family. Like it's really important for some reason. As if… it's all actually real." I bite my lower lip and feel myself drifting into my own thoughts.

"What do you mean?" she asks slowly.

"It just seems like it's all been a part of a dream. Like it's too good to be true. I've never felt this way about anyone and if…" I trail off, not really sure how to continue.

"Oh." Kate suddenly sounds as if she's just had an epiphany.

Wanting to be in on it,. "Oh, what, Kate?" I demand the way only a sister can.

"Nothing." She smiles widely.

"Spill it!" I insist.

Katherine shakes her head and grins. "You just like him. That's all."

"You already know that." Confused why she would state the obvious. She places one hand on her chin and appears to be concentrating rather hard for a few moments.

"No. You're definitely in deep," she accuses. Then lightens her tone. "Are you sure you guys have never…"

Seeing where she's heading with this, I cut her off instantly. "No, we haven't. It's not like that." I let out a slight huff, giving her a disapproving look. "I've already told you that."

Innocently, she shrugs, and in a high tone adds, "Just checking!"

I hear Gavin make his way out into the family room. Instantly, I feel my face burn with embarrassment. If he's heard any of our conversation, he doesn't let on. When he approaches with three plates full of food, I get up from where I'm sitting on the floor and attempt to help him. He hands me two plates and sets his down on the table beside us.

"Thanks." He smiles warmly as I unload his arms. "I'll be right back with our drinks." Then directed at Katherine, he grins. "Then your slave labor may commence." We all laugh as he exits the living room.

"He definitely is something," Katherine mumbles to herself and laughs.

We spend the rest of the afternoon entrenched in Kate's projects. Though it isn't what I'd call rigorous work, it's definitely time consuming. Mom calls to check in on us and proclaims we shouldn't worry about dinner this evening. She's ordering pizza, and there will be no arguing with her as she kindly mentions when I attempt to protest. By the time she and the rest of my family arrive for dinner, Katherine, Gavin, and I are still completing her to-do list. We enlist the help of others after dinner and are able to complete everything within an hour or so.

Before heading to bed, I make my goodbyes to everyone since we'll likely be on the road before any of them even get out of bed. Knowing this will be hard for Mom, I save her for last. In a long hug, she whispers in my ear, "Night, honey. Good luck tomorrow. I know you're nervous, but you'll be fine. Besides, if Gavin's put up with all of us..." She points to

Dad and Kai who are currently harassing Gavin. "You'll have it easy."

I can't help but laugh as I pull away from her. "No kidding!" I quickly hug her once again and whisper, "Night," as I turn to walk upstairs for the evening.

We plan to leave as soon as possible to beat any traffic along the I-5 corridor. I've packed everything, leaving only my bag of toiletries and a change of clothes in the bathroom. Just as I'm settling into bed and about to turn off the light, I hear a light knock on my door.

"It's open," I call out in a normal voice, thinking it must be one of my parents. To my surprise, it's Gavin. I greet him with a welcoming smile, which he returns, leaving me slightly at a loss for words.

"Hey." He holds my eyes as he steps into my room. "Are you still planning on running in the morning?"

When I remember how to speak again, I mumble, "I wasn't planning on it since we want to beat the morning traffic. Did you want to?" I ask hesitantly. *Crap. I didn't even think to ask him his plans.*

"Let's run after the long drive tomorrow, if that's okay? I don't think Liz will be home tomorrow if we get there after seven thirty. She mentioned something about a morning meeting when I spoke to her earlier."

Gavin walks over to the side of my bed, and I sit up a little straighter. "That sounds fine. I'm sure after being cooped up in my 4-Runner all day, we'll need exercise."

Gavin smiles sheepishly and looks down toward me. In a whisper, he bends toward me, "I also came up here to say goodnight." He leans toward me slowly and kisses me softly on the lips. "Night!"

"Night!" I hazily reply.

"Get some rest. We have a lot of cooking to do tomorrow." Gavin brushes my nose lightly with his finger and kisses me once more. "See you in the morning!" Before I can say another word, he pivots and walks briskly out of the room, shutting the door quietly behind him.

Even though we make it to Gavin's sister's house by seven, we still miss her. Gavin calls her as soon as we are close to her house, but she has an appointment on the other side of Seattle at eight. She gives Gavin the combination to the garage door and tells him where to find the things we need.

It feels awkward walking into a stranger's home and taking their food. Since it's Gavin's sister, I'm a little more at ease. Her home is in a Seattle suburb. For having two kids, it's huge and immaculate. There are drawings hung on the oversized stainless-steel refrigerator that were obviously created by children as well as photos of kids themselves.

"That's Mason." Gavin points to a curly, blond-haired boy wearing a green soccer uniform. "And that's Gretchen in the princess costume. I know she's going to love her birthday present." He reaches over to me and squeezes me from the side. "Thanks again for helping me pick it out. We'll give it to her this weekend."

"They're adorable." I laugh lightly. "I can't wait to meet them."

Gavin opens the fridge and takes out the contents which are clearly marked for us. He also plucks the note his sister has left for us and chuckles aloud, shaking his head. "Liz has thought of everything, I see." He hands me the note and continues to gather things from the fridge. "Apparently, everything else is in a box in the garage."

I look over the list briefly. "Wow! It's a good thing my 4-Runner is big!"

"I know," Gavin states in a serious tone. "I think she forgot something though."

Wondering what it could possibly be, I can't help but ask, "What?"

"The kitchen sink should be on that list somewhere, I'm sure." He rolls his eyes, shaking his head.

The room's suddenly filled with loud laughter. Within a few minutes, we have cleared out the contents from the fridge and loaded them into the ice chest, to put into the 4-Runner. Once inside the garage, I realize that most of the things she wants from out here are for Gretchen. There's a small pile of gift-wrapped boxes in a bag next to the non-perishable items.

"I hope you don't mind. I told Liz we'd take Gretchen's gifts, so she'll be surprised." Gavin smiles as he reaches for the bag of presents.

"Not at all. We have plenty of room. Do you think we'll even need to stop by the store?"

"Yes," he sighs, rolling his eyes. "But we'll go out after we look through these things more carefully. I know we'll need milk and eggs for sure."

Typical of Washington weather, it begins to rain as we ascend the pass. By the time we reach the top, large, beautiful flakes of snow float everywhere. Though the roads are still clear from the plows, Gavin pulls over at the first turnout to put our vehicle into 4-wheel drive.

I'm surprised when he pulls off the highway before we

reach the town of Leavenworth. We follow a well-maintained road for a couple of miles before turning into a snow-covered driveway. There's no trace of any vehicles, so we must be the first ones to arrive. Gavin drives steadily down the winding driveway under the canopy of snow-filled trees for another few minutes before I see any signs of civilization. As we round another corner, I see a cabin-like structure, but I wouldn't by any means describe the home on the other side of it as a cabin. "Wow!" I whisper. "You call this a cabin?"

Gavin looks at me sheepishly "Um... yeah... I guess? Were you picturing something different?"

Taking it all in, I realize the first structure is actually a three-car garage. The house itself is technically a wooden house made of logs, but it's much more than a mere cabin. It's two stories, with a large peak in the center. As we approach it further, I see large windows facing the exquisite lake behind it. "We definitely won't be roughing it, will we..." Sarcasm rolls out of my mouth.

"Hey." Gavin smiles defensively. "I told you we wouldn't." His version of a cabin is at least the size of my parents' house, if not bigger. And there were six people living in our house. Gavin pulls the 4-Runner up to the house as close as possible and puts it into park. "Want to take a look around before we unpack?"

"Why don't we unpack everything, then we can look around since the snow's let up?" I suggest instead.

"Sounds good. I'll open the door and bring things up from the car to you, if that's okay. Most everything goes in the kitchen. There's no point in both of us tracking in the snow."

Once alone inside, I can't help but take in the enormous great room. Even though it's spacious, there's a cozy feel to it. Two distinct sets of oversized furniture fill the room. The one at the entry surrounds a large television while the other faces a view of the lake. Between the two clusters of furniture is a kitchen bar. The rest must be tucked behind the granite countertop with six barstools on the side closest to us. Setting my personal belongings on the couch closest to the door, I turn to see Gavin approaching with two bags.

I quickly retrieve them from Gavin as he pivots and returns to the car. On my way to the kitchen, I spot two hallways to the left and right of the kitchen. I'm curious where they lead but focus on the task at hand. I unload the bag to make sure nothing needs to go into the fridge before returning to Gavin.

I'm greeted by Gavin and a large pile. Gavin motions his head toward the 4-Runner. "I'll pull it into the garage, so we won't have to scrape windows when we leave." He kicks off the snow from his shoes and carries a cooler into the kitchen.

"Is there enough room? I don't want to take anyone's spot." I look anxiously toward the door before following him to the kitchen.

"You're taking mine. Besides, Dad parks in the garage attached to the house and unless my sister and her husband take separate cars, there's plenty of room. Can you put these in the fridge?" Gavin sets the cooler on the floor next to the fridge to make it easier for me.

"It's the least I can do," I mutter since I have no idea where to put the remainder of the groceries. The fridge's safe. As I look around the countless cupboards, I shake my head. I wouldn't have a clue how to organize those.

In one short stride, Gavin reaches out to give me a light squeeze. "Thanks," he whispers before kissing me softly on the forehead and leaves the room, causing my stomach to dip and my heart to race.

Will I ever get used to this? Suddenly, I feel completely unhinged. I take a few deep breaths to calm myself once alone and savor his musky scent before getting back to work.

Pulling out the first item from the chest, I find it's dripping from the melted ice. Crap. I need towels. Towels... Where would they be? I look around for the obvious drawers and search. Luckily, on my second pull of the drawer, I hit the jackpot. I don't like going through people's things, but coming from a big family, I know it's necessary. Within a few moments, I'm drying everything off, emptying the ice chest.

Before I know it, Gavin snakes an arm around me from behind, nearly scaring me to death. I jump into the fridge and bump my head on the higher shelf. "Ouch," I mutter and laugh quietly as he spins me around.

I feel the vibration of laughter from Gavin's chest. "I'm so sorry. I didn't mean to startle you." He pulls me closer into a bear hug and rubs my head softly.

"I'm okay." Rolling my eyes, I laugh at the situation. "I just didn't hear you come in."

"Well," he sighs, locking his eyes directly onto mine with full force. "Would you believe me if I say I just couldn't help myself?" Gavin grins sheepishly, and it takes me a moment to remember how to respond.

I let out a deep breath slowly and grin. "Hmmm..." is all I get out before he leans forward and kisses me tenderly on the lips. Though it's a slow and passionate kiss, it ignites a flame throughout my entire body. My arms wrap around his neck and the next thing I know, he lifts me to his level. Even though the fridge is wide open at my back, I feel as if I'm on fire. Minutes or months could pass, and I wouldn't be any the wiser.

It isn't until a bottle clanks that I'm brought back to reality. The door has swung and now rests on Gavin's arm. I force myself to pull away and make words form at my lips. "Um…Gavin…" He interrupts me with another breathtaking kiss before I can continue.

It'd be so easy to get caught up in the moment again, but for some reason, I'm determined to stay with my line of thought. "We should probably get these groceries put away and go to the store before your family comes."

Gavin slowly places me back on the floor with a wide grin spreading across his face as he steals one last kiss. "You're right," he whispers. "But I've been wanting to do that for days." A mixture of excitement and longing shine through his eyes, making my heart stutter. "It's nice to be just the two of us again for a change."

"I couldn't agree with you more," I whisper in return, reaching up on my toes to kiss him one last time. As I pull away, I sigh heavily, catching my breath again. "But we really do have a lot to do," I sadly remind him.

I can feel him chuckle before the sound escapes his mouth. "I'll make you a deal. I'll wipe, and you can put things into the fridge."

Rolling my eyes, I can't help but laugh in return. "Sounds like a deal."

It takes twenty minutes to put away the groceries Liz had sent with us. Gavin makes a list of things to purchase at the store as we put everything away, so we won't have to search through it again later. When we finally put the last canned vegetable into the cupboard, Gavin takes my hand.

"Want me to show you where you'll be staying? I'm sure you'd like a few minutes to settle in. I'll show you the rest after we take our bags upstairs."

"Sounds good." I walk toward my bag, but like the gentleman he is, Gavin beats me to it. He has it thrown over his shoulder before I can protest. Knowing it's useless to argue, I shrug and follow him down the hallway to the right. At the end, there's a stairway leading upstairs.

"Mind if I keep my things in here, too?" Gavin asks as we approach the stairs. "Of course, you'll have the room to yourself, but I'd like to keep my bags out of the way, if you don't mind?"

Confused, I ask, "Where will you be?"

"Um, tonight, I'll be in the guest room Liz's kids will sleep in, but when everyone arrives, I'll be downstairs."

I realize then that I'm taking his bed *again*. "Oh, Gavin," I say in disapproval. "I'll take the couch. It doesn't matter to me either way. You should sleep in your bed. I've already put you out enough."

We reach the top of the stairs, and he guides me through the first door on the right. "Here it is." He motions. He walks in, setting both of our duffel bags on the floor next to the queen-size bed. "Alex, how many times do I have to tell you, you're not a burden." He shakes his head and takes my hands in his, capturing my thoughts with his delicious, golden-brown eyes. "It's not a problem. The couch folds into a bed."

After a few heartbeats of staring into his eyes, I

remember my argument. "Then I'll take the couch." I
attempt to sound as stubborn, but it's useless under his stare.

"Hardly, Alex." Gavin's eyebrows raise in challenge. "Do
you honestly think my family will let that happen? Or yours
for that matter? What kind of hosts would we be if we made
our guest stay on the couch in the family room? Besides, you
ought to know me better by now." He waits for my
surrender with a thin smile spreading across his face.

"Once again, you're being ridiculous. Gavin... but... if
you insist..." I shake my head in defeat.

"I insist," he states firmly. Once I concede, he smiles
impishly. He pulls one of my hands to the door. "Shall I
show you around?"

Gavin eagerly leads me from room to room in the
enormous house. He explains his parents bought this place
when he was a kid. Each has a room designated as his or her
own. There's one guest room, making it five bedrooms, but
Liz's kids now claim it. All bedrooms, except for the master
suite are located on the second floor. Liz's room and the
guest room are connected by a joint bathroom while Gavin
and Will each have one of their own. He laughs as he
explains how Liz threw a fit about having to possibly share
the bathroom, but since hers was the largest, she should
have no room to complain.

My question from earlier is answered when I follow the
other hallway on the main floor to another staircase to the
basement. There's a pool table and a bar stocked for
entertaining guests, along with another set of couches and a
large TV area to lounge in.

Photos spread throughout the entire cabin of Gavin and
his family. I make a mental note to take some time later to

look at them more closely. Suddenly, I want to know everything I can about Gavin.

When we return from shopping, we're surprised that no one else has arrived. Gavin and I just finish putting everything away when he suggests, "With the oven in full use tomorrow, should we start making pies?"

Not being able to withdraw myself from his gaze, I simply nod. Eventually, I remember I have a few great recipes I'd love to share. "What are your favorites?"

"Well, I thought we might do a couple of the traditional pumpkin for starters, then maybe a few others." Gavin eyes me suspiciously, knowing I have something up my sleeve.

"Sounds good. How about apple and a cheesecake, too?" I've already made sure we have all the ingredients when we unloaded everything. "We can also make some appetizers tonight as well," I suggest eagerly. "Then there'll be less to do tomorrow."

"As usual, you surprise me, Alex." Gavin quickly closes the gap between us, bending to brush a kiss across my lips. "My family will love it, thanks." Then he turns to gather ingredients for making the crusts, leaving me almost breathless. Knowing I need to focus and can't let him be a distraction, I sigh and get to work whole-heartedly.

It amazes me how well Gavin and I work together in the kitchen. We're in tune with one another and accomplish a lot in a very little amount of time. Since we need numerous pies, we increase the size of the recipe to fit our needs. Before we know it, we have everything ready to fill the pies, except for the crust.

Just as I'm ready to roll the crusts out on the counter, Gavin looks up and smiles slyly. "You have a little something... Here..." He lightly touches the side of my cheek, in what I think is an attempt to remove flour. But instead, he picks up more with his other hand and sweeps it across my nose. "And here..." he chortles, slowly bending down to kiss my lips gently.

Not to be outdone, I bring my hand up to his face and wipe flour across his chin and barely manage to contain my laughter as I state, "You seem to have some here, too," and I kiss him gently.

Gavin unleashes his golden-brown stare fully onto me. For a lingering moment, I'm utterly speechless. Suddenly, his eyes turn mischievous around the edges. From the corner of my eye, I catch his quick movement to pick up more flour with his hand. A split second later, he holds his other hand above my head. He grins widely as he releases a shower of flour and bursts out laughing.

No longer holding my composure, I let out a spasm of laughter and prepare for revenge. Before he has time to react, I sweep up some flour into my hand and throw it in his direction. He tries to dodge it, but I'm quick with my other hand and get him from the side he's least expecting. Of course, he retaliates, as do I. Before I know it, we're both covered, laughing hysterically. Finally, when neither of us can stand it anymore, we double over in convulsing fits, gasping for air.

Then I hear an unexpected throat clear. "Uh... Hi." A snicker escapes before the deep voice states, "You must be Alex."

Straightening, I cringe as I face the stranger behind me. As I turn, there's a man resembling Gavin in the living room. Though he's lighter hair and is slightly older, he gapes in our direction with both shock and amusement across his features. *What in the world should I say?* "I... Uh... I," I stammer as I take in the scene he's witnessing. I can't help but shake my head in disbelief and embarrassment.

Gavin chuckles loudly and suddenly wraps an arm around my waist to help me hold my composure. He tussles my hair, to free some flour, grinning widely at his handiwork. Without taking his eyes off me, he announces through stifled laughter, "Alex. This is my brother, Will." He grins impishly at me before turning to face his brother with a smug expression on his face. "Will, this is Alex."

Will shakes his head, fighting to contain his obvious amusement as he reaches out his hand to mine. "It's nice to finally meet you, Alex. I've heard so much about you." I wipe the excess flour off my hand onto my clothes before reaching out to shake his hand.

Will eyes Gavin suspiciously, until finally, he can't maintain his composure any longer and joins us in a burst of laughter. We explode in hysterics until none of us have the breath to continue, and tears fight to escape.

Finally, when we've exerted ourselves entirely, Will reaches out and hugs Gavin, saying, "Nice to see you happy, Gav. I've missed you." He pulls back from his hug to fully assess the situation. Now he, too, has flour all over him. "Obviously, you've arrived early." He looks around further, examining the contents on the counter. "Pies?" he suggests.

Gavin chuckles lightly. "Yeah, we have all the ingredients for apple and pumpkin ready. We were just working on the crusts when you came in."

"Crusts..." Will speculates. "I thought for a moment it was snowing inside the house, too." Obviously, Gavin's sense of humor runs in his family. I can't help but be impressed with their ability to quickly come back with such sly remarks.

"Well, you know..." Gavin rolls his eyes and surveys the room.

Finally, I come to my senses. "We'd better finish and clean this up." Not wanting to meet his father the same way, I quickly ask, "What time's your dad coming?" Before either can answer, I set into wiping up the floor with a towel I'd used earlier.

"I was expecting him here," Will announces as he grabs another rag. He begins to help after throwing another towel to Gavin.

"Me, too, actually," Gavin states as he gets to work on the counters. "Have you tried calling him?"

"No. I'll wait until we're through here." Will shakes his head and smiles widely in our direction.

Within a few minutes, we have the majority of the mess cleaned up. All that's left is what's on our clothes. Gavin suggests getting the pie crusts into the oven before changing. Knowing it won't take long, I roll some out on the counter as he washes the dishes.

Will, seeing there's nothing for him to do, states, "I'll get out of your hair and finish bringing in my things." He smiles slyly at Gavin before snickering, "Boy, I sure hope those pies are good!!" Shaking his head, he walks out the front door.

After placing the crusts in the oven, Gavin turns with a strange expression on his face. "Um..." Appearing at a loss for words, he tilts his head to the side and eventually smiles. "We have about twenty minutes to get ourselves cleaned up."

Since our things are in his room, I follow him out of the kitchen. As I pass the mirror above his dresser, I gasp loudly at my reflection. From behind me, Gavin snickers. He quickly closes the gap between us to place both of his arms around my waist. Holding me from behind, his eyes meet mine in the mirror.

Though his eyes have the usual effect on me, I attempt to glare at him. *How could he have let me meet his brother like this?* It's mortifying. Though my clothes look like his, the flour's not just lightly sprinkled all over my body; it's in clumps, and my hair looks like a rat's nest.

He keeps the full force of his stare on me until I melt, and he knows I'm nowhere near being mad at him. Gavin nestles his head into the base of my neck, whispering, "You're beautiful," as he kisses me lightly on the neck.

This sends chills down my spine. I slowly turn to face him as he keeps his arms around my waist. Without the mirror, the entire full force of his golden-brown eyes penetrates my every being. I'm at a loss for words, as my mind goes blank. Keeping his eyes on mine, he slowly leans toward me. When he's within inches, I close my eyes to inhale his delicious, musky scent, bringing my arms to his neck. As his lips touch mine, he closes the distance between us by picking me off my feet.

Though my brain is mush, my body has an instant reaction. I return his kiss by pulling him as close to me as possible. I wrap my legs around his waist as my hand runs through his thick, brown hair while the other clings to his back. One of his hands remain at my back, pulling me closer to him as his other guides the kiss at the base of my neck, making each one more passionate than the next. Time has no meaning.

Eventually, we're left breathless and gasping for air. Gavin slowly sets me down but doesn't let go. He kisses me lightly once more before shaking his head and clearing his throat. "Um... Alex, we don't have much time before the crusts are done..." He steals another kiss before finishing, "We should probably get cleaned up..." Kissing me again in a way that feeds the inferno burning inside me, I can't help but be caught up in the moment.

When I'm forced to stop kissing him because I can no longer breathe, my mind clicks back on, making me aware of our surroundings. Will's somewhere in the house, and Gavin's dad should be here anytime. I certainly don't want to meet him looking like this. Embarrassed because I've never lost control like this before, I look up sheepishly, to see Gavin's wide grin.

He lets out a quiet laugh. "You okay, Alex? You're suddenly nervous about something."

Crap! He knows me too well. I blush at the accusation, knowing he's right. "I'm fine," I whisper. "Not sure what has gotten into me," I tack on at the end, meaning it for only my benefit, though it's said aloud.

Gavin shakes his head and whispers, "Me neither," leaving us both giggling lightly. "But I'm not about to complain..." he mutters into my ear as he hugs me tight.

Gavin pulls back but keeps his hands at my waist as he looks me over with care. "You'd better take a shower. I'm not sure that flour will come out if you don't. There's shampoo and everything you should need in there. I'll set a towel out for you and use Will's bathroom." He glances at the clock.

"Take your time. I'll make sure the crusts are out of the oven before they burn and then put the apple pie in." He leans in one last time for a light kiss on my forehead, whispering, "See you downstairs," as he drops his hands to leave.

It takes longer than I imagined to get out all the flour from my hair. I shampoo at least three times before my hair feels normal again. Eventually, I put conditioner in and finish with my shower.

To make up for my long shower, I dress quickly in the first outfit I put my hands on. A pair of dark jeans and a blue V-neck sweater. I quickly run a towel through my hair again to keep it from dripping everywhere. I pull a brush hastily through my hair, but it's still so wet, it sticks to my head. Finally, I throw it into a French braid to keep it out of my face, as well as make it look presentable.

Returning to the kitchen, I hear faint laughter from across the house as I enter the hallway. As I enter the kitchen, I realize Gavin's dad has arrived. Will's in the middle of describing the scene he found us in, shaking in laughter and barely able to finish.

"...Dad, you should have seen it. Gav just picked up the flour and tossed it at her..." There's another deep laugh, this time from his dad. "And she holds her own, giving him a run for his money..." A deep gasp. "I've never seen anyone as competitive as him. Finally, they just couldn't take it anymore and burst out laughing..." Will almost snorts as he tries to continue, "That's when I let them know I was here." He bursts out in hysterics before adding, "You should have seen the looks on their faces... Utterly priceless."

Gavin's dad chuckles and shakes his head as Will wipes his face with his hand. They have their backs to me, and

I'm unsure how I should introduce myself. I take a deep breath to calm my nerves, and this alerts them to my presence.

"Hey, Alex." Will smiles at me. "I was just telling Dad what he missed. I can't believe you two cleaned this place up so quickly. He wouldn't have believed me if it weren't for the flour I still have on my shirt!" As I look at his navy sweater, I see the evidence of our mischief.

Utterly mortified, my face turns crimson. Finally, I muster the courage to introduce myself, "Hello, Mr. Wallace. I'm Alex." I smile sheepishly before remembering my manners. "Thanks for inviting me."

With a light laugh, Gavin's dad returns my smile. "You're very welcome. I'm so happy to finally meet you and glad you're well enough to be here. Please, call me Peter."

"Hey, Dad," Gavin calls from behind me, "when did you get in?"

"Just a few minutes ago." He chuckles, eyeing Gavin suspiciously. "Will just informed me of the fun I missed out on."

Gavin lets out a bellowing laugh and shrugs. Then he walks over to his dad to welcome him with an enormous hug.

I notice all the men in Gavin's family are tall. Each easily over six feet, with Gavin being the tallest, though Will's just a hair shorter. Their dad's the shortest, by only about an inch. Each have the same body type as well. Broad shoulders, muscular and narrow waists. I wonder... Are they all as athletic as Gavin?

Their differences are subtle. Gavin and Will have dark-brown hair, whereas their father's is lighter. Mr. Wallace has blue eyes, though both his sons are golden-brown. His mother must have had brown eyes.

The timer goes off. I walk to the oven, take out the apple pie, and set it on the counter next to the other crusts Gavin set out earlier, as they continue to talk.

"So, what's on the agenda for this evening?" Peter asks everyone.

"Before it gets dark, we should take the snowmobiles out. What do you think?" Will asks.

"Sounds great," Peter agrees. "Just let me unpack my car first."

Then they look to Gavin and me as if they're waiting for our response. Gavin, who stands beside me, looks down and smiles. "So... What do you think?"

I've never been on a snowmobile. Unsure, I ask Gavin, "What do you want to do?"

"I'd love to show you around. It'll be fun. Have you ever driven one before?" he asks.

"Um, no," I admit.

"Well, I can teach you, or you can ride with me. Either way, we'll have a blast!" He grins in excitement, then looks to his dad and brother. "We'll get ready and meet you in the garage."

Within twenty minutes, Gavin's helping me Velcro my last glove into place. He found a snowsuit from his sister for me to wear as well as thick gloves and goggles. She must be about my size; everything fits perfectly. Since we're the first to arrive, Gavin opens the garage bay to push the snowmobiles out.

After he has three of the four out there, he turns to me and smiles. "Do you want your own, or to ride with me?"

"I'm not sure," I admit honestly. "I have no idea how to work one of these. Is it easy?"

"Have you ever driven a motorcycle?" he asks, raising an eyebrow, obviously curious.

"No." I shrug. "Maybe I'll just ride with you, if that's okay."

Gavin grins at my choice. "We'll take it easy. I've already witnessed more than I can stand of you being injured," he teases at the end with a wide smile.

He takes a deep breath and suddenly he's serious. "I think I would literally lose it if anything happened to you." he admits, shaking his head to rid himself of some dark thought. When he sees me getting defensive, he catches me off guard by placing his hands on my shoulders, looking deep into my eyes. "Alexis, don't worry."

I start to say something, but he quickly brushes a loose strand of hair behind my ear and bends to kiss me gently. "I won't let anything happen to you," he whispers, making me shiver, and it has nothing to do with the snow outside.

When we hear the front door of the house open, we quickly pull apart. "Here, let me help you with that helmet, now that your gloves are on."

Riding the snowmobiles is exhilarating. It's amazing to be out in the hills going down trails far too narrow for a car. The view is spectacular. Though it's lightly snowing, the clouds are high, and I'm able to capture the vast hills and valleys with scattered trees in the distance. We're following a trail, with Will taking the lead.

I have to admit, Gavin's an excellent driver. One of the perks of riding with him is having permission to put my arms around him without feeling awkward in front of his family. Even through layers of snow clothes, I still catch his musky scent from time to time. It causes me to inhale deeply and want more. I can't squeeze him closer to me. Will I ever get enough of him?

"Are you doing okay?" Gavin asks so that only I can hear as his dad and brother pull further ahead for a moment.

I sigh as I'm brought back to reality for a moment. "Yeah. It's amazing!" Though part of my response is my closeness to Gavin.

I can feel as well as hear Gavin chuckle loudly. Then he asks, "Wanna catch up with them?"

"Sure." I giggle. Preparing to go faster, I wrap my hands around my forearms in front of Gavin, squeezing him tighter. The force of being pulled back is bewildering. A rush of adrenaline soars through my veins. The endorphins left behind make the ride invigorating. I can't help but laugh as we quickly close the distance between his father and us.

Without knowing it, I realize we've made a large loop because we're suddenly back on the road to the cabin. As Gavin parks, I slowly release my grip on him. My arms are stiff from holding on so tight, so I flex them and stretch as we come to a stop. Once off the snowmobile, and our helmets have been removed, Gavin turns to me with a wide smile spreading across his face. "So... Did you like it?"

I can't contain my emotions as I beam. "Yeah. It was amazing!"

"Maybe we'll go again before we leave," Gavin suggests, taking off his gloves.

"Sure, I'd love to!" I grin back at him, removing my own gloves.

Will walks over to us, grinning from ear to ear. "So... did you have fun?"

"Yeah, I can't wait to do it again!" I laugh lightly at my sudden enthusiasm.

Will motions to the snowmobile. "I'll put it in the garage for you. Why don't you guys go inside. Maybe you'll figure out something to eat before I get in there. I don't know about you, but I'm starving."

"I'm sure we'll be able to dig something up. Liz packed enough for an army," Gavin teases as he grabs my hand, leading me to the house.

After taking off our snow gear and leaving it in the mud room, Gavin and I venture into the kitchen. "What do you feel like having?" he asks as he looks into the fridge.

Realizing how ravenous I am, I hope we find something that doesn't take a lot of time. "How about enchiladas?"

"You're reading my mind," Gavin teases as he pulls everything out from the fridge.

As soon as he's done, Gavin gasps. "Shoot. We left Gretchen's gifts out in the open. Do you mind if I go put them away?"

"No problem. I'll start dinner. I'm starving," I admit as my stomach growls loud enough for him to hear.

Gavin grins. "Sure. I won't be too long. Liz asked me to wrap a few things, too. I promise I'll try to hurry." He touches my cheek lightly then turns to leave the kitchen.

As I look around at everything set out on the counter, I realize this kitchen's a dream to work in. There's ample space, and it's equipped with everything necessary. I quickly pull out a pan and brown the hamburger, adding spices along the way. I also take this time to grate the cheese and set the table in the dining room. Since Gavin hasn't returned when the meat is ready, I quickly throw everything together and get it ready to place in the oven. Once that's done, I wash the few dishes I used as well as make a salad for everyone. Gavin arrives just as I'm pulling out a can of corn to add to dinner.

"Wow! Smells good," he says in a playful tone. "You work fast." He surveys the kitchen. "Is there anything left for me to do?"

"Not really," I admit. "Once I warm up the corn, we just have to wait until it comes out of the oven."

Just then, Will and Peter come into the room. "Hey, what's for dinner?" Peter calls out.

"Enchiladas," Gavin exclaims. "Your favorite!"

"Wow, I can't wait!" Peter admits. "I was hoping I'd get some of those while you were here." Will and Peter pull out barstools as Gavin and I lean on the counter across from them. "So have you heard where you're going yet next year?" Peter directs obviously at Gavin.

Conversation shifts to Gavin's trip to Florence. Apparently, they've been there before. They talk about all the sights and architecture. I listen eagerly, though having never been outside of the country, I don't have much to contribute. When the timer goes off, I take the enchiladas out of the oven and place them on the dining room table in the other room.

I don't even have to say anything. Before I put the dish on the hot plate in the middle of the table, suddenly all three guys pull out chairs at the table, continuing their conversation about Italy. I take the seat next to Gavin, and we fill our plates.

"Wow, Gavin, this is great!" Peter exclaims. "I can't believe how hungry I am."

"Thanks, Dad." Gavin smiles. "But the credit goes to Alex. My contribution only consists of pulling some things out of the fridge."

"You cook, too? Girl, you amaze me." Peter's admiration is evident as he takes another bite.

"Thanks," I reply humbly.

"Yeah, she has that effect on people," Gavin says as he pats my leg under the table. "Do you know she even speaks Italian?"

My cheeks flush as embarrassment rushes through me now that the attention of the table is turned to me. To keep from doing anything foolish, I quickly take another bite of enchilada and chew it carefully.

"Do you know where you'll be going next year?" Will asks me.

"Um…" I clear my throat lightly. "I'm not in architecture. I'm an education major," I quietly say.

Will seems embarrassed by his mistake. "Oh," he whispers.

To make him feel more comfortable, I add, "I've always wanted to go to Italy, so I took Italian in high school."

"Alex will have degrees in elementary education and an English Language Learners endorsement," Gavin offers to his family. "Though she'd probably survive easily in Florence, if given the chance. She's way better at Italian than I can ever hope to be. I will definitely add Italian as an elective next semester."

"There's no doubt about that." Peter shakes his head and laughs. "I'm sure you'll be able to pick it up easily enough while you're there, too." Peter then turns his attention to me. "Have you ever thought about studying abroad?"

"Well, not really, though my advisor suggested I travel to Italy because I have enough credits in Italian. I could consider it as a minor if I continue to take classes since my AP credits transferred. She also said it would help me teach others English as a second language." As I finish, I see Gavin's jaw has dropped. I thought he knew all of this, but I guess I might have forgotten to mention that last part.

"You should consider it," Peter warmly suggests. "Eleanor and I always encouraged travel with our children. Obviously, I travel a lot for a living, but she always loved to experience new things. It's a life-changing experience." Peter looks happily lost in thought for a few moments before he continues, "Europe has so much history and deep culture, not to mention the architecture…" He grins at Gavin.

"Speaking of architecture," Will interrupts, "if you're not an architecture major, then how did you meet? Gavin hardly ever leaves that studio."

Before I can say anything, Gavin smiles and simply states matter-of-factly, "She knocked me head over heels on my butt." He gives me an impish grin afterward.

Please kill me now. As I recall the memory, I want to crawl under the table. Both Will and Peter look bewildered at Gavin's explanation; their eyes dart from Gavin to me. To my extreme mortification, Gavin continues to go into detail about the specifics of our incident. Though to give him credit, he mentions the coffee shop with Sophie beforehand. By the end of the explanation, they're laughing hysterically. I have to admit, I join in the laughter by the end.

Peter's still snickering when he states, "You must be one heck of a runner to knock someone like him over."

Before I have time to react, Gavin interjects, "You should see her play soccer! If we weren't on the same team, she might be able to take me." Gavin lets out another soft chortle at the memory of our practices. "If you think I'm intense, you haven't seen anything."

Trying to stifle his laughter, Peter states, "Let me get this straight." He takes in a deep breath to steady himself. "So she cooks, runs, plays soccer, speaks a foreign language, and can kick your butt?" Letting a loud laugh escape, he pats Gavin on the back. "Son, I think you've found a keeper!"

"I know," Gavin whispers softly as he reaches out to pull me close so he can kiss the top of my head.

Though my embarrassment continues, this declaration humbles me greatly. I could easily turn the table on him, having each of those qualities mentioned about me be focused upon him, and still be telling the whole-hearted truth. Instead, his admission has left me speechless.

For the remainder of the meal, I'm lost in thought. I try to follow conversations, but I find myself only being able to focus on Gavin. After dinner, to calm my nerves, I volunteer to clear the table, encouraging the guys to watch the game they were hoping to catch the end of.

Will and Peter quickly head into the basement to watch TV on the larger screen. When Gavin gets up, he takes his plate to the kitchen with him. Thinking he's joined them, I'm surprised to find him in the kitchen when I enter. "Hey," he says as we're suddenly face-to-face in the kitchen. "How are you doing?"

Not knowing what to say, I stare at my feet. He slowly

places his hand under my chin to make my eyes meet his. "You're kind of quiet. Is everything okay?" His face is filled with concern. "I didn't upset you, did I?"

"No," I whisper as I take in the full depth of his deep, golden-brown eyes. "I'm okay," is all I can muster under his hypnotic stare. Finally, I take a deep breath and add, "I guess I'm not used to all that attention. It's kind of embarrassing," I admit sheepishly.

"Alex, you have no idea how amazing I think you are," he shares.

Gavin stares intently into my eyes and I can't help but smile. "You're not so bad yourself, you know." I lean up, extending my arms around his neck and hug him. Taking in the full aroma of his musky scent, I draw in a deep breath and for once, I find being in his arms completely relaxes me.

He takes a deep breath and exhales slowly, letting my head rest on his chest.

Eventually, I hear a cheer from downstairs, reminding me Gavin's family's waiting for him. I pull back, leaving my arms around his neck and smile. "Go… Spend time with your family. I'll finish up and join you shortly."

Gavin hesitates for a moment but hears another cheer from his father. He quickly squeezes me tightly and says, "Thanks."

We spend the evening watching TV. After the game's over, we watch a movie since it's still early. Gavin scoots closer to me on the couch as the movie begins. Eventually, he puts his arm around me and pulls me into his chest. Nestled on the couch, I feel myself slowly relax, and the exhaustion from the day sets in. I quickly lose the battle with my eyelids and drift off to sleep in Gavin's arms.

17

WINTER WONDERLAND

THE NEXT MORNING, I wake feeling completely confused in a strange room. As I take in my surroundings, I remember being at Gavin's, but I have no idea how I got upstairs to this room. I roll my eyes in embarrassment as I think of Gavin carrying me all the way up here. He should have just woken me. Though I'm grateful for his kindness.

I glance at the clock, 5:13. Thankful I won't disturb anyone, I get up and get ready for the day. Remembering the kitchen's pretty far from anyone, I might as well start our Thanksgiving meal. Not knowing when Liz will arrive, I won't start the turkey until Gavin's awake.

I head to the kitchen. I make a green bean casserole, put the potatoes on to boil, and begin making a macaroni salad. After that, I start the sweet potatoes, and a Jell-O salad for the kids. I'm just slicing bananas into the salad when I hear a barstool slide out from behind me. I turn around, expecting to see Gavin, but instead, I find Peter, still in his pajama bottoms and t-shirt, smiling at me.

"Good morning, Alex," he whispers. "I was expecting Gavin."

I look at the clock and realize it's a little before seven. I shrug and say, "I guess he's sleeping in. Can I get you anything to eat?"

"Sure, what do you have in mind?" Peter gets up from the stool and turns on the coffee maker.

"Pancakes?" I suggest as I pull out the mix from the cupboard.

"Sounds great. Want help?" he offers.

"I've got it."

As I set to work on making the batter, I offer, "You have an amazing home here."

"Thanks, we enjoy it. Most of my fondest memories are here," Peter sighs, and my heart goes out to him. He looks at me and shakes his head. "You know, you're our guest. You don't have to wait on us."

"I know," I sigh. "I love to cook. I do this for my family when I'm there. Coming from a family of six, Mom never turns down help when she can get it." I chuckle at the thought.

"You and Gavin are a perfect match then. Since his mom passed, I live for the days he comes home. He's an incredible cook. She taught him everything she knew." He grins proudly at the memory. "She would've loved you. You both have a keen sense knowing when to ground Gavin when he needs honing in." He chuckles and shakes his head. "Gavin's always been such a determined little thing. Once he sets his mind to something, nothing stops him," Peter sighs deeply. "I'm just glad he's decided to let someone special share it with him."

"Oh," is all I manage to say before he continues.

"You know how focused he can be, right?" He raises an eyebrow in my direction.

"Yeah. Though, focused is an understatement," I tease.

"We were so worried about him after Eleanor passed. She did her best to encourage him to focus on his goals like soccer, college, and his career so that she'd know he was happy after she passed." He smiles and shakes his head again. "From the time he was knee high to a grasshopper, he's always been goal oriented. He was never satisfied unless he could do it the best, or at least better than everyone else.

"Once his mom got sick, he had numerous friends, but always kept them at a distance. He'd go out in groups and kept himself busy by playing sports or being on various teams. Unlike his brother, Will, who dated frequently, Gavin's never let himself get close to anyone in that way, at least to my knowledge."

As much as I'm dying to know more, I'm not sure how I feel about hearing such private information about Gavin without him telling me himself. But if I'm being honest, I haven't heard any new information, so I let his dad continue.

"Then one day, I call him, and he states, 'Dad, I'm bringing my girlfriend, Alex, home for Thanksgiving.' I have to admit, I almost dropped the phone." Peter chuckles at the memory. "Not that he hasn't dated, but he's never had anyone worth bringing home. Then he's talking ninety miles a minute, telling me how great you are, that he took you to our favorite restaurant in Spokane, and he's already been home to meet your family."

Not knowing how to bring it up, I ask hesitantly, "Did he tell you about my accident?" I ask hesitantly.

"He said you'd been in a car accident, and he's helped you get to and from campus." Peter looks a little confused. "Isn't that the case?"

"He told you he witnessed me being hit by a car while I was running, right?" I clarify.

Peter suddenly looks at me with shock. "Um, no..."

To fill him in, I tell him about our classes together and mutual friends before the accident. Then I fill him in on the details to the extent of my injuries and of Gavin assisting me after the accident, making sure I clarify he's been nothing but a gentleman the entire time.

Since I feel comfortable with Peter, I talk honestly about Gavin without hesitation. "You know, Gavin's an amazing guy. From the moment I knocked him over, I haven't been able to get my mind off him. In fact, on the morning of my accident, I'd been so focused on him, I hadn't even seen the car." I suddenly gasp. Shocked at what I've just admitted, mortification flows freely as I beg, "Oh, please don't tell him. No one knows that. He'd feel awful. It's not his fault I was such a stupid klutz that day. Please... Please don't tell anyone," I plead.

Peter winks and whispers, "Your secret's safe with me. I'm just thrilled to see him happy. I'm sorry you were hurt, but at the same time, I'm glad Gavin's taken this opportunity to let you in." Peter suddenly stands, walks around the counter, and surprises me by giving me a hug. "Thank you, Alex."

Confused, I can't help but ask, "For what?"

Peter's face is overcome with emotion. "For sharing with

me, and for making my boy show he's turned into one heck of a man. I'm so happy he's found you." After another hug, he pours himself a cup of coffee before sitting while I go back to cooking.

As if the aroma of food invites them, within a few minutes, Gavin and Will appear. We sit for breakfast filled with laughter as I'm told stories from Gavin's childhood. Shortly after we finish, Will and Peter slip downstairs to watch more football as Gavin turns on the TV upstairs, staying to help prepare Thanksgiving dinner.

He looks around the kitchen and then walks to the fridge to examine the contents. "Is there anything for me to do?" He closes the door and walks to me. "Just how long have you been up, Ms. Manning?"

I impishly grin. "Since five." I poke him lightly on the chest. "You can put the turkey in the oven if you want?"

Gavin rolls his eyes, grinning widely in my direction. "Good, at least I'm not utterly useless." He bends down for a quick peck on the lips before turning to the turkey as I finish cleaning up from breakfast. When he finishes, he grabs my hand, leading me downstairs to watch the game and visit with his family.

It isn't long before we hear the pattering of little feet on the stairs. We turn to see Mason bounding down the stairs. As he gets to the bottom, he shouts anxiously, "Papa, Papa, Papa," running to climb into Peter's lap.

Peter grins from ear to ear, the way only a proud grandpa can. He hugs him fiercely and nestles his hair. "Hey, buddy! Where are your parents? You didn't drive here by yourself, did you?"

Mason laughs as if it's the funniest thing he's ever heard.

"No, silly." He takes a deep breath. "I can't drive... My feet don't reach the pedals!"

"Well, you look pretty big to me," Will exclaims as he gets off the couch to steal him away from Peter. "Come here, you! Give Uncle Will a hug!" Mason squeals with delight as he's torn from Peter and given a bear hug by Will. Will lifts him high into the air and pretends to almost drop him, making Mason squeal even louder with glee.

"Again! Again!" Mason cheers. Of course, Will complies, making Mason almost reach the high ceiling above him before he lets him drop. Mason screams in excitement.

When Mason's set down, Gavin asks in a hurt tone, "Hey, what about me?" Mason's eyes light up and is on Gavin's lap before I can blink. After a quick hug, Gavin asks, "Are you ready to play in the snow today?"

"Yeaaaaa!" Mason eagerly exclaims. "I have a new sled. We have to find a big, big hill!"

Before anyone can say another word, Liz enters the room, carrying Gretchen on her hip. "Gabin! Gabin!" Gretchen squeals in a way only a three-year-old can as she pushes away from her mom to get down to the floor. She runs into Gavin's open arms to hug him, as well as share his lap with Mason. I scoot over to make room for them on the couch, grinning at how well he does with children.

"Hey, sweetie! How's my favorite three-year-old?" He hugs her once again. "Do you want to play in the snow today?" he asks eagerly.

"Yep, I wanna build a snowman!" She beams in delight.

With a wide grin spreading across his face, Gavin chuckles. "I think that can be arranged. Uncle Will's good at making them, too!" Just then, Gretchen's attention is directed to Will. She hops off Gavin's lap to run to him, giving him an enormous hug as well.

"So... Are you making dinner today, or are we only having turkey this evening?" Liz raises an eyebrow in Gavin's direction when she sees him resting on the couch. She snickers before adding, "I'd better get started if all we have is the turkey in the oven."

"No worries, Liz. Everything's already taken care of, knowing those two!" Peter interrupts, eyeing us suspiciously before Gavin can respond. "You obviously haven't opened the fridge or looked in the garage."

"What?" Liz asks in disbelief. "It's only eleven thirty, and you're already done with everything?"

As I predicted, Liz's about my size. Unlike her brothers, she has the coloring of her father. Remembering the pictures around the house, I notice she looks more like her mom though. She has wavy, light-brown hair past her shoulders and crystal-blue eyes. She, too, is athletic, appearing to work out often. Like her brothers, she has a flawless complexion and would be considered beautiful by any standards.

Gavin chuckles at her uneasiness. "Yep, Alex, as usual, was up before the roosters and had almost everything done before I even made it to breakfast." He looks at me in admiration before returning his attention to his sister. "By the way, Liz, I'd like you to meet Alex. Alex, this is my sister, Liz."

"Oh my goodness! I've forgotten my manners," Liz exclaims. "So... this is the infamous Alex I've been dying to meet." She raises an eyebrow at Gavin before directing her attention to me. "It's a pleasure to meet you."

My face heats as I stand to shake her hand. "Nice to meet you, too."

"Where's Phil?" Will asks as Gretchen climbs off his lap to play with the toys Mason's pulling out of a closet.

"He's unloading the car. I wanted to make sure everything's ready for dinner, but apparently I'm too late." She smiles sheepishly at Gavin. "I should have known you'd have handled it. Sorry for jumping to the wrong conclusions when I came in and found no one working in the kitchen."

"No worries, sis." Gavin giggles as he reaches out to hug her. "Let's go upstairs so you can inventory what we've got, then you can finish. We're mostly waiting on the turkey to come out of the oven at this point." He then looks at her kids and raises his voice so they easily hear. "I've promised to take some kids out to play in the snow."

Both kids giggle in delight. As Peter states, "I'll bet I can make an even bigger snowman than Gavin. What do you think, kids?" He then roars with laughter as both kids run to hug him ecstatically.

"That sounds like a challenge to me," Will chirps in. "Why don't I get you guys into your snow clothes, and then we'll go outside to play." It doesn't take long before both kids bolt upstairs to change their clothes.

After showing Liz what we've done, I can tell she's pleased. She insists I join in the Winter Wonderland fun with Gavin and the guys.

I'm not sure who has more fun outside, the men or the kids. Phil joins us shortly after we get outside. The guys make snowmen while Gretchen and Mason show me what a snow angel is and insist I make some, too. Eventually, the guys lob snowballs toward one another. The kids and I join in on the fun, but we're no match for them.

Eventually, Gretchen gets cold. Though her dad offers to take her inside, she insists I go with her. Remembering there's hot chocolate in the cupboard, I suggest we make some for the guys when they are ready to come in. Gretchen's grin spreads from ear to ear at this idea.

To my surprise, Gretchen insists she sit on my lap when we enjoy the cocoa. For the remainder of the day, I have a second shadow. I can't help but be flattered.

The dinner goes off without a hitch. It's filled with laughter and welcomed conversation. Though I'm a little embarrassed when the whole, "How'd you meet" thing comes up again, as well as the incident with the pie crusts. But overall, it's enjoyable. Gretchen won't let her mother help in any way and insists she stay next to me. After I assure her it's okay, Liz relaxes and enjoys her meal without the welcomed interruptions.

Every now and again, I feel Gavin's gaze land on me, or he brushes just the slightest part of me in casual conversation. Of course, I'm completely unhinged and at times almost breathless. It's all I can do to maintain coherent conversations with everyone. Thankfully, no one notices my odd behavior.

After dinner, Gavin and I continue to play with the kids. We go downstairs to put on a movie. As predicted, Gretchen curls up on my lap as Mason lies himself down on the other couch.

After placing a blanket over Mason and propping his head up with a pillow, Gavin sits next to me on the couch. As he puts his arm around my shoulders, Gavin leans in with an enormous smile and whispers, "I think you have a new best friend." He pecks me on the cheek as he reaches for my hand. Though we watch the entire movie, Mason's out within a few minutes and Gretchen shortly thereafter. I'm far too comfortable to suggest moving.

As soon as the movie's over, the kids wake. Once upstairs, we celebrate Gretchen's birthday. We light a candle into one of the pumpkin pies and sing 'Happy Birthday.' Afterward, Gretchen rips into her presents. Like a typical three-year-old, she's excited to open her gifts. She hardly has one open before she moves onto the next. Gavin's dress and tiara are a hit. As soon as she opens her last present, she strips down, right then and there, to put on her new dress. Gavin also bought Mason a toy car and a picture book about WSU from the campus bookstore. The kids play for the remainder of the evening with their new toys.

Around eight, Phil announces bedtime. Gretchen's immediately at my side, pleading, "Alex, you read my story?" With her wide blue eyes flashing at me, there's no way to resist.

"Of course, Gretchen." I chuckle at her eagerness as she pulls me to their bedroom. As we leave, I hear Mason asking Gavin to tuck him in.

As soon as I have Gretchen changed and ready for bed, Gavin and Mason enter the room. Gretchen insists I sit on her bed while Gavin and I take turns reading a few of their favorite stories. By the end of the second book, Gretchen's fast asleep. After a tiring day, Mason loses his fight with sleep halfway through the third book. We sneak out of the room and spend the evening visiting with his family.

As usual, the next morning, I'm wide awake early. I

quietly make my way to the kitchen, trying not to disturb anyone. Being hungry, I make breakfast for everyone. With a crowd this size, Mom's favorite breakfast casserole will be perfect. I'm almost finished when I hear the patter of little feet. Gretchen emerges from the hallway moments later.

"Good morning," I quietly whisper. "Want to help with breakfast?" I offer.

She eagerly accepts, and we finish the casserole together. She helps me set the table and make a fruit salad. Gretchen giggles the whole time, helping herself to parts of the salad when she feels too hungry. While we wait for the casserole, she pulls me over to the coffee table to color in one of her many coloring books.

We're finishing a page when Gretchen stands and shouts with such enthusiasm, I'm startled. "Gabin!"

"Hey, Sweetie!" Gavin chuckles as he picks her up. "Did you sleep well?" He greets me with a warm smile but keeps his attention on her.

"Yes! I cooked!" she trills, pointing to the kitchen.

"Wow, you did it all by yourself?" He feigns being shocked.

"No...silly." Gretchen chuckles. "Awex helped me!" She points to the floor and runs back to me. "Color?"

"Sure." Gavin joins us on the floor. He greets me with a side hug and whispers in my ear, "Good morning. At it again, are you?" He raises an eyebrow, waiting for my reaction.

He seriously has no idea how little sleep I require. I impishly grin. "Yeah, I was up, so I thought I'd start breakfast. It'll be ready in twenty minutes."

He locks his eyes with mine and squeezes me from the side. "You're absolutely amazing."

Between his words, golden-brown eyes, and delicious, musky scent, fresh from the shower, I'm left utterly speechless. I manage to roll my eyes and shake my head in disagreement. *I haven't done anything special.* After all, he's the one who's been taking care of me. "It's just casserole. Nothing special. You've been such a gracious host, it's the least I can do."

Gavin shakes his head but says nothing. Gretchen demands his attention to the coloring page she's selected, and we spend the next few minutes coloring. It isn't long before the aroma of the casserole fills the house. Will and Peter are the first to arrive, followed almost immediately by Phil and Liz. Mason's the only one who's yet to appear.

"You didn't have to cook again, Gavin," Liz calls out as she enters the room. "You could've slept in," she suggests as she walks to fill up her cup. "I would've been happy to make breakfast."

"Um... I slept in this morning myself." He grins in my direction before adding with a hint of sarcasm, "Apparently, Alex doesn't know the meaning of sleeping in... I've yet to see her sleep past six... unless she's under the influence of medication." He teases and waits for my reaction.

I playfully scowl, shaking my head before confessing, "I guess it's just one of my character flaws... My family hates it!"

This makes everyone laugh, but it's Peter who says through laughter, "Well, we'll reap the benefits of it!"

Will chuckles as he adds, "Don't worry, we won't hold it against you."

The timer goes off, and Liz stops me from getting up, "I'll get it. It's the least I can do. I can't remember the last time I slept until seven... It seems Gretchen has a new best friend. Thanks so much for watching her this morning."

"It was fun!" I smile at Gretchen who's still at my side.

After returning from placing the casserole on the table, Liz points in the direction of the dining room and says, "Shall we eat?"

After breakfast, Liz insists Gavin and I do something fun and relaxing. For the rest of the day, we're not allowed in the kitchen other than to eat since we've prepared and cleaned everything for the past two days. Gavin and I accept this graciously and continue to spend time downstairs with our new shadows.

When Peter suggests going into Leavenworth, Gavin, Will, and I go with him. Liz and Phil stay behind because she wants the kids to nap. Peter volunteers to drive and soon, we all pile into his silver SUV, with he and Will up front while Gavin and I sit in the back.

As if captured in a snowglobe, the quaint Bavarian town is decked out in lights and Christmas decorations. Small flakes of snow float down from the sky, slowly covering the freshly cleared roads and sidewalks. It's as if I've stepped into a slice of Germany as we drive down the streets looking for a place to park.

A strong gust of wind makes me thankful for my hat, scarf, and gloves as I step out onto the sidewalk. Within an instant, Gavin's there offering his hand. His breathtakingly gorgeous smile and hypnotic, golden-brown eyes make me completely oblivious to the cold weather. Nothing exists but him. He chuckles lightly before stealing a kiss on the cheek, causing my body to heat. He straightens quickly, pulling my arm through his before shutting the door behind us. Will and Peter take the lead while we walk hand in hand a few steps behind them.

Like most tourist towns, Leavenworth doesn't disappoint. It's filled with small shops filled with little trinkets and baubles found in a Bavarian Village somewhere in Germany. We walk through a few of his family's favorites, as well as ones I find interesting. Even though I'm not a fan of shopping, I enjoy this time with Gavin and his family.

In a shop filled with Christmas decorations, I buy Kate and Ben an ornament for their wedding. It's an exquisite hand-painted ball with "Our First Christmas" and the date inscribed. I also find an intricate snowglobe to add to my mother's collection for Christmas.

While I finish paying, Peter and Will move onto the next store. When I leave the enchanting shop, we find Will and Peter sitting at a coffee shop, a few doors down.

"Want a latte?" Gavin suggests as he reaches to take the bags from my hand. "I could use some coffee."

"Sounds great." I shiver as another gust of wind comes up from behind us. Since Peter and Will are already seated, Gavin and I head in their direction to join them.

Before Gavin sits, he points to the direction of the car. "Mind if I take these packages to the car?" he asks the group.

Peter hands him the keys. "Will you take these, too?" Peter hands over another two bags.

I pick up our order and return to the table. Will and Gavin are talking, so I sit and casually follow along, contributing when I can. Eventually, the conversation turns to my sister's wedding.

"When is your sister's wedding?" Peter asks.

After I finish swallowing, I reply, "In three weeks. The first weekend of winter break."

"Boy… With Liz's wedding, there was so much to do." Peter shakes his head and chuckles at some unknown thought before adding, "I got off easy. All I had to do was sign my name to a few checks, show up, and walk her down the aisle… Eleanor and Liz did everything."

"I think Kate has it under control. Gavin and I helped her a lot this week. I can't believe how many little things need to be done." I roll my eyes, reminding myself when it's my turn, I'm keeping it simple.

Will shakes his head and laughs. "Gavin and I felt the same way with Liz. Mom made us help her with whatever she thought we were 'capable' of doing… Which was way more than we bargained for…"

Peter replies with a chortle, "You boys didn't have it that bad. If I remember… You were graciously rewarded."

Catching onto their mood, I laugh. "I just want something simple when I get married. No need to go to such extremes." Suddenly, I remember Kate's latest request. "She has me walking in three-inch death traps! I hope I don't trip going down the aisle!"

"That would be something worth watching," an all-too-familiar voice teases from behind. "I'm sure you'd love to be in crutches again!" The sarcasm's thick in Gavin's voice, making me blush a deep shade of red.

"I'm sure I'll manage to stay out of those." I smirk back at him. "I've had enough of being a gimp, thank you!" I add on curtly with a grimace.

With that, we all burst out into laughter.

Gavin sits beside me and pulls me into a hug before whispering in my ear, "I'm sure you'll look stunning. Besides, I like having you around. Crutches did have some advantages."

Rolling my eyes, I sigh. I'm sure he'll get tired of me eventually. Though it'll be different when he's not around all the time. My heart pangs at the thought, and I force myself to focus on the guys in front of me.

Thankfully, the conversation changes, and I feel myself relax. Eventually, we make our way through more shops before returning to the cabin. We spend the remainder of the day playing outside with the kids in the snow, then watching movies in the basement until bedtime.

After the movie, Gavin and I return to his room to get ready for bed. He takes a shower while I get myself ready for bed. I quickly change into my pajamas and get out a book to read from my bag while I wait for him to finish using the shower in his bathroom.

I attempt to read, though it's extremely difficult to concentrate on my book as I wait for him. My thoughts are consumed with everything that's happened this week with Gavin. It feels like I've known him forever... Yet, it's barely been months. My heart races, and blood flows quickly through my veins every time I think about him. As ridiculous as it is, I can't get enough of him. My lips curl up into a smile as I realize maybe my sister is right... I'm falling for him... hard. He's the most amazing person I've ever met. He's gracious, honorable, kind, caring, and let's be real... He's incredibly gorgeous.

I must be daydreaming about Gavin more than I realize because when the bathroom door opens, I jump. Gavin comes out in merely a pair of shorts, drying off his hair with a towel. I let my eyes discreetly trace over the planes of his body, and I'm once again in awe of his utter perfection. Without looking at me, he walks to his duffel bag and grabs a shirt. He turns and catches me staring. His lips slowly turn up as he grins impishly.

Like a kid who's been caught with their hand in the cookie jar, a heavy wave of embarrassment washes over me. My cheeks heat and yet, I can't help but gape at him wide-eyed. His hypnotic, golden-brown eyes captivate my attention, and I lose track of all coherent thought.

Eventually, he takes the two necessary steps over to the bed and stands before me, our eyes locked, and my breath hitches. His free hand reaches out, pulling me to a standing position while the other holds his shirt. Without a word, he wraps his arms around my waist. *Ohmigod. He smells incredible. Can I bottle this smell?*

"I'm so glad you're here," he whispers softly. He leans in for a long embrace, squeezing me so tight, I'm almost lifted from the floor. His face nestles in my neck as he continues, "Thanks for coming with me."

I take in a deep breath of his delicious, musky scent and eventually remember how to talk. "Thanks for inviting me," I finally whisper back.

"God, I don't know what I'd do without you." Gavin squeezes me tightly again, then pulls his upper body back to look me in the eyes. "My family completely adores you."

Once again, I'm at an utter loss for words. I simply grin and shake my head in denial. How can he have it so backward? It's him who's completely amazing. He's...

Before I can finish that thought, I'm interrupted by

Gavin's irresistible lips. What starts out slow, quickly turns into an inferno. I grasp my hands in his hair while he envelops me. Before I know it, my feet dangle from the floor, and we're ravenously out of breath yet yearning for more. To regain my breath, my lips trace his cheekbone, his neck, and his mouth, and I fight for my breathing to be under control. My hands trace the planes of his chest and his back. *Is he real?*

A light giggle escapes my mouth, and Gavin pulls away, looking puzzled he sets me on the floor again.

"Oops, I did it again." I smile impishly. "I lose all conscious thought when you're around," I mutter aloud, but more to myself as I bury my head in his bare chest, taking another deep breath.

Gavin's quiet laugh vibrates through his chest. "I'm not complaining... Besides... You have the same effect on me."

He reaches over to where he's dropped his shirt and starts to put it on. I want to stop him, but I regain control of myself. I step back while he puts on his shirt, but once he's accomplished his task, I reach my arms around his waist and hold him tight.

"I'd better let you get some sleep," he begrudgingly whispers in my ear. "I'll see you tomorrow." He bends down and kisses me once more before whispering, "Goodnight, Alex. Sleep well!"

He turns and walks away after one more peck on the cheek without saying another word, leaving me reeling. All I manage is to watch him walk out the door. I have to admit, it takes awhile to regain my thoughts and finish getting ready for bed.

18

SAFE TRAVELS

"ACCORDING TO THE NEWS, there's a storm coming late this evening. We might want to hunker down or get on the roads before it comes. It's supposed to last through Saturday evening, which will make the roads a mess Sunday," Peter suggests as Gavin walks into the kitchen the next morning.

"We'll take off today." Gavin yawns as he enters the kitchen, then looks to me. "If you're okay with that?"

"Of course," I agree, knowing I'm expected at work on Monday.

We spend the morning with his family. When the guys take the kids out to play one last time, Liz and I make lunch. Just as we're finishing up, she stops and faces me. "Thank you, Alex."

"It's not a problem." I shrug. "I love to cook."

"No, that's not what I mean…"

"Wha…"

Before finishing my thought, her arms fly around me in an enormous bear hug. It takes few seconds to respond but when she whispers, "Thank you so much for bringing this side of Gavin back to us."

Bring him back? "What do you mean?" I ask when she releases me.

"I mean, I've never seen him this happy. *Ever.* Not even before Mom was sick. He's had it harder than all of us. He loves with his whole heart, and I've *never* seen him look at anyone the way he looks at you."

What do I even say to that? Wait… she thinks he loves me?

Thankfully, she goes on before I have to respond, "Alex, you're the best thing that could happen to him. Thanks for being you."

"Okay…" I draw out.

"Seriously. He needs someone like you in his life. I absolutely love that you knocked him on his butt and are just as competitive as him. He's gonna get a run for his money, and I can't wait to sit back and watch."

The front door slams open, and the snow party has been moved inside. I look to Liz and with a knowing glance, she shrugs, understanding we can't continue this conversation.

Liz jumps into action, helping the kids remove their snow clothes as I put the finishing touches on lunch. We settle in the dining room and share one last meal before Gavin and I head off to school. Just as we finish, Peter points out that it's snowing.

From the looks of it, the weatherman was wrong, and Gavin wants to get back to campus before the roads get bad. We quickly say our goodbyes and have our things loaded in the vehicle.

We don't even make it to Othello before our visibility turns to crap. My SUV handles well in the snow, but it's already taken us four hours just to get to Othello. We're supposed to have been to Pullman by now, but the weather's not cooperating.

Gavin spots a hotel and pulls into the lot. Shaking out his hands, he says, "I don't think I can white-knuckle this drive any longer. Let's see if we can find a place to stay for the night and continue in the morning."

Since neither of us have said much for miles, due to the conditions of the road, I whole-heartedly agree.

"You're in luck. I've got one last room," the middle-aged woman announces when we inquire about the room.

"We'll take it," Gavin and I say in unison, setting the process of renting the room in motion. As long as we're not on those treacherous roads, we'll take anything.

We stop in the hotel's restaurant to eat dinner before heading to the room. The snow falls heavily through the window, and we're relieved to be off the roads. Gavin tells me the trip usually takes less than four hours in total, and we're barely halfway there. We call our parents to let them know about our unplanned pit stop so they won't worry. Everyone's relieved we're off the roads and safe for the night.

Everything falls into place, until we reach our room.

There's only one bed.

No couch.

No extra blankets.

Barely room to walk around, even if there was.

"Um..." Gavin starts, but I cut him off.

"We'll share the bed, Gavin. It's cold in here, and I'm not arguing with you."

"But I..." Gavin starts and the lights flicker. "Crap. I

really hope we don't lose power. They'll have a generator, right?"

"Gavin, I'm not arguing. Especially, if we lose power at some point. I refuse to wake up tomorrow morning and find you with hypothermia on the floor just because you're trying to be a gentleman." I punch my fists to my hips, letting him know I'm not budging on this. For a long time, we have a stare-off.

Eventually, he resigns with a nod. *Yes! Victory. God knows, he can be stubborn.*

We take quick showers and get ready for bed, should the power go out. We pass the time watching movies. With only the bed to sit on, Gavin stretches out his arm, and I easily fit next to him. There's a chill in the air, even with the heater on, so we curl up under the covers.

I'm really nervous at first and take awhile to settle in. Gavin absentmindedly brushes his hand under my shirt and sensations soar through me. I have no idea what I'm supposed to do.

My hand comes up to his chest, and I can't help but trace his hard muscles. I've spent nearly the last month with him and still can't get over how hot he is. I lift my head from his chest and am met with the most hypnotic stare. *Crap. Can he read my mind?* He bends slightly and brushes a kiss to my lips, and I get caught up in the moment.

I turn to face him, and he pulls me close, not breaking our kiss. I run my hands through his thick hair and kiss him for all I'm worth. The next thing I know, I'm straddling him, and he's running his hands under my shirt. My body's on fire, and I can't get enough. We are full-fledge making out, and I absolutely love it. I've never felt so alive.

I have no idea how much time passes as we explore each other's body like we've been given a map and there's hidden treasure. Before things get too carried away, I force myself to pull back.

"Uh... Gavin." One more kiss because I can't resist him.

"Yeah," he asks when I pull away once more. He looks adorable as I stare into his delicious, golden-brown eyes. "What's wrong, Alex?"

"I..." *Nothing's wrong. I just don't know how to tell him.* "Umm... Nothing... I just..." Gavin sits up and pulls me with him against the headboard. "I've never done this..." I admit, and confusion fills his features.

"Um... we've kissed before," he teases.

Geesh, Alex. Put your big-girl panties on and tell him the truth. What's the worst that can happen? This is Gavin we're talking about, I internally scold myself. "That's not what I'm saying..."

He reaches out to touch my face, and the sincerity in his eyes slay me. I know I've been a fool and can tell him anything, and he won't judge or be upset. "I've... I've never been with a guy... like this."

"Um... Alex." He clears his throat. "I've never done this before either."

What does he mean? He's never...

"Alex... don't get me wrong. I'm enjoying this. I've never done anything like it either."

Is he saying what I think he's saying? Gahh... I just need to tell him so we're on the same page and can go from there, with no guessing. "Gavin... I'm still... A... Virgin. I'm not on birth control, and I'm not sure I'm ready for more than just making out."

I'm expecting judgment, but I should've known better. This is Gavin, after all. A sheepish smile spreads across his features, and I swear his cheeks redden. When he finally talks, it's low and barely above a whisper, "So am I. I'm not planning on taking this too far. I don't have protection either."

"Okay…" I draw out, not sure what to say.

"Alex, we'll go as slow as you want. I have no problem waiting. I've waited my entire life for you and until we're both ready, it's not happening." He holds my gaze until it sinks in. He reaches for my hand and squeezes it.

He's serious. There's no doubt in my mind. "Okay," I whisper in agreement.

"Come here," he gruffly whispers and pulls me to his chest. "Let's slow things down and get some rest." I glance to the clock and see it's nearly eleven. Gavin flips my body and adjusts it so we're spooning. As he places an arm under my neck and pulls at my waist to bring me closer, I can't help but fall for him further.

Our breathing slows, and he reaches over to switch off the lamp beside us before returning to cuddle me from behind. He places an arm around my waist and kisses my neck lightly. The weight of the day releases, and I want to stay like this forever. Just as I'm drifting off to sleep, Gavin rocks my world when he whispers, "I love you, Alex. I'll wait forever, if that's what it takes."

19

COMING TO MY SENSES

WAKING up in Gavin's arms is one of the best feelings ever. My head lies on his chest, listening to his steady heartbeat and slow breathing. My leg is thrown over his thigh, and my arm snakes around his waist. He smells absolutely heavenly, and I just want to take a moment and take him in, as his words from last night play on a loop through my mind.

He loves me. Gavin Wallace loves me.

I know without a doubt I feel the same, even if I was too chicken to say the words. I didn't want to ruin the perfect moment. My fingers absent-mindedly stroke the contours of his abs as I take everything in.

Sometime during the night, Gavin took off his shirt, and I'm relishing in this closeness. He has a light dusting of chest hair and as I look up to his chin, I notice for the first time a day's worth of growth is evident. I'm dying to reach out and touch it but restrain myself.

I'm so lost in thought about these nuances that I jolt when his chest rumbles, and he whispers, "You might give me a complex if you keep staring at me." He glances at the clock. "Good grief, woman, don't you ever sleep?"

I start to pull away to let him sleep, but he stops me. "I don't think so..." He pulls me close and kisses the top of my head. "This is the first morning waking up with you in my arms. I've been dreaming about this since I met you. There's no way I'm letting you go so soon."

"This is something I could get used to," comes out before I give it any thought.

"I sure hope so." Gavin chuckles. "If I have anything to say about it, this will be the first of many mornings we spend together."

That right there is why I have fallen for this man. His off-the-cuff remarks always bring a smile to my face. When I can't contain the emotions building in me any longer, I let them out. "I love you, Gavin."

"I think I might just love you more, Alex." He pulls me in for a kiss and every thought I've ever had goes right out the window. I don't care that I haven't showered, brushed my hair or even my teeth. He must not care either because this quickly becomes the hottest kiss I've ever experienced.

By the time we pull apart, we're both panting and our cheeks are flushed. His hair is perfectly disheveled between my hands running through it and his bed head. When I look into his eyes, I don't think I could ever be more attracted to him.

"God, you're beautiful, Alex." Gavin's lips turn up as he roams his golden-brown eyes over my body.

I never knew a body could heat from sheer looks alone. Whew.

"What do you say to grabbing some breakfast and making sure the roads are clear before getting on the road?"

Not wanting to leave the comforts of his arms, I hesitate.

"Or we can stay right here for a bit longer. We don't have to check out until noon," he teases. "Since it's only seven, there's plenty of time to decide."

"I'm sure we'll think of something to occupy our time," I tease as I pull him in for another amazing kiss.

THE NEXT MORNING, it feels strange to wake in my apartment without Gavin. We both have a full day ahead of us, so we thought it best to stay at our own places to be well rested. Since the ground is covered in snow, I skip my morning run and am surprised to hear a knock on my door a little after seven.

Wondering who would be here at this hour, I look through the peephole and am pleasantly surprised. When I open the door, there's Gavin in a thick winter jacket, pink cheeks from the cold, and a hat covering his thick hair.

I don't even get to greet him properly before he whisks me into a hug and pulls me close. He plants a mind-numbing kiss on my lips and steps into my apartment, closing the door behind him.

When he sets me down a few moments later, I'm out of breath. "Well, good morning to you," I tease.

An impish grin forms on his face as he takes off his hat and coat. "Sorry. I've missed you."

"I've missed you, too," I admit.

"My apartment isn't the same without you. Since I

knew you weren't running today, I thought I'd walk with you to class. You're back on the schedule again for work, right?"

"Yep, I'm working from one until eight." I walk into the kitchen and pull things out for breakfast. "Have you eaten?"

"Nope." He shrugs. "I couldn't wait to see you."

We quickly eat breakfast and head to campus. Since my class is further, he kisses me once again before we part ways.

Later that evening, it's like déjà vu. Gavin and Josh come in for dinner. Though this time, I'm not nearly as nervous and manage coherent thoughts around them. He asks if I'd like to come over tonight, as if it's not a big deal, and I eagerly accept. It may seem weird, but it felt strange being alone in my apartment last night.

THE NEXT FEW weeks fly by. When Gavin and I are not working or in class, we're together, either with friends or just the two of us. Everything seems perfect until he has to go away for the weekend, and I can't go with him.

Since I've taken so much time off with my accident and plan to take most of break off as well, when a co-worker asks if I'd cover her shift so she can attend a family event, I don't hesitate to agree. Unfortunately, Gavin chooses that same day to meet his uncle in Spokane for the weekend. As much as I'd like to meet him, I'll have to wait until another opportunity comes along.

When I get home from my shift Friday evening, I run into Sophie in the parking lot.

"Hey, stranger," she greets me with a hug.

When she releases me, I ask, "What are you up to? I'm just getting home. Gavin's in Spokane visiting family."

Sophie's eyes light up. "Are you up for going out? Erin and James are out of town, and Josh is working."

"Sure," I eagerly accept. "Let's go to my place, so I can change. I can't believe how much I miss him," I admit to Sophie as we enter my apartment.

"That's to be expected, considering you've spent 24/7 with him for the past month or so. Of course, you miss him," she teases.

We make ourselves comfortable on my couch as I contemplate her words.

When I don't say anything right away, she continues, and my world implodes. "I can't imagine what it's going to be like when Josh goes to Europe for a semester. Sure, a lot can happen in a year. Who knows if we'll even be together by then, but I can't help but think about it, you know?"

Holy crap. I haven't thought about it. What's going to happen to Gavin and me? This is all so new. Should I even be thinking about something that far off? But... What's the point of even starting something as serious if it has an expiration date?

Gavin says he loves me, but will he want to do the long-distance thing? I can't stand being apart from him for two days, how can I spend a semester apart?

"Alex, are you okay?" Sophie's voice fills with concern.

Not wanting to admit I'm in the midst of freaking out, I automatically reply, "I'm fine."

"You look fine all right. Come on, Alex, spill it." She challenges me in a way that only a close friend can.

Crap. I should've known better. This is Sophie. I sigh in

frustration as I contemplate where to begin without sounding like a raging lunatic.

"Honestly…" I start but still don't know where to begin.

"No… Lie to me," she teases.

I chuckle and slowly let out the breath I didn't know I was holding and shake my head. "Everything you just said hit home, I guess."

Sophie cocks her head to the side, then asks, "What's bothering you the most?"

Where do I begin?

"Well, first there's the fact that I've fallen head over heels in love with Gavin. Then there's the fact that he claims to feel the same way. But since he's going away next spring, what's the point in starting something that has an expiration date?"

"Alex," Sophie chides. "You can't think like that."

"Sophie, for the first time *ever*, I've fallen for a guy. He goes away for the weekend, and I can't stop thinking about him. Like… I feel crazy for the amount of time I've spent missing him. If I can't handle this for a weekend, how will I handle going home for the holidays, summer vacation, or when he goes to Italy for an entire semester? I don't know. Maybe I should end things now, before things get too deep."

Tears fill my eyes at just the thought of ending things with Gavin. Somehow, in such a short time, he's become an important part of my life, and I have no idea what I'd do without him.

Sophie rushes to me and pulls me into a hug. "Alex, now you're just being silly. Why would you end things with someone because you're feeling something for him?"

"That's just it," comes out in sob. "I care about him too much."

"Oh, Alex." Sophie pats my thigh. "You'll get through this, and I'm sure it'll be with Gavin still in your life. I've known him for years. He's not the kind to enter a relationship lightly. You guys really have a connection."

"I know," I whisper as I wipe my face free from the couple of tears that have managed to spill over.

"Seriously, Alex, promise me you'll talk with him about this. Get your fears out in the open, and you'll feel much better."

"That's so much easier said than done," I groan, knowing she's right. I need to talk this over with Gavin. "How do I even bring it up…"

Sophie's quiet for a moment and chews on her bottom lip as she contemplates. "I'm not sure. But I know it needs to be done. You can't live in fear of '*what-if.*' You can only focus on '*what's happening now*' and go from there. You could be hit by a bus tomorrow, though your odds are considerably lower, given your recent accident… but you get my point. Stop worrying about the future and let it take care of itself."

After a moment to let her words sink in, I concede, "You're right. I'll talk with him."

"I usually am," she teases, and the subject's changed to her plans for winter break.

Gavin's a sight for sore eyes when he walks through the door to my apartment Sunday afternoon. Even though I've worked the past two days, I've had plenty of time to think about my conversation with Sophie. I'm determined to talk about my fears with him tonight, so I can put myself out of my misery.

My fears are temporarily forgotten when he swoops me into his arms and plants a kiss on me that could make me forget my own name. I wrap my arms around his neck, and he picks me off my feet in a well-practiced move. I instinctively wrap my legs around his waist.

My fingers run through this thick hair as his arms wrap around my back. I find myself deepening the kiss as I let all my pent-up emotions flow out of me. All too soon, Gavin lowers me to the floor and breaks our kiss.

An eyebrow quirks, and a smile that melts my heart fills his face. His deep voice sends shivers up my spine when he asks, "Miss me?"

"Maybe." My face heats as I neither confirm nor deny. God knows, I've missed him like crazy, but I'm not about to admit how much, especially after the emotional rollercoaster of a weekend I've had.

"Well," he draws out. "I've missed you." He pushes a piece of hair from my face and brushes another kiss across my lips. Though we've texted and called while he was away, there's nothing like being here with him in person.

We walk into the living room and settle on the couch. He pulls me close, and I snuggle into him, his arm draped around me. I inhale deep, and his musky scent seems to wash away the tension I've built inside me. *How can he have this effect on me?*

Gavin places a finger under my chin to draw my eyes to his. "What's got you so worked up that I visibly feel you relax, Alex?"

Instantly, my body tenses. I have no idea how to even bring up what's bothering me, but with his golden-brown eyes boring into the depths of my soul, I know it won't be long before he finds out.

I sigh, wondering where to begin.

"Alex, have I done something to upset you?" His eyes widen and guilt crushes through me.

"Other than being perfect for me," I mumble, then I raise my voice so he can hear, "No."

"What is it?" His tone is demanding. There's no way he's going to let this go.

"It's just… Well… I'm worried," I admit and avert my eyes to the ceiling. There's no way I can look him in the eyes and admit my fears at this point.

"About?" he prods.

Geesh, Alex. Rip off the Band-Aid and get this over with. "Where this is going," I barely whisper. My internal monologue's much bolder than I feel at the moment.

Gavin cocks his head to the side. "Where's what going?"

My heart races and then drops to my stomach. Oh, God. What do I do now? "Um… You and I," I finally admit.

Gavin blanches for a second then regains his composure. "We're dating…" comes out as a cross between a statement and question, as if he's suddenly unsure. He's quiet for a few moments, then slowly asks, "Are you breaking up with me?"

The second his words come out, pain rips through me. My breath hitches, and my eyes fill with tears. "No," I whisper.

"Then what is it?" comes out a bit defensive.

I take a deep breath and brush at the tears threatening to spill over. "I'm afraid."

His hand caresses my cheek, and tortured eyes bore into me. "Just tell me, Alex."

I sigh heavily again before letting everything pour out. "This weekend was harder on me than I thought it would. It got me thinking… What things will be like… When we're apart over the holidays, this summer, and when you go to Italy."

"Alex…" Gavin pulls me into a fierce hug.

I can't help but hold him close. I never want to let him go. But I need to get the rest of this off my chest, so it rolls out of my mouth like a freight train that's lost its brakes. "I've fallen so hard for you, Gavin. I'm worried about getting in way over my head if we have an expiration date."

Confused, Gavin's eyebrow quirks. "Who says we have an expiration date?"

"I barely made it through one weekend, and you were only a couple of hours away. What about when you're on the other side of the world?"

Gavin shakes his head. "Who says I have to go alone?"

What on earth is he talking about?

Before I can voice my question, he blurts out, "Come with me."

"What? I… I can't…"

"Alex, you're fluent in Italian. You're close to making that your minor. You've always wanted to travel. Let's go together."

When he puts it like, it makes sense, but I can't just drop everything and go around the world. "I have classes, a job… I can't just follow you around the world on a whim. We just started dating, for crying out loud."

"Alex," he demands my attention. "It'd hardly be a

whim." He's right. What we have between us is hardly whimsical. "I love you, Alex. After spending the weekend apart from you, I don't know how I would spend a semester apart either. Please consider this…" he almost begs.

Relief washes over me. Then I remember something and can barely contain my excitement. "Well, I *am* meeting with my advisor this week. I'll look into the options of studying in Florence. I might have to take extra classes next semester to compensate, but I might be able to manage."

Gavin pulls me to him and lifts me onto his lap, so that I'm straddling him. He kisses me for all he's worth, and my worries fade away.

THE MOMENT I lay eyes on Gavin Tuesday afternoon on campus, I rush to greet him. My excitement causes me to jump into his arms as I scream, "Ohmigod, you're never going to believe it!"

He easily catches me, but I can tell he's caught off guard because he sways a second before steadying himself, and he chuckles. "What am I not going to believe?"

"I did it! It's really happening. I'm going to Florence with you. My advisor said she would help me work out all the details, including filling out forms for additional financial aid. She says I'd be the perfect exchange candidate."

Gavin swings me around and kisses me as if we aren't in the middle of campus, surrounded by hundreds of people. "I have some amazing news, too."

He sets me on the ground before he explains that he has an interview for an internship on Friday afternoon. It's unexpected, but it's for a prestigious firm outside of Seattle. He'd been hoping to hear from them and just got the news before meeting me.

His dad arranged for him to fly in Friday morning and return before finals begin.

"Dinner's on me! Let's go celebrate," Gavin cheers as he takes my hand, and we walk back to my apartment.

20

STUDY DATE

AFTER I RETURN from my morning run, I notice a text from Gavin, and I can't help but smile. I wasn't expecting him home so soon. He was supposed to come back from Seattle later this afternoon, so he must've caught an earlier flight.

> **Gavin: Want to meet me at the top of Holland to study?**
> **Me: Sure. What time?**
> **Gavin: How does ten sound? Latte's on me.**
> **Me: Sounds great. See you soon.**

When I arrive on top of campus, Gavin's there, a latte in hand. He looks handsome in dark jeans and a button down. He's dressed nicer than usual, so my heart picks up the pace when I see him. *Damn. He looks hot. How does he do this to me?*

He reaches out a cup in my direction. "Here's a latte for you."

"Thanks." I take a drink, but nothing comes out. "Um,

Gavin, this is empty. Are you sure it's the right one?" I look to his cup. He must have made a mistake when he handed me this.

"Yeah, that's your cup." He takes a drink of his and smiles. "I'm drinking straight coffee."

"Well, there's nothing in here." I shake my cup. It feels heavy, but nothing sloshes the way it should, if there's liquid in it. I'm confused. I look to Gavin who's standing in front of me, grinning for some strange reason. Why on earth does this amuse him?

"Take off the lid and see if something's blocking it," Gavin suggests as he steps directly in front of me to face me.

"Okay," I say with great uncertainty. I stop walking and fiddle with the lid to get it off carefully, in case there is liquid waiting to spill all over me. But before I have it completely off, I notice out of the corner of my eye as Gavin places his cup on the ground and kneels for something. I look to him in confusion.

Gavin's on one knee and looks really nervous. He clears his throat, and I forget about the cup.

"Alex, I started falling in love with you that morning you ran into me. From that moment, our paths continued to collide until we took matters into our own hands." He places his hands over mine around the cup I'm holding as he continues, "The way I feel for you only intensifies each and every day. There're so many things I genuinely love about you."

"Oh, Gavin..." I start to say but get interrupted.

"I almost lost you once, and even though at the time we didn't know each other well, I knew there was something between us. I knew I just couldn't wait around any longer and not let you know how I felt about you."

He takes a deep breath and rolls his eyes slightly. "Sure, you thought I was just being polite and honorable." He takes another deep breath. By now, he has the full power of his eyes upon mine, and I can't do anything but hold onto his deep intensity as he continues, "But the truth is, I don't want to waste another minute not letting you know how I feel. If I've learned anything in my short life, it's that time's precious and meant to be spent with those you love."

Ohmigod, where is he going with this?

Gavin takes the lid off my latte, but all I can do is stare into his golden-brown eyes, filled with love and compassion. "And, Alex, I truly love you. I want to start spending the rest of my life with you as soon as possible." *Ohmigod, is he...?*

Gavin takes another breath. "Alexis Marie Manning, will you marry me?"

Holy crap! He did! Tears spring to my eyes as I'm overcome with emotion.

Gavin directs my attention to my latte. In the round cup is a piece of silver-striped satin neatly tucked like a flap, into itself, in a triangular shape. I hear Gavin's eager voice say, "Go ahead. Lift it up." Pulling carefully onto the triangular top, it reveals an exquisite diamond ring. My mouth gapes as I take in the beauty of the ring before me.

The ring's sunk into the satin so that only the top is visible from this angle. It's made of multiple diamonds. The center stone is round and radiant with two smaller stones bordering it. The band on either side of the smaller stones resembles braided knots, holding the stones into place. In front of the large stone is a smaller band with three diamonds set into a past, present, and future setting, with knot-like braids lining the outer two diamonds that match the other larger band. It's so beautiful, I've never seen anything like it. I'm speechless as I take in its meaning.

"Alex, do you like it?" Gavin nervously asks.

It takes me a few heartbeats, but I'm finally able to close my mouth and take my eyes from the ring, to focus on Gavin's brilliant eyes. "Oh, Gavin," is all I can whisper as my hand comes to his shoulder.

I fumble around for a moment, but eventually, I pull him to a standing position, so I can I wrap my arms tightly around his neck. Tears break the barrier of my lashes, and I can't get close enough to him.

Gavin apprehensively pulls his head away to read my expression. Concerned, he whispers, "Alex, are you okay?"

"Yes," I whisper through my soft sobs.

"Yes. What, exactly?" he says hesitantly, making each word sound like its own sentence.

I haul in a deep breath, determined to tell him my answer. "Yes, I'm okay... Yes, I like it... Yes, I'll marry you."

Now it's his turn to be shocked. After he fully comprehends my answer, he pulls me tight into an enormous hug, spins me around, as laughter escapes loudly from his chest. "You have just made me the happiest man on Earth!" He sets me down on the ground and places his enormous hands around my face. "Thank you," he whispers as he tilts his head slightly and slowly places his lips on mine.

Once our lips meet, his hands move to the small of my back, and he lifts me to meet his height. I gasp, and he takes advantage of my lips parting, delving in with his tongue and making this kiss the best one I've ever experienced. I pull him closer, not wanting to let go of any part of this incredible moment. I wrap my arms entirely around his neck and pull my legs to his waist. Not caring at all about the fact we're in public. Our kiss could last for an eternity, and it would still be too short. I love this man, and there's no denying it.

Loud clapping and cheers eventually bring me back to reality. I release my hold, and he sets me on the ground where he kisses me lightly once again and pulls away with an enormous smile on his face.

"I love you, Alex." He quickly bends down to kiss me again.

"Gavin, I truly love you, too," I whisper in his ear.

He steps back and takes the cup from my hand and removes the ring. He takes my left hand in his and slowly places the ring onto my finger. "I hope you don't mind. It was my mother's." He kisses my finger lightly once he has it in place. "My sister and dad insist you have this when I told them my plans. They know how happy you make me and wanted to be a part of that joy."

Not knowing what to say, I fiercely hug him once more. He holds me tight until I pull my head away, leaving my arms locked around his waist. "I love you, Gavin!"

Gavin grins widely. "I might just love you more. Do you know what today is?"

I stare at him, wondering if I should know, but all I can come up with is "Saturday?"

"Besides that, silly." He bends down and kisses me once on the nose.

I'm left staring blankly at him as he steps back and holds

his arms out wide, looking around. I, in turn, do the same, but don't really get what he is referring to.

"Um," he hesitates and smiles widely, "Four months ago today, you came blazing around that corner and knocked my whole world upside down." He chuckles at the memory.

I giggle as I remember the ridiculous events of that day. Gavin steps closer to me and places his arms around my waist once again, staring at me in silence for a few moments.

"And I wouldn't have it any other way," he whispers in my ear and embraces me tightly.

EPILOGUE

"ARE YOU READY, HUN?" Gavin asks as he takes my hand to lead me off the plane.

Adrenaline fills my veins as we walk down the short aisle. When I read the Italian signs, I almost scream with excitement. I can't believe I'm finally here in Italy of all places.

"You bet I am!" I squeeze his hand and reach up on my toes to kiss his cheek.

We'd announced our engagement on Christmas after my sister returned from her honeymoon. I was afraid my parents would object since we hadn't known each other long, but everyone was ecstatic to hear the news. Dad just grinned knowingly. Apparently, Gavin had done more than attend an interview when he was home last.

When we returned to Pullman for spring semester, I took twenty-two credits so I could travel abroad a year later. With Gavin getting placed in Pullman for fall semester, we planned our wedding for summer.

My dreams came true when I walked down the aisle in my parents' yard in front of our closest family and friends. Gavin looked sexy as ever in his dark-gray suit. I wore a simple white wedding dress with little fanfare. Our bridal party was small. Only Kate, Will, Sophie, and Josh stood up for us. Instead of going on a honeymoon right away, we chose to wait until this trip to Italy. Though I must say, our wedding night was one I'll never forget. Gavin was perfect in every way imaginable.

When we're done with classes this spring, we plan to travel across Europe for the summer before returning for our last year in Pullman. Who knows where I'll do my student teaching, we haven't planned that far. We'll have to see where Gavin lands a job, but as long as we're together, I'll be happy.

Gavin and I have rented an apartment in Florence for the semester. We'll attend University and immerse ourselves into the culture as much as possible. My skin pricks with goose bumps when we make our way through customs, stamp our passports. and verify our visas.

"Enjoy your stay, Mr. and Mrs. Wallace," the customs agent says as he hands us our papers.

"We will," I eagerly reply.

When we exit the airport, Gavin pulls me to the car waiting for us. The driver loads our luggage, and Gavin pulls me to the door. He brushes a kiss on my lips, and my body heats with anticipation.

"Are you ready for the adventure of a lifetime, Mrs. Wallace?" Gavin asks as he pulls away from my lips.

"Only with you, Mr. Wallace. Only with you." I pull him in for one more kiss and get in the car.

"I love you, Alex," Gavin whispers in my ear.

"I think I might love you more." I smile in return.

"Andiamo a casa."

"Let's go home, Alex," he repeats in English, and I swoon with excitement.

The End

ABOUT THE AUTHOR

Amanda Shelley loves falling into a book to experience new worlds. As an avid reader and writer, sharing worlds of her own creation is a passion that inspired her to become an author. She writes contemporary romance about characters who are strong and sexy with a twist of sass.

When not writing, Amanda enjoys time with her family, playing chauffeur, chef and being an enthusiastic fan for her children. Keeping up with them keeps her alert and grounded in reality. She enjoys long car rides, chai lattes and popping her SUV into four-wheel drive for adventures anywhere.

Amanda loves hearing from readers. Be sure sign up for her newsletter and follow her on social media. Join her reader's group Amanda's Army of Readers to talk about her books and stay up to date on her latest information.

www.amandashelley.com
Readers group:
https://www.facebook.com/groups/AmandasArmyofReaders/
Newsletter: http://eepurl.com/gfluuj
Goodreads:

https://www.goodreads.com/author/show/19713563.Ama nda_Shelley

facebook.com/authoramandashelley

twitter.com/AmandShelley

instagram.com/authoramandashelley

amazon.com/author/amandashelley

bookbub.com/profile/amanda-shelley

ACKNOWLEDGMENTS

I'd like to thank, you, the reader. Though this isn't the first book I've published, it's the first I've written. This story showed me I wanted to write on a regular basis. Your support means more to me than you'll ever know. Feel free to contact me at amandashelley.com or leave a review at your favorite retailer.

Mickel, thank you for being the first person to talk through Alex and Gavin's story. Your support and belief in me pushed me onto an entirely new path in life. Though I'll always love pineapple on my pizza, your thoughts have still been valuable to me.

I can't thank my beta readers enough with this book. Cara and Jackie, you two are the best. I love that I can always count on you to get my stories where I need them to be. The fact that we can talk about fictional characters as they are real, makes my life complete.

I'd like to thank Susan Soares for editing this book. It

wouldn't be what it is without you. I appreciate your flexibility and support.

Thank you also for Julie Deaton for making this book pretty. I cannot thank you enough for catching all my mistakes and helping me bring this book to completion.

Thank you to Krys Janae for making my beautiful cover. I fell in love with it long before I even finished this book. It's been a huge motivator in helping tell Gavin and Alex's story.

Most importantly, I'd like to thank my family for their love and support. I can't believe the journey this book has brought me on. From writing while you were napping, to talking about these characters as pre-teens, I hope each of you get the happily ever after you deserve. Remember, you're in charge of your destiny, and I will love and support you through it all.

ALSO BY AMANDA SHELLEY

Resilience: Book One of Resilience Duet

Resolution: Book Two of Resilience Duet

THE RESILIENCE DUET

Resolution

BOOK TWO

AMANDA SHELLEY

Samantha never saw Enzo coming.

As the dust settles from her divorce, her life is full. She doesn't
have time for distractions. She's too busy running her own
company and checking off numerous items from her kids'
demanding schedule to have a life of her own.

Then he walks into her kitchen with his breathtaking green eyes
and a mischievous grin. He's there to surprise his father - her
contractor, but his presence makes everything off kilter.

Enzo's perfectly content with his adventurous life as an elite rescue
pilot, until a harmless prank turns on him. Instead of surprising
his father, he finds his world thrown off course by the beautiful
woman with a sexy smile, wicked sass and the mouthwatering
ability to keep him on his toes.

With his limited time on leave, is she worth the risk to his heart?

Making The Call

Dani

As a bestselling romance author, most assume my life's glamorous, filled with combustible chemistry, and most of all, romance. Ha! I can only wish. With a deadline looming, I've escaped to my family's cabin on Anderson Island to free myself from distractions. My plan's great, until a man, who could pass as a cover model on one of my books, comes to my rescue. Is there chemistry? Sure. Is he everything I'd look for in a guy? Absolutely. But will my career be at risk if I give into my desire?

Luke

For a player, women line up outside the locker room. For coaches, we're lucky to get in the game. As the youngest NFL coach in the league, I live, eat, breathe, and even sleep football. To gear up for this season, I return to my home on Anderson Island for a much-needed break. When Dani literally crashes into my life, my mind's suddenly on the sexy brunette with a sailors mouth, rather than my team's next play. She has me dusting off another playbook entirely, making me wonder, did I make the right call?

Coming Soon

Drew: Book One of thePerfectly Independent Series

My heart races, palms sweat and knees go weak.

I've never seen anyone like Drew in a science lab. He's made me a firm believer in chemistry existing outside a textbook.

Then his ego and entourage show up.

Nope - No thank you. Moving on. I mean... who has an entourage in college?

When our professor announces we'll be stuck as lab partners, I nearly lose my mind - and not in a good way.

I can't afford the type of distractions Drew brings.

Preorders now available

https://amandashelley.com/books-by-amanda-shelley-2/